BELIEVERS
AND
HUSTLERS

BELIEVERS
AND
HUSTLERS

a novel

SYLVA NZE IFEDIGBO

ISKANCHI
PRESS AND MEDIA

ISBN: 978-1-957810-02-7

Published in 2022 by Iskanchi Press
info@iskanchi.com
https://iskanchi.com/
+13852078509

Book Design (Cover and Text Layout)
by Ayebabeledaipre Sokari @ayeskreatif

For
Daddy
Chief (Sir) Sylva N. Ifedigbo (KSJI)
Agubanze
For the gift of your books that sparked this.

"Every age has its pseudo-problems created by its fake prophets and pseudo-philosophers."

— **Marty Rubin**

ONE

Of the many things Ifenna believed God would hold against Nigerians on the last day, using the name of His Son as a prompt to cut cakes, he was certain, would bring the most punishment. Growing up, it was something he found both funny and perplexing, at birthday parties and wedding receptions. He always imagined God rising from His throne, pacing around and throwing a temper tantrum like one whose freshly repainted car was scratched in traffic. Those thoughts came to him again this morning, as the MC announced the cutting modalities after the dignitaries gathered around the cake.

"Ladies and gentlemen," he said. "My dear people of God, we will cut this magnificent cake at the spelling of the name, Jesus."

The large gathering cheered. Usually, "cutting of the cake" was an elaborate ceremony at every Nigerian party, complete with an order of proceedings of its own. It takes a village to execute, as a throng of well-wishers, appointed by the MC, flank the celebrant. The role of this group of observers was to make drab patronizing comments of the

1

process afterward. They would gather around the decorated cake, like characters ready to take a bow after a play, while the moderator counted down and, depending on how comical his performance, a loud cheer from the audience would bring the show to a climax.

Dropping the event brochure he was using to fan himself on the chair, Ifenna joined the rush of photographers and others, who, like him, were armed with their mobile phones and heading toward the stage. Maybe, because the church needed much media buzz for the feat they claimed to have achieved, they had graciously reserved seats in front for journalists. Ifenna endured the nudge of elbows and bodies on either side as he forced his way to the front of the stage, to a position he knew would give him a good shot. He needed to capture the image for his report, especially since he missed snapping one earlier during the actual ribbon-cutting ceremony. Just a few photographers were allowed in, with the promise that the official pictures would be circulated to all journalists later, but Ifenna didn't want to bank on that. This was going to be front-page news in all the papers the next day, and he couldn't return to his editor with excuses.

"Give me a very big jay," the MC said, after allowing some time for the dignitaries, who had formed a crescent around the table, to stretch out their hands toward the knife.

The MC's well-trained voice reverberated across the auditorium speakers as he dragged the words "very" and 'big' for effect. He was a veteran Nollywood actor, one of those faces popular with the ritual-themed movies Ifenna watched growing up back in the nineties. He had since become born again and now had the prefix "Evang." to his name. His face now featured more on church revival posters than on home movie DVD jackets.

A more rewarding career, Ifenna thought, given the layers of folds the MC had accumulated at the back of his neck, which glistered this morning with sweat, like fried turkey oozing oil.

"Jaaaaaay!" the audience chorused in response.

"No, no, no. That jay was for you. Not for my Jesus. I say, give me a biiiiig resounding jaaaaaay!"

The response from the audience was deafening this time. The MC smiled in satisfaction. "An elegant and exquisite eee."

Ifenna took some shots of the dignitaries in front of the cake and steadied his hands to catch the moment when they'd cut, when the audience would roar even louder. That was when their smiles would shine brightest. He adjusted his phone camera lens to ensure he had everyone in focus and made a mental note of their names and designations for the photo caption. The editorial policy at *The Nigerian,* the newspaper house he worked at, required not more than five people in one group picture, but some occasions were exceptions to the rule–like when ten legislators squeezed in with the visiting US president after he addressed a joint session of the National Assembly, or when the Super Eagles won the Nations Cup and all twenty-two players, and their coaches appeared in the frame. Ifenna was certain this picture would be another exception.

"And if you want to make it to heaven," the MC said, "give me a fantastically sweet eeeessss."

Beaming at the center of the pack gathered around the cake was Pastor Nick or Daddy Founder, as he was popularly known among his congregation. He stood tall at almost six feet, dwarfing everyone else, with broad shoulders that gave him the look of a rugby player. Though he wore a priest's collar shirt, the way the blazer hugged his frame perfectly suggested a wealth higher than a regular priest. Ifenna always admired the man's suits when he saw him preaching on television. They were the kinds with price tags that ran like telephone numbers in city boutiques; the kinds Ifenna looked forward to owning someday.

Pastor Nick's wife, Pastor Nkechi, whom the church members called "Mummy General," stood beside him. She looked like a bride on her wedding day, smiling like a toothpaste model. Pastor Nick's left hand rested firmly around her waist as if guarding his trophy. To his right was the vice president in a white flowing agbada with the Armed Forces remembrance emblem, which had just been launched the week before, pinned to his chest. Pastor Nick stooped slightly and whispered something into the vice president's ear, and both men shared a quick laugh. As if not to leave his wife out, Pastor Nick turned and said something to her too, and her face melted briefly into a smile. Only the three of them had their hands on the knife. The others, a medley of politicians, including two serving African Presidents and a former British Prime Minister, businessmen, and four top men of God— some of whom came from the US—had their hands stretched in the direction of the cake, as if it was a sacrifice they were praying over.

The MC, who stood very close to the cake, walked backward as he neared the end of his countdown to make sure he was not in the pictures. Already many of the photographers had signaled him, the way you'd shoo an animal away, to step aside. Ifenna noticed that two nozzles were set up just by the foot of the table to burst out in celebratory fireworks once the cake was cut. He once attended a wedding where one of those lights caught the bride's veil and flared to her hair extensions, causing a bit of a frenzy and filling the hall with the smell of roasted meat. The man sitting by his side at the table that day, who, by the color of his outfit, was the groom's relative, told his wife that this was not a good sign, that the marriage was destined for doom. The woman was nursing a morsel of amala and had nodded her agreement, then added that the bride needed to go for immediate deliverance, which made the eavesdropping Ifenna chuckle. Now, Ifenna decided that to make his picture even more dramatic, he would delay his shot to capture the flames as they popped.

"All right, now, let me have a dignified uuuu…"

Ifenna glanced at the cake. It was the reason for the whole ceremony, baked in the shape of what they said was now the single biggest church in the world. The brochure said it could sit over a hundred and twenty thousand worshippers. It resembled a football stadium, covered on top by a huge golden dome that ran the length of its circumference. On the top of the cake was an image of a cross and Pastor Nick, clean-shaven and smiling his trademark grin that had made him the darling of the young people who were the bulk of his congregation. Beneath, the text *Heaven's Gate Cathedral* was written in blue calligraphy font.

Earlier, the MC had remarked that the church had made the former record holder, also a Nigerian church, look like a rat hole, and the congregation greeted the remark with thunderous laughter. Though he did not mention a name, everyone knew what church he meant. The comment had reminded Ifenna of the argument in the danfo earlier that morning while on his way to the event.

Two passengers in the danfo had dragged each other over who had more anointing between Pastor Nick and Bishop Makinde. An announcement of the commissioning of the new Rivers of Joy Church Global Headquarters (aka Heaven's Gate Cathedral) by the vice president had been aired over the bus radio. The first passenger, a young man who had a book over his face, told no one in particular that the church being commissioned was now the biggest in the world. Perhaps, to help everyone get a picture of what that meant, he added that it was bigger than Bishop Makinde's church. The comment was greeted by murmurs of both surprise and disapproval. A well-rounded woman, who had a baby with nostrils leaking mucus strapped to her back and who, just a few minutes earlier, had cursed the bus conductor in Yoruba following a disagreement over her change, countered, insisting that the claims were false. She declared that Bishop Makinde's church, also called the Retreat Camp, remained the biggest church in the world.

"You don't even know what you are talking about." The first passenger doubled down, lowering the book he was reading to his lap. "We are talking Guinness Book of Records stuff here. You are mentioning Retreat Camp whose sitting capacity is not even up to that of O2 Arena in London. Forget it. Let me tell you something, this is my church. I know what I am talking about. That edifice is worth over ten billion and was completed in record time. You think the vice president would go to commission a mushroom church?"

It was only then that Ifenna looked at the cover of the book the young man was reading: *Thinking at The Next Level; How To Think Yourself To Wealth* by Rev (Dr) Nicholas Adejuwon.

The woman seemed deeply disturbed by what must have sounded like blasphemy to her. "When Bishop Makinde started his ministry, your pastor was still a child," she said, saliva escaping her lips. Her hands made patterns in the air like an opera conductor.

Ifenna easily identified her as a Makinde follower with her jewelry-free ears, bare neck, and a wristband, with *"Be ye holy"* inscribed on it, dangling from her wrist.

"In fact," she continued. "Who is your pastor's father in the Lord? Where did he get his anointing from? Who planted him? All these small boys will just sprout out of nowhere and start claiming anointing. You are saying billion, billion. How did he get the money? Every time, money. What of holiness? Does he preach salvation?..."

"Give me a loud eeessss!" The MC's voice rang through the auditorium.

It was followed by a loud chorus of 'JESUS!' that filled the air, accompanied by claps and trumpet sounds that lasted for several minutes. The celebratory fireworks popped and the dignitaries, done with the all-important assignment, exchanged banters as they made their way back to their seats. As the euphoria died down, the church band started playing the tune to "To God be the Glory."

Satisfied that he had captured as many good shots as he could amid the pushing and shoving that greeted the last moments of the cake cutting and fireworks, Ifenna made his way through the throng back to his seat.

Something the woman with the baby in the danfo said earlier came back to his mind as he sat down. Her comments prompted the passengers to take sides and voice their thoughts. She had referred to an incident that happened about a year ago, which Ifenna had not given much thought to until then. Someone, a pastor, had died at the construction site of Heaven's Gate Cathedral. It was said to be an accident and that he'd gone to inspect the construction work and stepped on a loose platform that gave way, and he fell to his death. Not much else was thought about the accident then, and nobody bothered to ask any further questions.

Ifenna remembered that the church had made frantic efforts to brush the news away quickly. Pastor Nick had wanted the news headlines to circulate around the construction of his church, not a death that occurred there. The news editor at *The Nigerian* had issued an internal memo about it back then. Now the woman in the danfo pointed to the death as a reason to be suspicious of Pastor Nick, insisting that there was more to the story. When she got the attention of the other passengers with her speculation, and they prodded her to say more, she declined and turned her attention to her crying child, using her mouth to suck out the mucus from the baby's nostrils.

As Ifenna thought of it now, his curiosity, which was what made him interested in journalism in the first place, became fully activated. *What if it was not an accident? What if the young pastor committed suicide or was pushed to his death?*

It all seemed a distant possibility, but the journalist in him took over. He had an opportunity to at least ask. There was going to be a media parley at the end of the ceremony, during which Pastor Nick was going to take questions from journalists. They called it a World Press Conference, perhaps because there were some foreign journalists mainly from Christian cable networks in the mix, but it was really just a well-controlled charade.

All the journalists who got passes to the ceremony were handpicked, and the church's media team gave them the question to ask Pastor Nick. This was the usual style for Rivers of Joy Church. Usually, they compensated the journalists handsomely for being good sports, so much so that journalists often lobbied to be sent to cover the church's events. There was always a fat "thank you" envelope, fatter than the usual brown envelopes journalists got for covering corporate events. And after running the story with as much a favorable spin as possible, they further credited their bank accounts in appreciation. That was how Pastor Nick became one of the most popular preachers in the country and a darling of the media in less than ten years of establishing his church.

Ifenna's mind churned. The implication of deviating from the script could be grave. He thought of his editor, who had been explicitly clear on splitting the proceeds of the assignment down the middle. Plus, Ifenna wasn't the editor's usual choice for this type of assignment, but Bolanle, the *Religion & Spirituality* desk reporter, had got sick, battling difficult early months of pregnancy. Ifenna was surprised to receive a call from the editor asking him to cover the cathedral commissioning the next day.

"The usual rate for normal press conference is like fifty K," the editor said on the phone. "This one is a big event. I am certain it will be double. So, omo Ibo, we will share it fifty-fifty. No games. You know I will always find out how much was shared."

As if that was not enough, Bolanle also sent him an SMS from her sickbed asking him to remember her and share some of the goodies with her since he was the one benefiting from her illness. So, now, Ifenna feared losing the entire package by asking a question different from the designated one the female church staff had slipped into his hands as he signed in at the entrance earlier that morning.

"You will be the third to ask a question during the press parley," she'd instructed in what Ifenna called LAFA (Locally Acquired Foreign Accent). It was difficult to keep his eyes away from her breasts, the bulk of which was not covered by her low V-neck blouse. "You will collect your envelope from me at the end when you sign out."

Ifenna suspected that she was familiar with Bolanle and must be somewhat disappointed to see him. He knew she wouldn't give him that envelope if he deviated from the script, but he was also thrilled at the possibility of giving a different slant to his reporting, something different from what all the other papers were going to say.

"We will now prepare for offering," the MC announced after the band finished their rendition of 'To God be the Glory."

Ifenna looked up at the podium, surprised.

"Yes, I know some of you will say but this is not a church service, so why are they doing offering, but I ask you, how can we not thank the Lord on a day like this?" the MC asked.

"This is the time to dance and thank the Lord for the great thing he is doing in the life and ministry of our Daddy Founder, Pastor Dr. Nicholas Adejuwon. The ushers are already distributing the offering envelopes. Collect it and do something big for the Lord. Challenge Him on this occasion so that he will open the storehouses of heaven in your life. Connect to our Daddy Founder's anointing and sow that seed—"

He was interrupted by someone who came to whisper into his ear. He held the microphone away and listened, nodding in agreement to what he was being told. Just then, one of the female ushers handed Ifenna a pack of envelopes with the inscription *"The generous man will be prosperous and he who waters will himself be watered – Proverbs 11:25."* He took one and passed the rest down the row.

"As I was saying," the MC continued. "Daddy has told me to tell you that there is a special blessing for those who give bountifully in this ceremony."

He looked in the direction of Pastor Nick as if to seek confirmation. "So, don't hold back. This is your opportunity for a breakthrough. Ushers, please. There are also POS machines in case you don't have cash. We are very cashless-economy compliant."

The MC chuckled into the microphone and continued, "I am also told that an account number will be on the screen any moment from now for those who want to do transfers. While you get ready for thanksgiving, the choir, I have just been informed, will entertain us with a special rendition of the "Hallelujah Chorus," which is dedicated to our Special Guest of Honor, His Excellency, the vice president of the Federal—"

Squeezing the envelope into his pocket, Ifenna got up and started walking toward the closest exit.

A MEDIA ROOM INSIDE THE Cathedral held the press parley. There was a lectern in front beside a slightly raised platform facing rows of single chairs fitted with microphones. Large screens plastered the walls across all sides of the room, complete with a hanging projector and a teleprompter. Only one who understood the power of the media, like Pastor Nick, would make such investments in a space for the media in his church. By the time Ifenna arrived, the room had filled up. A guard, with gym-instructor biceps, verified everyone at the door. Two television crews were already set up on either side of the room, and about half a dozen microphones from different news houses fought for space on the lectern.

Ifenna sat on one of the seats in the front row. Reporter chatter filled the room. Ifenna knew many of them; they were faces he had encountered on the job. He was a metro desk reporter and often had to comb the city for some of the best human-interest stories, which otherwise never made the news. Magistrate courts offered the best stories. The cases sent there for adjudication ranged from the surreal to the ridiculous. From violent husbands to cheating wives and homicidal children. His hunt for news also often saw him covering corporate press conferences, and that was where he often met some of the reporters in the cathedral media room. They would compare notes and have quick chitchats as they waited to collect their brown envelopes, but he was not friends with any of them.

This afternoon he wasn't looking for idle talk; a bigger matter occupied his mind. In the time since he walked out of the church auditorium just before the thanksgiving, he had thought of a million ways to ask about the pastor who died at the site. The August sun stung like darts to his skin, contrasting the chill of the auditorium. It was that short period of the dry season in August when the tear glands of the skies dried up. When he was younger, his parents referred to the period as August Break, and it was usually followed by days of torrential downfall, the skies making up for the lost time.

Ifenna had sought out a kiosk to have a cold drink and enjoy some shade while waiting for the ceremony to end so he could go for the press parley. Sitting there, nursing his bottle of soft drink, he googled the incident on his phone to see what extra information he could find. Everything he came across was the same brief statement the church released: there had been an accident that led to the death of one of its officials. A prayer that his soul finds rest. There was just one post on Nairaland by a lady who said she was a former member of the church. She gave the name of the pastor who died. All the other major news outlets did not mention the pastor's name. The Nairaland poster had indicated that the dead pastor was one of Pastor Nick's close assistants. If this is true, Ifenna thought, why is there such little information about it? Especially since Pastor Nick is a news darling and would have made the loss a major topic in his interviews.

By the time he walked back into the cathedral complex to locate the venue for the press parley, Ifenna's mind was made up. He needed to decide on how best to put his question. His heart pounded as he settled into his chair and waited for the parley to begin. Not long after, someone came in to call the room to order, signifying that proceedings would soon commence. It was the lady who spoke in LAFA at the media accreditation. She had been sitting then. Now that he saw her standing, that her curves were accentuated by the tight skirt she wore, he concluded that she was beautiful. She introduced herself as the media assistant to Pastor Nick and began to lay the ground rules for the meeting.

"We want this to be as orderly as possible. One question

at a time. You all have your turns. Please do not ask follow-up questions. As you can see, Daddy Founder has had a busy day, and we cannot keep him for longer than planned. So, please ask your question and allow the next person to have their turn. I know most of you are already familiar with how we do things here."

She paused and scanned the room, her eyes settling briefly on Ifenna before moving on. "I see a few new faces around. I hope we can all act accordingly so we can wrap up what has been a historic day for our church and our country in grand style."

Someone asked if the church had a prepared press release and a picture of the vice president commissioning the cathedral, which had been promised.

"Sure, I almost forgot." She smiled. "Your media packs are right underneath your chairs. Reach out and pull them out."

A flurry of activity and some murmuring greeted her comments as the reporters discovered the packs in a compartment under their chairs.

"The packs contain the official press release, pictures, some facts about the church, including the certificate we received from the Guinness Book of Records, and your envelopes," she continued, satisfied that the packs had made the right impression on the reporters.

She waited for everyone to inspect the content of the packs before adding, "I believe everyone is happy now."

Ifenna felt some relief. It was unlikely that they would retrieve the envelope from him for asking a question outside the script, but he felt excited, too. The wads of crisp notes in the envelope suggested that the amount exceeded his editor's estimation. Thoughts of what he would do with his share danced through his mind. Salaries at *The Nigerian* were late by two months now, and there were talks that the coming recession would squeeze out what life was left in the economy. His jalopy, which he also used for kabu kabu, conveying passengers from the Island to the Mainland to augment his earnings, had been broken down for a while, and the mechanic said some parts of the engine needed to be changed. Now, he finally had the money to fix it.

For a moment, he wondered if asking the question was necessary. A voice asked what he would do with the information and what difference it would make. Even if there was something there to report, Pastor Nick had the muscle to kill it. All it would take was a phone call to his editor, and the story was off. Would it be worth it? Ifenna heaved a deep sigh.

Just then, Pastor Nick sauntered into the room, led by a bodyguard in a long black jacket, smiling and waving both hands like a politician arriving at a campaign rally.

TWO

The limousine sped onto the Lekki-Ikoyi link bridge on the heels of the siren-blaring police escort van. Though a traffic build-up clogged the route toward the toll plaza, the map indicated it was the fastest route by half an hour to the Civic Centre from their Banana Island residence. Pastor Nick and his wife, Nkechi, were the only passengers in the limo. They were heading to the banquet, part of the ceremonies celebrating the commissioning of their new mega-church complex.

Nkechi sat at one end, close to the window, away from her husband, who was on the phone. A large Bible occupied the space between them. It seemed out of place there, like a piece of decoration of very little value. Looking at it now, Nkechi wondered if it had ever been read, if its pages had ever been opened for a ministration. It seemed to only serve the same purpose the rosaries on the rear-view mirror served, an identity. How else are you reminded that the car belongs to a man of God? She turned her attention away from the Bible and leaned toward the window.

Dusk settled over the sky. There were a few joggers,

ears plugged with earphones, running along the pedestrian lane. A speedboat sped through the water eastwards, leaving a trail of waves. Two of its passengers were trying to take a selfie against the backdrop of the colorful lights on the cable-stayed bridge. Nkechi admired the lights, the beautiful colors they gave off, which pierced through the gathering darkness. She had read in the papers that the bridge, which connected Lekki Phase 1 and the Ikoyi district, had cost the state government close to thirty billion naira. She thought it was worth it. If nothing else, it provided moviemakers with an iconic image for their establishment shots of Lagos.

The figure "thirty billion" resonated in her mind. It had punctuated her husband's speech earlier that day at the commissioning ceremony. Her husband had announced in his speech that the cathedral had cost that much. For a moment, she imagined what that amount of money would look like if she was to see it in cash and how many rooms it would fill if withdrawn in one thousand naira notes and stacked in a heap. Growing up in Enugu the daughter of civil servant parents, that kind of money existed only in her imagination.

As children, she and her friends never counted beyond millions. When someone was said to be a millionaire, it sounded like the peak of wealth, and she had wondered how that person slept at night, whether they had different stomachs, ones that let them eat expensive feasts. So, it had felt a bit surreal, listening to her husband declare earlier that he was a billionaire to thunderous applause from the congregation. And even though this was the life she lived now, she still hadn't fully come to terms with it. Would she detest it one day? Regret it?

She shifted in the car seat and threw a quick glance at her husband, who was now scrolling through his tablet and mumbling. They wore coordinated outfits. She had on a chic red gown by Armani, while he wore a black suit with red detailing on the side and collar. She had chosen the style after seeing a picture of Alicia Keys and Swizz Beatz at the Grammys. Her husband, always particular about his outfits, had loved it and said it would make him look like a Rockstar. She remembered how long it had taken him to settle on the black bow tie to wear that evening, discarding several options because he didn't think they sat well. She was pleased with his final choice, a hand-woven piece she'd bought him on one of her recent trips abroad.

"What do these people mean by my church is believed to be the biggest?" He asked without raising his face from the screen. "It is the biggest, damn it! Did they not see the certificate from the Guinness Book of World Records? What is this believing business about?" He spoke to himself in an irritated tone but loud enough for her to hear. "These people are just incompetent."

Nkechi stayed quiet. She adjusted her frame again on the seat, crossing and uncrossing her legs at the ankle before turning her attention back to the window and the street hawkers around the Lekki Phase 1 roundabout who were running after the car. They probably hadn't seen such a car in a while. Her husband was obsessed with reading about himself, and though he sounded like he was irritated, she knew it pleased him that he was all over the news.

"And why are we not yet on CNN?" He dialed a number on his phone.

When they first met, he had seemed like someone

focused on improving himself. He always had one of those *How-To* books in hand: *How To Attract People To Yourself*, *How To Speak And Get A Standing Ovation*. When he spoke, he could easily reel out whole paragraphs from books by Norman Vincent Peale and Stephen Covey. After they got married, he included titles on parenting, being the perfect Christian husband, and building an unbreakable marriage. Then, he found TD Jakes, and it was like he got possessed by a spirit that multiplied all the other tendencies he already had by many folds.

Even now, as she listened to him ask someone on the phone when his special interview with CNN would air, Nkechi remembered the day they met, almost twelve years ago. She had just finished her final year undergraduate exams in Nsukka, and her coursemates had organized a party to celebrate. She wasn't typically a party person but had gone along because she didn't want the five thousand naira she'd contributed to go to waste. At least she would have some pepper soup and drinks. So, while her colleagues danced, she had remained seated in a corner of the lounge, sipping from a bottle of malt and cheering those who danced.

A young man had come to sit beside her. His mild but inviting perfume–she would later learn it was Tom Ford–first caught her attention before his smile. She knew at once that he wasn't one of them, an undergraduate. The perfect cut of his shirt, the glistering chain of his wristwatch, and the confident air that hung around him like a halo told her so. He also claimed to be not much of a dancer, which she would later find untrue. They had talked for the rest of the party, sitting side by side, their knees touching, his hand straying to hers often. He was the kind who could talk on end, and before the evening ended, she knew he had gone to the Yaba College of Technology and worked with a Big Four firm in Lagos as an auditor. He was in Enugu on an official assignment and had come down to Nsukka to see an old friend doing his master's program. This friend, a friend to one of Nkechi's coursemates, dragged him to the party.

Nkechi fell in love with him, the kind of love that made her run away from home in Enugu to Lagos just to be with him in those idle months post-graduation. And when she was posted to Rivers State for her Nation Youth service, she promptly redeployed to Lagos to be with him. And when her parents hesitated to give their consent to their marriage because he was a Yoruba boy and they couldn't stand the idea of their Ada getting married to an "ofe mmanu," she called their bluff and followed Nick to the registry in Ikoyi.

"Pastor Bode said Doctor Panam confirmed at the last minute. He'll be performing tonight," Nick said, looking briefly in her direction then back at his tablet.

Again, she did not respond. They weren't talking. Or, more appropriately, she was not talking to him. Six weeks had passed since she vacated their room. When they first moved into their mansion in Banana Island, she complained that the house was too big and she did not need a room to herself. Her parents slept in the same room, she said, and the idea of husbands and wives staying in separate rooms was bad for marriages. The room had been set up, all the same, furnished like an alternate master bedroom. Following their quarrel, she'd been grateful to move into it. She suspected he was having an affair and confronted him with her evidence one night after their bedtime prayers, and in the heat of the argument, he'd smacked her across the face.

The head butler had returned a pack, which contained two unused condoms from one of his jackets in a pile being sent for laundry.

"What was she doing searching my jacket pockets?" he asked, flustered and obviously more embarrassed that he had been caught than at the fact that he was cheating.

"That's not the point, Nick," she retorted. "What were condoms doing in your jacket? You sure didn't buy them to use with me!"

That was when he'd swung his hand at her. "Do not talk to me like that. I am your husband."

The slap had sent her storming out of the room, slamming the door behind her. It was shock at first, then anger and disgust. She stayed away from their room. Initially, she thought it would be for a few days and hoped that her absence would extract some remorse from him, but he continued to act like he didn't even notice she was gone, so she gradually moved all her things into the other room.

It wasn't the first time they'd fought. The issues began barely two years into their marriage. Initially, they had seemed benign: flashes of temper, impatient angry retorts, and unnecessary arguments. Nkechi didn't complain about it to anyone. Arguing was expected in a marriage; all the women said so. Plus, his work was incredibly stressful at times, leaving him grumpy and distant. Then, he began to stay out late and hit her, once causing her a miscarriage. Back then, she had moved into the guest room of their two-bedroom flat in Yaba and stayed there for a month.

It had seemed then that their marriage was headed for the rocks, but he had found Bishop Jakes one day and came home to tell her he was going to start a church. He had been unusually boisterous that night, buzzing like a bee at the sight of a honeycomb. He had even stopped by her favorite suya spot on his way home to buy a wrap of ram kebab. It was the first time he had said a full sentence to her in weeks, and the way he spoke like all was well between them intrigued her in a way that erased the anger that had been lodged in her heart for weeks.

He told her he had a vision, that God had inspired him to build a place where His people would not feel like their conscience was constantly under judgment, where worshippers would not feel guilty and unworthy for being themselves. He had spoken in a matter-of-fact tone as if convincing her made his theory true. Like if she believed in what he saw, it would make his own view clearer. Most people, he said, just wanted to sleep well at night and did not want to be told about a God that condemned them. He was going to preach a new gospel to bridge that gap.

"I need you by my side on this journey, Nkay," he had said, going down and clutching both her legs. "I need you to complete me, to be my pillar. It will be our church, mine and yours. We have equal shares in the registration documents, I promise you. Please, Nkay, let's forget the past and begin afresh."

And, as if delivering the punch line in a rap contest, he looked up at her and added, "And we will be rich. I mean, like bastardly rich. I promise you. I will buy you a yacht and take you to see the world."

So, she'd stayed. Not because of the money–she hadn't imagined he would be able to pastor a house fellowship, let alone to talk of a megachurch then–but because she thought then that her husband's plan was a direct lifeline from God to save her marriage.

Now, the limousine slowed down as they approached Lekki Admiralty Toll Plaza. A family, probably members of their church, in a saloon car in the lane beside theirs, waved. Nkechi knew they couldn't see the inside of the limo, but they must have seen the customized plate number as they pulled up and were waving with the hope that she and her husband were inside. Instinctively, she waved back. It was the kind of effect that her husband had now come to have on people; this celebrity life she now lived, which made her practice a smile whenever they were out in public and wave like a British royal at strangers. It made her feel powerful at times, though she knew it was him the crowds waved at–his charm, powerful messages, promises of prosperity and the absence of disease, products of the seeds he made them sow.

The limo slowed down. There was a bottleneck in front. A danfo had crashed into the back of an SUV just ahead of them, taking off the bumper, and the drivers of both vehicles were close to blows. A police officer jumped down from the escort van in front to divert traffic and create space for them to switch lanes so they could get away from the melee. The traffic was heavy. It was that time of the day when the people made the return journey home in the outskirts of the city. Nkechi saw the looks on the drivers' faces as they reluctantly shifted to let their convoy through. She thought of how she went from the person who complained about the harassment of siren-blaring convoys to the one doing the harassment.

"It is a necessary evil," her husband had said the first time he started using police escorts a year into his ministry. "You know how unsafe Lagos is and all the envy we're accumulating. All these pastors, I tell you, are not happy that our flock is growing so fast. We need to take some extra care now. Remember what the good book says about faith without action."

As the limousine drove through the toll point, Nkechi reached for her mini makeup kit and hand mirror. The Civic Centre, the venue of the banquet, was a long drive after the toll plaza, so she needed to touch up her makeup. She knew many of the women there envied her for being the lucky one to grace the spotlight with the flamboyant Pastor Nick. Many, she knew, wanted her place. She had figured long ago that being humble and meek served no purpose. She wasn't about to roll over for them. It did not matter how she felt toward him. The condom incident had got her guards up, but she would always reinforce her status as his wife. When the limousine pulled up at the entrance of the Civic Centre, she would step out holding her husband's hand and beaming her practiced smile for the cameras. She would lean slightly on him on the red carpet to pose as the picture-perfect couple the tabloids had crowned them to be. And when they were invited to open the dance floor, she would plant her body against his and sway her waist. She would dance hard enough to make her husband's lover, if she was present, choke on her own bile.

THREE

Ifenna had two stories to file for the next day's edition of *The Nigerian,* and he was running late. The tip of his fingers ached as he punched away at his laptop. He sat at his favorite spot in the newsroom, next to the window overlooking the street. He preferred its view, the one of Allen Avenue. Anytime he experienced writer's block, he got up and looked out at the bustling traffic, the human beings in a race to secure their stomachs for the night. Something about it made his creative juices flow. In the evenings, the position afforded him a good view of the prostitutes who lined the road. He liked to watch them ply their trade: the turf wars, the negotiations, and the way the flashy cars they jumped into when a deal was successfully negotiated, drove off in a hurry.

The newsroom was quiet. It was just 11 am. Most of the reporters were still out gathering their stories. They would start trickling in after lunch. From 2 pm to 5 pm, it would be like a war room with reporters and editors rushing against the deadline, arguing over what should go in as they wrote and rewrote headlines. Some reporters would finish their work on the floor or lean against the walls, laptop in hand. Ifenna hated to be caught in that madness, so when he could, he preferred to finish his stories earlier and only hang around to ensure his editor signed off on them.

A cup of coffee and a copy of the day's *The Nigerian* sat beside his laptop. The banner headline announced the latest GDP figures. The economy had recorded a negative GDP growth for a second quarter. All seemed set for the declaration of a recession, the economists were saying, though Ifenna thought Nigeria had been in full-blown recession for over a year already. The cover image, however, was of the commissioning of Heaven's Gate Cathedral, one of the shots he took at the cake-cutting ceremony the day before. He had been pleasantly surprised to see it. Though he knew his editor would be bullish about the story at the editor's budget meeting, he half-expected that it would be pushed to one of the inner pages, perhaps running along with his news story on Page 5. The newspaper, half-folded up with the image facing up, felt like a trophy for him.

Ifenna sipped some coffee even though it wasn't hot anymore. The bitterness made him smack his lips, and his back hurt from stooping over to type. Relaxing on the backrest of the wooden chair, he stretched and cracked his knuckles. The story he currently wrote was about a man who'd killed his mother because his pastor told him that she was the witch responsible for his failures in life. Like someone possessed by evil spirits, the man had gone home and started beating his mother, stripping her naked in the process. Before the neighbors could come to her rescue, she was dead. The story fascinated Ifenna, not because there was anything new about stories of people killing their parents for rituals, but because of how convinced the man was that he'd done the right thing when Ifenna interviewed him at the scene just before the police took him away. His contact at the Sabo Yaba Police Station had informed Ifenna as soon as the call had been placed to the station. As a metro reporter, he had moles within the police and courts who gave him juicy leads. When he got to the scene of the crime in Makoko Waterside–a shanty ghetto town built on stilts–the police van was also just arriving.

The man, whom the assembled neighbors called Lati but who the police notes identified as Latunde Barika, had shown no remorse. Sitting in handcuffs just beside his mother's corpse, which was covered with a worn Ankara wrapper, he had insisted that he had finally broken the chains of poverty and looked genuinely surprised that people were making a fuss about it when all he'd done was secure himself a better life.

"Look at me now," Lati had said during their short interaction. "Next month I go complete tarti-seven yez. No progress for laif. My wife e leave me go cos of say I no fit take kia of am. See for where I dey live. I don try try. Wetin I neva do? Anythin I start go jus scatter. No job. No moni. No wife. I know say e no normal. How can it be my own mama that is winching me? My own mama?"

"But how you sure sey na she dey responsible for your wahala?" Ifenna had asked.

"Yes nau. Na the pastor tell me. He see it clearly. She be winch. All her childrens, no one is fine. My sister marry, two yez, the husband die. My other brother is doing conductor work. Last month, e fall commot for danfo, trailer hit am, e still dey hospital for Igbobi. I go an meet Pastor to look at my destiny and see what is worry our family, and when he pray for me he see it clearly. Mama is our problem. Do you know that even Baba Ijebu I play, winning number yesterday, Mama use her winch to change it? I miss it. How can sombodi be wicked like that to her own childrens?"

"So, the pastor say make you kill her?"

"I no plan to kill am. True to God who made me. I just beat her because I am angry. I am shock. How can my mother be the one suffering me? So, I beat her. I did not know she will die. But that one too is okay. Pastor said a winch e suppose to die. Me I believe God e use me to do good work today."

"Who is this pastor? Where e dey stay?"

"Na for Ibafo e get prayer house. Very powerful man. Na one of my fren carry me go. E pray for that my fren an wash him head with anointed ororo and his life change. Two weeks no pass, e get job. So, me too I go for my own blessings."

"So, e no pain you as your mama die so?"

"E no pain me lai lai. I thank God. I sabi say my problem e don finish now."

As the police dragged Lati into their van, Ifenna thought it ironic how Lati believed his problems were over when they may actually just be starting. Ifenna knew that if the police did not simply put a bullet in his head after having fun torturing him, they would dump him at the Awaiting Trials Unit of Kirikiri Prison and forget him there. He had been to the prison a few times to interview inmates, some of whose stories made his eyes watery with tears.

In the story he now wrote, Ifenna thought of how this was a symptom of a society gradually losing its soul, the real-life implications of the unemployment numbers that the Statistics Bureau put out quarterly. He was going to relate it to the coming recession and try to establish how the economic situation was turning the poor into monsters, even against their will, and how the rich would soon have nowhere to run.

IFENNA'S PHONE VIBRATED. IT WAS a flash from Bolanle. A reminder. she had called earlier about her "cut" from the Rivers of Joy Church press conference, and Ifenna had promised he would send her something that morning. Bolanle was an open book, a free spirit. She knew the latest city gossip: whose husband was sleeping with who, which billionaire was a front for ex-generals. She gave up information about her own life as easily as she gave up that of others. Once, she had told the entire newsroom that her husband was a one-minute man, just to make her point that premature ejaculation wasn't enough excuse for a woman to leave a marriage. After the room had fallen into a shocked silence, she'd continued.

"Why are you people looking at me like that? Baba Seun doesn't last more than a minute, but we have three children. We're happy. He knows other ways to satisfy me."

Ifenna had liked her after that. When they spoke earlier that morning, she had admitted to him that, no, she wasn't having any early pregnancy issues. She was just away to attend an interview in Ibadan.

"You should be finding job o,' she told him. "This salary they are owing. You never know. Me, my mind is no longer in that place. I can't shout jare."

Ifenna asked how the interview went.

"It went well o jare. It's one small company like that that is looking for a communications manager. I have another one today in Lagos, a reporter role with a new evening newspaper. But it is that Ibadan one I prefer. You know that is where my parents live. If I get that one, I will just be going from my parent's house in Molete and be saving all my money. You know Ibadan is not expensive like this Lagos. I really want that one."

"What about your husband? You will leave him here?"

"Baba Seun? Does he have an option? All of us will go na. Do you know they are also owing them? He said they are even retrenching some staff. Two of his friends got their letters yesterday. I don't even know where this country is going. As I am here now, I don't even have money to cook for my children. That is why I'm calling. That Pastor Nick parole, how far? Send me my share now, abeg."

Ifenna got up from the chair, stretched, and used his palm to suppress a yawn. His second story was almost done. He hadn't enjoyed writing it as much as the first, perhaps because the details disgusted him. A man had impregnated his thirteen-year-old daughter and insisted the devil was responsible. Rather than being concerned about her daughter, whose life was now damaged, the wife had seemed more upset about the shame it would bring to the family now that the NGO had insisted on a public trial.-

It was almost noon. Ifenna would finish the story later. He would go to the bank across the street to send some money to Bolanle, then have lunch before coming back to finish the story. He would also see his editor, who he knew was expecting his share of the money.

A few reporters were beginning to arrive the newsroom. Ifenna shook hands with some as he walked out.

"Baba, I see your work for cover today. Nice one," Jide, a sports reporter who walked with a cane because polio had left his left leg deformed, said, referring to the cover page image.

"Thank you," Ifenna said with a proud smile.

The sun shone brilliantly. It was the third straight day of the August break, and rain would likely fall the next day. He hoped Sikiru, his mechanic, would finish fixing his jalopy that day so he wouldn't have to worry about jumping buses in the rain. There were few things Ifenna dreaded more in Lagos, so he had given Sikiru some money from the Rivers of Joy media parley envelope. It had felt good counting out the crispy notes, aware that Lilian, who lived on the ground floor, could see him. She had moved in not long ago, and Ifenna had eyes for her. He once saw her in her short white nurses' gown, which stopped midway between her hip and her knees and exposed her thighs, and it had made him imagine her undressing in front of him, his penis throbbing inside his boxers. That morning, when he gave Sikiru the money for the repairs, she was washing her clothes on her veranda and had a wrapper tied around her chest. Ifenna had gone across to her to make some conversation after Sikiru left, asking if it was her off day and pointing out he lived on the second floor and had seasons one through eight of *Grey's Anatomy* if she was interested in coming around some time to watch.

The traffic on Allen Avenue was beginning to build up, with okadas and kekes buzzing past. As he stood on the other side looking for some space to cross, a vehicle, some meters away, started hooting. Initially, Ifenna did not worry about it. It was not unusual in Lagos for drivers in traffic to honk their horns just for nothing, but the honking continued, making him look in the direction of the car. Then he noticed the driver of the car was trying to get his attention, his hand sticking out of the window and waving. The traffic moved a bit, and the car inched in front of where he stood. It was his editor.

"Omo Ibo, Come and see me in my office immediately you get back." he said.

Before Ifenna could respond, the traffic moved again, and his editor drove off.

IT WAS ALMOST TWO O'CLOCK when Ifenna got back to *The Nigerian* office. The deposit had taken so much longer than he envisaged. There had been a queue when he got there. He'd expected it to be done in thirty minutes, but as the lines moved, people continued to claim spaces in front of him. He would have left but he knew Bolanle would raise hell if she didn't get her share of the money that day. One of the bank staff who wore an orange t-shirt with "Ask me about internet banking" boldly printed on it approached him to talk about enrolling for the bank's mobile and internet banking services, indicating that Ifenna would not have to be on such long queues for simple transactions.

"You will just do it fiam, on your phone, in the comfort of your office."

Ifenna had heard a lot about the online services but was still very skeptical. One of the first stories he covered after joining *The Nigerian* was about a woman who committed suicide after fraudsters gained access to her internet banking profile, wiped her account clean, and all four million and six hundred thousand naira was gone. The bulk of the money was a loan she just got from a market women co-operative society to invest in her aso-oke business. They said she'd first rushed to the bank in bathroom slippers when she started receiving debit alerts that she knew nothing about, her hair like the aftermath of a whirlwind. It was the early days of the Central Bank's Cashless Policy, and even the bankers were a bit confused about how she was in Nigeria while someone was using her card to shop in Texas, United States. They said she paced around the banking hall while the bankers tried to figure out what was happening as she held her head and cried. She left the banking hall much the same way she rushed in and jumped on an okada before anyone could stop her. Later that evening, news broke that a woman had jumped off the Third Mainland Bridge to her death. Since then, Ifenna, who covered the recovery of the body by local fishermen and later went to interview the bank staff, decided that internet banking and all its relations were not for him.

Now, as he entered the office, he felt pressed. The amala and ewedu he ate at Iya Amala Joint after leaving the bank was hot, and he had eaten it in a hurry. It now felt like the amala had melted everything in his stomach and flushed it toward his rectum. Should he rush to the toilet or go see his editor first? The meeting would probably be brief. Plus, the man must be getting impatient now. He jogged up the stairs to the first floor, where the editors had their side offices.

Ifenna pushed the slightly ajar door open and entered. The editor was at his desk, eating from a cob of roasted corn while reading a copy of the day's *The Nigerian* spread out in front of him. The table was largely bare but for his open laptop, some pieces of coconut in a small transparent plastic bag, and the box telephone. Scattered all over the wall were plaques and framed certificates of awards and training he had gathered over the years. The man's favorite line was "I have paid my dues," and he was always quick to direct everyone who disagreed with him to his office wall to see that he was an experienced and professional journalist, not what he called moin-moin reporters of nowadays." He wore his days in the pro-democracy struggle like an invisible cape of honor though Ifenna believed that many of his claims of being detained many times by the State Security Service (SSS) in their Shangisha dungeon were false.

Ifenna reached into his pocket and pulled out the envelope containing the fifty thousand naira he had chosen to give to the editor.

"I am here, sir," he said, announcing his presence, though the door made a loud creaking sound when he pushed it, like something that needed oiling at the hinges.

"This is from yesterday," he added when the editor looked up before dropping the envelope on the table.

"That's not even the matter now," his editor said, lowering the corn in his left hand into the plastic bag with the coconut. "There's a big issue."

Ifenna could sense that the man was troubled, the way his eyes bulged, and a vein seemed to divide his forehead into two halves. "You know I didn't read your story yesterday before passing it to print. I just thought you slammed the press release they gave you there as usual. What is this here? What rubbish is this?"

It was only then that Ifenna noticed that his editor

was reading his story from the commissioning: "Death and Secrecy: The Making of a World-Record Cathedral." He had half-expected that the editor would change the title because that was really the bulk of the editing they did, rewrite headlines to make it sensational, depending on who was paying the piper, without looking at the details in the body. When he saw that it ran the way he presented it, he had felt pleasantly surprised, but it was clear now that the man hadn't even paid any attention to the story at all.

"What were you thinking? Such a headline. Death and secrecy?"

Ifenna remained quiet, lifting the weight of his body from one leg to the other to control his urge to use the toilet, which was getting worse from his boss's words.

"Just look at this." His editor began to read excerpts from the story.

… but the story not being told is about the grand cover-up of the death of the young, charismatic Pastor Felix Azinge, who fell to his death from a scaffolding during the construction of the edifice. Though it was said to be an accident, information available to this reporter seems to suggest there is more to this narrative than meets the eyes. When confronted with this, the founder and general overseer of the Rivers of Joy Church, during his media parley with journalists, declined to comment on it. Perhaps, we can conclude that just as Christ had to shed his blood to establish the church, there had to be some bloodshed for this gigantic edifice of great architectural accomplishment to be born. What is left to be known is ….

THE QUESTION IFENNA WAS SUPPOSED to ask Pastor Nick at the press parley was about the plans the church had to support the less privileged, especially those in the communities closest to the complex. The two reporters who asked questions before him had kept to the script. The first asked what inspired the project, and Pastor Nick seized the opportunity to retell the story of the message he received from God. One morning, as he prayed for a new temple that would bring people from every corner of the world to worship him in Nigeria. He'd gone on about how Nigeria was special in the eyes of the Lord and how it would be the root of the new mission, like Antioch in the times of the Apostles. The second question was about the cost of the project. Ifenna guessed that the lady who'd asked the question was a groupie of the pastor, the way she started off with eulogies.

"I feel so privileged to meet you, sir. I am so in awe of the great work you are doing in our time. You are a blessing to this generation."

The only thing she seemed to have left out was a declaration of her love for him. Her encomia left Pastor Nick grinning from ear to ear, bowing slightly in feigned humility *and* declaring, with the pride of a father announcing to his friends that his son won a tennis game, that the building cost a little over thirty billion naira. Just so no one doubted his claims, he added that all the marble used was of the finest Italian granite, and all the materials for the interior were sourced abroad. He also added that he had ordered an organ "bigger and better than the one in the Westminster Abbey in England," and the entire complex had its own independent power and water supply systems.

Then, to cap it all off, he'd added, with his voice many pitches lower for effect, "And we did not take a dime in loan from the bank or from anybody. Everything you see was paid for in full, even the tarring of the road leading to the church, which Julius Berger is handling. We are not owing a dime because our God is not a God of debts and insufficient funds."

Ifenna had been sufficiently irked by the time the applause ended, and it was his turn to ask a question. Somehow, the anxiety was gone, and he did not stand like the two earlier reporters.

"Pastor, there are people who believe the death of the young pastor at this site during the construction was not an accident. Some people believe he may have been pushed in a cover-up homicide. What is your comment on this?"

Ifenna watched the smile drain from Pastor Nick's face, as if in reverse slow motion. The room went silent; perhaps, even the other reporters knew this question was not part of the script. He saw the pastor and his beautiful media assistant exchange quick glances; her eyes showed she was as confused as he. Then, in an instant, the smile returned to his face.

"Who are these people thinking these things? I have not heard of any such claims."

"But sir, this is a real perception out there. There is a report that you had a disagreement before his death. How true is that?" Ifenna pressed.

"I have no comment on that." Pastor Nick fiddled with his wristwatch as if to indicate that he was running late for something else.

"But, sir—"

The media assistant interrupted him. "Please, that will be enough on that matter. You can seek further clarification after this press conference, and I will be happy to oblige you. Like I said in the beginning, it's been a long day for everyone. We need to keep to time, and the Pastor needs to go rest and refresh for the banquet. Next question, please."

Ifenna sat back, relieved. He had the response he wanted for his story.

"WHAT KIND OF ALLEGATION IS this?" Ifenna's editor asked now, after reading the short excerpt. "What are you insinuating? Who are you to make such a careless allegation of the man of God? Do you know how powerful Pastor Adejuwon is in this country?"

"I had a good source that provided the lead, and as a journalist, I had to follow the lead."

"What rubbish lead? You are following lead? That lead will lead you out of a job very—" His desk phone rang. He picked it up on the second ring once he recognized the caller ID.

Ifenna swallowed hard. The urge to take a shit had disappeared, and he was back in his Institute of Journalism class, sitting in front as usual.

It was an MC 301 class on News Writing. Professor Babajide was walking around the class, the high sole of his shoes knocking the floor as he did. He spoke in his polished English accent, his baritone voice reaching the ends of the room.

"Journalists are nothing without their sources, and when you get a lead from a credible source, follow it because if it smells like a rat, it probably is a rat, and right there is your story."

"Yes. Yes. No. I am with him now." The editor spoke into the phone. "Yes. I was just about to … no, yes. I will send him over from here. Yes. Okay. Thank you."

Ifenna's heart began to do backflips.

"Chairman called me this morning," the editor started after dropping the receiver.

Chairman referred to the rarely seen publisher of *The Nigerian*. In the time Ifenna had been there, he had seen Chairman only once in person, a chance meeting on the staircase. He'd come to take a picture with the editorial board to mark the tenth anniversary of the paper. Whenever Chairman attended any of his many society functions, he took up the paper cover no matter what other more newsworthy pictures there were. And during elections, the paper was available only to his friends who were mostly members of the ruling party. The editors spoke of him like a demigod, like they feared the idea of his very existence. To hear that he had called made the boot soles in Ifenna's chest quicken their steps.

"Apparently, Pastor Nick called him to complain about your story," the editor now spoke slowly, in a solemn voice, like someone about to deliver incredibly sad news, rubbing his two palms together and moving his swivel chair from side to side.

"You know Chairman doesn't call unless it's a serious matter. He was very angry that we ran a story like that about the man of God. So, I am afraid, Omo Ibo, we must let you go immediately. Go straight to HR now and submit your ID card. They are expecting you."

Ifenna stood petrified. So many thoughts swerved through his mind. He wanted to ask whether *The Nigerian* was a media house or a crony patronage house. He wanted to ask what the "Integrity and Truth" motto of the newspaper meant, if Chairman really asked them to sack him, or if the decision was a knee-jerk reaction to save face. He wanted to ask about his outstanding salaries and the contributory pension that had been deducted but not remitted into his Pension Fund account.

But when his lips finally parted, he heard himself say, "Sir, my name is Ifenna, not Omo Ibo."

The editor regarded him for a while, the way you would peer at a neighbor's child who'd just peed on your Sunday best. Then, he picked up the corn and coconut— the latter with his left hand and the former with his right— and took a bite of each, indicating the finality of the conversation.

Ifenna made to leave, but on second thought, he turned around and grabbed the envelope he earlier dropped on the table.

FOUR

The persistent banging on his door woke Ifenna up; it felt as if someone was pounding a gong right on his temple. He jumped up like one who'd just wet the bed, surprised he had slept on the three-seater couch in his living room rather than in his bed. The television, which hung on the wall, was turned on, set on Hip TV, and played Davido's new hit "Dami Duro," a little too loud for the early hour. As he picked up the remote from the center table to turn the volume down, the bang on the door sounded once more.

"Who is it?" He barked, looking at his wristwatch before shuffling toward the door. It was just about 6.30 am.

"We want to go out," answered a grumpy female voice, followed by the footsteps of the person walking away.

Ifenna recognized the voice, deep and raspy like someone with a cold. It was the wife of the man who lived just above him, Tunde. The lady and her husband were of a special mettle, like two beings cut from the same cloth. They were both very uncultured and rude. The man carried himself like he owned the building, perhaps because he and his wife had two cars. And this was the reason for the altercations he and Ifenna always had.

The way the compound was built, there was only one long space that ran the length of the building itself where tenants could park their cars. It was such that they had to park in a straight line, and when anyone wanted to go out, they had to ask others parked behind to drive out first.

Everyone understood the situation and responded promptly when they were called to drive out, but not Tunde and his wife. When they came down, they would neither apologize nor acknowledge that others were waiting. It did not help that they had two cars, against the tenancy rules of one car per tenant. Now that his wife was pregnant, Tunde had to drive out both cars, causing delays that irritated Ifenna, especially on the mornings he was in a hurry to leave. In contrast, when they were the ones being blocked, his wife impatiently slammed on her neighbor's doors.

Ifenna looked around for his car keys. Sikiru, his mechanic, had returned his jalopy the evening before, and he had driven it out to a beer parlor, determined not to feel bad about losing his job. He had returned past midnight, and because the gateman, Nuhu, was already asleep, he had parked the car just outside the gates so that no one could drive in or out of the compound. He located the keys in his trouser pocket, momentarily realizing he still had his work clothes on. Stifling a yawn, he pushed his feet into his slippers and made for the door.

The other tenants were already downstairs with their groggy faces and bad breath. Everyone waited for Ifenna, and it seemed they had been waiting for a while. He imagined some of the men being dragged up from between their wives' legs, their Saturday morning sex truncated by the call to drive out. He felt some guilt for delaying them. Anyone could read the complaints in their eyes as he walked toward the gate slowly because he was still sleepy and had a headache.

When he got back to his flat, the power had gone out, and the blades of the ceiling fan were making the final slow-cycling rounds. Ifenna cursed as he kicked off his slippers. His headache was now more pronounced, throbbing on both sides of his head just above his ears. He remembered the bottles of beer he *canceled* last night; how he kept telling the female attendant with breasts like pumpkins to make sure the bottles were "mortuary standard" each time he ordered a replacement; and how she said, '*This one don die finish,*" as she set the bottles in front of him.

The music had been loud, and the DJ had a good head on his neck. Ifenna had risen from time to time to dance, a glass cup in hand, screaming the lyrics of the song or just mumbling some words. He decided he had to sleep off the hangover but not without light. He worried his sleep would be labored. He sweated a lot without the fan on. Just then, he heard a generator come on outside. He remembered he had run out of fuel in his generator days ago and cursed, more because he now also had to contend with the noise of generators in finding sleep. He dragged himself first into the toilet to empty his bladder, spilling urine all over the toilet seat, before peeling off all his clothes slowly and collapsing face down on the bed.

IFENNA IS WALKING ALONE ON A LONELY BUSH PATH. It is evening. The grumble in the sky announces impending rain. He quickens his steps, balances the load of firewood he'd fetched

43

for his mother firmly on his head. He is just fourteen, and the only item of clothing he has on is a pair of khaki knickers. He is approaching the last ridge on the path when he hears footsteps from behind. He turns to check but there is no one. He continues walking, and the footsteps behind grow louder and closer.

From the sound, it is clear there are more than one person, maybe about three, but each time he looks over his shoulder, Ifenna sees no one. To be sure his mind is not playing tricks, he stops walking and listens. The footsteps also stop. The only sound he hears is that of his heart pounding against his chest, but as soon as he starts walking again, the strange footsteps seem just some distance away from him. Ifenna's hands are shaking.

A slow breeze passes through the bushes, making the trees sway and crackle. Ifenna, who is now descending the last ridge, begins to run, and as he increases this pace, the footsteps also begin to run. Lightning flashes through the skies. Thunder vibrates his feet. Then, darkness falls. The footsteps are now right behind him. Ifenna feels his foot strike a stone, and he falls. The bunch of firewood thunders to the ground.

"He is the one trying to ruin us. We must deal with him," a voice says.

Ifenna gets up and drags himself along the dusty path, he tries to make out any face in the darkness.

"Let me strike him on the head," a different voice says.

"No, we will not kill him. Let us cut off his legs and make him miserable forever," a third voice quipped.

Ifenna wants to talk, to tell them they had the wrong person, to scream for help, but it is as though his vocal cords had been severed. He feels the three faces a few inches from his own, peering down at him. Suddenly, lightning flashes, illuminating the darkness long enough for him to glimpse their faces. He knew them. Pastor Nick,

Chairman, and his editor. He tries to scream again, but this time, all three men wrap their hands around his throat.

HE WOKE UP TO HIS phone ringing. It was his mother. K'naan's "Wavin Flag," the special ring tone announced her. Ifenna allowed the phone to ring its course as he sat up on the mattress and looked around. The mattress was drenched with sweat and had formed the outlines of his bare body. He could feel his heart pounding, still feel their hands around his neck. Though he knew it was only a dream, he reached up and rubbed a hand over his throat.

The phone started ringing again. He grabbed it and ended the call; he never allowed her to expend her call credit on him. Ifenna took a moment to take a deep breath, trying to clear the dream from his head. As he re-dialed her number, he noticed that he had over ten missed calls and knew immediately that his mother would already be very worried. The time on the phone's screen was *1:58 pm*. How had he slept that long?

She picked on the first ring.

"Mummy. Good afternoon," he said, trying to sound normal.

"May Jehovah be praised. You're alive." He could hear his mother heave a sigh of relief.

"Of course, mummy. Onwelu ife melu? Is anything the matter?"

"Kedu ebe phonu gi di sinci m' kpo balu gi?" she asked in a mixture of English and Igbo. "I have called over twenty times."

Ifenna chuckled at her exaggeration. "I was sleeping."

"Sleeping? You did not go to work today? Odikwa nma?"

"It's Saturday, Mummy."

"But you told me you work on Saturdays?"

"Eh, Mummy. But not every Saturday," Ifenna tried to keep the irritation from his tone.

His mother had invited him several times to come along with her to the last Friday of the month vigils in her church, but each time he told her he had work and could not attend.

"Odinma," she said in a way that suggested she wasn't satisfied but also not keen on pushing the discussion. "Well, it is good you are at home," she said after a brief lull.

Ifenna could feel that the concern had left her voice and given way to excitement.

"I wanted to tell you about last night's vigil. It was a special encounter. Do you know I almost did not go? That waist pain was just holding me down all through yesterday. It must have been Satan trying to block me from what God already had planned. I just struggled and went. Bia k'ifu, it was powerful. The man of God who ministered came from Jos. Onye Awusa o. I didn't know Hausa people had such powerful pastors. Jehovah be praised. When he started praying, ebe nini a na e shayki. Everywhere was shaking. Ah, you needed to have been there. It was like we were lifted to another realm."

Ifenna put the phone on speaker and dropped it beside him on the bed. His mother's church stories bored him. They had been raised Catholics, he and his sister, Nkoli. Their late father was passive at best, attending Mass compulsorily only on two occasions in a year, Easter and Christmas, and when family friends invited him for a christening of their new baby or to celebrate an anniversary. Otherwise, on Sunday mornings, he would hand Ifenna and Nkoli a fifty naira note each for offertory and tell them he'd see them later as they left with their mother. When they returned, they often found him dressed in a wrapper tied around his waist, his legs crossed on the table, watching CNN, empty bottles of Guinness Stout littered at his feet. He was usually in a happy mood and would jokingly ask them what Fada said in their own church because the Fada at his own told them to drink and be merry because the kingdom was at hand.

It was their mother who took them to Mass at St. Mathew's Church in Orile, holding each child in either of her hands as they trekked. It was she who made sure they attended catechism, who prepared them for their first Holy Communion exams, who made sure that after they became communicants, they were always in a state of grace to receive the body and blood of Christ at Mass. Their mother led the women to cook the best party Jollof Ifenna ever tasted during the annual bazaar, coordinated the women during their football matches to mark Mothers' Day, and, once when the cardinal visited to hold confirmation, she read the speech as the chairperson of the Catholic Women's Organization.

Then, their father died, and it was as if something inside her died, too. She'd been strong, at first. When sympathizers came to see her, she talked with them as if nothing had happened and rebuked those who shed tears in her presence, but when she returned to Lagos after the funeral, she seemed to sink into her own dark hole. She started talking about the enemies of the family and how they had succeeded in killing her husband.

"How does an active, healthy man, dimkpa mmadu,

suddenly slump and die?"

She insisted that the illness that killed her husband without warning was projected into his body, and the same people were now after her and her children. They wanted to have the village to themselves. She wasn't going to let it happen. She started attending midweek evening fellowships at Power In The Blood Ministries. Then, she stopped attending Sunday Mass at St. Matthew's all together and started dragging Ifenna and Nkoli with her to her new church.

Once, when they got home after service, she took out all the effigies of Jesus, Mary, and Joseph in the small altar they had in their living room, together with the flowers and rosaries, and set them on fire in the backyard. The pastor had preached from Exodus 20:4 about graven images. People who used items of any kind to pray were offending God and no better than the idol worshippers in the village who prayed to gods made of wood. The way they prayed changed. They no longer knelt. Instead, they stood and held hands. Their mother led the prayers, speaking in a high pitch, as if she were scolding God, and calling on Holy Ghost fire to consume her enemies.

Ifenna watched his mother become another person. He saw the transformation clearly on the Sunday she took them to a different church, which they had to take a bus to get to. The walls were freshly painted in a cream color and had a smell that tingled his nostrils like insecticide spray. The pastor, whose hair was mostly grey, wore an oversized coat that looked like a parachute and kept a stern face.

"To defeat the enemy, you have to be holy in both body and spirit," he preached. "For we battle not against flesh and blood but against principalities and evil powers, and against the rulers of the darkness of this world."

After that sermon, Ifenna's mother stopped wearing jewelry and threw away all her hair curlers. She chopped her hair off and began to wear a hat when she went out. She also began to read the Bible so intently and made Ifenna and Nkoli memorize whole verses from a daily devotional she told them to keep under their pillows.

"Hello Ife'm, are you still there?" she asked now on the phone.

Ifenna had got up from the bed, spread the bedsheet across the length of the mattress, picked up the phone, and said he was there.

"So, that is how the man of God called me out. I was shocked. He said there was a widow here with two children who has been seeking favor for her children to no avail, that today was my day. I did not wait for him to tell me to; I walked out myself."

"But Mummy, how did you know it was you he was referring to?"

"I was convinced in my spirit. And I was not wrong. The man prayed for me when I came out. He prayed for me. Ah, Ife'm. I have not felt the anointing so strong. Then, he started speaking, prophesying. He confirmed everything I have always said. That your Uncle Bonny is evil. Oburo ezigbo mmadu cha. He is the one behind all our misfortunes."

"Are you saying he called Uncle Bonny by name, like he really said his name?" Ifenna asked, fanning himself with a plastic hand fan he received as a souvenir at a colleague's wedding.

"He didn't have to. When he said there is an evil strong

49

man in my husband's family, I knew who he was talking about already."

Ifenna wanted to mention to her that there were other men in the family. His father had three other brothers, and it could have also been any of them, or even none of them, the man was referring to, but he decided to let her continue.

"He said your father did not die an ordinary death. He said misfortune is already visiting the person who did it. Did your Uncle Boniface not have a motorcycle accident last month? Did he not injure his leg and is now walking with crutches? That's the misfortune! And it will not stop until he dies and goes to hell. Wicked man."

"Mummy!"

"Ogini? He should not die? The Bible said suffer not the witch to live. In fact, that's also why I am calling. The man of God gave us special prayers to say for two weeks, every day at midnight. I will text you the Bible verses after. I already sent it to Nkoli. I just hope she can be waking up to say it properly in school, but you must say it, Ife'm. O di ezigbo nkpa."

Ifenna was silent. He had received many such prayer points and Bible verses, including calls over the years from his mother, telling him to fast or sit vigil overnight. And even though he never followed through, he always indulged her by not arguing about it. When she asked, he always assured her he had followed all of her instructions.

"Did you hear what I said?"

"Yes, Mummy."

"Good. And there is some hopeful news too. The man of God said you were born with a star and that you will be great and very wealthy. He said that there was something going to happen soon in your workplace that will elevate you. Maybe you will be promoted, or you will win an award. I don't know, but he said we should get ready to testify over your life."

Ifenna wanted to chuckle at the irony. *Surely, there is something wrong with the man's vision*, but he could not tell his mother he had been sacked. He knew what it would do to her, so he said, "Amen."

"Ngwanu. Let me leave you to rest. Hope that anointing oil I gave you is still remaining?"

"Yes, Mummy."

"Ka o di mgbe ozo. Take care."

After the call ended, Ifenna sat back in bed, and for the first time, he gave serious thought to the events of yesterday. It was the second time he had been sacked from a job. The first time, his mother was hysterical. She was convinced it came from the same enemies who killed his father. She'd run to her pastor, a short, balding man who spoke as if he had hot food in his mouth. He corroborated her claims and declared Ifenna needed special deliverance prayers because the enemies were bent on making him a pauper. By disempowering the first fruit, these enemies would ruin the entire family. His mother must make a special first fruit offering in January of every year, the pastor insisted.

Ifenna had been amused by it all. Though he had submitted himself for the deliverance prayers because he still lived with his mother at the time and couldn't escape it, he knew very well what had caused his termination. So, when the pastor, all sweaty and husky with a Bible in one hand and a bottle of olive oil in another, circled him speaking in tongues and asking the spirit of failure to depart, he thought instead of how he hated working at the place and how, in a way, his job loss was a good thing.

It was his first job after NYSC, in a bank as a contract staff. He wasn't working as a teller like many fresh graduates. That was what made the job a miraculous blessing from God, according to his mother. He worked instead at the bank's head office in Marina, in the communications team, with a desk and laptop to himself. The bank published a monthly magazine, and he had been recruited as part of the editorial team. Besides the attractive pay and that he had no big revenue targets to chase, it was something he thought he would enjoy doing. But a few weeks into his stay, he knew it wouldn't be for long. He found it quite nauseating that the bank held an hour-long prayer session every Monday and Friday at seven o'clock in the morning. The session, led by the bank's MD herself, compelled everyone, regardless of their faith, to join. And, of course, she kept an attendance roster at the door.

The MD was from a well-known family who controlled massive interests in various sectors. She was as popular for her feat in being the first female bank MD in the country as she was for her love for elaborate jewelry and taste for corporate jets. But she was also deeply religious, or so she wanted everyone to believe. The bank's financial statement had a line item on tithes in which she paid ten percent of the bank's annual profit to her pastor. Ifenna had always admired her. She had gifted a new female hostel to his university and was later bestowed with an honorary doctorate degree at his convocation, but he could not understand the need for the compulsory prayers in a work environment. So, after the first two weeks, he started skipping the sessions, appearing only occasionally, and making sure to be late. This did not go unnoticed.

His boss, the communications manager, however, existed to please the MD. She could kiss the floor on which the MD walked. Ifenna thought it was disgusting, the way she carried the MD's handbag when they were out at functions and called her, a woman of a similar age bracket, "Mummy.'"

And she expected her staff to do likewise, to call her 'Mummy' too, to compliment her clothes and hair every morning and to never leave the office before her. So, the communications team idled away on their systems and made like they were busy long after work hours until "Mummy" left for the day.

It wasn't long before Ifenna started breaking this rule, too. After a corpse was found—a victim of robbers—close to Orile Bus Stop, he decided it was too dangerous to go home so late, no matter the amount of olive oil his mother rubbed on his forehead before he left in the morning. At five o'clock in the evening, when he finished all his work tasks, he bid everyone goodnight and left.

Six months into his employment, his manager called him into her office for a feedback session. She didn't explicitly mention his failure to attend prayer sessions or his habit of leaving early but told him he wasn't a "good enough team player," and Ifenna understood exactly what sins he had committed. His overall ratings were poor, she said, though the pieces he wrote for the magazine were beautiful. The same day, he received a letter from Human Resources, terminating his contract for not meeting the expectations of his role.

It amused Ifenna even now, how just three months after

his termination, the MD of the bank was arrested, along with her senior management, by the Financial Crimes Agency for the reckless granting of credit facilities and mismanagement of depositor funds running into billions of dollars. A year later, she was sentenced to jail. By the time he joined *The Nigerian* two years later, the bank had been acquired by another bank in a liquidation deal. He remembered the banner headline on the day's copy of *The Nigerian* announcing the deal, how it had thrilled him so much that he went into the restroom to laugh. In a way, he thought now, perhaps his mother's prayers worked after all.

Dizziness spun Ifenna's head as he got up from the mattress. His stomach growled. The generators outside had reached a crescendo. Many of the other flats had turned theirs on to watch the English Premiership matches. Ifenna walked to his small kitchen, holding the wall for balance as he did. He found a plastic bottle of malt that had lost its chill in the fridge, uncapped it, and gulped down its contents, all the while thinking of what to eat. He did not feel up to walking down his street to the restaurant. The place would be bursting with people who were there not to eat but to see the football games for free. It was his usual spot to go on Saturdays because he didn't subscribe to the premium Cable TV bouquets that aired all the matches, but he didn't think his headache could handle all the noise. He did not also want to cook. Only then did he remember he'd bought some roasted groundnuts on his way back from work the day before, which he had yet to eat. A bowl of soaked garri and groundnuts would cure his hangover.

Bolanle called as he began to drink the garri, which he had soaked in water with a little more sugar than necessary, with groundnut floating atop like a plastic bottle in a puddle. He had noticed her name among the missed calls on his phone earlier and made a mental note of returning the call.

"Ife," she called his name as if it was a Yoruba name. "Which kain story I dey hear so?"

"My sister. That is it o. Na so we see am," Ifenna said before stirring the bowl of garri a bit more, having bitten some undissolved cube of sugar in the last spoon.

"Just like that?"

"That is it o. They said Chairman was vexing that I asked Pastor Nick difficult questions."

"Aeyaa. Pele!"

"Me I was surprised that Chairman and Pastor Nick. I mean, is that man Christian or Muslim sef?"

"Eh, forget what you see outside o. Everybody goes to Pastor Nick. All these rich men you see. Why do you think he is so powerful? Ah! Many of them are like Nicodemus. They go to the man at night."

"But what does he do for them?"

"Ife, if you ask me, na who I go ask? There is something about Pastor Nick that attracts people to him like ants to sugar. He has such a sweet mouth. Have you heard him talk? And they say his prayers work too. Plus, he rarely preaches about hellfire o. No time for that one. That makes people like him more. Me sef, I will not lie to you, I like the man. Very generous somebody. But sha, I know it is not pure. There is something behind that we can't see. I fear the man very much too."

Ifenna remembered his dream from earlier and wondered how dangerous the man could possibly be. How afraid he had been at the pastor's voice in the pitch darkness saying he would be taught a lesson. He wondered if his job termination was the lesson or if he should be worried that the man would still come after him. Then, just as suddenly as it came in, he pushed the thought out of his mind. Dreams rarely came true.

"You see that question you asked him, eh," Bolanle continued. "Hmm. Me too I heard something that time it happened o. Abi whether Pastor Nick felt threatened by the other pastor or that he was planning to go and start his own church? Whatever sha. It really doesn't seem like it was an accident."

"That's no longer my problem now," Ifenna said dismissively.

A brief lull hung between them as he tried to silently chew and swallow a spoonful of garri. The power suddenly flicked back on and shouts from the neighborhood children echoed through the vents. Ifenna sighed in relief as the blades of the ceiling fan began circling again. The first whiff of cool air felt so good. The television came on next, a blank blue screen as the decoder loaded.

"So, wetin you go do now?" Bolanle asked, sounding concerned.

"What can I do? I can't fight them now. Abi na my papa company?"

"No, I mean about getting another job."

Ifenna paused. His lack of an answer for this bothered him. When he lost his first job, he hadn't worried so much because he still lived with his mother. Plus, most of the people he served with hadn't even got their first jobs yet, so in a way, it had seemed like he was simply back to the starting line after a false start. The economy was a lot better then, as well. The papers boasted that Nigeria was among the fastest-growing economies in the world. Oil sold at over a hundred dollars; prosperity was in the air. So he hadn't worried much.

First, he got a marketing job with an insurance company, which required convincing people to take out policies as an alternate form of savings. Insurance was so hard to sell, and because they were paid only a bonus of the amounts they brought, Ifenna soon got frustrated and left. He then got a writing gig with a new online magazine where he had to rewrite news stories stolen from other news websites. The more stories he stole, the more he earned. It was so easy, and the pay had been regular. That was when he'd bought his jalopy and moved out of his mother's house. After six months, the pay stopped being regular. By the twelfth month, they owed two months' salary to all their employees, and then the website got sued for copyright infringement after they copied an investigative report done by a prominent newspaper without giving credit. The website was taken down. Ifenna moved on with the laptop they provided him and for some months pitched his articles to different publications, some of which accepted and paid, until the opportunity at *The Nigerian* came along.

"I don't know, frankly," he said. "But I will work something out."

"It is well with you, eh. I know you will. You are a very smart guy. God will help you. Don't worry; if I hear of anything, I will let you know."

"No problem at all. Thanks," Ifenna said, eager to get back to his garri, which was swelling so fast.

FIVE

Pastor Nick flipped to the second page of the sheet in his hands, swiveling his chair a little to the right and then to the left in a semi-circular pattern. Enya spewed from the speakers, and he tried to align the side-to-side chair movement with the rhythm of the music, gliding his head slowly as he read.

He was going to have a meeting with his ghostwriter, Kofi that morning. The themes for the discussion were written on the paper he had in his hands. It had been lying there on his table, untouched for over a week. If not for his secretary's reminder the night before, he wouldn't have remembered that he had a meeting with Kofi that morning. The attention following the commissioning of the Heaven's Gate Cathedral, a lot of which he had stoked himself, had been somewhat overwhelming and had impacted some of his other activities. It had been one media engagement after the other since then, with television and radio stations falling over one another to host him on their breakfast shows. The meeting with Kofi mattered more to him, so he had told Bimbo, his media assistant, to cancel an appearance on a radio show that morning so he could get in early to the office and prepare.

On an A4-sized printing paper, Kofi had drawn out the outline of Nick's biography. Bimbo had suggested he should have one written. With his increased popularity and the Heaven's Gate Cathedral feat, more people wanted to hear his story. A biography, Bimbo insisted, was just what he needed to ride the waves of his success for a while longer. A book would also be good for the ministry. Initially, Nick objected, saying he was still too young, that biographies were things you did at the twilight of life and at the peak of your career, but Bimbo convinced him otherwise. Think of it as a sign of accomplishment, she'd said, of being a highflyer among your generation. Like Obama.

Kofi, more Lagosian than Ghanaian, spent most of his life in Lagos and had agreed to ghostwrite the biography. Already he had written Nick's fifteen motivational books, sprinkling them with scripture so they'd pass for religious texts. He was a whiz kid of sorts with a very smart mind and a depth of knowledge on every topic, which Nick sometimes found intimidating, given his young age. The first time they met, with his dreadlocks like the strands of a wet mop and lips blackened by years of cigarette use, Nick had been concerned about being seen publicly at the posh eatery in Victoria Island with someone like Kofi. He'd barely looked like he could write the alphabet, let alone write a book. Bimbo knew him from the ad agency where she used to work and swore to Nick that Kofi was the perfect man for the job.

"Well, he's a bit eccentric and rough at the edges but very talented," she had said.

Kofi had resigned from the agency because he believed he could write a Nobel prize-winning book. The story idea was well-formed in his head, but somehow, none of the publishers he'd sent the synopsis to shared his enthusiasm. By the time Bimbo contacted him to write for Nick, actually to turn around and finish a manuscript Nick had been struggling with for close to a year, Kofi was broke and more Bohemian than she remembered, reeking of cheap alcohol and interspacing his speech with some Patois, like someone eager to connect with his lost Jamaican roots.

He took the job even though he said, as a Jah Rastafarian, he did not believe in the Christian god. He'd done a great job with the manuscript, which quickly became Nick's first bestseller. A non-disclosure agreement and a retainership deal followed. Now, five years after, it seemed like Kofi had given up on the Nobel prize dream since the money Pastor Nick paid him was like winning the Nobel prize anyway.

The plan he had developed for writing the biography required a weekly two-hour session with Nick over a period of two months to interview him on each of the themes he had outlined. Nick nodded as he came to the end of the list. The last chapter would be titled: "The Heaven's Gate Story." Nick thought that was a befitting climax for the book, one he would be happy to talk about. He flipped to the first page and set his eyes on the first item—"The Formative Years"— which was up for discussion at their meeting that morning. Kofi had written two subtexts underneath it like bullet points to provide more context:

Description of early childhood
Remarkable experiences that helped shape your life, etc.

Pastor Nick stopped swiveling the chair. Enya had since

given way to Luciano Pavarotti, another of his favorites. He let his thoughts float briefly with the music, shutting his eyes and moving his head to the rhythm. He opened his eyes after a few minutes and looked at the paper again. His childhood wasn't an aspect of his life he liked to think about. He decided there were two distinct parts to it.

The first part was a happy one. They lived in Ikorodu, a suburb of Lagos, he and his parents and his two sisters. They were not rich, but they also weren't poor. Their life was simple, draped in joy and his father's big dreams for his children. He remembered his father's authoritative baritone voice ringing through their small house, calling them to gather around the television to watch *Speak Out* on NTA so they could learn new words from their fellow children, to go have their siesta in the afternoon because it helped their brains to develop properly, and to not speak vernacular like uneducated fishermen because those types of people had no future. He recalled their morning devotions; how he and his sisters shuffled to the parlor with sleepy eyes following their father's banging on their room door; and how they sat smug and listened as he read a passage from the Bible, his favorite King James Version, before repeating the same lines of prayer. Usually, by the time he finished, Nick and his sisters would have all fallen asleep in their kneeling positions.

Pastor Nick's face melted into a smile as he recalled acting war films with stick guns with the other children in the neighborhood and being called Rambo because he sprang the best enemy ambushes and all the other kids wanted to be on his side. At school, he was called "The Prof" because he was always first in the class and represented the school in the annual debate competition. He was a smart child, his teachers said. He could be a lawyer or a doctor in the future.

But then his father died, and everything changed. It was as if someone put a pin to the floating balloon that was their lives, and everything in it emptied out with a burst. One incident, the memory etched into his brain like a hot iron brand, shaped much of that second part of his childhood. It was so fresh on his mind, like it had happened just yesterday.

Owo Blow and his boys came just before dawn that day. The sound of their knuckles against the door made Nick jump up, setting off a parade of boot soles in the left of his chest. He had stayed up late the night before to watch the telecast of WrestleMania on NTA and had fallen asleep on the long couch in the sitting room. The television channel had closed, and the television shrieked, like freshly cut onions poured into hot groundnut oil. The sound compounded Nick's brief confusion, and all traces of sleep disappeared from his eyes as they adjusted to the bright light of the long fluorescent lamp hanging above. His first thought: robbers. There had been two robbery incidents in the neighborhood the past month, and the residents had met and agreed to compose a group of local vigilantes to keep watch at night, though no one had come up with a schedule yet. Nick leaped toward the television and turned the knob to turn it off, striking his left toe against a wooden stool in the process. The pain traveled like needle pricks to the rest of his body, but he held himself from screaming as he stood still in front of the blank television, waiting to hear the banging sound again. He started to wonder if it had come from his dream when the fists pounded on the door again.

Nick almost jumped out of his skin. He could now hear voices. They were barely audible, but he was certain there had to be at least two people. The louder of the two demanded that the door be opened, or they would break it down. Nick did a quick analysis. It was just him and his two sisters in the house with no money for the robbers to steal. What if the robbers killed them for a wasted venture? The last time the robbers had struck the neighborhood, they'd shot the man of the house and mocked him for being lazy since he had only one thousand naira in the house.

The order to open the door came again, this time louder, angrier. Just then, his sister, Maryanne, rushed into the sitting room, a wrapper over her chest, awoken by all the banging. Nick turned around to meet her eyes, the questions in them. With his index finger to his lips. As he turned back to the door, his eyes fell on the wall clock hanging next to the picture of their late father. It was almost five o'clock. Already morning. He rolled the curtains away and turned the keys just as another round of banging started.

Owo Blow was their landlord. Everyone knew him by the nickname he'd acquired many years ago for his exploits in Operation Wetie when he was a thug for a first republic politician in Ibadan. He launched in as soon as the door creaked open, kicking it back with such force that it threw Nick to the floor. Three of his boys wielding machetes followed him in, eyes like the red of hibiscus. The smell of weed waltzed in with them and made Wura, Nick's other sister, who had also come out of the room, to start coughing. She suffered allergies from strong smells.

Nick picked himself up slowly, grateful that his head hadn't hit the edge of the center table. Seeing it was Owo Blow at the door and not the dreaded robbers should have brought some relief, but Nick's panic grew instead. He knew why the man was there. He had come about a week earlier, just before dusk, his prayer beads in one hand, a burning cigarette in the other, kicking at everything in his path and issuing threats of eviction. It had been his boys' hefty heaps of muscles and dangling skull pendants that had held Nick's attention that day, the way they all stood sentry like bodyguards without a will of their own. Owo Blow had given a one-week ultimatum on that visit. Now, their time was up.

"You should have let me break the door down before you opened," Owo Blow said in Yoruba, irritated about the time it took to open the door. He was not a very patient man, especially when he was in a particular mood.

Nick and his sisters exchanged quick glances full of concern but said nothing.

"See, they even have light," Owo Blow said, making like he only just noticed the light bulbs were on. "You can pay for NEPA but you cannot pay my rent, abi? Ka ni da fun gbogbo yin. All that nonsense will end today."

Nick wished then that there was a power outage. Their line had been disconnected many times because of unpaid bills, but each time the men from the power company left, after cutting and taking away the cable that brought in power from the high street pole, they got Brother Emma, the electrician who lived on their street, to reconnect them. Other times they bribed the power staff to allow their illegal connection for a little while longer.

"Where is that unfortunate mother of yours?" Owo Blow said, looking around, his fist folded tightly.

"She's not around," Nick stammered.

"So, she knew I was coming and decided to run away, abi?"

"No, sir," Nick protested, raising both hands into the air to deny Owo Blow's accusation. "She traveled," he added in Yoruba and then, feeling that information was insufficient, added, "She went to look for your money."

Owo Blow had made clear during his last visit that he would throw them out if his outstanding rent wasn't paid in a week. They weren't sure if he was just bluffing, if he was really going to make good his words this time, but Nick's mother did not want to wait and find out. Completely out of options in Lagos, she decided to make the trip to Ondo to seek help. She had relatives there who farmed a cocoa plantation. They held some hope to end her family's ordeal.

"I wish her a safe journey," Owo Blow said. "But running away will still not save her." His words seemed to amuse him. He began to laugh hysterically. When he finished, he turned to his boys, who looked confused and unsure whether to join him in the laughter or not and signaled by snapping his finger that they should begin to throw everything outside.

As if on cue, Wura and Maryanne, who had been standing silently near the entrance of the passageway that led from the sitting room to the rooms, threw themselves at Owo Blow's feet and began to beg, but he regarded them like trash on a wet path, stepping away from their hold on his legs.

"Hurry," Owo Blow said to his boys. "Throw all of this rubbish outside immediately."

Two of the boys lifted the single-seater couch and started heading toward the door, while the third one bolted for the television. Nick stood in his path, but the boy pushed him aside in the same way you'd dismiss a buzzing housefly with the back of the hand. A birthday card sat on the television, the only gift Nick got for his thirteenth birthday two days earlier. His mother had delayed her travel just to give it to him and sing him the birthday song because that was all she could afford. Owo Blow's thug flung the card away and lifted the television box from the base before realizing it was still plugged in. He hissed, dropped the television, and bent down to fiddle with the connections.

Nick joined his sisters. They needed more time. Surely their mother would come back that day with the money. Owo Blow should have mercy. They had nowhere else to go.

"Have I not been merciful to you enough?" Owo Blow said, as if he'd read Nick's mind. "For a good two years. A whole two years' rent. Who does such a thing? Is it until I gift you the house before you know I have been merciful? I have told your mother, two-bedroom is not for everybody. If you cannot pay, you leave."

Two years earlier, the brakes of the danfo that Nick's father had been riding in failed. It was a regular commute from Obalende to Ikorodu, a bus filled with passengers heading home from work. Nick's father had worked as a secretary at the Ministry of Housing on Lagos Island, and that day, he had left work a little earlier. He'd got promoted and wanted to rush home to break the news to his family. The driver lost control of the bus, which hit the curb and flipped onto its side. Five people died.

Owo Blow came to the house to pay his condolences, remarking that Nick's father was one of his long-time tenants and a very trustworthy one who never gave him any headache. He declared that he would waive the rent for the two-bedroom apartment for twenty-four months as a way of supporting the widow and her three children. The group of sympathizers had briefly suspended their mourning and applauded, and even Nick's mother, who was inconsolable, had managed to smile through her tears. The news of Owo Blow's generosity had traveled far. Even a local fuji musician sang about it in a record, pouring encomiums on him: "Owo Baba, the one who does Sadaqah for the downtrodden as Allah enjoined."

The rent waiver turned out to be a relief, as the downturn in the fortunes of the Adejuwons following the death of their patriarch became dire. Nick's mother, who hardly finished primary school before being married off to the young civil servant working in Lagos, did not have a job, and her husband's salary had been just enough to raise their three children and maintain a respectable lifestyle in the suburb of Lagos. Nick's father had insisted that Nick must attend boarding school at the Federal Unity College, though the Babangida government had just started the Structural Adjustment Program, which implored on citizens to "tighten their belts."

Adjusting to their father's passing required some major changes. Nick's mother used the entitlement the ministry paid her to start an akara and ogi business in front of their house. Nick withdrew from boarding school and became a day student at a nearby grammar school, the one his father once described as a glorified madhouse and vowed that no child of his would attend. The only good news was Maryanne, a year older than Nick. She had won a Christian charity scholarship that would take care of her school fees until she was done with secondary school. Wura, who just turned ten, had only recently sat for her common entrance exams.

It had been a delicate balance since then until Owo Blow jumped back into their lives six months ago and upended it. A vacancy had been created in his harem after he decided to send his first wife away, and he wanted Nick's mother to fill up that space as his new wife. When she declined because she did not want to remarry yet nor become someone's fourth wife–also because Owo Blow wasn't the kind of man she would want to be with–the harassment started. For bruising his ego, he promised to taunt her until she *begged* him to be his wife.

First, he declared that she could no longer use the front of the house for her akara and ogi business. She didn't take him seriously until he sent his thugs to enforce it one morning, a few days after he made the declaration. There were over ten of them beating up the customers, pouring away the ogi and looting the akara. A few weeks passed, and when that did not win him any new affection in her heart, Owo Blow suddenly declared that they owed him rent. No, he never made an offer of a waiver to them. No, he was a good Muslim and did not drink alcohol, so he could not possibly have been drunk on the day they claimed he uttered such nonsense.

The thugs worked at Owo Blow's commands like a fun sport, lifting, dragging, pulling, and smashing. They hummed some of their favorite fuji songs as they went on, sharing jokes and throwing banters. Meanwhile, Wura and Maryanne had taken their protest outside, screaming and crying. They attracted a crowd of neighbors and passers-by, some of whom were also Owo Blow's tenants–he owned five properties in that area–and others who knew of his notoriety as a chieftain of the National Union of Road

Transport Workers (NURTW). When people found Owo Blow and his boys at work harassing Nick and his family, they stood aside, heads resting in the groove of their palms or hands folded across their chest, and watched. They dared not interfere.

Nick watched on in silence as their belongings were gathered into a rough heap in front of the only home he had ever known. It was a small heap because they did not own much. He willed himself to cry like his sisters, but he felt numb, his sense of feeling frozen. He stood a little away from the crowd; they appalled him, how they all stood and did nothing. Some of them were faces that came to see his father to help them write letters because he was the educated one.

He thought about the story his teacher told them in school about apartheid in South Africa and how Black people were oppressed by the whites because they did not have power. He wondered if, perhaps, the Blacks felt the same way he felt that morning, a mixture of anger and shame. Then, he decided it was different. Their teacher told them the Blacks fought back. Even the children resisted. The teacher told them of the riot by school children in Soweto that caught the world's attention. This was different. He could not fight back; he could not do anything to Owo Blow and his boys as they threw out the last of the items from the house. He watched on as they used a big padlock to lock the entrance door, and Owo Blow turned around to face the crowd with both fists raised as if celebrating a feat. Nick wished the ground would open and swallow him when some people in the crowd echoed the thugs hailing with a chorus of "Owo Blow!'"

Owo Blow said loudly that nobody should use their kaikai to spoil his palm wine, and he was not responsible for anybody's poverty. It got him some more cheers, which felt like puffs of pepper spray into Nick's eyes. And, as though nature had conspired with Owo to perfect the humiliation, dark clouds gathered above and began to trickle down in droplets, slowly at first, like an announcement of terrible things to come, and then in faster, angrier torrents.

THE DESK PHONE RANG, STARTLING PASTOR NICK AND PULLING HIM out of his reverie. He let it ring one more time. *Kofi must be here*, he thought, and his secretary was calling to inform him. He pulled the chair closer to the table and threw a quick look at his wristwatch. Ten minutes to nine. Kofi, in all his bohemianism, was never late to an appointment. It was one of the things Nick found endearing about the young man.

"Is he here?" Pastor Nick asked, after touching on a button to answer the call without raising the receiver.

"No, Daddy," the secretary replied. "He called me a few minutes ago to cancel."

"To cancel?"

"Yes. He said he had been calling you, but you weren't answering."

"Calling me?" Nick reached into his jacket pocket and retrieved the phone with his direct line, the one he gave out to only a small circle. Three missed calls flashed on the screen. "Did he say why he was canceling?"

"No, Pastor. He only said he would call you to reschedule. But the way he sounded on the phone, I suspect maybe he is not feeling okay."

"He is healed in Jesus' name."

"Amen!"

"Remind me to call him later. What else do I have today?"

"Pastor JohnPraise is coming at eleven for a meeting, and then at two o'clock, you are meeting with the pastoral care team in your conference room."

"Okay. I don't want to see anybody until Pastor JohnPraise comes."

"Yes, Pastor."

Nick thought it was a good time to review the church accounts. He didn't trust anyone else with the details of his financials, not even his wife. He was grateful for his accounting experience from working in a Big Four firm because he could manage the complex inflow and outflows and have the books in good shape for whenever his benefactors wanted to have a look. Booting up his desktop monitor, he launched the accounting software and stood up. He needed a drink first.

The coffee machine sat on an elevated platform in the far-right corner of the expansive office, which was the size of a basketball court. As he approached it, he decided instead to grab a drink from the refrigerator, right next to the coffee machine. He had been trying to cut down on a long-time habit of drinking coffee because his doctor said he needed to reduce his caffeine intake to protect his heart. He bent slightly to pull open the refrigerator door. A framed picture of him and his wife Nkechi sat on top of the refrigerator. He was holding her from behind, and they were both smiling at the camera. Behind them, the Eiffel tower sprang up into the skies. He remembered that holiday two years ago during which they had also visited the Notre-Dame Cathedral and worshipped at a church of mostly African migrants in the Château Rouge area. Nkechi had insisted on Paris. It was the city of love, and they needed some time together to rekindle theirs. Their rapidly expanding ministry had been keeping him too busy, she had complained. He agreed when she began to nag about it, and it really turned out to be a nice trip. Their smiles in the picture seemed like a distant memory given how things were currently between them.

He grabbed a bottle of apple juice from the refrigerator and closed it a little too forcefully, making it shake slightly and dislodging the stand of the picture frame, which collapsed and slammed face down on the top of the refrigerator. Nick regarded the frame briefly, and then as if deciding the fallen picture was a good reflection of how things were, he started toward his chair, uncapping the bottle of juice as he walked away.

SIX

Pastor Nkechi and her team walked with long strides down the hallway toward her office in the East Wing of Heaven's Gate Cathedral. Sarah, her personal assistant who was carrying her Chanel handbag, strode in front. Bayo, Nkechi's executive assistant and public speaking coach, padded beside Sarah. Timothy followed behind Nkechi. He was her police orderly, and today he wore the new police camouflage uniform, a pistol dangling from his waist. The last three members of the entourage took up the rear: Nkechi's personal photographer, makeup artist, and stylist.

They entered the building through the emergency exit doors, a regular escape from the throng always at hand at the main entrance. Crowds of women and children chanted, "Mummy General, we love you," and asked her to touch them or give them money. Other visitors hung around the entrance too. Bank marketers looking to sell a new product, fashion designers pitching the latest styles, representatives of various women groups looking to invite her to a function, journalists sniffing around for news, and church staff who wanted to discuss matters they could not take up with her husband. They surged toward her, each whispering their own ideas to her as she walked through the masses. Already, her husband had taught her the art of engaging with such audiences, how to nod, wave, smile, stop briefly to listen, make a face as though in deep contemplation about what was being said, and then pass them on to her personal assistant with the promise of *looking into it.*

That morning, she did not want any such delays. Her schedule was packed. People already waited in the area outside her office, people who had confirmed appointments, but most of whom she wasn't probably going to see. Everyone stood as she and her team entered. She flashed her practiced smile and waved politely, asking everyone to sit down before walking into her expansive office.

When the cathedral had been designed, her husband told her he intended to make her office something the nation's First Lady would be envious of. And indeed, Nkechi had been impressed with the outcome. The place felt more like home than her real one. It had an African-themed interior decoration, abstract paintings that lined the wall, Chesterfield sofas, and a private suite complete with a jacuzzi, massage room, and a soft bed.

On her white office desk sat an iMac, a copy of the Bible, and a set of the day's newspapers, carefully arranged by her assistants. There was also a tray with correspondences, the ones that survived her assistant's screening and merited her attention. Usually, she started the day by going through them, mainly invitations to church programs and requests for support, deciding on which to be accepted and those to be politely declined. Then, she would start the meetings rounds. Her secretary would send in the waiting visitors who had appointments, one after the other.

This morning, however, a crew from *Allure Magazine* had come for a special photoshoot. She was going to be on the cover of the September edition in their "Top 50 Most Influential Women in Nigeria" series. A section of her office already looked like a mini studio with cameras and lights set ahead of her arrival. She regarded them briefly as she took off her jacket and hung it on the hook.

"How long is this going to take?" she asked Sarah.

"One hour forty-five, two hours max. They'll be taking only five shots."

Nkechi mentally added an hour to that estimate. From experience, she knew that these things lasted longer. "Call Sister Anwuli," she said, looking now at Funmi, her secretary who just joined the team from the outer office. "Tell her I will be an hour late and that I will not spend more than thirty minutes there."

"Yes, Mummy General," Funmi said, then added, "Madame Carole, the French Ambassador's wife, called earlier. She wanted to remind you of your meeting over tea tomorrow at her residence."

"Oh, right. Please put it on my schedule for tomorrow."

"But Pastor, you're already scheduled to attend the prayer meeting the governor's wife is hosting for wives of elected state officials tomorrow morning," Sarah said, flipping through the pages of her small notepad to confirm her information.

Nkechi shook her head slowly and sighed. She lowered herself onto her office chair. "Any suggestions, Bayo?"

Bayo, fiddling with his phones, looked up surprised. "I am sorry, Pastor. I was a little distracted."

Nkechi looked in Sarah's direction. "The oyibo woman is lonely in this Lagos and just looking for friends. The other appointment has more value for the ministry."

"I concur," Bayo said, a little too loudly.

"Look at this one. What are you concurring to?" Nkechi made a face and rolled her eyes. Everybody laughed.

"Funmi, cancel with Carole. Tell her we will reschedule," Nkechi said after letting a few seconds pass.

"Okay, Pastor,' Funmi nodded and left the room.

"You can call them in. I'm ready now," Pastor Nkechi said, referring to the *Allure Magazine* crew.

"I DON'T WANT TO BE disturbed for the next one hour," Pastor Nkechi told Funmi through the intercom as her next guest walked in.

The man took off his dark glasses as he approached the table. He was clean-shaven and wore a striped jacket over a Polo shirt with denim pants and sneakers. He walked like someone carrying something heavy under his arms, his shoulders slumped in on themselves. As he got close, Nkechi eyed the black folder he had in his left hand.

"I am sorry for keeping you waiting," she said as they shook hands. "I hope you've been well taken care of?"

"It's not a problem," the man said, smiling and dropping the folder on the table. "Your secretary was a good host."

"Please, sit."

The man surveyed the room, a suspicious look on his face as if looking out for hidden cameras before pulling out one of the low-arm visitors' chairs.

"It's just us," she said as if to assuage his worries.

"Madam, I really must repeat that I am not comfortable meeting here. The walls, like they say, have ears."

"This room is completely soundproof."

Her husband had made sure of that. He had joked to her that he intended to stroll to her office and make love to her right there on her office table. No one would be able to hear their moans of pleasure.

"Cameras?"

"None."

The man looked around again. "It's also not safe for me to meet you here, especially given the nature of the assignment. In my line of work, discretion is important, and we do well to protect ourselves and our clients, too."

"Well, you're here now, so let's get to it. Next time, we can make other arrangements." Nkechi was eager to find out the revelations he had told her last night on the phone.

The man opened the folder and shuffled through the contents. Two postcard-sized photographs and a few sheets of paper rustled at his touch. "We found not just one but two leads that may confirm your suspicions." He handed her the photos.

Nkechi held the two pictures apart in both hands, her eyes roving from one to the other and then back again. In less than a minute, she felt a cocktail of emotions run through her, from surprise to anger and back to surprise again. She knew both women. The picture in her right hand was Bimbo, her husband's media assistant who was engaged to Kunle, one of the lead choristers in the church. Nkechi knew when Bimbo started attending the church; she became a convert during one of the programs they held at the University of Lagos auditorium in the early days. She also remembered that she'd become her husband's media assistant because she worked in an advertising agency and had many contacts in the media. Nkechi also thought about how Bimbo had called her "Mummy" and often came to her for advice, particularly about her relationship with Kunle.

The other woman in the second photo was a junior pastor's wife. She was a rather reclusive fellow who always smelled of baby formula and said very little at the ministry programs. This woman had a baby not quite six months old whom she always had strapped to her back. To Nkechi, she seemed to possess very little in terms of talents, besides her big hips, which even she, as a woman, often thought were remarkably too wide for a woman so slim.

"I suppose you are familiar with both ladies?"

Nkechi didn't respond. His words were like hot, dry pepper poured into her stomach.

"There may be more, we cannot say for sure right now, but in the two weeks since you asked us to track him, these are the two we know he's been seeing. There are pictures of them together in the folder."

Nkechi let the pictures drop from her hands. She had expected the private detective would find something, but the identity of the women involved left her feeling heart wrenched on the one hand and disappointed on the other. She looked up at the man whose face bore no emotions. He must have done this many times, Nkechi thought, delivering news that confirmed the worst fears of the spouses of rich men. He came highly recommended from Peju, who thought the wives of men of God ought to be proactive in discovering the people tempting their husbands.

"Frankly, I am lost for words," Nkechi finally said

before picking up the pictures and staring at them again. "I know them. This is unbelievable. I mean, what on earth is he doing with her, for God's sake? The woman just had a baby." She tossed the picture of the Pastor's wife toward the man.

"There may be reasons to question the paternity of the baby," the man said, ignoring the picture and crossing his arms against his chest.

Nkechi thought of the possibility. The woman's husband was sent to Abuja as part of a team to plant Rivers of Joy Church in the nation's capital. He was rarely in Lagos. A cold chill shivered her body.

"My God."

"We have other documents here, too." He eyed the open folder. "Hotel bookings, flight tickets, bank deposits, properties—"

"Wait, properties?" Nkechi asked, leaning forward

"Yes. Your husband bought a house in Ikeja GRA for the other lady."

"But he told me it was for business ... that he was going to rent it out purely for business."

"The property is in her name."

"Jesus!" Pastor Nkechi stood abruptly. "You're telling me the duplex with eight flats in GRA was bought in Bimbo's name?"

"Please, keep your voice down, Madam." The man looked around the room again.

Nkechi did not bother reminding him that the room was soundproof. She took a few steps away from her chair toward the replica of Ben Enwonwu's *Tutu* that hung on the wall. Her heels hurt from standing on the Louboutin during the session at the single women's conference. She had spent more time there than planned because most of the girls had questions for her. The questions focused on how to be a successful wife, how to build a happy home, how to keep a man, questions to which she had offered template responses that painted perfect pictures of her life as a married woman and co-founder of the fastest-growing church congregation in the country. She stared at the painting and remembered her husband telling her the original was lost in 1975 and then boasting that were it to ever be discovered and auctioned, he would buy it for her. She sighed and walked back to her chair.

"What else?"

The private detective told her he had evidence of her husband's travels with Bimbo to London, the city he was in this very minute. He was there on the invitation of another pastor to minister at the special thanksgiving service. The detective revealed they both flew to London in a British Airways flight, though Bimbo was in Economy Class so as not to raise any suspicions. Also, they were staying in different hotels right across the street from each other.

"But our eyes on the ground have seen her arrive at his hotel at night in a taxi and then leave in the morning," the man said.

Nkechi felt stupid. She had been the one who insisted Bimbo be her husband's media assistant, even after Bimbo admitted she was having an affair with one of her married bosses. Then, after seeing Nkechi's expression, Bimbo had hurriedly added that she'd been attending Rivers of Joy Church and no longer wanted to be involved in such an unholy act. At the time, Nkechi had thought it was a god-sent solution. Bimbo working for the church would lead her down a better path. She had told Nick to hire her, though he'd wanted someone with more experience.

"Can I smoke?" The man tapped the breast pocket of his jacket, feeling for his pack of cigarettes.

"No … sorry, no.'

"It's fine. Can I use the restroom?"

"It's that way," she said, pointing.

Nkechi's eyes followed the man as he walked to the left side of the office, toward the visitor's toilet. He was much taller than she had imagined him to be when they spoke on the phone. Initially, she wasn't keen on calling him, and even after Peju made the recommendation and sent her his number, she had ignored it for two days. Finally, at Peju's insistence, Nkechi made the call.

Peju and her husband were the founders and pastors of Living Spring Church, a growing ministry in the Apapa axis of Lagos and not a direct competitor to Rivers of Joy Church. One Sunday, Peju invited Nkechi to preach during a program they held in the church. Nkechi had gone to help Peju raise funds to upgrade her car. Pastors often did that–invite a pastor with enough star power to motivate their congregation's generosity. And it didn't get better than Nkechi and her husband. Peju had confided that she needed to raise at least thirty million to change her two-year-old Range Rover to a newer model. After preaching for about fifteen minutes, during which she had the audience on their feet twice clapping for her, Nkechi had raised more than enough for her friend to get her desired vehicle.

"Our Mummy cannot be driving in a car that can stop her on Third Mainland Bridge," Nkechi had declared. "It is time to test your faith in God. I have come here to bless somebody. Sow a seed and ask God of something today and see what will happen in exactly seven days' time. I need just ten people, only ten people, that will give a million each."

Pastor Nkechi had ended up raising thirty-five million, and an obviously elated Peju insisted she joined her for lunch at their house, just the two of them. Peju's husband was in America to attend a ministers' conference.

After seeing the private detective today, Nkechi remembered the conversation she and Peju had that day over lunch. They were both old girls of federal unity colleges and shared tales of boarding life. They'd talked about fashion and vacation locations and the accusations made against Bill Cosby. That was when Peju asked her how she was dealing with all the female groupies around her husband. Not one to discuss her family matters with third parties, Nkechi tried to shrug it off even though the condom incident was still fresh on her mind.

"What can I do?" she'd said, holding the fork with a piece of fish, midway to her mouth. "One must just continue trusting on God for discipline and faithfulness."

"You mean you aren't bothered?" Peju asked, dabbing the edges of her mouth with a napkin. "I'm not saying your husband isn't disciplined, but you see, with the fame comes all these women. I see how they're always all over him. Surely that must bother you sometimes."

"If I keep worrying about it, my blood pressure will rise, and if I'm unwell, all those women would have won."

Nkechi was eager to move on to another topic. "That reminds me, are you attending the prayer meeting with the governor's wife?"

Peju ignored the question. "Pastor Nkechi, I don't

think you are taking this thing seriously at all. You don't want some woman with children to come out of nowhere and lay claim to all the things you and your husband are toiling for today. Did you not hear of the Baptist minister's wife who had four children for her husband? Very beautiful couple. They were in their sixties. Baba was always celebrating his wife on the pulpit and professing his love for her. People called them everywhere to minister to married couples and share testimonies about the secrets of their love. When the man died in that plane crash last year, another wife showed up with four children of her own."

"You're kidding me," Pastor Nkechi said, opening her eyes wide.

"I kid you not, Pastor. I know the couple. The man had an alternate family hidden away in plain sight in this same Lagos. And guess what? This other woman was their church member. And if you see the ages of the children, it seemed like once he knocks one up, he moves on to another one. Eight children, all boys."

Nkechi's stomach churned in disgust.

"And that is why we, wives of ministers, need to look out for our husbands. By doing so, you also protect yourself and your children. The temptation out there is too strong."

Pastor Nkechi wasn't sure if her host was looking for gossip or if she had some of her own to share.

"Well, I guess that's why we must continue to pray hard for our husbands."

A female help in a kitchen apron brought in the tray of dessert and balanced it on the table before retrieving the empty plates. The ladies waited until she left before continuing.

"We must pray, yes," Peju said, scooping some ice cream. "But we must also act." She paused as if to see the effect her words had on Nkechi.

"Act how? By monitoring them?"

"Exactly. Keep an eye on who they are with so that we're not taken by surprise. That way, you can do what you need to do to nip anything in the bud. But you can't act when you wallow in ignorance. Does the Bible not tell us that my people suffer for lack of knowledge?"

"You say these things as if you will go and glue yourself to your husband's body so you can follow him everywhere. I mean...you just told me about the lady who thought she had a happy home, yet her man was cheating. I don't know how you can achieve such diligent monitoring."

Peju took a quick look around to ensure they were alone in her dining room. She leaned forward toward Nkechi and spoke in a whisper. "You don't have to do it yourself. There are professionals who do this job at the right price. They will track everything and give you the details whenever you want it."

At that moment, Nkechi's thoughts swerved to the condoms and how much she wanted to know who her husband was sleeping with, but she was careful about revealing anything about her personal life to anyone. As concerned as Peju seemed, Nkechi was still skeptical about being open with her. So instead, she acted like she wasn't worried.

"Sounds interesting," she said offhandedly. "I didn't know we had private detectives in Nigeria."

"And they are incredibly good, too. I will send you the number of the one I use," she was whispering again. "In fact, most wives of rich men here in Lagos use him."

"Pastor Peju, I appreciate it, but I am not quite sure I'm inclined to do this. I mean, I don't suspect my husband for anything, and it wouldn't make any—"

"I will send it to you anyway. Save the number somewhere, just in case," Peju said, cutting her short and reaching for a cupcake.

PASTOR NKECHI DID NOT REALIZE the investigator had returned until he dragged the chair. The legs scratched the tiled floor, rattling her from her memories.

"Sorry," she said. "I was a bit carried away by my thoughts."

"I understand, Madam," he said. Then, as if feeling the need to show some empathy, he added. "Take it easy, please. The details of this preliminary report are all contained in this folder. How we progress from here is entirely your call, Ma."

"What options do I have? What can I do with this information?"

The man sat back, his right hand scratching the back of his head. "Usually, we charge for such advice, but I'm happy to share a few ideas for free with you."

The topic appeared to excite him. The muscles of his face relaxed for the first time since he'd arrived, and it looked like he was going to smile. "If, for example, you are done with the marriage and want to destroy him for what he's done, you can leak this information to the media and boom, everything will be up in flames. But you can also decide to confront him with this evidence and see if he admits guilt and shows remorse. Some people make mistakes and can retrace their steps when confronted with facts."

He paused to allow Pastor Nkechi to consider her options. "Alternatively," he continued. "You may decide to quietly take care of the women involved and keep your marriage and lifestyle."

"By take care, you mean?"

The man nodded. "Yes. Remove them out of the picture."

"How many people will I be taking out of the picture? When will it end? Would he not just move on to other women?"

"Well, you could also take him out of the picture. I only recommend this option if you're sure everything comes to you when he's…gone."

"Are you suggesting I kill my husband?" Nkechi scanned his face to see if there was any way none of this was real.

"The winner of the game is the one who plays it," the man said frankly. "It all depends on what's at stake and how much you want it."

SEVEN

The idea of starting a blog came to Ifenna as he eavesdropped on the conversation between two passengers one morning as they crawled in traffic toward The Island. It had been two weeks since he lost his job, and he was now a part-time kabu kabu driver. He figured that a good way of surviving in the interim, until he got another job, was to put his jalopy to use. So, early every morning on workdays, he dressed up like one off to work and then stopped at Adekunle, close to Yaba Bus Stop, to pick up passengers, usually workers hurrying to work on the Island.

Most times, he went from Yaba to Eko Hotel Roundabout and there, he would pick a fresh batch of passengers heading to Lekki Phase 1. After dropping them off at their destination, he'd run the Lekki Phase 1-Ozumba Mbadiwe Street route, all the way to TBS, to complete his morning round. Sometimes, on his way back to Yaba, he got flagged down as a taxi and made some extra money. He would then return home and stay indoors until evening when he would go out again for the evening rush. It was too risky being a taxi or kabu kabu driver during the day outside of the rush hours. Too many hawks waited to suck your blood. Area boys collected taxes for every passenger you picked at the bus stops they controlled. Local government transport forces looked for their emblem or stickers; LASTMA officials waited for you to make the wrong turn on an unmarked road. Policemen looked for *something for pure water*, and there were vehicle inspection officers, who everyone called VIO, just being savage in the way they went on, seemingly without human feelings.

Ifenna was particularly scared of the VIO. He had heard of and read about so many tales that he didn't want to get a first-hand experience. They wore white uniforms like the navy, but you would find out soon enough that there was nothing innocent about them when you got caught in their net. Their main job was to check for *roadworthiness*. Ifenna did not wish to put his jalopy to such a test; his tires were worn, one of his brake lights needed to be changed, and the passenger's side mirror had disappeared while the car sat at Sikiru's mechanic shop. The Toyota Corolla 1996 model — nicknamed *First Lady* in Nigeria's tradition of naming cars it didn't manufacture — had become so important to his survival that he couldn't risk it being impounded by VIO, so he stayed at home during the day and kept up with the social gossip online.

When the idea of starting a blog came to him on Third Mainland Bridge that morning, the traffic heaved with congestion. It had rained earlier, around four o'clock, and whenever it rained in Lagos, the traffic grew a potbelly. Ifenna cursed as an okada squeezed into the space between his car and the one in front. Both the bike rider and the passenger, a young man in a suit with a knapsack on his back, probably a bank staff, weren't wearing helmets. The first time helmets had been enforced by the law, for fear of contracting an infection, passengers often placed handkerchiefs on their heads before wearing the often sweat-stained helmets. Everyone seemed to comply after the police started arresting defaulters, often seizing the bikes if a passenger wasn't wearing a helmet, until the monitoring fizzled out like most things in Nigeria.

Once the line moved a little, the okada leaped into the next lane, escaping a collision by inches, and curved into another lane. The driver of the danfo that almost hit them spread out the five fingers of his left hand and yelled something in Yoruba about the rider's family being unfortunate. How ironic, Ifenna thought, that a danfo driver was bitter someone else drove recklessly since that was their stock-in-trade.

Ifenna stole a look in his rear-view mirror at the passengers in the back seat. They hadn't paid him yet. Of the four, two were finishing their night sleep, heads thrown backward and mouths ajar. The lady between them had headphones plugged into her ears and her phone pressed to her face. Was she listening to music or watching YouTube videos? The fourth passenger had his eyes on the road, like he could make the cars in front disappear just by looking at them.

Ifenna turned up the volume of his radio a little. The host said something about the president leaving again to the UK for treatment, this time for an ear infection. One of the two passengers hissed before wishing the president deafness. It drew some giggles from his seatmates. Soon, a discussion started on the health of the president and how stupid everyone had been to have elected such an old man. The passenger in front who made the initial comment noted that it was shameful leaders were so quick to go abroad to treat their ailments when they left the hospitals at home in rot. The other rider mentioned the billions budgeted for the Aso Rock Clinic and wondered why, despite such huge funds, they could not treat an ear infection here.

Though Ifenna enjoyed listening to his passengers' arguments, he kept quiet. Topics were always centered around economy, politics, ethnicity, football, or religion. Sometimes, the discussion went full circle, touching on all topics from the time Ifenna drove from Yaba to the Eko Hotel Roundabout. Other times, the discussion morphed into a shouting match between two vocal passengers. What amazed Ifenna was how very easily strangers meeting for the first time could form friendship or foeship, united or separated by Nigeria's many problems.

Now, the discussion went from the president's ear infection to the reports of villages near Jos being sacked by herdsmen on a killing spree, then it swiveled to the upcoming World Cup qualifier match the Super Eagles had that weekend with South Africa in Uyo. At the foot of the Adeniji Adele bridge, a huge electronic billboard displayed an advertisement that caught Ifenna's attention: a special power-packed crusade in preparation for the 'ember months. He barely caught the words as he tried to keep his car in line as the traffic merged from four lanes to three, but the glimpse was enough to nauseate him. Classic, he thought. Church adverts always competed for billboard space with product brands. One of the passengers, the one in front who first reacted to the president's story, said something about how the man on the billboard was a big fraud. He had attended the man's church once and seen him selling tickets to heaven for one million naira per person.

"He had white handkerchiefs, about a hundred of them, and he wanted a hundred people to sow a million-naira seed. When you came out, you received one handkerchief. And he was telling people: 'Don't miss heaven. This is your opportunity to *make* heaven. Come out now or be left behind.' I don't know o; I just felt there was something very wrong about it all. I left and never went back."

"Is that not Apostle Godswill Nimbe that curls his hair like a woman?" The other passenger asked.

"Yeah, that's him."

"I know him. I once attended a program where he ministered. Do you know what he did there? In the guise of speaking in tongues, he called the names of foreign currencies from dollar to pound to yen to lira, everything. He was just mixing them up. Well-rehearsed rendition o, and the people were screaming in awe. When he was done, he told us that God was speaking to him in foreign currencies. Anyone who went up to him and made a pledge to be redeemed in foreign currency would get a special blessing from God. Guess what? That was the period when the dollar was scarce, when the Central Bank tightened access to forex. Later, it occurred to me that the man was simply mopping up forex from his congregation for his own use. Omo, I was like, this guy is bad."

"It's just sad the things some of these men of God do. Haba now! And people keep falling for it. See, eh, I have one cousin confined to a wheelchair since he had an accident when he was eight. So, every time he would see this guy, what's that his name again now? The one that does that Miracle Rain on TV?"

"Bernard Madu?"

"That's him, my brother. So, every time he would see Bernard Madu performing miracles and raising people from wheelchairs and curing blindness, you know all that sort of stuff, he asked his mother to please take him there too. You see, the boy had been stretching his hands to the television as the man often requested viewers to do, so he could pray for them to receive their own miracle, but it never worked. He was so sure that if he could meet the man one on one, the healing would happen. That's how the poor mother contacted me o, as somebody they know in Lagos. They live in Warri. They had to come all the way. Too much trouble traveling from Warri to Lagos with somebody in a wheelchair. When they got to Lagos, I had to take time off at work, and we made the trip to the church in Ejigbo. My brother, that was when our troubles changed gears."

"What happened?"

"We went there on a Tuesday afternoon. They said the man of God does healing sessions only on Thursdays. Come and see the crowd. People from all over the country, some arriving in chartered buses. First, you must buy a form and register for Healing School, twenty thousand naira. Then pay for sleeping space, five thousand naira per night, and this space, I am telling you, is just a six-spring mattress on a bare floor in open hostels. And there, you must purchase food and drinks. Nothing's provided. Then, there is anointing oil and healing wristbands that you must buy for accreditation. Only those who are accredited can attend the Thursday session. The rest either go away or stay until the next Thursday to try again. So, you can imagine, everyone was hustling to go in. We paid fifty thousand to make it. The boys' mother was desperate. I am sure that was all her life savings. Thursday came. The healing session was recorded and televised. The place was like an open studio, cameras everywhere. Before the man came, there was a lot of singing and praying. Everyone was hyped up, expectant. They kept telling everyone inside to pray and sing hard and have elevated faith so they can be among those the spirit will move Pastor Bernard to pray for."

"Wait, you mean, even after all the trouble of making it into the session, not everybody is going to be prayed for and healed?"

"Exactly. They made it clear that your faith would heal you, such that if at the end of the show, you were leaving with the ailment you came with, it was your fault for not having enough faith. When the man finally arrived, he started calling people out after singing some solemn worship songs, you know how he does it on television? *'There is a man here that is paralyzed in the left hand: come out. There is a woman here who the doctors have told is barren: come out.'* Like that, like that. He prayed for each of them and then pronounced them healed, and that person would start screaming and jumping in celebration. He called out twelve people that day. Out of a hall of over two thousand people."

"Only twelve?"

"My brother. I couldn't believe it when the man said a short prayer, and they suddenly said it was over."

"But on television they make it look like so many more were healed, like the few you see there are just a few the time allowed them to show."

"My brother, the thing is a television show, simple. There is a crew of white people running it. It's very well-orchestrated. There's even a director pointing out camera angles, directing when the audience should cheer loudly and when the show should end."

"You don't mean it."

"Do I look like I am joking? And you know the thing is, even those twelve people who'd been 'healed' could've been actors planted there for the show of it all. If you ask me eh, nobody was really healed of anything that day. Everyone else went away feeling guilty that they hadn't mustered enough faith. They probably grew even more determined after seeing those twelve healed. You needed to see that my cousin. He was inconsolable. Later, you know what the boy told his mother? That maybe he wasn't healed because his mother didn't buy a big enough bottle of olive oil."

"Ah, just look at that," the other man said, shaking his head in pity. "I have been saying it. All these men that say they have the gift to heal people only do so on television. Why can't they just be healing people everywhere? I mean, if I have such powers, then I'd be going from hospital to hospital."

"My brother, that's it o. Since that day, if I see any miracle advertisement, I just shake my head."

Ifenna dropped the man off at Obalende Park. After eavesdropping on their conversation, Ifenna wondered if it'd be interesting to host a forum where people like that man could share stories of their unpleasant encounters with men of God. He imagined a big hall with cameras, like the testimony sessions the men of God often held where people shared stories of their exploits. The thought amused Ifenna as he stepped on his accelerator. It would be an interesting gathering. Perhaps if people narrated their disappointments with men of God and shared stories of their tricks on camera, it would make others less gullible. He thought of his situation—losing his job over a news story — and decided such a forum wasn't possible. Men of God were too powerful, and people feared to question them openly. No one would ever confront church officials on camera.

But then he thought of a blog. He often saw the types of stories the man had just told online on people's Facebook posts or as comments to posts on Nairaland. He could curate them in a blog and post every new story he encountered. It could be his fun pastime that may eventually lead to a job. As he drove past Bonny Camp Cantonment, he started to think of a name.

THE THOUGHT OF LILIAN, THE nurse from downstairs, coming over that evening to visit him made Ifenna giddy with excitement. He had seen her going out just as he drove into the compound from his morning kabu kabu round. Usually, when he encountered her like that, he waved and it thrilled him when she smiled and waved back. She had a smile that radiated happiness. It made him want her even more.

That morning, he decided not just to wave. He stopped and beckoned at her. She wore a pair of tight-fitting jeans and a chiffon top. As she walked over to him, Ifenna noticed she wasn't wearing a bra. Her nipples pushed out on both sides of her chest, and his penis grew hard in his trousers.

"You still haven't come to see me o," Ifenna said. He had learned it was best to start with an accusation and then, in trying to deny it, they would agree to your request.

"It's not like that o. You know how things are," she said. "Sometimes, as I'm coming in, you're going out, and most times, I don't even see your car in the evenings."

"Ehen? So, I am the cause now, eh?"

"Chill, jor," she said, leaning forward so that her breasts were inches from his face. The smell of her perfume filled Ifenna's lungs. "I'm just saying, we've both been busy."

"Oya. So, when are you going to come?"

"This evening, if you'll be around. Around eightish?"

"I'll be around for you," Ifenna said, winking at her.

"Go, jor." She tapped his shoulder playfully. "I hope you can stay awake. We're going to watch a movie."

Her response thrilled Ifenna even more. If she was already issuing a pre-warning about staying up all night, did that mean she had other ideas in mind?

"Movie, abi? No problem."

"I just hope nobody will break my head sha."

"Break your head? Who?" He pretended he didn't know the answer. It was a question girls asked when they wanted to know if you had a girlfriend.

"I don't know. You tell me."

"Nobody will break your head, jor."

"Okay, o. I got to go. I'm going to my tailor's shop in Oshodi before traffic on that side gets too busy," she said.

"Hope whatever you're getting is something that shows those curves," Ifenna said, flirting some more and watching her reaction.

"You're just a naughty boy," she said, smiling shyly. "Let me be going, jor."

Ifenna watched her walk away, his trousers bulging.

Though he was eager to get home and go on his laptop to start creating the blog, he decided to clean up first, put his one-bedroom apartment in shape for her visit. It had been a long while since he swept his place. After sweeping and mopping, he arranged the table where he usually dumped everything he came home with and tidied everything in a neat pile. In the kitchen, he washed the piled-up plates and decided he needed to step out and buy some drinks to put in his refrigerator. Next, he went into his room. Though it was her first visit, Ifenna did not want to risk anything. He had long learned that first impressions mattered. Once, a girl back in university, whom he'd spent months wooing, declared to his chagrin that she was not going to sleep with him the day she finally paid him an unscheduled visit in his off-campus room because his mattress was disgusting and the entire room smelled like rotten eggs.

He went out to buy some packs of juice and malt cans from the kiosk down the street. He also bought some eggs and noodles, which was the only food he could prepare without qualms. He was already ascending the stairs to his apartment when he remembered he didn't have any condoms. So he climbed down again, walking further down the street to the pharmacy.

Satisfied that everything was set for Lilian's visit, Ifenna settled in front of his laptop to begin working on his new blog. He had settled on a name earlier: *The Bad Shepherds*. Now he thought it was too short, so he switched it to *Exposing the Bad Shepherds and Unchaining the Sheeps*. He thought *sheeps* sounded better than "sheep," and though the computer underlined it red, he left it that way. He also decided he would post anonymously so nothing could link him as the person behind the blog. So, he created a new email address to remove all traces of his real identity and started to design the layout. After graduating from the university, he had taken some graphic design lessons where he learned how to write short codes that enhanced the themes of free blog sites. By the time the layout was done and the blog ready to be launched, it was almost six o'clock in the evening.

Ifenna wondered what post to launch the blog with, later deciding on an article that captured his feelings about the kind of Christianity that had taken over the country to better indicate the kind of content he intended to publish on the blog. He was in-between secondary school and university when his father died, and his mother's Christianity took a new route. By the time he finally got into university, he was already choked by it all: the long prayer sessions, the speaking in tongues, and the continuous tales of demonic attacks and vengeful enemies.

Though his mother insisted that he joined the Christian Union, which to her was the closest "Bible-believing" fellowship that aligned with the beliefs of the church they now attended, he had been nominal at best, attending a few Sunday services in his first semester and then stopping entirely in his second. In his second year, he joined a different fellowship, the Campus Love Universe, which, at the time, was the hip and happening fellowship on campus, with their loud music and dancing and liberal doctrines that allowed women to wear trousers and keep their heads uncovered. It was where all the beautiful girls on campus went, and he had gone there because a girl insisted she couldn't date anybody who was not a Christian–her idea of being Christian meant attending her campus fellowship.

When he went home on certain weekends, he followed his mother to her church, but he no longer closed his eyes when the pastor ordered, and when they passed the offering box to him, he dipped his empty clenched fist in and dropped nothing. By the third year, Ifenna decided to stop attending the campus fellowship after a scandal broke. The new Daddy of Campus Love Universe had been caught having sex with one of the fellowship sisters, a fresher, in his room, which members called Holy of Holies. The news trended on campus because Daddy was a popular fellow, his popularity stemming from his ability to speak in tongues. He once held a class to teach members of the fellowship how to speak in tongues. Before the scandal, he'd been seen as a very holy person. Many had been shocked at the news, even more so when it turned out to not be an isolated case. Stories immediately emerged about other fellowship presidents and their sexual escapades too, rape even springing up in the mix.

None of this surprised Ifenna. He had long concluded that campus fellowships were social clubs, an alternative to joining cults. Though he enjoyed the singing and the dancing, he found the hypocrisy and the pretenses of holiness by the fellowship leaders quite jarring. It amazed him even more how students handed so much power to these leaders under the excuse of getting closer to God.

Just as he finished typing his first blog article, Lilian knocked on the door. He checked the time: quarter past eight. He didn't know that much time had passed since he opened his laptop. He had planned to shower before she arrived and change into something nicer to make the right impression. Now, there was no time. He shut his laptop and went for the door, grateful that she had, at least, kept her word of coming over.

Lilian wore a short gown and some light makeup. Her lips glowed. Ifenna froze at the door.

"You look lovely," he said eventually.

"Let me enter, jor," she said, smiling and pushing him slightly. "You want your neighbors to see me entering your house, abi? You know they like to gossip."

"What's my business with them? They can say what they like," Ifenna said, letting her in and bolting the door afterward. "Neighbors can't visit each other?"

Lilian stood and looked around, her eyes swerving from the small bookshelf hanging on the wall to the now-arranged table and three-seater couch.

"Your apartment has more space than ours."

Ifenna smiled. "Rent is also slightly more."

"I will gladly pay the extra for more space. My apartment feels like a matchbox sometimes. You can't even stretch your legs in it."

Ifenna laughed. "Sit down, jor." He motioned to the couch.

Lilian sat down and crossed her legs. Her gown barely covered her thighs. "Nice apartment," she said, looking around again.

Ifenna thanked her as he pointed the remote to the television to turn it on.

"So where is the Grey's Anatomy I was promised?" she said as the television came on.

The television, set to a sports channel, showed wrestling. Ifenna changed it to one of the Nollywood channels.

"It's here somewhere," Ifenna said. "What can I get you to drink?"

"Just water. Shebi it is cold?"

"I believe so. There has been light for most of the day."

As Ifenna walked into the kitchen, he asked how it went with the tailor.

"Don't mind the woman. Another member of her family died today. Last month it was her aunty. Today, her uncle's second wife. The woman keeps killing her relatives with her lies. Material that I gave her almost two months ago, she has still not done it o. Lagos tailors can disappoint for Africa."

"So you went all the way to Oshodi for nothing?" Ifenna asked, pulling his lone side stool and setting a bottle of water and a glass cup before her.

"More like. But I collected my material from her o, before next time it would be her grandfather that died. Rubbish."

Ifenna chuckled as he sat down at the other end of the couch. "Your blood can be hot," he said, shaking his head.

"What was I supposed to do? Leave the material with her for another two months?"

As she poured some water into the glass cup, Ifenna looked intently at Lillian. She had been to the salon since they saw each other earlier. She had fixed on new weaves with straight jet-black strands that reached down to her nape.

"What?" she asked, meeting his eyes.

"Just admiring your hair," Ifenna said.

She flipped the hair to the side and smiled. Ifenna thought he saw her blush.

"Oya, come and put on *Grey's Anatomy* for me now," she said, turning her attention to the television.

Ifenna got up and picked the television remote control

from the table. He had Season One of *Grey's Anatomy* saved in a flash drive, which he had plugged into the television earlier. He switched the viewing from the decoder to the flash drive to play. Soon, the first episode appeared on the screen. A woman woke up from her couch, wrapped a towel around her and began to pick up her clothes. He'd watched the episode so many times and mentally repeated the lines of each character. The series, along with *24* and *Prison Break*, had been popular during his final year in the university. He particularly enjoyed *Grey's Anatomy* because of his fascination with the human body and surgery. He also liked the sex scenes, which he often fast-forwarded to when he was watching it alone, his penis erect and yearning for a release. He was genuinely surprised when Lilian said she hadn't ever watched the show.

Gradually, Ifenna shifted closer to Lilian on the couch until he was right next to her. She didn't seem to mind when he placed his left hand across her shoulder. She rested her head on his hand while keeping her eyes focused on the television. From time to time, she exclaimed things like: "What is wrong with this Alex Karev guy? Gosh, Izzie is so pretty. Wow, Doctor Burke is so hot. This Chief guy is mean o. He behaves like our CMD at the hospital."

Soon, she leaned on Ifenna completely and rested her head on his shoulders. He began to run his right hand over her lap, first drawing patterns with his index finger and then deploying all fingers to reach further up her lap. She gave him a *what-are-you-doing?* look but did not stop him. Ifenna leaned in for a kiss, planting a peck first on her lips and withdrawing, expecting to be pushed away. When she did not, his mouth went to hers again, and their tongues met and rolled over each other.

"You're a good kisser," Ifenna whispered when they briefly pulled apart to get some air. She giggled. Her hands were behind his head. He pulled her closer, and they resumed kissing.

His hands ran all over her lap, reaching underneath her gown and further up. Then he reached her breasts and started kneading them, which made her moan ever so slightly. He lifted her from the couch, and they kissed, standing face-to-face. He ran his hands over her body, reaching her buttocks, finding her breasts, and running through her hair. Satisfied that she wanted it as much as he did, he eased down her zipper, and soon, the gown was on the floor. Ifenna unhooked her bra and flung it away. The sight of her breasts was even better than he had imagined and sent a new wave of sensual excitement to his groin. They stood firm, with the swollen nipples pointing forward, inviting him. He grabbed each breast and sucked them while she let out soft moans. As he did this, her hands reached into his shorts and started stroking his erect penis, which throbbed under her hand. Not wanting to delay any longer, Ifenna pushed her back on the couch and took off her lacy underwear.

"You are so beautiful," he whispered, admiring her fully naked body on his couch.

Lilian smiled and writhed, wiggling her hips as he planted kisses from her forehead to her lips and down to her cleavage. Then, he took each leg and kissed her inner thighs, stopping just before her vagina. It made her gasp in anticipation, and Ifenna took his time to pleasure her even more. When he sensed that she was very wet and his own erection was beginning to ache, he pulled his t-shirt over his head and stepped out of his shorts. He was about to take her when he remembered the condoms and rushed naked into his room to get them. She let out a big moan when he finally slid into her after tearing the pack with his teeth impatiently and rolling the condom over his penis with trembling hands. Ifenna let out a moan too as he began to thrust, easing all of himself into her, gently at first and then increasing in speed as she dug her fingers into his back and called to God like she was in some kind of trouble. Soon, their bodies rocked in rhythm, their moans a loud chorus, the sound of the television like distant whispers.

Ifenna rolled down to the bare floor afterward. She soon joined him there, resting her head on his sweaty chest as they caught their breath. Ifenna thought it was special, climaxing together; it had never happened for him before. He worried that the neighbors heard them in the final moments. Then he wondered if she always shaved her pubic hair or if she shaved that day in anticipation of something happening when she visited him. He decided it was the latter, the way she offered herself without any resistance. Next, he wondered if she had a boyfriend somewhere, if there was a chance to have a relationship with her, or if they would just be compound mates who fucked from time to time.

"Jeez. That was the best fuck I have had in ages," Lilian said, wrapping her legs around his.

Ifenna chuckled. He liked how she expressed herself like a free spirit.

"Now you have to rewind the show for me. God, I'm so hungry now." Lilian stifled a yawn.

"Let me get you some juice," he said, lifting himself up.

After each of them drank a glass, Lilian asked if he had

any food in the house. Ifenna offered to make noodles for her.

"Noodles ke? That one is not food now," Lilian said. "I have soup downstairs. Do you have garri that we can use to make eba?"

Ifenna nodded.

"Okay. Let me go and bring the soup."

Lilian picked her gown from the floor, pulled it over her head, and turned her back to Ifenna to help her zip up. He reached out to grab her breasts briefly after fastening the zip, and as she walked toward the door, he slapped her buttocks, making her giggle.

Ifenna sensed she was going to spend the night in his apartment, which meant he might not find the time to publish the article on his blog. So, he reached for his laptop and powered it back on. The article was already in the draft. He ran his eyes quickly through it one last time, and just as he heard Lilian return at the door, he clicked the publish button.

Nigerian Men of God or Con Artists?

I am about to stir the hornets' nest, for, in Nigeria, no issue can be as sensitive as religion. My apologies to those who might be offended by this piece, but what must be said must be said.

For the avoidance of doubt, I believe in the existence of God and in the reality of heaven and hell, but I also know where to draw the line between spirituality and deception.

At some point in my life, I believed the only hope left for the nation was the religious institution. I am not alone in this conviction; many Nigerians think so, too. The nation appears to be on the verge of breathing its last breath with a combination of bad leadership, corruption, and tyranny, all driving the people to desolation. Like always, everyone turns to the heavens for help. This massive return to God is evident in the rapid spread of Pentecostalism, new generation churches across the land, and an increased call for prayers for the nation by the few founding fathers who are still alive.

Today, however, the whole religious revival fever has generated its own problems. It has given rise to a new set of chief executives going by various names such as general overseer, supreme shepherd, founding bishop, and the likes. These individuals—who set up their churches, driven perhaps by a foresight of the boom that lay ahead—have turned into kingpins as their congregations transform from mushroom gatherings into business empires and exceptionally large conglomerates.

Gradually but steadily, a new bourgeois class has emerged, this time around in the vineyard of God and thus unquestionably divine. We watched as the focus shifted from intercession to save our nation from final collapse to a grandiose scramble for the same old root of all evils: money. Pastors, who tasted the pleasures and comfort of the elite class by virtue of their headship of various churches and the unhindered assess it gave them to the commonwealth of their congregation, are now determined to sustain their position by spreading a new gospel of prosperity.

Under this new revelation, they make everyone under their spell believe that God never wished for anyone to be poor and that every child of God could become rich if they could be bold enough to put the Lord of the harvest to test. This translates into giving more from their meager earnings to sustain the ministry, and indeed, the pastor's new standard of living.

Religion has become business, with the key players acting in no way different from our civil leaders.

What we have today are mega-rich, celebrity, superstar, stage con artistes parading with the name "men of God." I am *seriously amused when I watch their broadcasts on television. I advise any freethinking individual who wants a laugh to tune to those broadcasts when they can.*

From the onset, they emphasize not what the Bible says but a stage-managed effort to delude and, by extension, hypnotize their highly gullible congregation into parting with more naira notes.

Today's "man of God" stands on the pulpit in a polished Italian suit, the type whose price tags read like telephone numbers. Depending on his preferences, his hair could be in jerry curls or a bushy afro, cut into a style like a Boys-II-Men member. He speaks with an annoying accent, mostly American wanna-be, for the desired effect, which he has cultivated and perfected over time. Much of what he says is incomprehensible, thanks to this accent. Occasionally, he goes to the glass stand where his Bible is and reads out a verse, then spends the next fifteen minutes explaining it. Most of his talk is about wealth, prosperity, and miracles, and we sometimes see some of his listeners rising and jumping senselessly into the air, which spurs him on. It goes on and on and on.

It is no secret that a good number of these superstar "Men of God" have built business empires. Agreeably, every individual has the right to own and operate a business, but when the capital for this stems from ripped-off, innocent churchgoers, it becomes morally questionable. Owning private universities can be said to be the current craze among them. These are universities that a greater percentage of their congregation cannot send their kids to because of the fees. Owning eye-popping SUVs and flashy rides is now minor and if you think your state governor's convoy is intimidating, wait until you see one of our more prosperous "men of God." Holiday trips abroad are a normal way of life, and hey, like the banks, they keep opening new branches nationwide.

Like showbiz celebrities, they are not spared of controversies. We have read about one pastor attacking another on the pages of newspapers. We have read about their illicit affairs with female members of their congregation and how their marriages are collapsing because of one flimsy issue or the other.

Now, would we be right in always attacking our civil leaders for corruption and deception when our religious leaders are worse? Would it be wise for us to continue to fall prey to these self-serving individuals who claim to be speaking for the Supreme Being when, clearly, they're just toying with our sensibilities?

I have a feeling that this was what Karl Marx had in mind when he said that religion was the opium of the masses, a potent item to make them sleep to their reality.

So, I've started this blog as an outlet for everyone who feels the way I do and wants to scream about it. You now have a wall to do so for free. We should also highlight their actions and utterances here. If you have clips, pictures, inside stories, or personal experiences of your own that you would like to share, just send me an email, and I will publish it here.

EIGHT

Ifenna stirred and stretched in bed. The bedroom wall light was on, and the rays made him squint as he tried to open his eyes. He could make out Lilian standing in the middle of the room close to the wardrobe with her back to him. She had just come out from the bathroom and was running a towel over her naked body.

"You're up already?" Ifenna asked.

"Oh, he's finally awake," she said, turning around to face him with a smile. "Sleepyhead."

"Come back to bed, jare. Where are you rushing off to so early?"

She giggled and hung the towel on the wardrobe door. "Do you know what the time is? I'm on the morning shift. I need to be at the hospital by seven o'clock. I said let me just shower here so when I get back to my place, I will just dress and be on my way."

Ifenna followed her every move as she bent down to pull her undies up her waist and felt blood rushing to his groin. Memories of their night filled his head. They made love two more times after eating the dinner of eba and egusi soup and settling back to watching *Grey's Anatomy*, sprawled on the floor on the duvet Ifenna spread out because the couch could not fit them both. A sex scene in *Grey's Anatomy* by Meredith and Derek had inspired the first of the two instances. They started kissing, watching that scene, and Ifenna pulled her up from the duvet, backed her against the wall and took her from behind. The second happened later in the bedroom. She had slept off while leaning on him in the living room. After attempting to lift her and failing, he led her gently into the bedroom.

There was a power cut just when he got her to lie down on the bed, and he rushed out to put on the generator in the balcony. By the time he got back into the room, she was wide awake as if she had never slept. As he joined her on the bed, she asked to cuddle. Soon, she was straddling him and riding him with her back arched in deep pleasure and guiding his hands to the right places as she came down on him.

"Not going to work today? You normally leave early," Lilian asked, adjusting the band of her underwear around her waist.

"I think after what you did to me last night, I need extra sleep," Ifenna said, which made her laugh as she picked up her bra from the foot of the bed.

The thought that she was now officially his girlfriend thrilled him. He didn't even get to ask her. They'd been lying with their eyes on the rotating ceiling fan above when she asked about his occupation. She had just come down from riding him, and they were both still breathing in heaves and relishing the aftertaste of their lovemaking.

"I'm a journalist," he replied.

"For what paper?"

"*The Nigerian.*"

She paused for some time. Her next statement indicated they now had something going.

"I like openness in my relationships. I don't tell lies, and I hate to be lied to," she said.

Ifenna wondered if she knew he was lying about working at *The Nigerian*, that he got sacked and was currently jobless. But at her mention of a relationship, his worries lessened. He was deciding what to say in response when she continued. "I don't do office romance. That's why I've never dated any of the doctors at the office. I don't know what a compound romance will be like, but I'm willing to see how this goes."

Ifenna pulled her close and kissed her, and neither of them said anything again until they fell asleep.

Now, Ifenna sat up in bed and tilted his head as he watched her slide on her gown. He had a coy smile on his face, and he remembered how she had told him last night about her last boyfriend, who'd gone on to marry someone else while still dating her; how she only found out when she saw pictures of the wedding on Facebook; how she had been heartbroken for months and even considered suicide at some point. Though sympathetic for her, Ifenna couldn't help but feel lucky the relationship had ended.

"Whaaaat?" she said, blushing when her eyes met his.

"You are so beautiful," he said. "I could look at you all day."

She smiled. "You really have a sweet mouth."

"It is not sweet mouth. It is the truth. See that shape," he said, admiring her figure now inside the gown.

"Thank you," she said shyly.

"Must you go? I just want to be here with you, all day."

"I have to go o. You know I need to relieve those on night shift. I hate it when I am on night and the morning person comes late."

Ifenna got up from the bed and stretched. His hip ached slightly. He hadn't exerted them as he had done last night in a long while. "Where is your hospital located again?"

"Ikeja. Off Allen," she replied, leading the way out of the room. "Come to think of it, your office is around that side, abi? I normally see one signboard with *The Nigerian* on it."

"Yes. Our office is around there, but that's not where I report. I go there occasionally," Ifenna hurried behind her, stifling a yawn.

At the door, they kissed. He said he would call her, and she promised she would see him later that night. Ifenna considered leaving for his normal morning kabu kabu drive. He was already late, though. He usually left the house at five o'clock. It was half-past five. Though he was still sure to find passengers if he left then, he feared that before he made the round, VIO officers would have resumed work at their various checkpoints. It wasn't worth the risk. He needed the money, especially now that he had a girlfriend, but he worried if the officers stopped him, he could lose everything he had made that week. He thought of just going back to bed and was already back in his room when he remembered his blog and decided to see if his article had got any comments.

Ifenna found notifications for five comments to his article in his email. He clicked on the comment section of the blog. While setting it up, he had allowed visitors to be anonymous in their comments, but they had to adopt aliases.

112

The first comment was by Naijamanstar. Ifenna read it quickly, a bit anxious that it might be a rebuke.

> *Naijamanstar: Thanks for this piece. I am a Christian caught in this dilemma. I barely go to church anymore. Each and every time I go, it's all about money, prosperity, and more money. "Give your offering." "Pay your tithe." "Sow a seed." And it continues, "The church needs this and that." But when it is time for your children to go to the schools built by your genuine effort, you will be shocked to discover that the gates will be shut against them! It's all a parasitic relationship. I am about to go back to my parents' church, a very conservative and spiritual church that no individual can lay claim to as the founding bishop. It's all a sham. Something needs to be done to regulate church revenue in Nigeria. Maybe the Ministry of Inland Revenue should wake up to its responsibility by ensuring these churches are run like proper charities and not investment empires.*

IFENNA READ THE COMMENT AGAIN before clicking to like it and moving to the next one. It excited him. He thought it was a good way to start, the type of validation he needed to reinforce his thinking. The next comment was short.

> *Drunken126: This topic has just distracted my attention from the US Open Venus vs Serena match as it is something that I so agree with. If there is a God, and I sincerely hope there is, I wonder what He thinks of it all.*
> *Very well written.*
> *Now, back to the match!*

IFENNA THOUGHT DRUNKEN 126 SOUNDED LIKE a very prim and proper fellow, straight to the point when expressing his opinions. He decided he was a guy, in his mid-twenties, that he had to be from an affluent background to be watching tennis, and probably very smart. This made Ifenna appreciate his comment about the article being well-written even more. He was about to read the next comment when he heard the knock on the door. The rapidness suggested some urgency. He cursed under his breath. Only Tunde and his wife knocked that way. They must be ready to go out and wanted him to move his vehicle. He got up and shuffled to the door. Another round of banging started.

"Who is it?" He barked as he unhooked the door bolt, expecting to see Tunde or his wife and ready to express his disgust at the rude knocks.

"Na Oga Tunde, e wan comot," the person on the other side answered.

It was Nuhu, their gateman, standing there naked to his waist with a soapy sponge in one hand. Ifenna imagined he was on his morning routine of washing the cars in the compound. He looked like he was agitated, and Ifenna wondered if he now also smoked Indian hemp, the way his eyes were red.

"Okay, I dey come," Ifenna replied, relaxing the tensed muscles on his face.

Downstairs, Ifenna saw the reason for the panic in Nuhu's face. Tunde's wife looked like she was in labor. She writhed from side to side as her husband led her to his car, parked just in front of Ifenna's. She was also lamenting in Yoruba and tapping the back of her waist repeatedly as if there was something there that she needed to dislodge. An elderly woman followed just behind them, carrying a bag and offering words of comfort in Yoruba. Ifenna guessed her to be Tunde's mother-in-law. As he put his car in reverse and started to drive out, Ifenna caught the sticker on Tunde's car bumper: *Saved Family*. Ifenna had never seen it on their car before. It was the catchphrase for people who attended Saved Chapel, whose founding bishop always boasted that any Christian that generously gave to the church would not know sickness or poverty, and his members often echoed the same about their lives. The founding bishop had recently been in the news for buying a private jet, and when he was asked why he lived in such opulence, he famously answered that poverty was not a qualification for heaven. As if to buttress his point, he asked the reporter if Jesus was poor. When he got no reply from the reporter — maybe because it wasn't the type of question you gave an answer to — he chuckled to himself and said those expecting him to be poor because he preached about heaven needed to have their skulls examined.

This explained Tunde's rather proud nature of acting like he owned the compound. As Ifenna drove back into the compound, he thought of how, in seven days, there would be a party for the naming ceremony and wondered whether Tunde would invite him.

Ifenna returned to his laptop when he got back in. The next commenter on his article didn't seem very impressed and argued there were just a few bad eggs among the men of God and not enough reason to condemn them all, noting that religion was free will, and nobody forced anyone to pay any money.

JagaJagaMikky: If the churches do not force money out of their worshippers, they have done no wrong. They preached to you that God would multiply your seed, you believed it and gave them your money voluntarily. So, what is the big deal?

That the pastors live in splendor should also not give anybody headaches if they earn their incomes legitimately. If you think it is easy to convince people to part with their hard-earned money, go and start your own church.

Comparing our church leaders to politicians does not hold any dice. The politicians steal the money they should use to better our lot while leaving us in abject penury. The pastors collect what you willingly give them and nothing more.

Using the brush of a few to tar the rest is a tactic employed by those who have lost the argument. The church that I attend does not care whether you pay your tithes and offerings. Yes, it preaches that you should support God's work in any way you can, but no record is kept of those who offer and those who do not.

Church attendance is very voluntary, and so too is church offering. You can attend churches without making money part of your commitment if that will make it easier for you to listen to the gospel preached and make it to heaven.

AFTER READING THE COMMENT TWICE, Ifenna was annoyed, though he recognized the sarcasm laced through JagaJagaMikky's words. He seemed to be a devil's advocate. It interested him that two others had replied to the comment.

Naijamanstar: @JagaJagaMikky, I would just like to know what Pentecostal church doesn't preach money... even the one I attend that never made it an issue has recently made it compulsory to call out tithe payers for their tithes to be prayed for... and this was a direct order from the general overseer, with the argument that those who don't pay are denying the rest of the congregation the blessing from God.

InternetGeek @JagaJagaMikky, Not all Men of God in Nigeria are con artists, but we all know a lot of them are. The test is easy: if that pastor talks more of money than salvation, and if he uses the name of Jesus and God less than the word tithe and offering. If he uses the name of God five times but tithes and offering come up 41 times, run, my brother, run.

IFENNA CHUCKLED AT INTERNETGEEK'S COMMENT. he could have posted those same lines himself. When he worked at the bank, a cashier who attended Saved Chapel had told him a story. The founding bishop was a known proponent of the First Fruit gospel. He said that his members must give all their earnings in the month of January because Jehovah commanded it, and when they did so, it would open the storehouses of heaven for them. To ensure compliance, the church had fixed the first Sunday in February, when salary earners would have collected their pay for January, as First Fruit Sunday. The bank cashier knew that after her Christmas expenses, giving her pay to God in January would leave her broke, but to ensure she did not fail her pastor, she withdrew some money from an account of someone who was suspected to be deceased because their accounts had been dormant for a long time. She'd got caught. While she faced the disciplinary panel, she confessed she'd stolen the money to pay her First Fruit offering.

Ifenna wondered now, as he did then, if God accepted stolen money to keep His pronouncements, as interpreted by the men of God. He had no answers, but he was certain that Saved Chapel's founding bishop would fail InternetGeek's 419 test.

Another comment popped up on the blog. The commenter, Nkemkah119, who said she was Catholic, lamented that their new parish priest rejected the Camry the church had bought for his predecessor a year ago, insisting that the parish was big and should afford a four-wheel drive for his use. While the Pastoral council were still grumbling, he called their bluff and bought one anyway.

> *The latest one: last Sunday, he announced he will start collecting tithes. Can you imagine that? Tithe, in a Catholic church? Wetin Musa no go see for gate?*

The comment left Ifenna in stitches, holding the sides of the table as he laughed. When he finally got up from his laptop, there was an SMS from Nkoli, saying she was broke and needed some money. Damn it! He should've driven his kabu kabu that morning. But then he remembered his night with Lilian, her softness against his body, and the way his heart stopped when she smiled at him, and all his guilt disappeared. Something emboldened him, and he messaged his sister that he would send her some money later that afternoon. He decided to run his kabu kabu during the day, the presence of the VIO notwithstanding. He wanted to be home early so he could spend time with Lilian.

AFTER HE AND LILIAN FINISHED off the plate of jollof rice and fried plantain that she'd prepared in her apartment and brought upstairs in a flask, they made love on the couch. Just as they were settling down to continue watching *Grey's Anatomy*, Ifenna heard a knock. He answered the door to find one of his third-floor neighbors standing there, his face like the clouds heavy with rain. Ifenna's first thought was that the man, who lived alone and walked with the gait of a drunkard, had stopped at the wrong door after a night out at the bar, but when the man spoke, he sounded very sober. Tunde's wife had had a difficult labor, the man revealed, and the baby died shortly after he was born. He was knocking on doors so neighbors could go be with the devastated couple. Ifenna's mind went to the sticker he saw in the morning on Tunde's car. How cruel that the baby had not been saved.

NINE

Pastor Nick's convoy sped down Third Mainland Bridge. It was just a little past noon, and he was grateful that that axis of the bridge was free of heavy traffic because he was already running late to a function. A member of his church, a prominent one by the amount he signed monthly as tithe, was opening a new outlet of his international franchise eatery at the new Ikeja Mall. Nick had been asked to bless the outlet and declare it officially open. He was running late because his weekly meeting with his pastors had gone on longer than planned.

The pastors' meeting that morning had been special because Nick needed to address something that was spreading like a virus among churches in the country. In less than a month, there had been two high-profile disputes involving men of God, all bordering on internal rebellion. In one case, the pastor of a satellite church in Abuja had renamed the church and declared himself the head pastor after a disagreement with the general overseer in Lagos. For the other case, a pastor of an outlet church in Ikorodu had refused to be transferred to another location, insisting that he labored specifically for that outlet and could not be moved, and when those at the headquarter insisted, he resigned and started his own church, taking most of the congregation with him.

These stories troubled Nick. As a rule, he consciously monitored his pastors and dealt with dissent as quickly as it was founded, but he decided to use the meeting that morning to reinforce his principles so that if any of them was planning a rebellion, they would be drawn back into line. Not like he feared dissent; it was just the bad press that came with it that he detested.

The meetings held every Tuesday and was with a closed group of his closest pastors in the room, and the two pastors who were planting the Abuja church joined by video conference. This was his inner caucus, the kitchen cabinet with whom he was able to keep an eye on his rapidly expanding congregation and ensure that the church kept growing.

That morning, Nick had given a talk on loyalty. He handed out copies of a book called *Disloyalty in the Ministry,* which a pastor friend of his in London had recommended. The author, also a pastor of a church with branches across three continents, stated that to be successful, a church must be run in a strict and hierarchical manner that gave no room for disobedience or dissent. He said that the devil was an expert at destroying the church from within. He later talked about how to identify, avoid, and crush rebellion. As soon as Nick finished reading the book, he ordered twenty copies from Amazon.

Nick had been very frank that morning. He was a man with a special anointing, he said, and they were privileged to be working with him in a ministry ordained by God. Any of them who wished to draw from that anointing had to be loyal. He was explicit when he talked about disloyal acts and stated that he would not tolerate anyone challenging him, making statements that suggested he wasn't right on any matter, contradicting his views of the scripture, asking about the church's finances, not taking down notes when he preached, not clapping and shouting like the other congregants while he preached, not respecting his wife, gossiping about him, and envying his wealth and blessings.

The room had gone silent as he spoke, and he was satisfied with the fearful looks on their faces. He told them to read the book and ensure that its message was passed down the line to their junior pastors, church workers, and members. To reassure them, he talked about the benefits of remaining loyal; how the wealth would spread to all of them; how he would take the ministry to another level; and how they, who were closest to him, would be the first beneficiaries of the enormous blessings God promised for the Rivers of Joy Church. Then, he prayed, all of them holding hands to form a big ring, against the spirit of Lucifer, the chief source of rebellion.

The convoy reached the foot of the bridge at Iyana-Oworo and slowed down. Danfo buses congested the road as they parked along the curbs, picking up and dropping off passengers, and LASTMA traffic officials seemed to be having a torrid time getting them to keep moving. Nick looked out the window of his Range Rover Autobiography, which had been delivered to him two weeks earlier—a second one rode empty just behind him. It was part of the elaborate security arrangements he placed around himself. The two vehicles were exact replicas; he wanted to keep anyone looking to attack him confused.

The sun shone brightly. A broken-down BRT bus idled close to the pillars of the pedestrian bridge. Its occupants stood around its rear like a halo, watching as men busied around its engine. Hawkers milled about, their wares balanced on their heads, and Nick spotted two men—both danfo conductors—pointing clenched fists at each other by the side of the road, squaring for a fight. The shorter of the two, who wore a Chelsea jersey with a faded number five, swung his hand. The taller man, shirtless, ducked and threw his own fist. The sight amused Nick, and as the convoy made their way out of the holdup onto the ramp that led toward Gbagada, he thought of how easily he could have ended up as a bus conductor.

He picked up his tablet and tapped on Twitter. He had a handle, managed by his media assistant, Bimbo. Someone at the pastor's meeting had mentioned that he had now reached five hundred thousand followers. The numbers had grown exponentially since the inauguration of the cathedral: five hundred and eight thousand already. Nick smiled to himself, impressed. He looked at his latest post:

I decree that from today, everything you are believing God for will be answered with an earthquake. If you believe, reply with an Amen, and it will be so. IJN.

Funny, Nick thought, how these over fifty thousand people who had replied with an 'amen' believed he made the post himself and that they were going to have their prayers answered. He could now see why Bimbo believed social media was the next battlefield for ministries to win souls. She had said something about getting his account verified as well, which would put him in the same league as other top men of God, like TD Jakes. The thought made him smile again.

Looking at his profile picture, he decided he did not like it. His jacket looked too big. He immediately sent an SMS to Bimbo to change the picture. His appearance mattered a lot to him; he had been very deliberate in building his brand as a man of God, and he knew that to stand out in the crowd, he needed to look sharp, have an appearance that young people admired. He had accentuated his build by a disciplined routine at the gym, and as more money came in, he went from the nameless suit tailor in Tejuosho to the best foreign designers. No more modesty. That morning, he was wearing one of his new suits by Zegna. He liked Zegna because of its long history of dressing Hollywood superstars for the Oscars. He too was a superstar in the Lord's vineyard, he thought, and people needed to realize that just by looking at him.

As the convoy joined Ikorodu Road at Anthony Village and proceeded toward Maryland, Nick's thoughts fluttered to his next big project. He had been so focused on completing Heaven's Gate Cathedral that he hadn't bothered about expanding. His only effort at establishing a branch outside of Lagos was the church being built in Abuja. He wanted to go international.

During his recent trip to London, he had some meetings about establishing a London outlet. Essentially, he would acquire an existing church run by a Ghanaian, which would become the first Rivers of Joy Church branch outside of Nigeria. The Ghanaian agreed to sell on the condition that he could pastor in this new church. Nick didn't mind since

Ghanaians were generally more sincere than Nigerians, and Pastor Mensah looked meek. Still, Nick needed his lawyers to draw up papers structuring the deal properly to ensure that the ownership records were regularized with the UK's Charity Commission. This deal would be the springboard for his planned expansion across Europe.

If all went according to plan and the expansion happened, he would need to buy a private jet. Owning his own plane had been his dream since he started the ministry. He and Nkechi lived streets away from the University of Lagos Campus at the time, and he had printed handbills with the bold heading: 'How long has it been since you went to church?' The invitation was not to a church service but to a gathering of brethren to unwind over coffee and good music and have a conversation about God's unconditional love.

From the outset, the target audience had been people who felt inadequate by regular church teachings and those who were disgruntled and only attended church out of the habit of going. He had distributed the handbills himself, standing at the bus stop in front of the main campus gate, beaming his best smile at anyone who collected the handbill, and saying he looked forward to seeing them.

The first three meetings were in their sitting room. Then, he moved the meetings to a lounge that hosted parties at night when the numbers grew. He soon had to move the meetings to an auditorium on campus. Though the returns were meager, and he had offset the expenses with his own earnings, he'd felt like an investor, certain that one day he would reap big.

Nick wanted the jet to be this year's Christmas gift to himself. At his meeting with the pastors earlier that morning, he spoke to them about being more aggressive in winning new members who could give generously to God, ensuring he did not build a hundred-and-fifty-thousand-seat church to be occupied by rats and spirits. He didn't want to call for a special donation like some other pastors had done over the years. He just wanted to buy the jet, no hassle, no fuss, like picking something out at the supermarket. Maybe he could meet with his special group of benefactors. Owning a private jet would benefit him, sure, but it would also help advance the benefactors' interests. If he presented a strong pitch, he would get the funding. He'd own a jet by the holidays.

CHIEF PAUL EDOZIE, IN HIS red cap and leopard skin attire, nearly prostrated when he welcomed Pastor Nick.

"I am sorry I kept you waiting," Nick said, standing tall and squeezing the man's hand.

"We are blessed to have you," Chief Edozie said.

They were at the entrance lobby of the new Ikeja Mall. Nick had never been there before, and he marveled at its size, how it made the one in Lekki look like child's play. He knew one of his benefactors, a former governor of the state, owned a large stake in the complex, a fact that wasn't public knowledge.

Nick looked around, taking in the environment as Chief Edozie walked slightly ahead, leading him toward his international franchise eatery being opened. Most of the shops were yet to be occupied, but the footfall seemed very impressive already, with selfie-taking young people with knapsacks and colorful hairstyles milling around. Chief Edozie explained that the cinema was open, a main attraction for many people on the Lagos Mainland. Nick wondered if he'd made a mistake not investing in the project when his benefactor had first mentioned it to him. Over the years, he had got his hands on a rich array of choice real estate that held the bulk of his investments. He recently acquired an apartment in an exclusive location in Dubai, pleased to learn that his immediate neighbors to the left and the right were a former Nigerian Army General and the current Senate President. Hussein, the realtor who'd sold the property to him, swore that every who-is-who in Nigeria owned property in that neighborhood. Initially, Nick hadn't been interested, but after he found out he'd be the first Nigerian man of God to own a property there, he signed the bill of sale immediately. He wrote an extra cheque for Hussein and told him to make sure he remained the only Nigerian man of God there. He did not want to share bragging rights with any other pastor.

As they walked down the mall's hallway toward the eatery, Nick's bodyguards surrounded him. A few mallgoers had recognized him, and a crowd was gradually forming, some taking pictures with their mobile phones. Nick secretly liked the attention; he felt like a celebrity on the red carpet. Plus, it was good publicity for his church. Chief Edozie, a member of Nick's church, owning an eatery in this plush complex meant that Nick's followers were also prospering, that the ten percent tithe they paid was delivering promised prosperity.

A small crowd waited outside the eatery. The few that had seats stood up as Nick approached, welcoming him with claps and whistles. Balloons and ribbons decorated the doors. The staff, mainly young girls, stood like sentries along the corridor in their lemon-colored t-shirts and bright hair extensions. Both a photographer and videographer crouched at the ready. Nick smiled and waved as he walked through the party before taking his seat in front between Chief Edozie and his wife, who curtsied in greeting before shaking his hands.

Nick liked the couple. Always had. He had met Chief Edozie on a flight from Johannesburg to Lagos a few years earlier, and they had got talking as they sat side by side in Business Class. By the time they landed in Lagos, Nick had convinced the man that the issues he was having in his business were because he wasn't attending the right church. The very next Sunday, Chief Edozie and his wife showed up at Nick's church. Since then, the couple became committed members and contributed immensely to building Heaven's Gate Cathedral through their very generous donations. Nick would later inform them privately, after he had opened the eatery and declared a new beginning of unmatched business success, that he had decided to make them both elders in the church. He would make the official announcement next Sunday.

The opening ceremony was brief. Chief Edozie made a short speech welcoming Nick, which was his testimony of how he acquired the international franchise after many years of seeking it. The breakthrough came only after sowing a special seed at Nick's direction. Chief Edozie narrated how he was in his office one day when he got a call from the franchise owners, apologizing for not signing him on earlier and asking when he was available so they could come down to Lagos to sign the papers. The gathering clapped at Chief Edozie's every pause, and he acknowledged it by waving his hand like a tennis champion after winning a grand slam. At the end, he encouraged everyone to make their way to the Rivers of Joy Church.

After Chief Edozie's speech, Nick prayed, blessing all the food that would ever be cooked and served in the eatery and binding demonic spirits from walking through the doors. A silence hovered when he mumbled to himself, his eyes shut in supposed deep prayer before he symbolically anointed the doors with oil crosses. He then cut the ribbon with a pair of scissors and led the way into the eatery, where he prayed again before sounding the shofar. He had come along with the ancient musical horn used for Jewish religious purposes because he knew it would promote the impression that he was someone very grounded in ancient theology yet still modern and hip.

As his convoy drove out of the mall's parking lot at the end of the event, Nick opened the envelope that the elated Chief Edozie had slipped into his hands as he saw him off to his car.

"Just a small something for fuel," Chief Edozie had whispered as Nick feigned surprise and made like he was embarrassed by the gift. The content of the envelope was a cheque for one million naira. Nick folded the envelope slowly, tucked it in the inner pocket of his suit, and held his hand over it for several moments. A private jet would be his sooner rather than later.

TEN

Pastor Nick entered his wife's room unannounced. They had just returned from Sunday service, and she was sitting at the dressing mirror, using wet facial wipes to remove the makeup from her face. She saw him through the mirror, which was opposite the door, and she spun around, surprised. In the three months since she'd moved into the spare room, he hadn't ever been inside. He looked around the room like it was an alien environment. He was still wearing the blue-striped suit from church. He seemed to deliberately take his time before speaking. She kept quiet too and stared blankly, though she followed his movements with her eyes.

"We need to talk," he finally said. He stood in the middle of the room under the chandelier

"About what? Have you come to tell me you are taking a second wife?"

"Don't be ridiculous, Nkay," he said.

"So, what are you here for?"

He fell quiet again and paced about the room with his hands folded across his chest, the sole of his shoes tapping the tiled floor.

"I think it's time for this to end," he said, at last, straightening and slipping his hands into his trouser pockets.

"What exactly is ending, Nicholas?"

"You know what I'm talking about, Nkay. It has lasted for long enough. People are noticing. I mean, you were in church today, looking like you were bereaved or something. Do you know two different people came to ask me after service if you were okay? I don't want rumors to spread, and you know how these tabloids can be, so I have come to ask that we end this ... this misunderstanding. I mean, I get that you're angry and all, but it's been how long now? Three months? Four? It's time to fix it, especially since people are beginning to notice."

"Wait a minute," Nkechi said, her voice rising. "You're suddenly concerned about us because people have started to notice, and you are worried about what they will say? Shame on you, Nicholas. Shame on you."

"Well, you know very well that there's a lot of attention on us." Nick resumed pacing the room. "People are looking for bad things to say about us. Other pastors envy our rise to prominence. I know how much I spend on the media just to make sure we stay ahead of broadcasters with the wrong intentions. We can't be the ones giving them things to write about. So, for what it is worth, I have come to extend an olive branch. You know I love you. What happened was just an isolated event, a temptation that I fell for. It was just one careless slip. I have made peace with Jehovah, and I expect you to move it to the past where it belongs."

"In the past?"

"Yes."

"You're sure it's in the past?" Nkechi stood from the small stool and started to walk toward him. "If you really want to put this in the past, then you have to come clean."

"What else do you want to ask? You already know everything."

"No, I don't."

"Look, honestly, I just want to put this behind us. God has forgiven me, so why haven't you?"

"Who's the woman? Or is it women? And for how long has this been going on?"

"Some random lady I met. The devil used her to tempt me." Nick lowered himself and sat down on the edge of the bed, shaking his head in deep regret.

"Random?" Nkechi wasn't convinced.

"Yes. And it was just one time. I swear to you, Nkay. And I used protection."

Nkechi let out a laugh steeped in sarcasm. "Pastor Nicholas Adejuwon, you are such a shameless liar." She pointed at him. "You lie so much you make the devil look like a saint."

"Watch your mouth," Nick snapped. He sprung from the bed and walked toward the walk-in closet. "How can you call me a liar?"

"Because you are one, Nicholas," Nkechi followed him. "You really think I'll buy that story? You think I am a fool? It seems like after all these years, you still don't know the woman you married. I thought I knew the man I married, but now I know how wrong I was."

"Where are all these ideas coming from? How can you call me, your husband, a liar? You shouldn't speak to me that way."

"If you aren't a liar, can you explain to me what exactly Bimbo was doing with you in London?" She noticed the guilt creep into his face when she mentioned her name. "Tell me the truth. Or is she the so-called random lady? Tell me, Pastor Nick. You were at the pulpit today talking about fornication and adultery like some angel. Do you know how disgusted I felt sitting there listening to you say those things when I know you're having an affair with a lady whose husband-to-be you call your son in the Lord? Damn it, Nicholas! You amaze me. You really think I wouldn't find out? Let me tell you, I know everything. How you flew on the same flight as her, how you stayed in different hotels so that no one would notice, and how she slipped into your room every night for…for…special anointing." She let out a hysterical laugh.

Nick looked like he'd just been stabbed in the chest. He was too shocked to speak. When he finally did, his tone turned angry. "You've been snooping on me? That's what our marriage has come to? I see. Did you set up surveillance on me or what?"

"It doesn't matter. Were you with Bimbo or not?"

"Lower your voice."

"I won't!" Nkechi yelled. "Anyone that wants to hear should hear. After all, it's the truth, is it not?"

"Look, woman, shut your mouth. This must not leave this room."

"And what if it does? Are you scared of the scandal? You can lose your wife but you can't leave your church?"

"I'll have you know you aren't the only one who knows things around here," Nick barked before turning his back on her. "I know about you and Pastor Felix."

Then, as if to see if his shot had hit the target, he turned around again to face her. "Yes. I know everything."

PASTOR NKECHI WASN'T CERTAIN HOW long she slept. A few hours? The whole night? She pushed the duvet away and sat up. The room was dark. She tried to see if any rays slipped through the curtains to help her guess the time, but there weren't any. Perhaps it was early dawn. She used the back of her right palm to stifle a yawn and listened. Usually, a cock crowed in the early hours of the morning. Its call reminded her of growing up in Enugu, and she always wondered who in Banana Island kept such domestic birds. All she heard that morning, though, were generators humming to power the houses in the concrete jungle.

Nkechi tried to stand up. She had a headache. Her eyes felt heavy. She had been crying before she fell asleep, which made her feel like she had a cold, the way she continually sniffled. Had she cried in her sleep, too? She settled back on the bed as she remembered the fight from the night before. Her husband had left the room after revealing he had always known that she'd had an affair with Pastor Felix. Nkechi's stomach had dropped when Nick made the statement. She had wanted to ask him about the junior pastor's wife, whom the private investigator told her might've had a child for Nick. She stood rooted to the spot and wished the floor would open and swallow her. They stood staring at each other in silence, their eyes saying things their mouths found too heavy to voice. He had also told her to grow up. If he could keep her affair a secret from the congregation, so could she. She had remained quiet as he spoke, managing to wobble to the bed, climbing onto it, and burrowing herself under the blanket. Nick had slammed the door on his way out, the bang like a thunderclap.

She wasn't sure if she had cried out of guilt for having an affair or because a part of her still mourned Felix, as if her husband's mentioning of his name had awoken emotions she long thought were dead. When Felix had died suddenly in the freak accident at the construction site, she had been devastated, but she hadn't been able to grieve properly. Back then, she'd believed his death was God's wrath for the sin they committed. She had bottled all her sadness up and maintained a dignified mien, standing beside her husband at the funeral held at Vaults and Gardens in Ikoyi. She wore dark shades, not because that was the respectable way to appear, but to hide the depth of her grief. When she spoke to the other funeral attendees, she had struggled to moderate her voice, inhaling deeply, and speaking slowly, so her tone didn't betray her sorrow.

A week after the funeral, she went on a tour of the US in a roadshow to raise money for the completion of the Heaven's Gate Cathedral. She visited churches and handed out white handkerchiefs to generous donors. By the time she returned to Lagos a month later, the pain of Felix's death had finally faded. During her time away, she had even absolved herself of any guilt—or so she thought.

Nkechi found her phone beside the bedside lamp. Ten o'clock. She reckoned she slept for about seven hours. It hadn't been a deep sleep. It was filled with pictures of scenes from the past, carefully filed in her memory, playing back to her like a slow-motion video. The memories filled her with a kaleidoscope of emotions, some joyful, most sad. She woke up right at the scene of her and Felix's last encounter, just a few hours before he fell to his death.

They had become friendly, she and Felix. Always had been. He was smart, witty, and very kind-hearted, but she hadn't known this at first. Nick had made her the face of the building project with Felix as her assistant. Together, they had led a project committee that was largely figure-headed because, while they were custodians of the building plan and drivers of the fund-raising efforts, all decisions still had to be made by Nick. Another expensive IVF treatment had failed, and the doctor said she needed a distraction to help her escape depression, so Nick announced he was putting her in charge of the final phase of the project while he focused on the ministry. While she liked the role, she didn't like it that her husband appointed Felix, one of his acolytes, who dressed like Nick and mimicked his mannerisms when he spoke—a trend among the young pastors that irritated her—as her assistant. She had treated him with suspicion, just there as her husband's eyes to police her, and she made it clear from the outset he worked for her.

But all of that changed. Nkechi and Felix went to the site for inspection, and it started to rain with heavy winds that raised clouds of dust, throwing items in various directions. The two of them had been on the top floor inspecting the roofing, which had just commenced, so they ran down to the floor below to get shelter from the rain. Nkechi had lost her balance as she descended the stairs, her high heels buckled under her weight. Felix caught her before she could fall. He led her to a space where they stayed to wait out the rain. While they stood in silence, Felix told her a very funny story of how he became a drummer in a campus fellowship.

Nkechi remembered the story now. Her heart fluttered. He had made her laugh so hard that day. According to Felix, he had gone to see a friend in one of the female hostels on campus during his undergraduate days. Back then, male students were only allowed in the hostels from six to ten o'clock in the evening. The lady he went to see wasn't exactly his girlfriend, though he liked her. She had friend-zoned him, calling him a brother since they hailed from the same state. Most times, he went to see her just to eat free food, which had been the case on that fateful day. He had arrived at about eight o'clock. All her roommates were out. After eating concoction rice and dried fish, they had spent time talking, first about a difficult assignment and then to some campus gossip about an impending cult war. They got so carried away they did not realize they had missed the porter's warning bells to alert all male visitors of their obligatory departure. It was almost half-past ten, and this meant trouble. If he was found, he would spend the night at the security cell, which was not only a terrible experience but could also lead to other disciplinary academic actions. Felix was stuck in the room, and they had little time to think through any plan because her roommates would return at any moment.

They decided to tell the roommates that he was a female friend who was ill. So, he wore one of her wigs and lay down on her bed, covering himself up to the neck with her blanket even though the weather was severely humid. He faced the wall, and for effect, she brought out a half-used pack of Panadol and propped it on her table. Her roommates returned one after the other, and when they asked, his friend repeated the story, and there were concerned exclamations:

"Aeyaahh, has she taken any medicine?" and "Did she eat anything?" One of the roommates asked which of her friends it was because they knew most of her friends, and she said this one lived off-campus and had never been to the room. All the while, Felix pretended to be asleep.

"There was nothing I didn't hear that night," Felix said. "They talked about all sorts of things. Girls sleeping with professors, boys asking them out, and girls in a different hostel caught sucking each other's breasts and how they were marched around naked in the hostel. Then there were arguments about someone leaving sand from their footwear on another's corner and of someone not finding her pants where she hung it. I heard everything. I had to stop myself from laughing or turning around to see who was talking at a time. It was the hardest night of my life."

Felix said his friend who had to lie beside him nudged him many times that night because he was snoring so loudly, and then he had an erection while feeling her body against his, the softness of her breasts against his back.

"Honestly, I felt like my bladder was going to burst, but I had to hold it. I couldn't go to the toilet. My friend had to give me an empty water bottle after all her roommates left for lectures. By that time, I was shaking. It's a miracle I didn't piss myself that day."

As Felix narrated his story, painting a very vivid picture of his predicament, Nkechi had laughed so hard tears rolled down her cheeks. And at that moment, the dark clouds from the failed IVF lifted. Felix told her how the next morning, while his friend and the other roommates were out to have their bath, one of the roommates, a final year student and a born-again Christian, had come to tap him. Apparently, she had noticed he was a guy all this time. In exchange for not ratting him out, he promised to start attending the Scriptural Union (SU) fellowship and then, he encountered the Lord and became born again.

By the time the rain stopped, Nkechi and Felix left the site as friends. She felt drawn to him, his sincere smile, his well-kept beard, and the way he pronounced her name with his Yoruba accent. Weeks later, after they became friends, he confessed that the female hostel story was not true, that he'd read about it somewhere, but it still made her laugh, and she couldn't stop seeing him as the character in the story.

When he asked her if she was okay a few days afterward, she opened up to him about her struggles with having a child, the multiple failed IVFs, and the shame she'd felt when other women gave their testimonies of getting pregnant while she could not. Then she talked about feeling alone, the loneliness of being the wife of a busy man of God. Her husband was very bullish about his church, like a start-up founder looking to scale, concerned only about the growth of the numbers when sometimes all she wanted to do was hold him close in bed. As she started to cry, Felix reached out, slowly at first and then all at once, and pulled her close to him. He had held her, like one would hold a grieving friend, her head on his shoulder, her tears soaking his shirt, his hand stroking her hair.

The attraction grew. They started making excuses just to be in each other's company, fixing meetings only the two of them attended, supposedly to discuss the church building when they really just talked and laughed. He became her soothing balm, the one who made every worry disappear. He told her how his aunt sought a child for fifteen years and how she had conceived when she was almost fifty, even after the doctors said she didn't stand a chance. God gave her twin boys. Felix taught Nkechi about faith in a way she'd never heard before. He gave her hope that a miracle would one day come.

"There is no way God will not answer the prayers of one of his most beautiful creations." His words sent butterflies fluttering in the bottom of her stomach.

One day, they kissed. It had been so brief and sudden that afterward, she wondered if it actually happened, if she didn't imagine it because she had dreamed of kissing him so many times before. He had left immediately, and Nkechi thought he was disappointed in her because she instigated it. She had been priming him that evening, allowing him generous views of her breasts, casually running her hands around his chest; then, she leaned in while he spoke, and he had kissed her back. When they chatted later on BBM that night, as they did every night before bed, she was pleased to find that he had liked the kiss but had left quickly because it was the first time he had ever kissed a lady so beautiful.

The only time they made love was at his house. It was the culmination of many weeks of flirtatious messages, passionate kisses, and fondling inside her office. She showed up at his house unannounced on a Saturday afternoon. He lived alone in a two-bedroom apartment in Surulere. Nkechi had abandoned her driver at the Adeniran Ogunsanya Shopping Mall and taken a taxi to his place. The sex had been feisty, two horny beings eager to extinguish abominable passions. He had not bothered taking her clothes off; he had simply pulled up her gown before lifting her onto a table and parting her legs. When they were done, sweaty and panting, he had collapsed on the sofa and whispered: "What have we done?" His question jolted Nkechi to the present. What *had* they done? She straightened her gown, patted her hair back in place, and left without a word.

She had dwelt in the sweet pleasure of their lovemaking for the days that followed, like a teenager after her first time, pushing any guilt to the fringes of her thoughts and justifying it with the joy she felt. She even silently wished she were fertile at the time, that there was a chance of becoming pregnant with his child. She re-lived that day: how this man, who her heart beats for, had stood without his shirt, his trousers pulled down, firmly holding her buttocks and driving all of himself in and out of her, every thrust hitting against her heart, delivering sparks of joy. Even her husband seemed to know there was something different about her, from the way she sang when she led the worship session at the morning service the next day, like she was bringing the heavens down, how she pranced about like one who had found a new spring in her steps. They had just returned from service, and he'd been pouring himself a drink when he said it. She smiled, happy that he had noticed, and before ascending the stairs to their room, she told her husband that the Lord had been merciful to her in a special way.

When she and Felix met again the next Wednesday, which turned out to be the last time she saw him alive, he had expressed regrets for what happened, saying it was the work of the devil. He begged for her forgiveness. They spoke in her office at the church's temporary site. Sitting across from her on the other side of the table, he looked guilty and couldn't even look her in the face. Nkechi hushed him because she did not want to discuss the topic there and changed the subject to the building inspection they had planned for that afternoon.

NKECHI TRIED TO GET UP FROM THE BED AGAIN. Though she felt dizzy, she used her hand against the wall for support as she walked toward the toilet. Her bladder had been sending a discomforting sensation around her waist. The bathroom had always been her safe space. Growing up, she had been an introvert and often used her moments in the toilet as an escape. There, she would sit and let her mind run wild until someone rapped on the door to complain that she was taking too long.

As she sat down today, she thought about what her husband had said the night before about knowing about her and Pastor Felix. How much did he know? He had said he knew about it *all*, but did he know about that Saturday afternoon in Surulere? No one could have known about the sex, except if Felix himself had told someone, which she thought was unlikely. But the look on her husband's face last night suggested he knew more.

His eyes had been accusatory, like a justification for his own unfaithfulness. She remembered a moment many years ago when they were still dating. She had asked him what he would do if she ever cheated on him. It was a joke, the kind of question partners counting down to marriage asked each other during playful moments. The immediate change in his countenance had scared her.

"I will find the motherfucker and kill him. And then I will send you away," he had said with so much hate in his voice that she'd had to reassure him repeatedly she was just teasing, that she'd never cheat.

As Nkechi flushed the toilet, a thought crept into her mind that made her freeze: *What if Nicholas killed Felix?*

No, impossible. She dismissed the thought, shaking her head as if the gush of water from the tank would help dislodge such a crazy thought from her brain.

ELEVEN

"If I don't leave now, I'll be late," Lilian said, getting up from the bed and picking up her bra.

"Where are you running off to? I thought you were off today," Ifenna complained, stretching his naked body under the sheets.

"I have a workers' meeting at four."

"A workers' what?"

"Workers' meeting, as in church."

Ifenna's mouth dropped open in surprise. His girlfriend was a church worker? He had heard her punctuate a few statements with 'My pastor said,' which suggested that, like most young people in Lagos, she attended a church on Sunday and found what her pastor said inspirational, but he hadn't imagined she was so into it. He wanted to throw his head back and laugh in disbelief, but he thought it would embarrass her, so he just gave her a blank stare.

"Why are you looking at me like that?" she asked, pulling the jean trousers up her waist. "I'm a worker in church. Didn't I tell you?"

Ifenna shook his head. "What church?"

"Rivers of Joy. You know it, right? Pastor Nick?"

"Oh! Sure! I know it," Ifenna said, nodding. How could he not know the man responsible for his job loss? "They opened a cathedral recently, right?"

"Heaven's Gate Cathedral," she said excitedly. "God, that place really feels like heaven. Have you been?"

Ifenna shook his head again.

"You need to. Pastor Nick is such a blessed man of God. I love him so much. God. You need to listen to him minister. He literally brings down the glory from heaven."

"Yeah?"

"Yes. I even have some of his sermons downstairs in my room on DVD. You can borrow them."

"Okay," Ifenna said, though he knew it was never going to happen.

He got out of bed. Funny how his girlfriend was going right from his bed to a church meeting without any qualms at all. It'd be a good topic for his blog. Someone had sent in a story about a church in Lekki where all the girls went to worship on Sunday mornings after their nights of frolicking the streets of Lagos, and he thought of how it was similar to his own situation. The post had generated quite a debate in the comments section, with some saying the church was a place of repentance where sinners were welcome while others said the church itself was a joke because it had become a place for ladies to perfect their camouflage, making a mockery of God.

"I've never asked you what church you attend." Lillian ran a brush through her hair.

"Me?"

"Yes."

"Ah…does it matter?" Ifenna stood behind her and peered at her through the mirror.

"Well, yeah. I always told myself that my man must know and love God. I can't marry somebody who is not born again."

Marriage? Though the possibility of someday asking her to marry him had crossed his mind a few times, her mentioning it made him chuckle.

"Tell me, jor," Lilian said, turning around to face him.

"Tell you what, my darling?"

"The name of the church you attend."

Ifenna tried to remember the church his mother attended but couldn't remember its name. His pulse raced and he blurted, "Mountain of Fire!"

Lilian raised her eyebrows. "You? Mountain of Fire?"

Ifenna nodded. "Yes. Why?"

"You just don't look like a Mountain of Fire kind of person to me."

"Is there a way we're supposed to look?"

"Oh well, I don't know. Solemn, almost sad, in oversized coats and well-worn King James Version in their hands. Do you even own a Bible?"

Ifenna laughed. "Well, it's been a while since I went, to be honest. Like a year now."

"A year? Jesus."

"Sometimes I work on Sundays. Plus, the whole thing was suffocating, all the talk about the enemy and having to fast and all that. I think I needed a break."

"You need a new church," Lilian said smiling. "Come to Rivers of Joy with me. You will see the difference. I promise."

"Well, if it's anything close to the rivers of joy you give me, I will be happy to swim inside,' Ifenna said in a tone that made her giggle.

Once she left, Ifenna rushed to his blog, which he had continued to keep a secret from her. The blog was now almost a full-time job, like an infant needing attention all the time. His daily traffic had grown exponentially. After his first article, he no longer had to worry about content. His email was always filled with new stuff: stories of new occurrences, short video clips shot on mobile phones, screenshots of posts made by people on social media, of scandals, statements and activities involving men of God, and the personal experiences of people in different encounters. He had also received content about some quasi-Christian faiths like Eckankar and The Grail Message.

Usually, he would review the content, and if he found it appropriate, he would write a caption, choosing his words carefully to make it sensational enough to elicit interest before posting. He'd gone from two posts daily to six. He moderated the comments that followed because after the first major argument that degenerated into threats and abuses, he set some ground rules, which meant he had to read every comment and enforce censorship. Everyone was welcome to share their opinion and disagree with others, but no personal attacks or use of abusive language were permitted. Everything had to be civil. Sometimes he ignored certain comments when they helped advance the conversation or if the commenter made some important points.

Given that he was spending more time on the blog, he wondered how he could make money from the traffic. What brands would advertise a platform that called out men of

God and questioned their practices? It was like advertising in a pro-democracy publication in the heydays of military rule. One pastor had already mentioned the blog in his Sunday sermon after a post had been made about him supposedly delivering a young lady of her demons. The footage showed him pressing the lady's breasts, and the lens zoomed in to capture his bulging trousers. It had generated quite a buzz that spilled onto Twitter, and the pastor at the center of it all had pronounced Ifenna's blog as evil mechanization. The pastor placed a curse on the people behind the blog and forbid any of his members from visiting it.

Ifenna found sixty comments on the post he'd made earlier before Lilian came over. He looked at his watch. Three o'clock. He planned to make an evening kabu kabu round and decided an hour was enough time to read through the comments. Reading them was as enlightening as they were humorous. He had discovered the bulk of the people participating in the discussions were active churchgoing Christians who seemed to find themselves in some kind of bondage, living with the excesses of their pastors even when their common sense told them otherwise. They came to the blog to vent and, in a way, make fun of themselves. There were also those who came to defend what they believed in.

Once Ifenna posted a quote by a pastor who'd said those who did not pay their tithes were stealing from God. The exchange between those who believed tithing was an old testament teaching being misinterpreted by modern-day pastors just to enrich themselves and those who insisted tithing was a commandment from God and must be obeyed made an interesting read. Ifenna took sips from a bottle of stout as he regaled himself to comment after comment, many packed with Bible quotes to back their claims.

Someone who said he was a doctor at the Lagos General Hospital sent this morning's post to him. A woman who just gave birth had some complications leading to excessive loss of blood, but her husband wouldn't let the doctors transfuse her with blood because they were Jehovah's Witnesses. Against all entreaties, the man evacuated his wife from the ward, and while arranging for a vehicle, she'd died. When Ifenna first read the story, he was overwhelmed with disgust. Now, as he settled into the comments, he found that disallowing transfusions was an action many others were familiar with. Someone posted about a case before the Supreme Court in which a Jehovah's Witness couple sued a doctor for transfusing their baby, despite their making it clear they did not approve even though the doctor saved the child's life. The case had crawled through the judicial system for over sixteen years and finally made it to the apex court. The final appeal insisted that when parents refused blood transfusion for a child on religious grounds, the government should step in to enforce it, as the life of a child outweighed religious beliefs. As Ifenna read, he marveled at the blurred lines between common sense and faith. He paused to make sense of it all, of suing someone for saving your child's life because of some religious teaching and as much as he tried, he couldn't make any sense of it.

When he heard the knock, he thought it was Lilian. Perhaps she didn't go to the meeting after all. He quickly hibernated his laptop and rushed to the door. But it was Tunde, his neighbor from upstairs, who stood on the other side in a t-shirt and shorts. He probably wanted Ifenna to back his car out of the driveway, but Tunde stopped him when he made to go back into the room and fetch his car keys.

"No, I am not going out. I actually came to see you."

Ifenna frowned. Tunde had never visited him before, except for the night when he joined the other neighbors to go and condole Tunde and his wife on the passing of the baby. He stood by and pulled the door wider. Tunde walked in slowly and sat on the couch. Ifenna joined him after bolting the door. Then he noticed the forlorn look on Tunde's face, like the chaff of an orange after all the juice had been squeezed out of it.

"I'm sorry to barge in on you like this," Tunde finally said, raising his head but not meeting Ifenna's eyes.

"Ah no o, no problem at all," Ifenna said, concern now seeping into his veins.

The night they went to pay their condolence visit, Tunde had seemed unfazed, welcoming everybody and serving them drinks, explaining how God could give but take away as well. Ifenna had admired his strength, the way he joined them to discuss the president's gaffes during his recent trip to Germany. The image Ifenna had of Tunde from that night contrasted with the person who sat before him, who looked distant and defeated, like his neck carried his head with great difficulty.

"Thanks for the other day," Tunde said, referring to the visit. "I really appreciate."

Ifenna nodded his acknowledgment and waited. Tunde seemed to struggle with how best to broach the matter troubling him. His eyes were back to the floor, so Ifenna decided to ask him.

"Are you okay? Is anything the matter?"

Tunde sighed a deep one that conveyed the depth of his sadness. Ifenna shifted closer to him on the couch, hoping that would encourage him to speak.

"You see. The last two weeks have been the saddest of my life. Honestly, this has taken so much toll on me and is also taking a toll on my marriage." He paused.

Ifenna said nothing.

"I mean, it doesn't make sense. How does a healthy baby just die? I mean…I held him in my hands after he was cleaned, and he had the cutest smile. Next thing I know, the nurses are telling me he is no longer breathing, and just like that, he's gone. I mean, how can that happen? We did everything we were told. She did the antenatal from the third month. We did all the scans. She exercised. She drank all the vitamin pills. At the first sign of labor, I rushed her to the hospital; you saw us that day. Where did we go wrong?"

Ifenna felt he needed to say something consoling, to tell him it wasn't his fault and that things like these without explanation often happened in life. No need to split hairs trying to understand them. But before he could speak, Tunde continued. "And we did everything right in church. I paid tithes. Because this was my first child, our pastor said I needed to sow a special first fruit seed for safe delivery. I did, and this still happened."

"It's okay, Bro," Ifenna said, cutting in. He could sense Tunde was close to tears, the way his voice was beginning to break, his breathing deepening. "Just take it easy." He moved closer and put a hand on Tunde's shoulder.

"Do you know what annoys me the most?" Tunde asked, looking up at him. "Everyone somehow blames me. Can you imagine that? Like the fact that this happened is evidence I wasn't strong enough in my faith. Maybe I didn't give enough to the church."

Ifenna was taken aback. "Someone said that to you?"

"You should hear what the people from our church say to my wife and me when they come on their so-called condolence visits. How can you be using God to guilt-trip somebody on top of his grief?' The tears poured freely now.

Between sobs, Tunde told him that even his wife blamed him. She was attending a white garment church before they got married. When she was close to term, her mother had come with a message from the Mother-in-Israel of their church that said they both needed to come for prayers at the beach during the night, bearing certain materials. These materials, her mother said, needed to be sacrificed because the unborn child was possessed by some water spirit. If they didn't do this, the child wouldn't be born. Tunde had refused. It had all sounded silly, superstitious even, and he wouldn't be involved in such nonsense. His wife was fine with his decision at the time, but since they lost the child, she had borne her regret like a cloak, insisting that had the prayers been done and the sacrifices made, their child would not have died.

"Pure madness. How can she say that? I mean, is that not crazy?" Tunde asked, spreading his two palms as if demanding answers from Ifenna.

Tunde had needed a break from his apartment because his mother-in-law was haranguing him with this theory, causing a shouting match between the two of them while his wife sobbed in a corner. The woman had threatened to take her daughter away, and Tunde had stormed out because he was afraid he might strike her out of anger.

After Ifenna got him to stop sobbing, he retrieved the bottle of cognac he kept in his room. Consoling people wasn't one of his strong suits. Tunde didn't resist when he set the bottle and two glasses before him. They sat on the floor and drank like two long-time friends, and before long, Tunde revealed how, back in the university, he had been in the Eye Confraternity. He'd been part of many gang wars on campuses all across the southwest before he found God and repented. Then, he revealed that his wife, while they were still dating, had got two abortions because they were both from very respectable Christian families and couldn't have children out of wedlock. Next, he talked about his church called Saved Chapel. He explained how they never announced deaths of members because it would discourage membership; how the wife of his senior regional pastor, a woman in her fifties — who didn't wear makeup or jewelry because it was a sin — was sleeping with his friend who was the head organist; and how an elder had raped his domestic servant, but the church leaders helped hush it up.

Later that night, as he slept, Ifenna dreamt of Tunde and his wife dressed in all-white garments, holding red candles in their hands, and walking barefoot on the shorelines at Bar Beach. Ifenna was there, dressed in the cloak of a bishop complete with miter, leading them, a pot of burning incense in his hands. He was reciting words, pronouncing them loudly to cleanse their souls. They were chorusing their response as they walked along. The smell of the incense filled the cool night air, driving the solemnness of the event into their souls. Suddenly a strong breeze from the ocean put out the flames on the candles, and everywhere turned pitch dark. As he waited for the duo to light their candles, he heard the loud shrill of a baby crying, which startled him and made him drop the pot of incense to the ground. It made a loud sound as it landed, like a giant clay pot bursting. He woke up panting, thankful he had only been dreaming.

TWELVE

Freshly laid tar covered the road leading to Heaven's Gate Cathedral from the Lekki-Epe Expressway. It wasn't there the last time Ifenna was at the cathedral to cover the commissioning ceremony. Before, the road had been dusty, with a few puddles gathered after a downpour. He also noticed the pavements had been painted in blocks of white and black, the stretch now lined by royal palm seedlings.

A giant billboard of Pastor Nick's smiling face welcomed him at the parking lot. The text on the sign read: *"This is the gate of heaven; walk in, all ye that seek Him."'* Ifenna swallowed hard after reading it. It took some time to find a parking space in the expansive lot because of the throng of morning worshippers. Men in t-shirts with *Worker* printed on the back helped control traffic and directed cars to parking spaces. They seemed efficient, like policemen on the day a VIP passed by their route. Lilian explained that they were the workers of the Traffic Department. She was part of the pastoral care department, and they supported the man of God in areas of his ministry outside of preaching, including hospital visitation, visits to elderly church members, faith clinics, and counseling. She described a very organized network of teams, most of them pro bono, working across well-defined lines to ensure that the ministry was well run. Ifenna couldn't help thinking how lucky pastors were to enjoy so much free labor.

A lady with pink, low-cut hair received them at the main entrance, smiling warmly. Ifenna decided she would be more beautiful without the fixed eyelashes, but her perfume was pleasant to inhale. She uttered a few words of welcome and walked inside ahead of them, swaying her buttocks from side to side, and then directing them to a seat. At the entrance, there were many ladies dressed in jeans trousers and white t-shirts with a brooch plastered with Pastor Nick's face, curtseying, smiling, and leading worshippers to their seats. Lilian didn't like where the lady asked them to sit, which was close to one of the speakers at the back, so she pulled Ifenna by the elbow to another aisle as if to show she knew her way around. The usher stood back, looking flustered.

After they took their seats, Lilian whispered to Ifenna that the lady must be one among the new crop of workers recently admitted into the ushering department because she didn't look familiar. She said all the ladies only joined the church because it was trending. Ifenna made a sound in his throat. He'd noticed how Lilian's jealousy flared since the lady had met them at the door, but he did not want to comment on it.

The congregation stood, and a female voice rang through the speakers singing praise songs accompanied by a band. The congregation chorused their response, some clapping and others dancing. She introduced a new song, which elicited a scream of acceptance from the crowd. Ifenna knew the song, "Igwe," made popular by the gospel music group, Midnight Crew. He joined the clapping reluctantly, tapping his palms and murmuring his response to the song. He felt like an alien. Fraudulent. The only reason he agreed to come with Lilian was to make her happy. Now, in the pews, it seemed silly he accepted just to please a girl. If someone had told him he would do this a few months earlier, he would have sworn it was impossible. Making her smile mattered so much to him that he had agreed without any hesitation when she asked, though he said it would be just this one time. He knew now he shouldn't have come.

The praise songs soon morphed into a worship session, which lasted for about fifteen minutes before the prayers began. One of Pastor Nick's assistant pastors led it in the usual fashion. He called out a prayer point, proceeded to describe it for some time, and invited everyone to open their mouths and pray. A cacophony followed, with members of the congregation all praying loudly, some screaming, some jumping, some making strange noises. When the pastor seemed satisfied that the point had been sufficiently prayed on, he introduced another one, and the cycle continued.

Ifenna was familiar with the routine. It was similar to that at his mother's church and all the fellowships he attended in university. He always wondered how everyone went on and on praying over one prayer point for such elongated periods when he finished saying his own prayer in a few words long ago. Sometimes, he wondered if perhaps he had not prayed enough and repeated the same words he said earlier, moving his mouth and gesticulating with his hands until the moderator ended the session with a shout of "In Jesus name!" Mostly, he just stood and observed everyone around him to decide who was play-acting and who was genuinely praying.

This morning, Lilian captivated him. She had transformed into someone he didn't recognize, the way she snapped her fingers in the air, her eyes shut and her mouth whispering rapid words. She was almost screaming, yet he could not understand anything she said despite standing right beside her. Later that night, after they made love in his apartment, he would tease her about her moaning, saying it sounded the same way she prayed in church, and when she laughed and said that both sounds came from the same place in her soul, Ifenna would wonder if that was why she always called on God when they were in bed.

After the prayer sessions, Pastor Nick walked onto the beautifully decorated stage in his stripped-blue suit and long red tie. The congregation screamed "Daddy Founder" and clapped as he mounted the rostrum, preventing him from speaking for several minutes. It was sermon time, but he announced that a guest minister, 'a very good friend of his,' would be ministering. He then introduced this minister who'd come all the way from Port Harcourt. When the man came on stage, after bowing slightly to Pastor Nick, he began to reciprocate the praise he'd just been given in his introduction.

"I always knew Pastor Nick would make it," he said.

He was bald and didn't stand much taller than the lectern. A gold chain with a cross pendant dangled from his neck onto the brown short-sleeve safari suit he had on. Ifenna thought he looked more like an Igbo trader based in Alaba. All he seemed to be missing was the bulky armpit purse.

"Just look at this place." He waved his hand around the cathedral. "People have been talking. It is all over the news. I came today to see for myself the great things God is doing through my friend, Pastor Nick. Can somebody shout Hallelujah?"

"Hallelujah!" The crowd shouted in unison.

The man narrated a story of how he had always been friends with Pastor Nick. They had met at a ministers' conference in Benin when Pastor Nick had newly established Rivers of Joy Church. From the first time he saw Pastor Nick, he knew there was something about him. The Holy Spirit told him that Nick was the kind of person that should be his friend if he wanted to succeed, and he was happy he did not disobey.

"They say the cathedral broke the world record. I tell you, this is the least of the things we should be thanking God for today. Heaven has come to Lagos. Oh, you ain't listening to me this morning. I said heaven has come to Nigeria! It is not a mistake that it was named Heaven's Gate Cathedral because, indeed, it is the gateway to the kingdom, bestowed specially on us for a time like this. I tell you, just in case you don't already know, this is a church to cling to. If I were you, I would tie myself to this pastor and throw away the key, and I will say to the Lord, 'Father, bless me with the blessing of Pastor Nick.' Can I hear an amen?"

A loud chorus of "Amen!" echoed through the church, and some in the congregation sprang to their feet and waved their hands in the air.

"Turn to your neighbor and say neighbor, you arrrrre at the right place!" The man bounced around the stage.

Lilian turned toward Ifenna but didn't repeat the words. Instead, she directed him, with her lips in a pout, to someone, a lady in the ushers' uniform, walking up the aisle.

"You see that girl? She is a runs girl," Lilian said with a look of disgust on her face. "Yeye girl. I know her very well o. She just uses this church to cover things up. She lives in Lekki and drives a Prado, but she has no job o. As you see her so, all she does is follow rich men and sleep about."

When Ifenna didn't respond, Lilian added. "That's what she always does during service, walks up and down, up and down. And she is so rude. I don't even know how she's still an usher; everybody complains about her."

Maybe, Ifenna thought, the woman was using the church instead for marketing and had wisely joined the department that would allow her to meet men at the entrance and walk around during service, advertising her wares.

The pastor on stage was now saying something about the need to thank God. He read from Psalm 100 about entering His gates with thanksgiving and His courts with praise. The best way of showing thanks, he preached, was by giving. He went on to narrate stories of the many different places he went to preach and how those who responded to his call to give returned with amazing testimonies of how God transformed their lives. As if to bring the point home, he talked about how Pastor Nick was a testimony of giving, narrating how Nick had sowed into his own ministry many years ago after their meeting at the conference and what impact it had in his life and ministry.

"It is my turn today. I want you to touch three or four people and say to them: 'It is my turn today.'"

There was a flurry of activity as worshippers obediently

reached out to the people closest to them and chorused their response.

"I tell you something. Somebody will be enriched today. I don't know about you, but I know I will be enriched today. I said I will be enriched today. For the word of God tells me in 2 Corinthians 9: 11 that you will be enriched in every way, and through us, your generooosittttyyyy will result in thanksgiving to God. Can somebody shout a very loud Hallelujaaahhhh?"

The congregation responded with a loud chorus of "Hallelujah!" accompanied by whistling and clapping, many jumping to their feet and punching the air. Ifenna had a feeling that Lilian was controlling her actions because of his presence. He could sense her struggling to remain calm.

"You know one thing I have come to understand about God?" The pastor continued after the congregation quietened. "He is a practical God, and all you need to do is to obey His command. You know how soldiers say obey the last command? It is the same thing with our Father. And today, He has given me a command to give to you. He said He wants you to thank Him. Not for me o. Not for all the things that He has given you in abundance. He said you should thank Him today for your pastor. I did not plan this earlier. I am sure Pastor Nick is shocked, but I just got this message as I was ministering, and I must obey. And I know in my spirit that this is a special opportunity for somebody to tune into the anointing of this blessed man of God for a life-changing encounter.

"So, I am going to do this really quickly and get out of your faces. I will be calling for a special thanksgiving seed sowing today. Listen very attentively. Listen. Listen. Two categories. Those who want to sow a seed of thanksgiving for perfection for fifty thousand naira, to my right. To my left, those who want to sow a seed of glorious expectation, which is one thousand naira for every year you've lived. That is, if you are twenty years old, twenty thousand naira. Quickly. Quickly. Come out of your seats. I have just five minutes to do this."

He paused and walked over to the lectern, picked up his handkerchief, and wiped the sweat from his face. "Start coming out."

He walked back to the edge of the stage. "To my right, those sowing a seed for perfection. If you want God to perfect His works in your life, to perfect your marriage, to perfect your business, to perfect your academics, to perfect your plans, fifty thousand naira. Come out quick; we have no time. To my left, those believing God for something. Are you expecting a miracle or a breakthrough? You are expecting that wife, that husband, that baby, that contract, that new car, that new house, that promotion, this is for you. Sow according to the years you have lived. And if you want to do both, stand in the middle. Get up now. Up. Up. Up. Those at the back, you can run forward."

A mass movement of people shuffled forward, filling the aisle as they marched toward the stage. Lilian looked up at Ifenna as if to ask if he would go. He shook his head, and she didn't ask him why. She stepped out into the aisle and joined the stream of worshippers responding to the call. Later, as they drove home after the service, she told him he missed out on an opportunity for him to be blessed. She nonetheless sowed for him and filled two of the forms the ushers handed out, one for him for perfection and one for herself for twenty-six thousand, and Ifenna imagined what good things he could do with seventy-six thousand naira in his pocket.

Pastor Nick returned to the stage toward the end of the service. After the normal offering was held, the choir gave a special rendition, then three testimonies were taken of miracles courtesy of Pastor Nick's prayers. The congregation cheered with screams of "Daddy Founder" and applause that lasted many minutes, much louder than earlier. By this time, Ifenna was sufficiently disgusted and ready to leave. The man glided about the stage as he announced he had been nominated as one of those to receive national honors by the president, which was greeted with even more thunderous applause, infuriating Ifenna some more. The man responsible for his jobless state would receive a national honor from the president. Great.

Earlier, after Lilian joined the march to the stage, it struck him that this would make good content for his blog, so he took out his phone and started filming. The guest minister created the initial urgency to play on the people's psychology, Ifenna thought, to elicit prompt responses lest they missed out on the blessings so elaborately advertised. The man did not end at the five minutes he'd promised earlier and instead went on and on, hammering on why those still sitting should not miss out on this window of blessing. A guilt trip more than persuasion, really, the way he said things like: "You are not doing a good job and you are still sitting down? Don't blame anyone for your situation after today. You've been praying and fasting for a child and today God is sharing children in church, and you are refusing to accept?"

When it seemed he had reached the mark, as no one

else was coming out, he changed tactics and introduced a new category. He said the Lord had just told him to give room for others who He really wanted to bless but were still sitting for one reason or the other. "If you can sow a seed of between ten and twenty thousand, this is your last opportunity. Stand up now."

By this time, there was already a crowd in front of the stage, so he directed those in this new category to hold the closest pillar to where they sat as he prayed.

"This is the last chance. Don't miss it. Come out, come out. We are waiting," the man bellowed.

Ifenna's phone caught the scene of adults pushing and shoving for a chance to have their hands on a pillar, some preferring to wrap their hands around it as if the more contact you had with the pillar, the greater the certainty of the promised miracles.

After the man prayed and called down all manners of blessings on the worshippers who stepped out, he proceeded to warn them about owing God, warning that all those who made a pledge had to redeem it in a week for the blessings to take effect.

"You will be inviting curses on yourself and your family if you fail," he said.

Those who had the money were encouraged to pay right away. Ushers walked around with POS machines while the church's account details flashed on the screen for those who wished to use their mobile banking apps to make transfers. Ifenna found it all so nauseating. And when Pastor Nick took over the stage, the mere sight of him made Ifenna feel like soldier ants were creeping down his spine. Pastor Nick seemed in remarkably high spirits as he talked of the national honor and how he was the only Christian religious leader on the list of those to be honored. Ifenna remembered the morning after his sack from *The Nigerian*; how he had woken up hungover because he had tried to drown himself in alcohol the night before; how he had promised himself that, after he got a little sober, he would pursue the story that would bring Pastor Nick down. And though that resolve had waned in the weeks as he tried to survive while managing his blog, he now felt the anger take a new life in him. His heart pounded in his chest in irregular rhythm, and he feared he would stand up and scream his disapproval of the fraudulent man's words.

On their way home, after Lilian had stopped scolding him for not stepping out to sow a seed, Ifenna wondered how he could unravel the mystery surrounding the death at Heaven's Gate Cathedral site. Pastor Nick must have had something to hide. All Ifenna had to do was probe a little deeper. Then he remembered the lady who posted on Nairaland, the one through whom he'd learned that the late pastor's name was Felix, and he decided to contact her. Perhaps she knew something. Perhaps she would be willing to speak. The possibilities filled him with sudden excitement, and he looked across to Lilian. For the first time that day, he was grateful he followed her to church.

THAT NIGHT, IFENNA WROTE A new blog post. His thoughts were on Pastor Nkechi. She had sat on one of the elaborate chairs on the altar for much of the service, like the queen in an outfit that hugged her body and stopped just above her knees. He did not know much about her except that she was Pastor Nick's beautiful wife, but that morning, he thought of what more she could be, what she might have studied in university, the dreams she had while growing up, and the person she was when no one was looking. She seemed to already be living the best life possible as the co-owner of a huge ministry, a celebrity of a divine nature with many fans, and someone who could command people to walk in a particular direction with just the power of her faith. *What if this is not the life she wanted?* Ifenna wondered. *What if she feels trapped?* There had to be other wives of celebrity men of God who felt the same way. Nobody really cared about them beyond the shadows of their husbands. By evening his thoughts had formed into a blog post.

> *Is this anointing thing sexually transmitted?*
>
> *The call that men of God claim they receive is supposed to be a deeply personal mission to do God's work. We have been regaled time and again with so many of these beautiful stories of this special Saul On The Road To Damascus type encounters by your favorite pastors. How Mercy said "No," and grace seized them by the balls. Good for them. But it's only about them. How about their wives? Did they get the call, too? Or is this special unction from God sexually transmitted, passed on from husband to wife during some feisty spirit-filled "communion" on their matrimonial bed? How come their wives automatically become Pastor Mrs. and She-Bishops overnight, the moment their husbands open a church, or become appointed to head one?*
>
> *The case is even more interesting for the few among them who actually go through some kind of training in theology and ordination. How does the wife short circuit all that effort and years of understanding the Bible to attain the same status of grace by simply being their Missus? Do sperm cells carry genes*

that transmit Biblical knowledge from husbands to wives?

You see, most couples I know don't do the same job or, at least, not in the same office. Why the whole "Tales By Moonlight" about being called when really it's just you and your wife figuring out a potent stream of income? aka, founder/CEO and Vice CEO or should I say Bonnies and Clydes?

But that's only half of the story. You see, I have a feeling that many of these pastors' wives are actually trapped in their lives. Many, I suspect, are just floating about in misery, acting the part, marking time. Smart, beautiful women who should be breaking the glass ceiling in various professions are forced to partake in a call that did not ring on their phones. This is patriarchy, no? The holy form of it, I dare add. These women are forced to conform, to reduce their dreams and mold it into whatever shape of the box their husbands' superior calling to God comes in, to take their places beside them on the altar and look pretty (and God, do these men of God know how to select the prettiest ones for themselves), to subscribe to a certain moral standard (at least outwardly) that is not necessarily their cup of tea, to become extras in a puppeteer show.

Yes, I know they all enjoy the benefits. Well, most do. I mean, what in the world can be more beneficial than having your bills paid by other people's sweat? Who spits out a cube of sugar put into their mouth? You see them. I see them, too. The designer wears, choice accessories, and appearances that fit only royals. I suspect that for many of them, that's the compensation, the opium that numbs them into character. Of course, there are those who glow in it, who are actually the drummers beating the tunes their husbands dance to on the altar when they feed our bellies with their sermons that have just one aim, to reach deeper into our pockets to take more.

It will be great to read their stories. How did it feel the day their husbands first made the announcement? Did they say,

"Hi honey, I feel that I am getting this pull to start a ministry," or did he come home one day and say, "Sweetheart, I just got a fantastic idea on how we can become rich?" How did they react to it? Shock? Joy? Anxiety? Doubt? Were they like, "Oh, well, you and I are one so where you go, I go." Or did they protest, throw a tantrum or threaten a divorce? Well, a divorce might be extreme, but you get what I mean. And now, how do they feel being the spare tire general overseer–absolute bliss of biblical heights or misery painted in rainbow colors?

Like we say on this blog, it's just a random thought. It will be great to get your views on this, my people. Is the calling sexually transmitted? Can it be? Should it be? Should wives automatically acquire spiritual authority because they share a bed with a man who does?

THIRTEEN

"It feels good that I can freely smoke one of these during our meeting," the man said, lighting a cigarette with a pocket lighter.

He had to shout over the music, Dbanj's "Tongolo," blasting from the speakers. His cheeks formed dimples as he inhaled, and then he puffed white smoke from his mouth and nostrils. He repeated this in quick succession, each time huffing out white smoke that soon diffused into the smoke-filled air of the lounge.

Pastor Nkechi waited for him to finish silently. She had just arrived and sat near the edge of her chair, two hands clutching her purse. As he inhaled a cloud, Nkechi took deep breaths, trying to exhale the unease that had seized her.

"Hope it was not difficult finding this place?" the man asked, holding the burning cigarette away from his lips. He could sense her apprehension from across the table, the way the muscles of her face stiffened, and her jaw squared. *She is pretty, even in her disguise,* he thought. *Hers is the type of face you just want to cup in your hands and kiss.* How did the men of God always get the prettiest of wives?

Nkechi shook her head. She'd come in a taxi. It was the first time she used a taxi app service. Though she had been nervous initially, as she always was with technology, she had managed to figure her way around, setting up an account and hailing her first ride after downloading the app from the Apple store. Usually, she would have asked her personal assistant to sort it out, but she had to do it herself as part of her elaborate efforts to keep her being in an unnamed lounge somewhere in Egbeda a secret. The man insisted he would no longer discuss business in her office, no matter how soundproof she claimed it was. When he sent her an SMS with the address, she said no way. She never ventured to the mainland without her security detail, and this was not the kind of meeting she could take them along to. *Can you pick anywhere else? Somewhere closer?* she had texted back. *Maybe even Ikeja, around GRA.* But the man had replied: *See you there and please don't be late.*

Now, Nkechi glanced over her shoulder. They were in the VIP section, a space about half the size of a basketball court with couches set around low stools. She thought the place was quite full for that time of the day. Despite her disguise, she worried that someone among the heads, smoking, sipping drinks, and chatting loudly, might recognize her. At first, she had on a veil that could make her pass for a Muslim lady, and her dark sunglasses were thrown over her eyes, but she removed the glasses when she entered the lounge because it was dimly lit. Hopefully, her veil alone was sufficient cover.

"Relax, Madam," the man said, tapping away some ash from the burning cigarette into the tray at the center of the table. "You are safe, and I can assure you, nobody knows you're here. Nobody cares."

Nkechi shifted in her chair and leaned a bit forward to hear him more clearly.

"Have you been to this side of town before?"

Nkechi shook her head again.

"This is mainland mainland," the man said, sucking on his cigarette. After puffing out the smoke, he added. "You know there is Mainland. That will be like Yaba and Surulere. Then there is Mainland Mainland, like Iyana Ipaja, Igando, and Egbeda. So you are at the heart of the mainland. This is where I like to meet my clients. Just relax."

Nkechi smiled and hoped it masked her eagerness for the meeting to get on. She wasn't sure she would easily find a taxi when she was done or if the taxi app would work in this part of town, so she had asked the taxi that brought her to wait. The chatty young taxi driver with a big afro had regaled her with talks of being a graduate of chemical engineering and how he resorted to driving on the app because he couldn't find a job in his field. When she asked him to if he could wait, he hesitated in responding, so she promised to give him something extra for the wait. Even then, he had warned that he wouldn't wait for more than thirty minutes.

"Anything to drink?" the man asked, stabbing the butt of the cigarette in the ashtray.

"Thank you, I'm fine."

"Oh, I see. This place must feel too sinful for you to have a drink, right?" the man said, the sarcasm in his voice seeping through. "The other day, I was listening to an American pastor on CNN. He just bought a private jet, and they asked him why he spent so much money on a jet, and he said he didn't want to be caught with a bunch of sinners

171

inside a tube. A bunch of sinners. Just classic. You know you pastors have your way with words, eh. So maybe you don't want to be caught drinking with a bunch of sinners in a local lounge on the mainland," the man laughed.

"I don't drink," Pastor Nkechi said after his coughing stopped.

"Well, same thing. I guess alcohol is for sinners like me," the man said, beckoning to a waiter.

The waiter, not quite eighteen by Nkechi's estimation, held a notepad and a pen in hand and leaned toward the man so that his mouth was next to his ear as he took the order. Nkechi realized she didn't know his name, this private investigator she had known for almost six months. Peju, who had introduced him to her, had sent his name simply as Agent X. The first time they met, she had asked for his real name, and he had indicated that he did not divulge such detail about himself to his clients.

"Just call me Agent X," he had said that day, very business-like, with a face that indicated he would not entertain any further discussion on the topic.

Now, the very opposite of that person sat across from her, cracking jokes. She imagined that perhaps, after several meetings and exchanges of SMS, they had become almost friends, what with how much of her personal life he knew. It was to him she ran after the thoughts of the possibilities of her husband having a hand in Pastor Felix's death refused to be shaken off. The suspicion, like an occupying army, built a tent in her mind and continued to expand its territory every passing day. It was like a massive hand played a jigsaw puzzle in her memory, fitting parts together and giving her an illusion of a whole that did not seem real and fizzled when she tried to make sense of it. A few things she had not thought much about became curious; like how that day, she was supposed to go on the site inspection with Felix but hadn't because her husband had sent an SMS saying he was expecting the delivery of an important parcel at the office and wanted her to personally receive it. Felix had gone alone. The parcel never arrived.

Agent X retrieved a phone in his jacket pocket as the waiter left. He had a Bluetooth piece in his left ear, which he tapped and started speaking after confirming the identity of the caller. Nkechi tried to relax by sitting back. It wasn't just being recognized that worried her. There was also the fear of what the man was going to reveal to her. It had kept her awake at night since the day she contacted him and gave him the brief. She wanted answers, but she was scared of knowing because she didn't know what those answers would mean for her and her marriage. She really wished she were just paranoid, that the man would tell her she was over-reading meanings into random occurrences and that there was nothing that linked her husband to Felix's death.

The waiter returned with some ice in a small bowl, a bottle of VSOP, and a glass. He set them down on the table, closer to the man, and stood aside as if waiting for the man to confirm that all was intact. Agent X gave him a thumbs up, the signal that he could leave. Nkechi thought perhaps she should have asked for water. But it was too late as the boy rushed off swiftly to another table. Agent X concluded his call and reached out for the bottle.

"So, tell me. Where did your husband say he was on the afternoon of the incident?"

Agent X poured some of the drink into the glass and

added two ice cubes. He did not seem in a hurry to gulp it down. He held the glass and stirred by rocking it gently in his hands.

Nkechi leaned forward again, grateful that the man was finally ready to talk about the subject of their meeting. "When he sent me the SMS about the parcel, he told me he was joining the pastoral care team on a hospital visit. He had ministered that morning at a program organized by the Christian Association in Alausa. From there, he went to the hospital visitation."

Agent X took a deep breath. His eyes went from Nkechi to the glass in his hand. He looked intently as he rocked the cup, as if keen on seeing how fast the ice would melt. "Your husband didn't go to any hospital visit that day," he said after about a minute of silence. He gulped down all the contents in the glass and slammed it noisily on the table, with his face slightly squeezed as the liquid flowed down his throat.

"As a matter of fact, we have evidence that your husband was at the construction site that day. You might find the revelations shocking, but I guess that is why you came to us."

Nkechi dropped the purse on the table. Her head suddenly felt heavy, and her heart pounded against her chest. She supported her head by balancing it in the groove of her palm.

"Are you aware there were no laborers on-site that day?"

Nkechi nodded. The laborers had decided not to work that day. A colleague of theirs was sacked by the contractor the previous day, and they decided to protest it by going on strike.

The man nodded, too before pouring himself some more drink. "On the day of the incident, we believe your husband arrived at the site earlier than the deceased. We believe he drove himself because after the event at Alausa, he discharged his driver for the day. I believe he wasn't using the police escort then, correct?"

"Correct," Nkechi whispered.

"We spoke with the driver. We also spoke to the OPC people who were engaged as security for the site. One of the men on duty that afternoon told us that when your husband arrived, and they all gathered to greet him as usual, he gave them money and asked them to go and eat at one of the shacks down the road. There were three of them on duty. He told us they all left immediately and that your husband was surprised the workers weren't on-site and told them he would leave shortly as well after he spoke with the site engineer. None of them saw when the deceased arrived at the site."

"But it was the security men who reported the fall," Nkechi said.

"Well, yes. They found him when they returned."

"But they said they heard the cracking of the scaffolding and the thud as he landed."

"People lie, Madam. They were scared themselves. If the police were to take any action, they would have been the first to be arrested. So, you see, they had to give a story that sounded logical. It was also the best explanation there could have been to their mind. I mean, think of this: they return to find the corpse of someone familiar, someone that frequently comes to the site, on the ground with evidence to show he fell, so they assumed there was an accident while they were away."

Nkechi folded and unfolded her arms, then sighed.

"So, the question now is, what was your husband doing at the site? You just told me he said he was somewhere else. Why did he discharge his driver and drive to the site all by himself? Why did he need to lie? Truth is, we cannot prove if he had left the site when the deceased arrived or not. We cannot really connect him to anything. Perhaps, it was really an accident, and he also fabricated the stories to save himself because he was there. I can't say. However, something else makes us curious. We talked to our people inside the police, and we understand your husband went to great lengths to hush it up. He discouraged investigations into the death, saying it was the decision of the church and that they had accepted the will of God. I can understand people sometimes deciding to let bygones be bygones, but when the directive comes all the way from the Inspector General's office, I sense somebody was really desperate."

Nkechi recalled how her husband had been a little paranoid about the incident becoming a subject of police investigation, which would, in turn, generate negative media attention around the church—something he detested. The position made sense because they needed to keep every narrative about the church, especially about the cathedral, positive. Her husband called a meeting with all his top pastors with her in attendance the day after the incident and told them the implications of Felix's death, how it could become a dark shadow over the cathedral project and ruin all their efforts towards the opening of their cathedral. They needed to control the narrative, and that meant going on like it did not happen, not making reference to it publicly, not granting any press interviews to discuss it, and not speaking about it in any sermon. They were going to give him a befitting burial and place his parents on a monthly allowance, including annual payments on their house. It had all made sense back then. Now, though, it made a different sort of sense. She felt stupid and betrayed.

"Tell me, Madam, did your husband have any issues with the deceased? Is there any reason he could perhaps have wanted him dead?"

Nkechi shook her head.

Agent X sighed. "I'm not sure why you asked us to look into this, but the evidence points only to one fact: your husband knows something about that death that he is not saying. Perhaps, he was even involved. I think he and the deceased might have disagreed on something; maybe the deceased was looking to break away and start his own church. You know, those types of disagreements pastors have. Or there was a disagreement on the project or a woman. Who knows? Your husband obviously went to the site to confront him, making sure you were not there. Ensuring there were no witnesses. Then, an argument must have ensued."

Nkechi's throat tightened. Sweat dripped down her spine. As if to stop the man from making the pronouncement, she reached across the table and grabbed the glass, which had some drink in it. She was convinced that her husband, having found out about her affair with Felix, had ambushed him at the site and pushed him to his death. Agent X seemed bemused at how she gulped down the drink, and he signaled for more. He poured to about the halfway mark and watched as she tilted the glass into her mouth and swallowed hard, squeezing her face as the liquid flowed to her stomach. He decided he wasn't going to allow her drink anymore, even if she asked. He was a little puzzled. This was not the reaction he had expected. Initially, he had assumed she'd decided to leave her husband following the revelation of his cheating and wanted to dig into Pastor Felix's death to get some incriminating information she could use to negotiate a better deal after their divorce. Looking at her now, she did not seem pleased by the findings. It was as if the information was exactly what she dreaded hearing, like a source of renewed pain.

"You have all of this documented?" Nkechi asked.

"Yes."

Nkechi looked at her watch and shifted in her chair. She wanted to leave.

"We chanced upon something else while we were on this," Agent X said, leaning forward slightly with a serious face.

Nkechi looked up at him, a little bewildered, her eyebrows raised as if to ask what could be worse than what she already knew.

"Very interesting stuff," the man said, nodding slowly. "You'll want to see this, I assure you."

"What is it?"

The man smiled. "It's not covered by the other brief, so--" He sat back and pulled out another cigarette. "It's the type of information that is gold in the hands of the right person."

"How much?" Nkechi asked. She felt like soldier ants were crawling through her brain.

THE RIDE BACK TO THE Island was quiet. The chatty driver was probably too exhausted from waiting for much longer than he had thought and seemed just eager to get her to her destination. She had been surprised to find that the car was still outside the lounge by the time she emerged, the driver sleeping in a fetal position on his reclined seat. Nkechi appreciated the silence. She wanted to think through everything, but her head felt thick and hazy, like a harmattan morning. The two glasses of the alcohol she had gulped down in quick succession were taking their toll. Usually, when she and Nick went to banquets, she held a glass of wine but rarely took a sip. Now, worried about the smell on her breath, she brought out some menthol gum from her purse and tossed one into her mouth. Her chewing worsened the headache, though, so she wound down the window, hoping the cool breeze on her face would make her feel better. It didn't.

She was heading straight to Heaven's Gate Cathedral, where she'd left her car. Her plan had been to slip in and join the midweek service, but all she wanted to do was go into her office and take a nap.

What was she supposed to do with all the information Agent X had given her? He gave her two flash drives before she'd left the lounge. The first held details of his investigation on Felix's death, the people he spoke with, and their conclusion. And the second, he'd promised, consisted of other incriminating information. She had hesitated to take the flash drives. Her head was already full. A lot of things ran through her mind. She felt guilty all over again for Felix's death. And the fact that she lived with a killer scared her. She wondered if Felix was a one-off, something done out of anger or jealously, or if murder was something her husband had in him for various occasions. She feared for what he might do if he ever found out she had been snooping on him, and her fear turned into anger. She had to do something with the information. She owed it to Felix. She owed it to herself. Leaving him quietly and relocating abroad, the option she had been mulling over, was now out of the question. She needed to ruin him. She just needed to figure out how.

All she knew was that she needed to be careful. She couldn't act on impulse and do something stupid. She had not realized she was muttering until the driver pulled over by the side of the road and asked her if she was okay. She shook her head as if trying to shake herself out of a trance and forced a smile. As the car re-joined the road, she chewed her lip and stared out the window. Streetlights lined the road, fizzling every couple of moments as if the bulbs would go out any moment and plunge her into the darkness.

OVER THE DAYS THAT FOLLOWED, Nkechi searched the internet, looking at old news reports about the incident. She knew her husband had the media in his pocket, but she hoped to find anyone who could have taken more than a passing interest in the story. Maybe someone who'd written something critical about Nick or the church. She found very little, and just as it was beginning to seem like a hopeless effort, she came across a story in *The Nigerian* about the opening of the cathedral. The reporter had made a comment about the unresolved death of a pastor during the cathedral's construction. Finding the story hadn't been straightforward though. First, she found excerpts on a blog and followed the *Read More* link to *The Nigerian's* website, but it returned an error message, which suggested the story had been taken off the website. All the same, she noted the date the story ran. The next day, she would get her personal assistant to request that day's copy of *The Nigerian* from the church's library archives.

Pastor Nkechi locked her office door as she read the full report and decided she wanted to know more about the reporter, Ifenna Obumselu. She called the newspaper house and feigned that she was a Public Relations Consultant looking to locate a journalist she had worked with in the past. The rather impatient lady on the other end of the line, who chewed gum nastily as she spoke, informed her that he no longer worked with the paper. She hung up before Nkechi could ask another question.

Frustrated, Nkechi decided to check Facebook. She found him. The search threw up two profiles with the name Ifenna Obumselu. The first had no profile image and seemed pretty much inactive, so she studied the other profile with the picture of a young man who looked like a philosopher by the way his head tilted upward in contemplation. Nkechi grew giddy with excitement when she saw *Journalist* listed in the *Occupation* field. She jumped up from her chair and punched the air, but the enthusiasm quickly waned as she contemplated contacting him. The young man looked to her like an intern, not a real journalist. He couldn't really know anything, could he?

As the days passed, uncertainty crept into the back of her mind, and she imagined the implications of going public with the information—what that would mean for her life. She imagined her husband going to jail for murder and wondered what would happen to the church. She didn't have much of a life outside of her husband. Plus, maybe Agent X had been wrong. Perhaps he'd got his conclusions mixed up. Her husband couldn't be a murderer. Right?

FOURTEEN

Ifenna woke to a flurry of *Happy New Month* messages on his phone. November 1st. It was now three months since he lost his job. He slept on the couch last night, and his laptop lay on the floor, the screen halfway closed. He had worked late moderating comments on his blog.

Lilian worked the night shift at the hospital. He was grateful because her presence made it difficult for him to concentrate on his blog since she now practically lived with him. She had already moved a small box of clothes into his room and had taken over a portion of the upper section of his wardrobe for her cosmetics and makeup. It still shocked him when he pulled out panties from the bundle of washed clothing. Besides the distraction while he tried to work, he enjoyed having her there. She brought a warmth to his apartment that he never had before. He was in love with her.

Her laughter sounded like an orchestra, and staring into her eyes felt like standing on a beach and looking out at the calm blue sea. He had told her many times that he loved her, but she always told him love was too strong a word, that it shouldn't be said too early, which made him uncomfortable. Maybe her previous failed relationship had etched doubts about love in her heart; perhaps, she wanted some proof of his faithfulness, something to make her feel secure. If he introduced her to his family, maybe she would feel more at ease.

Ifenna scrolled through his emails. To increase the readership of his blog, he had opened a Nairaland account where he posted excerpts and the link to his blog. Sometimes his followers left comments on Nairaland after reading the full post on his blog. One notification in particular made him straighten up. The previous night, he had searched Nairaland for the post by Edowoman411. She was the lady who used to be a member of Pastor Nick's church. She appeared active on the platform, always posting about her daily experiences. Ifenna, posting from the *Exposing the Bad Shepherds and Unchaining the Sheep Blog* account, had dropped a comment on her old post about the incident at Heaven's Gate Cathedral site and asked if she could share why she stopped attending Rivers of Joy Church. Then he'd put a link to his blog for her to check out and an email address to send her story if she felt up to it. He hadn't expected a response so soon:

Check your inbox.

Ifenna grabbed his laptop to check his email, where her message sat at the very top. He clicked it open without hesitating. There was only a short text and an attachment. She said she had already written a detailed account of her experience and was going to publish it on her Nairaland profile, but since he asked, she thought his blog was a better home for it.

I have not told this story before because I feared for my life, but now that I am safely in Canada, where no one can harm me, I feel ready for the world to hear my story.

Ifenna opened the attachment. It was three pages long. The heading, typed in bold font on the first page, read:

How Rev (Dr) Nicholas Adejuwon aka Pastor Nick Sexually Manipulated Me for Two Years

This is a true personal account. I know there will be many who would attack me and accuse me of trying to bring down a Man of God. Well, good luck to you. I am well past the guilt and victimhood. And hell, I don't care what your opinion is. I am only sharing my experience to save others from manipulation and shame, to protect other young women.

SHE HAD FIRST ENCOUNTERED PASTOR Nick when she worked as an intern at a television station where he came for an interview. After growing captivated by his charisma and the way he explained scripture like a storybook he was quoting, she couldn't stop staring at his smile. All the ladies in the studio gushed over him and her producer, who had blushed when she shook hands with him, kept reminding them that he was married.

He was this smiling embodiment of a guilt-free gospel, and I wanted more of it. Of him. I had just graduated and moved to Lagos. I was finally away from my parents. I could do my own thing and be free. The first thing I planned to do was to find another church. I was done being a Catholic with the suffocating repetitive prayers and drab masses,

which was nothing like the moving fellowship sessions at the Pentecostal churches I attended on campus. So I decided Rivers of
Joy Church was perfect for me.

Rivers of Joy gave her peace, a reassurance that God's
abundant grace cleansed all her sins. She came to like
Pastor Nick's wife, Pastor Nkechi, whom she described as
gorgeous. She often drooled over the styles of her outfits.
Celebrities also attended the church, making it feel like it
was the popular, best place to be.

One day, after about six months of attending the
church, a worker approached me after service and said
Daddy Founder wanted to see me. I thought it was a mix-up.
What would Pastor Nick want to see me for? I wasn't even a
registered member, so how did he know me out of all these
people? But the worker had no answers and just encouraged
me to see him, saying I never know what the Spirit had
directed him to do in my life. I must confess, after the initial
doubts, I was thrilled about it all. *Being in the presence of this
powerful man of God must have special blessings*, I thought.

They met after service in his office. She had to wait
for over an hour because a long queue of people wanted
to see him too. Finally, when it was just the two of them
alone, he said he saw her when she dropped her offering
in the basket, and something told him he knew her from
somewhere. She reminded him of their brief encounter at
the television station, and he said he barely remembered the
interview itself but insisted something stronger was telling
him he knew her.

I was certain we hadn't met besides that one encounter,
so I was not sure what he was on about. I was very convinced
he was mistaking me for someone else.

He asked her how long she had been with the church and what department she belonged to. He expressed shock that she wasn't in any department and even scolded her for denying God her talents. Then he declared he wanted her to join one close to his heart: the Pastoral Care Unit.

By the following Sunday, I had joined. He also took my number and told me not to be a stranger.

Pastor Nick began to pay her a strange kind of attention. He found time to call just to check up on her, asking what she ate and how her day was. He started to send good night messages laced with prayers for God's protection so that it looked innocent, but she could sense the undertones. Next, he bought her gifts, a designer bag and a gold chain. When he invited her to his suite at the Eko Hotel one night, she did not hesitate. After a Hennessey and Coke, she sat on his lap when he asked.

We made love for the first time that night. He told me to kiss him as I sat on his lap, and things progressed fast from there. He took me in different positions all over the room as though he was sex-starved. He told me later in the morning that his wife was like a postcard, pretty on the outside but flat and empty in the bedroom. Making love to her, he said, was like having sex with a cold dead fish. At the time, this made me feel good because he said our night together was the best he had ever had.

IFENNA'S PHONE RANG, INTERRUPTING HIS reading. It was Lilian. Her colleague on the morning shift who was supposed to relieve her was unable to make it to work because of a family emergency, so Lilian had to cover the shift. She apologized and said she'd be late for the visit to his mother that they had planned for the afternoon. Ifenna said it was okay, eager to get on with the story.

The lady's real name was Abieyuwa Obazele. She and Pastor Nick began to have regular sex after their first night at the hotel. He maintained permanent suites in different hotels and invited her over often. When she started to feel uncomfortable about their affair, she couldn't say exactly. She only remembered the manipulation.

I began to feel like a slave to him. He subtly threatened me and my family. He said God had ministered to him about my family and that we were destined for prosperity, but he alone had the power of speaking it into life. At that time, my father had just lost his job as a Nigeria Airways staff, and things were tough back home in Benin. I needed to remain loyal. He also often boasted of people he had cursed and how his curse brought about their doom because he was an anointed man of God. Back then, I lapped up everything he said. I didn't realize he was manipulating me.

She got pregnant twice, and both times he'd insisted she got rid of the pregnancies. Despite preaching against adultery, fornication, and abortion in church, he sent her to a doctor friend who was a member of the church. The second abortion threw her into depression.

I felt guilty and ashamed of myself. I was drowning in darkness. I had no one to talk to.

While she battled this depression, she stopped going to see him, and instead of trying to understand what she was going through, he got angry. He tried to guilt her into sleeping with him some more, saying she was distracting him from the ministry, from his one true love: God. When she finally saw him again, in his office after service weeks later, it was to tell him that she couldn't continue with their affair. She wanted to be left alone. But fearing she would tell someone of their actions, he sent one of his close pastors to her to remind her about Psalm 105: 15 and repeated that she was the seducer.

When I saw that his pastors were aware of what he was doing but were prepared to cover for him, I stopped attending the church. I knew that no one was going to believe me if I talked about it, and even though I could prove it with loads of text messages and voice notes he sent me, I was too exhausted by life to do it. I just wanted to get on with life. But here it is now: my story. I don't care if you believe me. I don't care if you judge me. I have already made peace with God, and it is in my past. Now, I am starting a new life in a faraway place, but I wanted to alert others not to make the same mistakes.

Ifenna shut the laptop. His stomach flip-flopped. Normally, a story about a pastor sleeping with a church member wasn't surprising, but Abieyuwa's tale made him angry. Probably because it was Pastor Nick. His existing disgust for the man heaved bile into his throat. This would be big news when he published it, the type of story that could crash his blog with all the traffic of readers. He decided he would post her story word for word. Everyone should know the truth.

THE ROAD WAS SURPRISINGLY FREE on their way to Orile. Ifenna knew all the side routes through Surulere that cut off the traffic caused by trailers bound for the Apapa port along the Costain and Orile-Iganmu axis. It was a little past three o'clock in the afternoon when they set out. After covering the morning shift at the hospital, Lilian got home at about 2 pm and had to immediately get ready for the visit to his parents. She spent close to an hour deciding what to wear. Ifenna knew she wanted to make the right impression, the way she tried on each dress, looked in the mirror, and decided it was either too short or too revealing or too tight on her hips. Her apprehension thrilled him, and he stole glances at her as he drove. She had exhausted her questions on the kind of person his mother was, what she should say to what question, and if he thought his mother would like her.

Now, she was quiet, twiddling her thumb and looking out of the window. He hadn't planned to tell his mother a few days earlier that he was coming to see her with someone. She had called him to regale him with stories of weddings she'd attended and those whose invitation cards she'd received, mostly people he'd grown up with in their area. Ifenna knew his mother wasn't just giving him an update. She was telling him something, a song she had been singing for a while. He knew how it ended and how, after giving the updates, she would sigh and say she couldn't wait for the day when she would be the one sharing out invitation cards and selling aso-ebi. She would ask God what she did differently from others, why her son refused to talk about marriage. Ifenna hated when she talked like that, like a wrongly accused person, exhausted from screaming, gently pleading their innocence. When she got like that, he would, in trying to brush away the guilt it brought, dismiss it by picking a fight or hurriedly ending the call.

The day he told her about Lilian, his mother spoke

of Okwy, the second son of a man they all called Baba Yellow, bringing his wedding invitation card, but Ifenna had interrupted to announce he wanted to come and introduce her to a friend.

"Friendi gi'a, obu nwoke ka obu nwanyi?" she asked.

"A lady, Mummy. O nwanyi," he replied.

His mother stayed silent for some time, as if in denial. Then she said quietly, "When did you say you are coming?"

"Saturday."

"Okay. Ngwanu, ka odi mgbe nfulu gi."

Ifenna had thought she'd screamed, "Praise the Lord!" because this was the first time he was introducing her to a female friend. He hoped the visit would reassure her that he would also get married someday.

A male voice advertising a local alcoholic drink with aphrodisiac properties came onto the radio just as they turned onto Ayoola Street. Ifenna quickly rolled the radio knob until he landed on a music channel. Wizkid and Femi Kuti's "Jaiye Jaiye." He left it there and bobbed to the beat. His jalopy bounced in and out of potholes. The streets in Orile were narrow. There were cars and buses packed all along them, the drains overgrown and blocked. The last time he came to see his mother, it had rained the previous night and the street had flooded. He'd been forced to park his car at a filling station, nearly a mile away, and take an okada. The entire area where he grew up had degenerated into a slum, neglected by both the state and local councils. During that same visit, shortly after he dropped off the motorcycle in front of the compound he grew up and paid the rider, he heard gunshots. Everyone on the street started to run. After she bolted the door and drew her curtains, his mother told him that youth gangs were fighting a turf war in the area. Ifenna had felt sad, learning that some of the boys leading the gangs were ones he'd gone to primary school with, boys he rode skates with back then on the street. How could they be part of a gang? It used to be a peaceful area, or at least his childhood naivety had told him.

Banners hung from electricity poles advertising churches and sports betting centers. In some ways, Ifenna thought, they were similar—the churches and the betting centers were potent opium for people. Both thrived on the people's despair. Churches brought with them poverty and despair, the very things they promised to take away from their members' lives. The more they spread, the more the surrounding areas fell apart. He remembered when there were just four churches: St. Mathews for Catholics, St. Andrews for Anglicans, a Methodist church, and a Cherubim and Seraphim. Then, other churches started to spring up. Then, new churches popped up. The first to arrive was Deeper Christian Life Ministry, which forbade its members from watching television.

Ifenna remembered his friend Festus, whose family had moved to Orile when Ifenna was in Primary Four. Festus's parents had attended Deeper Life, and Festus was often clueless when other children in school talked about programs they liked on television. He would follow Ifenna home just so he could watch shows like *Speak Out, Terrahawks,* and *Telematch* on NTA. But what Festus lacked in television knowledge, he made up for in sexual knowledge. Because he grew up in a police barracks, he knew many things that children his age did not. Ifenna used to wonder back then at the irony of Festus attending a church that frowned upon watching TV but was the one who knew everything about kissing a girl and how to insert a penis into a vagina. Festus even taught the boys in school vulgar songs. The lyrics of one floated into Ifenna's thoughts as he turned into Bankole Street.

Our SO
Wit im big belle
If e take am faya woman
Her toto go burst.

He smiled as he remembered he and his friends singing to it while they walked home from school, walking right on that very street on which he drove now, their knapsacks dangling from their backs.

"What is it?" Lilian asked, noticing his smile.

"Nothing," he said, shaking his head. "I just remembered something."

"What?"

"No, nothing serious. Just the way we used to play on this street when we were kids. The street was not like this back then. You see all this area?" He pointed to his right at a cluster of dwarf houses with spray paints over them. "There was nothing here. It was vacant. They said it was earmarked for a flood channel, so nobody was supposed to build on it. We used to play ball there in the dry season. Then one day, somebody started construction, and local government people came and marked it with red ink, ordering them to stop work. It stopped for a while. But later, they continued. People on the street said the man, Baba Kassim, who was our landlord then, bribed the people at the local government with wads of note, and they just turned the other way."

"Can you imagine? Now, I am sure the street gets

flooded when it rains.' Lilian was irritated.

Ifenna nodded.

"But why didn't the other people on the street stop him? Or you guys didn't know the implication of him building there?"

"We knew, but Baba Kassim wasn't the kind of person you challenged. He was a powerful politician in the same party with MKO Abiola. So everybody feared him. He tried to buy everybody's silence. He dug a borehole in the new building and extended a tap by the road that was open to anybody to fetch from for free."

They stopped outside Ifenna's mother's house. There was a bold inscription on the wall.

This house is not for sale. Beware of 419 and especially my son, Kassim.

Ifenna pointed to it as they exited his car.

"That's how it all ended," he said. "Kassim turned out to be a street tout, and now his old man is having a running battle, protecting all the properties he acquired in the area from his son."

Ifenna and Lilian headed up the front steps. His mother welcomed them at the door, smiling and smelling of spices.

Ifenna's mother hugged Lilian. "My daughter, you are welcome."

She kept smiling as if to convince Lilian that she was excited to meet her. She apologized that she was still cooking and explained that she didn't get back home early from the market where she'd gone to buy fresh fish for the Nsala soup Ifenna requested. After they sat down and she set a cold bottle of water on the centre table, she invited Lilian to the kitchen. Although she said she needed extra help, Ifenna knew it was an interrogation.

Later, as they drove back to Yaba, Lilian would tell him that it felt like an ambush. All her well-rehearsed answers had vanished with a wave of nerves. But it went well, she said, and it seemed like they struck a chord. The conversation was easy, as if they had known each other for a long time.

While they ate at the dining table that evening, Ifenna asked his mother about Kassim, their landlord's son.

"Odika obido kwa go ozo," he said. "I noticed the message on the wall outside is fresh."

"That boy?" She held the morsel of eba midway to her mouth. "Do you know he was going to sell this house? In fact, he had already collected part payment from the buyer before his father got wind of it."

"No way."

"The man came here to tell me now."

"Baba Kassim came here himself?" Ifenna asked, surprised.

The man never went to any of his tenants' apartments. When he needed to collect his rent from a tenant, he simply sent his thugs to go and lock the gate of the apartment or compound with his own padlock, forcing the tenant to either rush and pay or go groveling at his feet, begging for more time.

"He did o. He is not the Baba Kassim of then that you knew. Nka abia go nu. Nwoke agba da go. You know he now uses a cane to walk."

"He does?"

"Yes, I told you he suffered a partial stroke last year."

Ifenna couldn't remember her telling him, but he nodded anyway.

"I just heard a knock one evening, and I went to the door and it was him. I didn't even know what was happening. He said Kassim told the buyer, one importer-exporter man in Alaba, that his father was dead, and he now owns the property. He told him the current tenants of the house owed him for two years, and he was free to evict them as soon as the deal was done. And I bet what pained Baba the most wasn't that he had to pay back the part payment his son had already squandered, it was that his son declared him dead while he was still alive."

"But na wa! How did Kassim think he could pull off something like that?" Ifenna spat out some fish bones.

"Does he care?" His mother poured some water from a jug into her cup and drank. "To think of all the celebration they must have had when he was born because a heir has come. Look at it now, the so-called son is the one killing him. The man told me if not for Kassim's elder sisters who are now married and doing well, he would be long dead. It was one of them who flew him to India for treatment when he had a stroke. So much for male child this, male child that." She gestured in the air with both her hands.

Ifenna giggled. Lilian laughed.

"Nwuye'm," she continued, looking at Lilian. "Don't worry about this you-must-have-a-male-child rubbish o. Nwa bu nwa. Every child matters. Anyone you give us, we will accept."

Ifenna was amazed at the way she called Lilian, my wife in Igbo, and how she was already talking of her bearing children, and for a second, he wondered if perhaps he had brought her too soon. His mother would think he was ready for marriage.

That night, after Lilian dozed off on the couch, exhausted from her double shift, Ifenna called his mother. He knew she'd be itching to tell him what she thought about his friend.

"She looks like a good girl, but…" she said.

"But *gini*, Mama?"

She sighed. "You did not tell me that she's from Calabar."

"Akwa Ibom, Mama."

"Hanine bu ofu. Are they not all the same?"

"No, Calabar is the capital of Cross River. Akwa Ibom is a different state entirely. They don't even speak the same language."

"Anugo'm, but what I know is that they are all ndi mba mmiri, and you know this mba mmiri people…"

"What is it about them, Mama?" Ifenna snapped, a defensive barb in his tone.

"I didn't say there is anything wrong with them. I am just saying before you get serious with her, she will need to come for deliverance."

"Mama!" Ifenna exclaimed. "Deliverance kwa? Maka gini zi?"

"Ge nti ka'm gwa gi. You know these people from riverine areas always have marine spirit problem. It doesn't matter where you were born. It's something in their lineage. Mothers pass it down to their daughters. Lilian has to be delivered, or else she will pass it to her daughter, too. *Your* daughter."

Ifenna wanted to ask her what these marine spirits looked like and if they ate food off their hosts like leeches. Did spirits even eat? He wanted to also ask her if *she* went for deliverance when she married his father since she was from Oguta, where a lake is situated, and if she possibly passed her own marine spirit to Nkoli. But when he spoke, he told her instead that he had heard what she said and not to worry, Lilian was just a friend, nothing more.

When the call ended, Ifenna thought about the widely held perception that demonic relationships existed between large bodies of water and the people who lived around them. It reminded him of a post someone had sent him, which he published on his blog a week earlier. It was a short clip of a lady preaching in a combination of English and Yoruba at a white garment church. The woman, the veins on her neck bulging, declared that there was no way anyone who ate Titus Sardine could make it to heaven without serious deliverance, that Titus was a product used by the queen of the coast to recruit new members for her marine kingdom. He'd had a good laugh that day as he posted it. Now, after speaking to his mother that night, it made him laugh all over again.

FIFTEEN

Ifenna got to the venue thirty minutes early. He wrote down *9.30 a.m.* on the piece of paper used to record attendance, which the receptionist had passed to him as soon as he indicated he was there for the interview. The place smelled of cheap air freshener and smoke.

"Sit over there," she said after Ifenna passed the paper back to her and gave her a *what next?* look.

Two others sat in the waiting area. Ifenna sized them up as he approached an empty spot on the bench. They seemed like twins, the way their heads bent over their phones, their fingers tapping away. Had they been waiting for long? It was clear to him that the interviews were yet to start, which meant his ten o'clock schedule probably wouldn't happen.

The email invitation had directed he should be there at least fifteen minutes before his session. Instead of making his usual morning trip to the Island, he had picked up passengers going to Ikeja that morning and, instead of going through Mobolaji Bank Anthony Way, he had gone through Opebi Link Road all the way to Alade Market where his last passenger alighted. Then he'd turned at Opebi Roundabout and headed to Oba Akran where the interview was to take place. Locating the address had been a bit tricky since the street numbers were a bit irregular, and when he finally did, he found no space to park his car. The one-story building had no parking stalls, and cars had already lined the side of the road leading up to it. Ifenna had had to park almost fifty meters away before running back to the building.

Now, he threw a glance at his watch and wondered why he had been so bothered, why he hadn't warmed the leftover rice from last night and eaten something before setting out. He still wasn't even sure he was interested in this job. Bolanle, his former colleague, had told him about the opportunity. She had called one afternoon to tell him she forwarded a link to his email and urged him to apply. The appeal had become necessary as he had ignored two earlier job suggestions. The first had been as an executive assistant to the CEO of a furniture company, the other a cabin crew of a local airline. This one was for an administrative assistant for what the advertisement referred to as *a new American company in Ikeja*.

"Just go and try." Bolanle had insisted on the phone, like a concerned mother admonishing a difficult son. "You never know. Don't be waiting for a reporter job to fall into your lap. Take what you can find for now."

Ifenna had sent in his resume, more to humor her for expressing concern than of any real interest in the job. He half-expected not to even hear back from them because all he had ever done was journalism. When they did reach out two days later, inviting him for an interview, he decided to come out of curiosity. There was something suspicious about companies that hid under a cloud of anonymity when trying to recruit staff. The job title had been so vague, but maybe they really were a cool American company, maybe a tech start-up looking to scale in Lagos, hiding their true name, so they weren't swamped with applications.

Another candidate, a lady with a brown envelope sticking out of the handbag dangling from her left elbow, arrived at eleven o'clock. She wore a grey skirt suit and seemed to have retouched her hair for the interview, the way it glittered in the morning light. Ifenna and the other two shifted on the bench to make room for her to squeeze in. Ifenna began to wonder if there was some mix-up in the communication. Maybe they were expected to take a written exam instead of conducting a one-on-one interview as he expected. Ifenna muttered a hello to the lady soon after she wiggled between him and the other two candidates. She replied with a stiff nod while rummaging her handbag. Soon, she popped in her earplugs and shifted away from him. Ifenna liked the smell of her perfume, but she clearly didn't want to chat. He glanced at his watch again and then took out his phone. He'd give it another ten minutes before asking the receptionist what was going on.

He had published Abieyuwa's story that morning just before he left the house and was eager to see how it was doing, but as he opened the browser, he found a story he had seen on Linda Ikeji the night before but had not finished reading. It was now trending. The Catholic priests of Ahiara Diocese had rejected the bishop ordained for them by the Pope. They didn't think he was qualified for such a job since he was not from Mbaise. It was the name Ahiara that got Ifenna's attention. He had first encountered it in his readings on Biafra. The principles of the revolution, popularly known as the Ahiara Declaration, were delivered in a speech by Emeka Ojukwu, the Biafran leader in Ahiara, on June 1, 1969. As he read the details of the story, Ifenna wondered if there was something in Ahiara's air that spread defiance. As he read further, he felt disgusted at how the bone of contention was not that the ordained bishop was incompetent or of questionable character but that he was from Awka Diocese. That the characters at the center were priests who ought to preach oneness, love, and respect made it even more disgusting.

Ifenna looked up from his phone. Two more candidates joined the waiting room. They walked in at the same time, both clutching folders and looking like they had just emerged from a race, sweaty and ruffled. There was no more space to sit, so they stood like commuters at a bus stop. Ifenna decided it was time to find out what was happening and why the interview had yet to commence. He walked to the receptionist who was polishing her nails and asked her why no one had come to talk to them.

"Eh, just wait now," she said, her eyes on her nails. "They'll come and talk to you soon."

"We've been waiting for a while already. Some people don't even have anywhere to sit."

She looked up at him slowly and rolled her eyes. "But the people standing aren't complaining."

"What kind of organization is this?" he demanded, raising his voice and resisting the urge to slam his fist on the desk. "I want to speak to somebody."

"Please, Oga, don't shout on me o." She dropped the nail polish and rose to her feet. "Is it not a job that you are looking for? If you don't want to wait, go! No one's forcing you to be here."

By then, the other candidates had gathered around the receptionist's desk, attracted by the raised voices. Ifenna could hear their protests rising to his defense, condemning the receptionist, demanding to be addressed by someone. Ifenna did not feel the need to respond anymore. He bit his lips hard and let his anger simmer, drowned by the voices of the other candidates. He already decided this wasn't the kind of organization he wanted to work for.

A man emerged from an adjoining door, hands in the air like one crossing a military checkpoint. He looked like someone who should be listened to, judging by his well-tailored jacket, protruding stomach, and the way his glasses balanced on his nose bridge. Everyone fell silent and turned to look at him.

"This is an office environment," he said. "You can't be screaming like it's a marketplace. Yes, I understand some of you have waited for a while, but we are sorting some things out. Impatience is not an excuse for you to turn this place upside down. That's unacceptable."

Ifenna wanted to tell him that it was unacceptable to invite people for an interview and treat them like their time didn't matter, but he kept quiet like the others. The man looked around like a school principal addressing a group of recalcitrant students. Satisfied that his reprimand had sunk in, he told them to return to the bench and wait.

"We need more chairs," the only lady among them said as the rest of the group began to shuffle away.

"We will arrange for more," the man said, looking in the direction of the receptionist.

As the rest walked back to the waiting area, Ifenna headed for the exit.

IFENNA NEEDED TO TOP UP on his fuel as he drove away from the interview venue. There were a few fuel stations on the side of the road. To be sure a station was selling the correct quantity of fuel, you needed to see danfos and kekes buying from there. They knew which stations had adjusted meters. Though the first two stations he drove past had large *Yes Fuel* signs, he drove on. The next one had a banner that read *Station Under New Management: One liter is now, one liter.* Ifenna stepped on his breaks and drove in. He found the notice funny, an admittance that the station must have been ripping customers off in the past. Just two cars were ahead of him on the queue. Though he saw the "No Phones" sign, he decided to send a quick SMS to Bolanle before it was his turn at the pump where the attendants would have stopped him from using his phone. He was eager to tell Bolanle about the interview, or lack thereof, expecting her to call immediately she read it. Then he checked his blog. He sat back in shock. Because he was going to be away from his laptop and unable to moderate comments for some hours, he had left it open. His latest post had over a thousand comments. He stared at his phone in disbelief for several minutes, not noticing the car in front had moved. The car behind his blared its horn. On the blog, there seemed to be a raging argument between those who accused Abieyuwa of trying to destroy a Man of God with her lies and those who used the story to further a Men-of-God-are-scum agenda.

By the time it was Ifenna's turn at the pump, the story was trending on Twitter and had been republished by most of the top gossip blogs in the country. Ifenna felt a fulfillment that made the irritation from the interview venue disappear. It was as if he just won an Olympic gold medal. He smiled at the fuel pump attendant, who had missed a button on her blouse and seemed happy to show off her silky pink bra. She tried to advertise a carburetor cleaning fluid to Ifenna, claiming that it helped the engine to work better when poured into the fuel tank, but he did not give her audience. He couldn't wait to get to his laptop.

Distracted, he didn't see the VIO checkpoint early enough. He would have taken the first exit at Under-Bridge Roundabout and followed the route through the State Teaching Hospital and Ikeja GRA onto Mobolaji Bank Anthony Way. By the time he saw the checkpoint, there wasn't much else he could do but drive toward it. Their van, painted in yellow and black stripes like an albino zebra, was packed by the side of the road, ready to give chase to any car that failed to stop. Several of the officers in their black trousers and white tops, like fifth-year law students, littered the road, some poking their heads into the driver's side of parked vehicles, others directing oncoming cars to the side, and a few others walking around with papers in their hands and drivers following behind, pleading. Ifenna slowed down and prayed he wouldn't be stopped, but an officer stood in the middle of the road, and Ifenna watched as his left hand went up into the air, indicating he should stop, while his right hand pointed to a clear space off the road. Ifenna heaved a sigh as he pulled over, keeping the engine running. He drove a few meters further up the road, so he could park properly and not obstruct incoming traffic.

The officer approached briskly. Ifenna watched him from the rear-view mirror. He was six feet tall, and Ifenna thought how that height would have been better served in a basketball court. The man stooped low as he took an interest in something behind the car. Ifenna suspected it was his broken taillight. It made him tighten his grip on the steering wheel. The officer walked to the side of the car and bent down to read off something on the rear tire. Ifenna thought he noticed an excited grin on his face as he approached the driver's window.

"Good morning, Officer," Ifenna said, forcing a smile.

"License and registration," the man said at the same time.

His name tag read *SN Babalola*. He had facial marks like Ladoke Akintola, the type Bolanle once told him was unique to people from Ogbomoso.

"Officer Babalola, make we greet now," Ifenna said, trying to relax the mood.

"Your papers, please." The man clearly was not in the mood for pleasantries.

Ifenna reached into the glove compartment and grabbed the folded bunch of papers, photocopies of his vehicle registration, roadworthiness, insurance, and proof of ownership.

Officer Babalola eyed Ifenna as he collected the papers. He touched his right thumb on his tongue to moisten it and began to flip through the papers, spending some time on each page and making a face like he was deeply studying it before flipping to the next. When he was done, he asked for Ifenna's Driver's License.

There had been a recent outcry by the public on the duplicity of the agencies on the roads and how the roles were not defined. This had forced the government to release a statement defining what each organization could ask from a road user. Ifenna was aware of this since he had covered the press conference by the commissioner for transport while still at *The Nigerian* and knew that VIO were restricted to inspecting the vehicle, and only the Road Safety had purview over his license. He decided not to argue the point. His wallet held the plastic card. He handed it over to the officer, who made the same serious face as he skimmed through it.

"Your tire is expired," the man declared, lifting his head from the license. Ifenna stared blankly back at him, wondering if he read that information off the card. "You're also driving around with a broken taillight."

"A keke bashed me yesterday," Ifenna said.

"Put on your headlight. The officer walked to the front of the car to observe.

Ifenna flicked on his headlights.

The man walked back to his side. "Put on your wiper."

Ifenna sighed. His jalopy's wiper hadn't been working for some time now, but he had been lucky never to have encountered rain when he went for his kabu kabu.

"Officer, the wiper developed a fault yesterday," Ifenna lied.

"Offence number three," the officer declared almost triumphantly. "I am suspending your roadworthiness certificate and impounding your vehicle. Your car constitutes a risk to other road users and yourself, and we cannot allow you to be perambulating all over the place."

"Officer Babalola, you can't do this, please." Ifenna unhooked his seat belt.

"What do you mean, I can't do this? Are you trying to tell me how to do my job?"

"No, it's not like that, Officer." Ifenna rubbed his palms together in apology, dragging out each word. "That's not what I meant. You see, Officer, like I told you, you know how rough these keke boys are. They're the ones that broke my taillight. As for the wiper, I will change it today. In fact, I was hoping to find these boys that do it in traffic."

"And what about the expired tire?" The man cocked his head at an angle like a prosecution attorney asking a defining question.

Ifenna wondered if he should reveal to the man that he never knew that tires had expiry dates. He decided not to; he knew how these things generally went. At some point, there would be negotiation on what fine he would pay, and the more guilt established against him put him on the weaker foot. Instead, he feigned surprise and told the officer in a matter-of-fact tone that he had only changed the tires a few months ago.

"I have to book you and impound your car until you pay. Three offenses. Each offense is twenty thousand naira." The man brought out a notepad from his back pocket and started to write.

"Officer. Take it easy now. I am sure we can work something out."

The man stopped writing and looked at Ifenna as if to find out how serious he was about "working something out." Ifenna knew this was the moment to pitch. He turned the car off, opened the door, and stepped out. A hospital ambulance with the siren wailing sped past. The breeze shook the papers in Officer Babalola's hands. Ifenna helped him hold them together so none of them flew off. The man made sure to retain his grip because that was his bargaining chip. When it was calm again, he placed the papers on the roof of the car and picked up a stone, which he used to hold them down. Then he turned to face Ifenna with a *make an offer* look on his face.

"Officer, you have to help your son." Ifenna had decided to take the pleading route, to make the man feel special and hopefully end the episode quickly. "I don't have much now. I am just a journalist hustling. All I have is one kay." Ifenna had earlier retrieved the one thousand naira he had in his pocket. He pushed it toward the man who eyed the money as though it was bird droppings on his Sunday best jacket.

"One thousand for what? It's like you don't understand what I am saying, young man. And you say you are a journalist. It's you people that will go and write rubbish about the VIO. VIO is doing this, VIO doing that. Now, you are here. Do you know how serious your offense is? Your charge is sixty thousand. Don't insult me."

"Officer, how can I insult you? Who am I? I'm just trying to reason with you. You know it's still morning. Just help me and hold this one, please." Ifenna pushed the money toward the man again.

"The least I can collect is ten thousand."

"I don't carry ten thousand on me!"

"We can drive to ATM."

Ifenna took a deep breath. His stomach sloshed. "Officer, even if we go to an ATM, there is nothing there. Please, help me."

The officer eyed him over. "If I impound this car, you will pay sixty thousand officially with abeg on top, and you will still pay for every night the car sleeps in our office."

"I understand, sir. That's why I am begging you. Okay. Let me make it one, five." Ifenna started to rummage his pocket to locate a five hundred naira note.

"I can see you are not serious. Do I look like a beggar to you?" Officer Babalola seemed infuriated. He began to write again on the notepad that had *Charge Sheet* printed across the top.

Ifenna decided to change his approach. "Oya, let's go to your office," he said, hoping his voice did not betray that he was just bluffing.

The man looked at Ifenna. He seemed taken aback, the way he narrowed his brows as he tried to understand the sudden change in tone.

"Yes, let's go." Ifenna continued, as if to make clear that he was no longer begging. "You think filling the charge sheet will make me scared? Oya, fill it now. You think I am scared? Let us go to your office."

Officer Babalola did not say anything. He turned around and continued writing on the charge sheet.

IFENNA LAY ON HIS RECLINED driver's seat. All the windows of his car were rolled down, but he was still sweating. The early afternoon sun needled his skin. His inner singlet stuck to his back. He adjusted himself on the seat, turning so that he now lay on his right side. His new position did not bring any new comfort. He hissed, looked at his watch, and hissed again. His phone, which had previously helped distract him from the discomfort, had just run out of power and gone blank.

He had been following the comments on his blog post about Pastor Nick and Abieyuwa, and it had been a steady stream. The majority of the initial comments were from those who condemned the pastor and expressed shock, but there were the skeptics and the active defenders who insisted the story was a conspiracy to smear the name of the man of God. Ifenna suspected they were members of Pastor Nick's online army because of the way they posted the same comments, obviously copied from the same script. Not getting to his laptop bothered him the most about his encounter with the VIO officer.

It had now been nearly two hours since Officer Babalola wrote his charge paper. Ifenna had agreed to follow him to his office, but Babalola insisted Ifenna would have to wait for him until he was leaving. Officer Babalola made him park his car beside the VIO van, facing the road. There had been several other cars held in a similar fashion, but they had left one after the other after the owners got tired of waiting and paid whatever the officers were demanding as bribe to be let off. Twice, Officer Babalola had come around, perhaps to see if he had changed his mind, but Ifenna remained adamant. He did not have the money he was being asked to pay, and he was not going to beg anymore either. He silently hoped that at some point, they would get tired of him being there and let him go. For him, it was a test of will, of who would blink first. He hadn't imagined he would be there for that long.

Ifenna sat up and looked out. The officers were still stopping and inspecting cars. He wondered if they would still be so dedicated to working under the sun if they weren't stuffing their pockets in the process. The windows of the van were all down. There were two officers sitting inside chatting. Ifenna had been hearing voices and thought there were more than two persons, but now he could hear them clearly. The louder of the two sat at the back. Ifenna suspected he was their boss, the way he had been sitting inside the van all the while, the buttons of his uniform undone to the stomach exposing a black singlet. It was to him the drivers went to negotiate and make payments before being freed to leave. The other looked smart, like a scholar of sorts with his glasses and uniform that hugged his slim frame. Black Singlet was saying something about how his friend, a Customs officer, sold the bags of rice they seized from smugglers at giveaway prices, when his phone rang. He raised it to his face and seemed to mentally reach a decision before placing the phone on his ear. The conversation was all in Yoruba, in decibels that suggested he was scolding the person on the other end. Glasses bit his nails as he waited for the call to end.

"Hope no problem, sir?" Glasses asked as Black Singlet ended the call and dropped the phone on the space beside him.

"Don't mind my mechanic. My wife wants to go to attend Bishop Makinde's Retreat Camp this evening, and I asked this idiot to come and service the car since morning. He is just now calling to ask me if anybody is at home."

"Oh, today is Retreat Camp," Glasses said. "There will be plenty traffic on that road tonight. I need to leave early."

"That is your church, abi?"

"It used to be."

"How? You people will be changing church like t-shirts. I thought you were passionate about Bishop Makinde? You always have one of his books with you."

"Yes o, Oga," Glasses adjusted the glasses, pushing it up his nose ridge. "I deeply respect the man of God, but my issue isn't with him. It is with my local parish in Ojodu. The pastor there is a complete idiot. They expelled me from the church." Black Singlet starred at Glasses without saying anything. "The pastor accused me of lacking understanding of spiritual things after I rubbished one of his bogus miracle claims."

"What happened?"

Ifenna could have asked the question himself as he adjusted on the seat, pulling up the backrest to the sitting position to listen in.

"Oga, you see, eh, there are some things somebody who went to school should not swallow quietly just because it came out from the mouth of a pastor. I mean, you can't just be spewing rubbish from the pulpit and assume all your congregation are fools that don't know any better."

Black Singlet asked him again, "What happened?"

"One Sunday, some months ago, our pastor shared a testimony about a miracle of how he drove his car with an empty tank from Yaba to Ikeja. He said he finished from a minister's meeting around Ajah late and forgot he needed to buy fuel. On his way home, around Yaba, he noticed the empty tank light was blinking on the dashboard, and there was no filling station open at that time. Then the engine went off in the middle of nowhere! Left with no other option, he prayed and called on the God of Bishop Makinde to come to his rescue. He started the car again, and the engine roared to life, taking him all the way to his home in Ikeja without going off."

Glasses narrated how the whole church had applauded the story and even broken out into a spontaneous thanksgiving to celebrate God for the miracle. The whole thing nauseated him because he knew better. The following week, it was his turn to speak during the men's midweek fellowship.

"They thought they were going to hear a sermon," Glasses continued. "The theme of my presentation was on car fuel tank reserve and their sizes. I took my time to prepare PowerPoint slides for the talk. I didn't study engineering in the university for nothing. I showed them, slide by slide, different car makes and the sizes of their fuel reserve. Then, I focused on our pastor's car model. Quoting from the car manual, I made them understand that when the fuel tank empty light blinks and the engine stops, it is a warning that the car has now switched to the fuel reserves, which holds up to fifteen liters of fuel. That amount of fuel can nearly take him to Ibadan without any prayers. When I was done, the room was so silent, you could have heard a pin drop."

"Was the pastor in attendance?" Black Singlet asked, shaking slightly from laughter.

"Of course! Right in the front row!"

"No way."

"He was there o, seriously. After my presentation, all the other men weren't quite sure how to react because he was sitting there. Normally, after the talk of the day, no matter how brilliant it was, he would come up and give a roundup of the talk, add a few of his own insights as if applying a seal of authenticity to it all before doing the final prayers. That day, he did not get up o. It was the assistant pastor that hurriedly said the final prayers and brought the fellowship to a close. The following Sunday, the pastor announced my expulsion, saying I was spreading blasphemy and insinuating that the God of Bishop Makinde was a liar."

Black Singlet, who had been giggling for much of the time, began to laugh, slapping the back of the seat in his front. Glasses joined him. Ifenna thought of the reception the story would get when he published it on his blog and the irony of it falling on his lap in the most unlikely of places. It suddenly didn't feel so bad being held there, and he thought about coincidences and how the universe sometimes played chess with people's lives using time and chance as pieces. He wondered if perhaps he had been informed of the job opportunity by Bolanle, which led to the botched interview and subsequently to the encounter with Officer Babalola just so he could hear Glasses tell his story.

SIXTEEN

Pastor Nkechi picked up her phone from the dressing table when she noticed the green light blinking. She was surprised to find three missed calls from Peju. Just as she set the phone back, another call came through. Peju again.

"Where are you?" Peju's voice held a barb of panic.

"At home. Why?" Nkechi sat down slowly on her bed.

"Have you been online today?"

"No. Why?"

Silence filled the other end of the phone as if Peju was contemplating what to tell her next. The hair on Nkechi's arms rose in anticipation.

"Come on, tell me. What is it?" she asked.

Peju sighed into the phone and still did not say anything.

"You're starting to scare me. What is it?" Nkechi snapped. "Why call me if you aren't going to say anything?"

"My sister," Peju said, like someone comforting a bereaved. "It is not like that. I just don't know how to say it. I thought you had already seen it."

"Seen what? I'm just getting ready to go out. I haven't been online."

Peju sighed again. "There's this trending story about your husband."

"What story?" Nkechi's heart raced.

"Somebody is accusing him of…"

"Accusing him of what, Peju? Tell me."

"It is a lady. You know that thing I told you, how all these useless single girls throw themselves at our husbands? I told you how it was important to protect your husband from all these daughters of Jezebel. I knew something like this was going to happen."

"Peju, if you don't tell me right now, I'm hanging up."

"I'll send you the link."

The line went dead.

As Nkechi waited for the WhatsApp notification, her mind went to Agent X, to the story he'd told her about her husband, and she wondered if he had released it. Perhaps he had found someone interested in buying it, maybe some pastor who wanted to see her husband's downfall, or perhaps an ambitious journalist who wanted a chance in the limelight. She wished she had bought it off the detective when he offered it to her. If anyone was going to bring her husband down, she wanted to be the one to do it.

She flipped to WhatsApp and hurriedly clicked on the link. Her heart stopped as she read through the first three paragraphs. Then she stopped reading and scrolled up to see the name of the blog, as if to determine if it was to be taken seriously. *Exposing the Bad Shepherds and Unchaining the Sheeps* didn't ring any bells. She started reading from the top again to make sure she hadn't missed anything. Sweat seeped through her shirt despite the air conditioning on full blast. The more she read, the more she felt like quicksand was dragging her down, choking her airway.

She startled at a knock. Sarah, her personal assistant, stood in the doorway as if unsure whether to proceed inside. Nkechi felt happy to see her, as though her sudden appearance would send the story about her husband away. She beckoned at her to come into the room. As she approached, Nkechi held up her phone.

"Good morning, Pastor," Sarah said, genuflecting slightly, a behavior she had refused to stop despite Nkechi's repeated pleas. "I take it that you have seen it?"

"I just did. This kind of thing was happening, and I am only just finding out?"

"I rushed over from the office to inform you about it so that you didn't stumble on it yourself. I didn't want to tell you about it over the phone."

"Someone sent it to me. It's trending, isn't it?"

"Kind of. Some other blogs have picked it up because you know how they like gossip, especially when a popular person is involved, but our communications people have zoomed into action. They should be able to take it down. Try not to worry."

"Try not to worry? You *have* read the story, haven't you?" Sarah nodded.

"Somebody just accused my husband of all that, and you say I shouldn't worry?"

"I understand how you must feel. But honestly, if you look beyond the hype of social media, there is nothing credible about the story. It's just gossip. We suspect someone just planted it to embarrass Pastor Nick. It's just their latest attack, and they went to use that useless girl to--"

"You know the girl?"

Sarah hesitated before speaking. "Yes, actually. She used to be a worker in the church. She was in the Pastoral Care Unit."

"It's true then. She's real. This is not some fictitious story."

"No, it's not, ma. The useless girl was sacked. She was a very annoying thing. I knew her well back then. The devil tried to use her to bring down the church, always jumping around like a dog on heat, looking for men to seduce. There was no atom of the Holy Spirit in her. She was sacked from Pastoral Care and asked to go for deliverance. Then she stopped coming to church. The next thing I knew, she started writing rubbish on social media."

Nkechi regarded Sarah for a while, admiring her innocent confidence and the way she lined her brows with pencil, making an arc at the edges that gave her an intimidating look. Sarah had been her personal assistant for two years now since she came out on top in the interview process. Sarah was young but very smart and enthusiastic. Her age notwithstanding, she provided intelligent advice dripping of wisdom far above her age, and Nkechi had come to trust her completely. On this matter, she willed herself to believe what Sarah was saying, but as hard as she tried, the lady's accusation kept bouncing in front of her thought, alongside Agent X's face that day at the lounge, telling her he had something incriminating about her husband. The detective's voice kept echoing in her head, and she had to squeeze her eyes shut to dismiss it.

"Where is my husband?" she finally asked.

"I'm not sure. He was at the cathedral briefly this morning before going out."

"Is Bimbo with him?"

"Bimbo is at the cathedral. She's coordinating the response to this nonsense."

Nkechi sighed and folded her hands across her chest. She looked across the room in the direction of her newly installed treadmill, and though she was staring at it, she wasn't actually seeing it. Instead, she saw the face of her late father, telling her she was making a big mistake by marrying Nicholas. They were in their sitting room in Enugu; her dad in his favorite single-armed chair directly opposite the television, and she was standing in front of him, face squeezed like a twig. Though her father's argument was based around ethnicity, which didn't make sense to her back then, she wished now that she had listened to him.

"I know you're concerned about the impact this will have on the ministry, but honestly, I'm not worried. Who in their right sense will believe that Pastor Nick had anything to do with that girl? They should have found someone more befitting to use in their conspiracy. It beats me how people can't just watch other people excel in peace. They must bring them down, even in the Lord's vineyard. Even if they publish a million blogs, we cannot be shaken by it. So don't worry, Pastor, God is fighting our battles, and even the gates of hell shall not prevail over us."

"I need to get to the cathedral," Nkechi said, rising from the bed abruptly. She needed to confront her husband, and she could not wait until he got back home.

"No, ma," Sarah said.

"What?"

"I'm sorry, Pastor. Please, ma, don't be offended, but we think you should just remain indoors today, or at least until

220

all of this is under control."

"We?"

"I discussed it with Bayo on my way here. We think it's for the best."

"I see. So you're telling me I can't leave?"

Sarah was quiet. She shifted her gaze to the floor, her hands clasped in front of her groin. Nkechi sat back on the bed. She felt weak in her knees. Though Sarah couldn't really stop her from going out, she knew it was probably for the best. Her legs might not be able to carry her, and she was likely going to cause a scene at the Cathedral, which would only make matters worse. Her plans for the day were ruined. She had planned to make a brief stop at the church before heading off to Nike Arts Gallery. One of the guest ministers at last year's Festival of Grace, an annual program they held in Rivers of Joy Church, had requested some bronze heads. It was she who'd taken the visiting ministers to the gallery and the Lekki Arts Market the day before they left and had watched in awe as they dwelt on the pieces like children in a toy shop. They had bought a lot then, but a few days ago, she received a message from one of them saying that he wanted some bronze heads to decorate their new office. She was to buy them and send them by courier to the good old pastor in Texas. She had planned to do it all herself so that she could be sure it was done properly. She didn't want to disappoint the man who had hosted her in his church during her trip to the US to raise money for the cathedral project. Now, disappointing him seemed like a trivial worry. She leaned back into her pillows and fought back the tears.

NKECHI GOT BACK INTO HER room and locked the door. She had just had a spat with her husband, and she suspected he might come barging in to have the last word. She stood there with her back against the door as if her weight against it, not the locks she had turned, would prevent him from gaining access. There was no knock. When it became clear he wasn't coming, which somehow made her feel disappointed, she walked toward her bed.

It was almost nine o'clock that night when he returned home. She had stood at her window overlooking the main gates of their mansion for a long time, waiting for his headlights in the driveway. Alone, she had counted the hours until her anger transformed into a headache, banging against her temples. Sarah had left with the crew from the church that came to record a short clip of her speaking in support of her husband. They had done the recording in the sitting room. She sat facing the camera with a Bible in hand and their wedding picture up against the wall behind. She read her script with a smile, saying how wonderful and caring her husband was and how hard he worked to shepherd the flock of the Lord. They were going to post it online and make it go viral. It would be the death of the accusation, the excited crew members told her. Already a counter-narrative of the accuser being a loose, misguided girl was already being pushed to discredit her. Someone had shared the story of her having a child at eighteen. Nkechi felt herself sinking deep in anger because though she now knew the girl's story was true, she had to keep up the appearance of the supportive wife. This came with a sickening feeling of utter helplessness.

After Sarah and the crew left, she felt so alone that she almost called her mother. Twice, she dialed the number she hadn't called in close to a year but ended it just before the first ring. Since her father died, she and her mother had barely spoken. Her mother blamed her for his death, insisting that he developed the high blood pressure that finally took his life after she eloped with Nick. It had got them into so much trouble with the church. When the child of Catholic parents married someone who wasn't Catholic, their parents were deemed to have fallen into sin and banned from participating in Holy Communion. Nkechi always thought this a very ridiculous rule. The parish priest and church council summoned her father to a meeting where he was reminded of the rule, and his blood pressure rose for the first time that night and never quite came down.

Attending the funeral had been difficult, and though she and her husband sponsored all the fanfare that went with it, including all the ridiculous requests the parish priest made, she had felt unwelcome. She couldn't mistake the accusation in the eyes of everyone when they looked at her, like she was the prime suspect in a homicide. Since she got back to Lagos from the funeral, she had not called her mother. She only inquired about her from Ike, her brother, who her mother now lived with in Port Harcourt. Strange how it was her mother she felt moved to call that afternoon.

When Nick's convoy made an entry into their compound, she marched to his room to wait, arms folded tightly around her chest. He walked in and pretended she wasn't there, kicking off his shoes and proceeding to unbutton his shirt while whistling the lines to 'Great is Thy Faithfulness,' as though he was celebrating something. If he was worried about the trending story, he didn't show any signs of it. He was about to go into the bathroom to shower when she leaped between him and the bathroom door. The balloon of anger that had swollen up all day inside her burst.

"How low can you go, Nicholas? How low? You are a philandering bastard, a dirty he-goat. You will not rest until you have dragged this family into the gutters and dragged the ministry we worked so hard to build along with you just because that thing between your legs cannot stay still when it sees anything in skirt. Are you not ashamed, Nicholas? Look at the kind of shame you are bringing to me. You thought it was me you were deceiving. Look now, there is nothing hidden that will not be revealed. Tell me, are there more women? Pastor Nicholas Adejuwon, how many more accusations should I expect?"

"Look, Nkay, I have had a busy day, in the name of God, just let me be. I need to shower," he said, brushing her aside and attempting to enter the bathroom.

"In the name of which God? The one who you are sinning against? Look, Nicholas, you can't push this matter aside."

"So, what do you want me to do?" He raised his voice too to match hers. "Sit down and start crying because of some unsubstantiated accusation online? Come on. That's the oldest trick in the book. I will not be the first man of God to be accused by demonic agents. It's all nonsense. I can't dwell on that."

"Look me in the eyes and tell me you didn't do it."

"Please, get out of the way. I need to shower."

"I said it." She clapped her hands in front of his face. "I said it. You cheat, mister man of God. You can deceive the whole world, but you can't deceive me. Let me tell you, if you like admit or ignore, I know you did it, and *you* know you did it. You disgust me. I regret the day I met you." She didn't wait for him to respond. She stormed out and slammed his bedroom door.

Now on her bed, almost panting, she dialed Agent X.

"Madam," he said right after the first ring. "You are not supposed to be calling me on this number."

"It's an emergency," she said. "That other story you have about my husband, what is it?"

"Madam, you know I can't tell you unless you're willing to pay for it."

"Do you still have it? You haven't sold it?"

"It remains intact."

Nkechi paused. A part of her had suspected the trending story was from Agent X. "You are sure the story has not leaked?"

"Positive, Madam. Why do you ask?"

"It has nothing to do with the story published on a blog by some lady accusing my husband of having an affair with her?"

"Oh, that? I came across it earlier today. I didn't make much of it, though. Sounded like gossip. Do you want me to check it out?"

"No. There is no use. I thought that was your story."

"Not even close, Madam. What I have got is real solid stuff, not society gossip."

"I want it."

"Pardon?"

"I want that story."

"I will send you a location to meet."

"One more thing. I need you to find out who is behind the blog that published that story."

SEVENTEEN

"Ouch! Take it easy!" Lilian squirmed, pulling her head away.

"Sorry,' Ifenna said, letting go of the loosened hair extension strand he'd been pulling at.

"Try not to pull so hard."

Ifenna made a sound in his throat to indicate he understood before grabbing the loose strand, sticking the pointed end of a pen into the braided area, and using his fingers to dislodge the braids.

They were in his living room. Lilian was sitting on the floor, her back to him and her body in between his legs while he sat on the sofa. The power had gone out, and Ifenna hadn't remembered to get fuel for his generator. A rechargeable lamp, which sat on the side stool beside them, provided light as he helped Lilian with her attachment braids. The day she came home with new braids from the hair salon run by some Togolese women down their street, Ifenna had marveled at how tiny they were, and she had praised the stylist whom she said had a special craft. They made them tiny and tight, which gave them more longevity, she said. The flip side, however, was that it was painful. Lilian had been hopeful that the pain would get better, but by two weeks in, she got home from work and declared she needed them out. Ifenna had been happy to help loosen them for her. He had endured many nights of her whining about the pain, writhing endlessly in bed, and denying him sleep.

"Did you know that at some point today, I just went into the toilet to cry because of this hair?" Lilian moaned.

"It hurts that bad?"

"Yes!"

"Wait, like seriously, it made you cry?" Ifenna chuckled.

"You don't understand. It was like there were a thousand soldier ants crawling through my hair and stinging me all over. Honestly, I felt like just tearing it off my head so I could have peace."

"Guess there is a cost for looking good."

"Abeg! This one is more than cost. This one is punishment, jare." Lilian stifled a yawn. "I cannot come and kill myself by myself abeg."

Ifenna laughed at the effortless humor in her words, at the unusual expressions that made up her language, at the way she said it, like one totally at peace with the world.

"Come. So, you were telling me. How did it end with the VIO people?" Lilian asked. "Did you finally follow them to their office?"

"For where? Don't mind those thieves. Do you know what happened? After wasting my time, they finally collected the two thousand."

"You mean it?"

"I kid you not."

"But I thought you only offered to pay N1,500?"

"Initially. But later, after like one-hour mehn, I told the Babalola guy I would make it 2k. The dude was acting like James Bond. He was telling me I must follow them to their office, that even if I offer him ten thousand, he won't accept, that he was going to 'deal with me.'"

"So he still collected 2k?" Lilian pulled the attachment she just finished loosening, separated it from her hair strands, and dropped it in the heap on the floor.

"They did o. What happened was when they were ready to leave, I thought, o*kay, they will now take me to their office.* Their boss called me and said the way he was looking at me, I am like a junior brother to him, and he wouldn't want to punish me, so he has decided to just pity me. Then he shamelessly told me to bring what I had. Honestly, I was regretting why I even added five hundred to it. If I had just shunned, they would have collected the one-five like that."

"So, they basically just wasted your time for nothing?"

"Precisely. But it was not a waste like that. You know how they say every disappointment is a blessing? While they were wasting my time, they gave me a story. Now I can write an authoritative article on how VIO set up roadblocks to extort money from motorists."

"Oh, cool. Was that what you were working on when I came in?"

"Yes," Ifenna lied.

"Just see how those VIO people played themselves. When the story is published, they'll wish they never stopped you."

Ifenna sat back and stretched. His lower back ached from stooping forward. When he offered to assist her, he hadn't expected it to take so long. Almost two hours later, they had hardly loosened half of the braids. His palms were oily. He ran his right palm over his own hair before scratching around the groove of his back. Earlier, he took his shirt off because of the heat. Now, he also felt like taking off his singlet. The sweat trickling down his back was sticky and itchy.

"Are you tired?" Lilian asked, turning her head slightly to look up at him.

"Not really. I just want to rest my back a little," Ifenna replied, stifling a yawn. "These NEPA people should bring this light, abeg. This heat is too much."

Lilian ran her fingers through the loosened part of her hair, using her fingers as a comb.

Ifenna picked up the pen and began to loosen another attachment strand. He remembered when he and Nkoli used to loosen Aunty Peshe's hair when they were younger. She was their mum's second cousin who seemed to visit them only when she wanted to make new braids and needed to loosen the old one. She had such long hair and skin that glowed like the sun; people called her an Indian queen. Her real name was Patience, but everybody pronounced it as Peshence, Peshe for short. Ifenna liked her because, whenever she came, she bought them popsicles and Okin biscuits and generally lit up the mood at home with her high-pitched voice and laughter that forced you to laugh, too. She always had the latest stories about everyone and told it in an Igbo that sounded different, more musical than the one their mother spoke. Then she'd stopped coming. Their mother got home and announced that Aunty Peshe was dead. He had locked himself in his room and cried that day, refusing to eat dinner.

Many years later, he learned that Peshe died of AIDS, that she had been a sex worker, the type that had permanent suites in cheap hotels where men came to meet them. Sometimes he wondered how her last days had gone and whether the dreaded virus stole her laughter before killing her.

"I didn't even tell you what happened today," Lilian said, tapping his knee and shaking him out of his reverie. "One of those stupid gossip blogs published a rubbish story about my pastor."

Ifenna's heart skipped. "What rubbish story?"

"Imagine o. One girl was claiming that Pastor Nick was sleeping with her o, that he was taking advantage of her."

"Seriously?" A frog in his throat made him cough.

"So annoying. I wonder how people just wake up one day and decide to bring down an anointed man of God. I mean, how can one be so foolish? Accuse Pastor Nick? That's how people bring curses upon themselves and their generations."

"You sound like you're very sure the person was lying," Ifenna said, slightly irritated.

"Obviously! I know the yeye girl. She was a worker in the church. I knew her then... always wearing short skirts and walking around as if she was hawking her body to the world. Very shameless animal."

"Lily!"

"I'm sorry, but I don't know what else to call her. Do you know she was advised in the church to go for counseling and deliverance? That was when she stopped attending church. Then, two or three years after, she remembers the pastor was sleeping with her?"

"But what if she's telling the truth. These things happen. Pastors are human beings, too. They make mistakes."

"Not Pastor Nick. Even in witchcraft, there is seniority. No be every pastor be mate."

Ifenna burst out laughing at her analogy.

"I'm serious! My pastor is a Holy Man of God. He is a spirit-filled man. Pastor Nick is a very handsome man and can get any girl in the church that he wants. Of all the hot babes he sees every day, he picks *that* girl? Come on. The girl is just looking for unnecessary attention, and she got it."

Perhaps it wasn't so much Abieyuwa the Nairaland girl but his blog that had got the attention from the story. When he got home after the encounter with the VIO officers, he had been surprised to find ten emails expressing interest to advertise on his blog and enquiring about his rates. Three of these were from churches looking to advertise upcoming programs. Ifenna had been so excited that he'd felt numb, surprised that he could make money from the blog, happy that the story had finally brought his blog to the attention of advertisers. Though he had hoped that someday his blog would bring him money, he had never developed a rate card, and now he had to hustle one up. He'd been working on one when Lilian returned, pitching up his own rate card after looking at what other popular blogs charged.

"Now everybody knows who she is. I never even knew she had a child at eighteen until today. Her real story is coming out now."

Ifenna had seen the child comment on his blog, and though some people were dwelling on it, he had dismissed it as idle talk, something manufactured by one of Pastor Nick's followers to change the narrative, which made Ifenna think that the pastor was indeed guilty.

"Why does it matter if she had a child. Does that make her claims less legitimate?"

"Are you defending the woman?"

"I am just playing the devil's advocate, just giving this lady the benefit of the doubt. I mean, I'm not saying her accusation is right or wrong. I am just saying that having a child doesn't discredit her. In fact, it should make her claim more serious."

"It should discredit her," Lilian turned her neck slightly to catch Ifenna's face.

"Why?"

"Clearly, she was a spoiled child. Somebody that had a child at eighteen, it says a lot about her. Lack of home training."

"I thought you weren't supposed to judge."

"I'm not. I'm just saying she has an agenda."

"An agenda?"

"Yes. When she was in our church, she wasn't bringing her child. Why? Obviously, she was trying to deceive people. That makes me more convinced she may even be possessed. And because the man of God resisted her back then, she has now come in another form. Then, just to see how useless the story is, she went to find an unknown blog to publish it. People will just be joking with the wrath of God."

Ifenna swallowed hard. He had made elaborate efforts to keep his blogging a secret, but he always worried that someday he would have to come clean and tell her about it. Now, he dreaded that day even more, seeing how she was going to take it. It made him feel a little uneasy as he tugged at her hair.

"Take it easy, love," she squirmed again.

"Sorry," Ifenna said, releasing the attachment.

"When you finish that one," she said, referring to the row of attachment Ifenna was working on, "You can stop. I am tired. Let's relax a bit."

Ifenna nodded though she couldn't see him do so. He tried to steady his fingers as he loosened what was left of that last attachment.

EIGHTEEN

Pastor Nick looked around the table with a satisfied grin. The four men were now discussing and laughing. The only agenda of the day's meeting was finished, and they were now waiting for their drinks to be served. These men were his benefactors, the unseen backbones of Rivers of Joy Church. He always felt like a child in their presence. In the earlier days of their relationship, he would sit by and listen to them talk about their many escapades in business and politics, about their many female conquests without having much to contribute. Now that he could contribute to the discussions, he still often liked to just sit back and listen to them banter, drawing out what wisdom he could from their wry humor. Meeting them had been a miracle, these four billionaires. He liked to think of them as his destiny helpers, a term he often used in his sermons to describe special people God used to fulfill His plans in a subject's life. The existence of the men in his own affairs made him believe the concept more when he preached it. He owed the men a lot, and that afternoon, as he shifted his gaze now from one to the next, he felt particularly grateful that God had blessed him.

The meeting had turned out more successful than he had expected. They rarely met physically. When they did, it was for something that constituted a threat to their collective interests or an issue that required their individual consent for an action to be taken. It was for the latter reason that he had summoned the meeting. His desire for a private jet had been the sole item on the agenda. It was almost December, and he was determined to unveil the jet to his congregation for the New Year. He needed their consent to proceed.

Gathering them together had not been easy. Usually, it took weeks to fix such meetings because of their busy individual schedules. This time, the meeting was delayed for two more weeks because Chief Arisekola Gbadamosi was performing the lesser Hajj in Saudi Arabia. Chief, now in his mid-seventies, was a popular face in most Lagos society magazines. He never missed any party of note in his crisp white agbada and cap that made him a distinct character in pictures. He was a Muslim by convenience, who drank his alcohol and wasn't bothered about the daily prayer times. By his own admission, the only reason he identified with the faith was because it permitted him to marry up to four wives. Otherwise, he was the party-loving, rich Lagosian who lived like there was no tomorrow.

Chief Gbadamosi's only affiliation to Islam was his performance of the lesser Hajj and the dozen rams and a cow he slaughtered during Ileya festivals. Only recently, he took a twenty-five-year-old friend of one of his daughters as a wife. The young lady, in her final year of university, was his current fourth wife, which had caused quite a ripple in social cycles. When, at their last meeting, one of the other men teased him about marrying someone so young, he boasted about his prowess in bed even at his age, which was why the young lady could not refuse him. Then he told them of how he once made love to her on his private jet during a flight to London and exaggerated about how he did it so well that the pilot almost lost control of the plane.

Though the group did not have an official leader, everything gravitated toward Chief since he had a unique way of telling stories that provided entertainment for the whole group. That afternoon, he had entered a bit of an argument with General Bature Gumi on whether the president, who had disappeared for over a month now, could rule from anywhere as his media assistants claimed. Rumors, which often rose above the iron-clad silence of the presidency, suggested that the president was in a hospital in Germany recuperating from a surgery. There was no consensus in the country though. Some said Germany, others said Saudi Arabia. But all seemed to agree he was bedridden. There was a public clamor for the vice president to be made acting president. In response, the president's aides came up with the theory that a president need not be physically present in the country to rule. General Gumi thought the president had done no wrong, and Chief, who barely managed to piece his sentences in English together without infusing a word in Yoruba, was attempting to cite sections of the constitution to the amusement of the others.

General Gumi was a retired army major general and a fine gentleman, in Nick's estimation. He had a way of speaking without raising his voice even when he was passionate about the subject, and he generally did not say a lot. Like the others, he knew how to enjoy his life, but there was a seriousness in him that only the regimented life in the military could have bestowed. Nick liked him because he asked the least questions whenever there was an approval to be given. That afternoon, he was the first person to agree to the request to help Nick obtain the private jet. While the others were still mulling the idea and shuffling through the two pages of documents in front of them, General Gumi had taken out his pen, ready to sign.

It had been a simple pitch. Nick had learned to keep it short and simple with the group. It was the secret to helping them reach a decision fast. Anything bulkier or more complex would have them turning and turning in the widening gyre. Though billionaires, they took a keen interest in where their money went and would not part with a dime if they weren't convinced about its destination. So Nick made sure the paper laid out before them was just two pages. The first page was his business case for wanting a private jet, while the second page bore the specifications of the jet he wanted and the cost.

Senator Enahire, a second republic senator who spent only two months as an elected legislator before the military struck but insisted on *Senator* as a prefix to his name such that it now seemed like it was his first name, was convinced once General Gumi signed. He was the first of the four men whom Nick had met. He had needed a little help and Nick had obliged him. They met at a filling station when Nick got into a confrontation with his police escort at the fuel pump. As usual for big men in the country, Senator was in a hurry and his police detail wanted to displace Nick on the queue so they could be served. The pastor had refused. The police detail threatened to whip him with a horsewhip.

As they argued, someone jumped down from the front of the Senator's Range Rover and approached Nick. The man in the Range Rover wanted to have a word with him. Nick recognized the man immediately as the owner's corner tinted glass window rolled down. The man was dressed in his Benin white attire, complete with coral beads and a haircut that seemed to be from the medieval ages. He was surprisingly apologetic for the action of his security detail and said he was late for an important meeting hence the hurry. It was still the early days of his ministry, and Nick wasn't as stylish as he was now. He used to wear a pastor's collar, which advertised his trade, as he moved around. It was the collar that had aroused the Senator's interest. He handed Nick a business card and asked him to call him.

It was Senator's sixtieth birthday in a few weeks, and he wanted to include in the lavish program a thanksgiving service because that was what big Nigerians did, but he was not exactly a Christian, and the widely held perception that he was a member of the Ogboni Fraternity was making it difficult for him to find a man of God willing to preach at the service. He had wanted one of the big names, but now, with the party close at hand, he was happy to make do with anyone. Nick looked the part, so he made him the offer when they met up in his presidential lodge at the Hilton two days after the filling station incident. He was also willing to pay handsomely. It had been an easy decision for Nick. Preaching at such a high-profile event, which was to be aired live on state television, was the best PR for his church. The money was just an added incentive. He accepted, and at the event, the elated Senator introduced him to the other three men. That was also the day Senator told him he'd make Nick the biggest pastor in this country.

"For me really, the issue is not even whether the president is right or wrong," Sir Augustus Nnamchi, the last of the four, said, interrupting General Gumi and adjusting his big frame on the chair. "The real issue is if the vice president you are all advocating for is ready to lead. The man doesn't inspire any confidence in me. He looks like a boy-boy that will rather quietly enjoy his spot in the shadows of his oga than be thrust into the big stage. The boy everybody is fighting for has not even uttered a word. He's too timid for my liking."

"Forget that timidity o. He is just acting humble. Wait until he gets power, and you will see another side of him," Senator said.

"Not this one," Sir Nnamchi insisted. "I hear all he does is drink akpeteshi and read newspapers in his office. You know he used to be a university lecturer—"

"Polytechnic," Senator interjected.

"Whichever one," Sir Nnamchi continued. "My point is that they should have left the man in the classroom. He is such a misfit. Imagine, since they came to power, he has not as much as granted an interview, and the few times he was given a speech to read on behalf of the president at some obscure function, he behaved like a jittery schoolboy in front of the school assembly. Did you not see the newspaper cartoon of him wetting his pants while being reprimanded by the president's chief of staff?"

The men all laughed. Pastor Nick joined in. Sir Augustus Nnamchi, who was always garbed in his blazers and bow tie, cut the picture of an old university professor — just that his blazers were the most expensive designers. What he lacked in terms of education, he made up for by accumulating honorary doctorate degrees from universities on a cash-and-carry basis. Recently, he acquired one from a university in Andorra.

This meeting was at Chief Gbadamosi's private beach house off the coast of Lagos, one of their secret meeting locations. The first time Nick came there, he was amazed at the luxurious, quiet serenity, how it was like a mini resort tucked away in the middle of the Atlantic. Two ladies walked in carrying two bottles of champagne on ice and five flutes. Nick admired how the men only drank once their meetings finished. Alcohol came in later after serious matters were off the table. The lady with gold hair extensions set the flutes in front of each of the men, and the other lady proceeded to pop both bottles before pouring glassfuls for all of them.

There was some clicking of glasses as the ladies left the room. Nick took a sip. Chief Gbadamosi always had the finest luxury selections. Nick recently saw a report that claimed Nigerians were only second to France in the consumption of champagne globally and thought of Chief Gbadamosi's contributions to the figures in the report.

"So, Pastor," Chief Gbadamosi said after also taking a sip from his glass. "What is this I hear about you and some girl and stories all over the internet?"

Nick coughed into his glass.

"You know I have a young wife," Chief said, as if in response to the questioning glances from everyone in the room. "She is always pressing her phone and looking at things on the internet. She keeps me up to date with the latest gossip. Yesterday she told me about a story of a pastor being accused by some lady of having an affair. I wasn't interested in all the talk, but you know women. I had to feign interest. So I just nodded in response. Then she showed me the picture of the said pastor, and I was like, this is Pastor Nick now. That was when I took the story seriously. I was like, so our pastor friend here also knows how to chop and clean mouth. I thought that was left for sinful men like us."

The other men burst out laughing.

"But Chief, that's not exactly correct," Nick protested.

"Which part?" Sir Nnamchi said, recovering from the laughter. "The chopping or the cleaning of mouth part?"

The question made the men burst out laughing again. Nick knew it was futile trying to deny or argue with them, so he joined in the laughter.

"How do you think they have the most beautiful women as wives, these pastors?" Senator said after he drank. "They are the original bad boys. They hold the playbook for chopping. See all those their worshippers throwing themselves at them for free."

"Ah, Senator. You know there is nothing free when it comes to women," General Gumi tipped his glass.

"I was just going to say that," Sir Nnamchi said. "That's why I wanted to ask Pastor what the problem actually was. Is it that he stopped chopping or that he did not pay adequately for the much he had chopped?"

Pastor Nick shook his head without saying anything. He ground his jaw and tapped his feet impatiently on the wooden tiles. How did this story get to this group? Now, he wondered how many more people had heard of it and how he must now be the topic in many gatherings. He hated to imagine it. Though he had been carrying on like he wasn't fazed by the news since it broke, he had been deeply angered by it and worried that it would dent the image he had worked so hard to cultivate over the years.

"You see? Our good pastor is now speechless," Sir Nnamchi teased.

"It is not like that," Pastor Nick said. "There is nothing true about that story, nothing at all. I don't know this girl and have never had anything to do with her. It's ridiculous how people can just come up with accusations that can ruin a person's reputation."

He had repeated those lines so many times in the last twenty-four hours that he now memorized them somewhat. He's had to lie so many times in his line of work that it was no longer difficult. When the story had first been brought to his attention, he had remembered her–Sister Abi with the well-rounded hips and face that looked carved right out of a fashion magazine. How could he forget her? Her hips were what attracted him to her at first. Then, he discovered how good she was in bed, and he became certain the universe had sanctioned the match. She was just the way he liked them: young, impressionable, and enthusiastic about the church. All he had to do was sweet talk, coerce them into falling in love with him, blurring the lines between being in love with God and being in love with him. That was the sweet spot, when they submitted their soul to him, and he became both their pastor and their God. With Sister Abi, it had been quite a feisty ride. Recalling some of their escapades gave him a hard-on even amid the scandal trending online. At the time, she was his steadiest girl of the lot. Then, like the lot of them, she started to suddenly misbehave, and he had to discard her quickly like a used rag.

"But the story said she was your former church member," Chief Gbadamosi said.

"Maybe she was. Maybe not. I can't say. I pastor a large

church, as you all know. I can't know every member."

"That's true." Senator nodded his agreement. "I wonder how you even manage to control traffic there on Sundays."

"So you really don't know this lady?" General Gumi asked.

"No."

Silence settled over the room for a few minutes before Chief Gbadamosi spoke. "These kinds of things generate unnecessary negative attention, and we don't want it. You know that, Pastor. I ask that you take care of it quickly. Whatever it is. Whether you know the girl, or if it's someone paying her to pour dust on you, you must end it quickly. Make it disappear. We don't want such negative attention, especially from the media. There is too much at stake here, and we cannot allow unfortunate people come and spoil things for us."

"No need to worry, Chief," Nick said, shifting to the edge of his chair to give his words a more serious edge. "My people are already on it. As we speak, they're clearing out whatever is left of the story online."

Chief Gbadamosi nodded slowly, as though he was struggling to believe Nick's assurance.

"We addressed the matter squarely and promptly," Nick added, seeing that his benefactors needed more reassurance. "If the woman wasn't making the allegations all the way from the safety of Canada, I would have pressed defamation charges."

There was another lull. Chief Gbadamosi emptied his glass and set it on the table gently.

"You should still report it to the police," General Gumi said. "They can push it to Interpol and smoke her out wherever she is. If you need help, you know what to do."

Nick nodded. Someone else had suggested that, but he'd waved it away, saying it was too much unnecessary trouble that would just give the story more attention.

"And the website that published it?" Chief Gbadamosi added. "Do you know who is behind it? My wife said they specialize in stories around men of God. You need to keep an eye on them."

Nick wondered why he had not thought of that. He nodded, a knowing smile playing on his lips, grateful for the idea that crept into his mind. Later, on the boat ride back to the jetty in Victoria Island, he called Bimbo and demanded that she find out who was behind the blog. The prospects of unmasking those trying to bring him down made him smile again as the boat tore through the water, leaving a million bubbles behind.

NINETEEN

Pastor Nkechi shifted her weight from her left leg to the right and then back to her left leg. Wearing high heels that morning was a wrong move. The discomfort was drowned by the excitement seeping in. She stole a quick glance at her watch and wondered how much longer she had to be there; she was eager to get to her office upstairs at Heaven's Gate Cathedral and to her laptop. A woman with a baby strapped to her back, the next on the long widening queue, walked up to the slightly raised platform on which she and her husband were standing. Pastor Jedidiah, one of her husband's assistants moderating the session, announced the woman's name before handing Nkechi an envelope and a piece of Ankara material to her husband. The envelope was puffy. It contained fifty thousand naira in cash. Usually, the church workers preferred the lower denominations. The envelopes looked better that way in pictures. Nkechi and her husband jointly handed over the items to the woman who genuflected in front of them before extending her hands, her lips spread in deep appreciation. The camera clicked twice. Nkechi flashed her practiced smile, and the elated woman left to make room for the next person on the queue.

They were at a charity program for widows, hurriedly put together by the church, part of the elaborate response to the accusation against Nick, something to keep the media mentions positive. The event hadn't even been on the church's calendar. The only charity event they held was the annual Christmas Heart of Love Party, during which the church hosted and gave out gifts to persons earlier identified and profiled by the Care for Humanity Unit as needy. Usually, Nkechi and her husband made elaborate efforts to come dressed to the event as some show of solidarity with the audience and took turns to ladle steaming jollof rice out of a clay pot into the plates of the beneficiaries, lined up like inmates in a refugee camp with plates in hand.

Someone, Nkechi suspected Bimbo, had thought up the idea of picking out a subset of the group they hosted at the annual party—widows—and quickly putting together an event just for them. It would help showcase Nick as a man concerned with touching lives, especially those of underprivileged women. His wife by his side, smiling at the camera, emphasized his humanity. None of this was lost on Nkechi. She knew the script.

The next woman in the queue was quite the drama queen, certainly above fifty in Nkechi's estimation, the way her hair looked more white than black and her hands like something out in the sun to dry. The blouse she wore was well-worn, made from Ankara and a wrapper that had the face of the opposition party candidate at the last governorship election. After she received the gifts from Nkechi and Nick, she took time to dance, standing on tiptoes and gliding to an inaudible rhythm. Then, without prompting, she gathered both Nkechi and Nick into a hug while shouting her thanks in what sounded to Nkechi like Yoruba. As the woman pressed her body against theirs, Nkechi thought she smelled like beef retrieved from the freezer after days of a power outage. It was suffocating. But what nauseated her more was her body touching Nick's. While the hug lasted, the audience of church workers and journalists clapped and cheered. Nkechi looked in their direction and her eyes settled on Bimbo, who stood there like the director of a movie production. That this woman was acting for the cameras would normally have irritated Nkechi, but there seemed an unusual peace inside her that morning, a certain feeling of having it all figured out. She smiled and joined in the clapping as the woman pulled out of the hug and screamed, 'Praise the Lord!'

For the first time in a long time, Nkechi felt she had the power to decide her fate, and it came with a thrill that rattled her bones.

"Hallelujah!" she called in response.

Last night, she had met with Agent X. Meetings with the private detective were always guaranteed to leave her either infuriated or depressed, but she was unprepared for what she found out this time. Agent X had given her the identity of the blogger. The name had sounded familiar, and while she tried to remember where she came across it in the past, Agent X told her that the blogger used to write for *The Nigerian,* and it had clicked immediately. She knew she wouldn't be able to sleep that night without sending him a message, but when she got home, she found that she had left her laptop at her office in the cathedral. The discovery, which she made just after kicking off her shoes and heading to the table that served as her study in her room and finding it bare, had left a feeling of a hydrant of peppery juice being pumped into the left of her chest. She felt like pulling at her own hair in frustration, but just as she was settling to the prospects of crying herself to sleep, as she did on many nights since she moved out of the master bedroom, her phone rang. It was the last person in the world who she expected–her mother.

Her first feeling had been apprehension as she picked the phone. Adrenaline pumped into her veins, diluting the peppery juice and leaving a numbness that spread through her entire body. As she pressed the phone against her ear, fear took over, and she half-expected to hear the voice of her brother, Ike, saying something had happened to Mama. When the voice came through, it really was her mother's, low-pitched but piercing as usual. The relief came in the form of a cold chill.

"Nke'm," Her mother called her pet name. "Kedu? How are you?"

Her mother spoke in Igbo, in a tone of someone who really wanted to know how she was doing. It was as though everything was good between them, like those lines erased all the issues that had happened between them. Nkechi swallowed hard before responding that she was fine. Her mother said she saw her in her dream a night before, looking troubled, sobbing, and walking naked on the street to jeers from the crowd, her wrists chained. Then, in another part of the dream, she had seen her daughter's hands freed, dressed in beautiful attire and laughing hysterically alone. The dream had left Mama Nkechi worried because she did not dream often and could easily make sense of it when she did. But this one had left her confused, and she decided to call and check up on her daughter.

Nkechi was grateful her mother had obviously not heard of the accusation against her husband. That had been one of the many thoughts that crept into her head initially when her mother started to speak, that perhaps the news had filtered to her in Enugu, and she was calling to have her "I told you so" victory lap. Nkechi worried not so much about her mother finding out, but for all the ridicule the families in her old neighborhood would give. She could imagine the women coming to visit her mother to feign sympathy while laughing at her behind her back. They would say something like: "She thought she was better than all of us just because her daughter didn't get pregnant in boarding house and passed JAMB in one sitting. Look now, see the disgrace she has become."

Nkechi quickly reiterated that she was okay, that all was well with her life. She spoke slowly in Igbo to inspire confidence, ensuring her mother that her dream was just a dream.

"I will light a votive candle for you in the church tomorrow," her mother said in English, clearly not fully reassured but not willing to draw it out longer. "Whatever is the matter, you will find a solution for it."

The call was short, with an awkwardness akin to divorced couples meeting themselves by accident in an elevator. But hearing her mother's voice had felt like a soothing balm to her heart. Nkechi fell asleep immediately after as though an orchestra of invisible mouths had sung her a lullaby. Her mother's promise of lighting her a votive candle brought a reassurance borne on memories. Growing up, her mother was a devout member of Saint Jude's society. Usually, whenever she had any difficult issues, she lit a candle at the altar of the saint in their local parish and knelt to pray. Though she had come to disagree with the idea of lighting candles in front of wooden images of long dead men to pray, Nkechi knew that Saint Jude, following her mother's prayers, would come to her aid, as she once believed as a teenager.

That night in Nkechi's dream, she was on a beautiful island. Flower petals heaved a pleasant scent that filled her mind with joy, like she was ascending into another realm. Birds sang in a language she strangely could understand. They invited her to dance, and butterflies fluttered about her head as she walked through the rows of dwarf flower stems, their wings painting the scenery in patches of beautiful harmony. As she walked through the plantation, revering in its ambiance and peace, she noticed a dwarf tower at the center. It seemed out of place, standing there like a shriveled old lady, with its medieval architecture, the type that immediately suggested something sinister in horror movies. She stood at the foot of the tower and looked up. Then she was at the top, overlooking a large pool of water. The flower plantation was gone now, leaving just an endless body of water that stretched infinitely into the distance. A being with a halo glided on the water, smiling at her, beckoning for her to jump. Nkechi hesitated. It seemed like a very long jump, like the tower was getting taller by the minute. Plus, she couldn't swim, so she shook her head. A slight wind blew, and the tower creaked at the foundation. The haloed face beckoned again. There was urgency in the way she signaled with her hands. The wind got heavier. The tower wobbled, creaked. Nkechi decided she would take her chances. Just as she was about to leap, she woke.

THE NEXT WOMAN ON THE queue had her hair covered in a hijab, which extended down to her waist. Her hands, the exposed bit, was marked in henna patterns.

Nick leaned close and whispered. "This one must be a Muslim."

Nkechi made a sound in her throat and smiled as she handed the envelope to the woman who wore a perfume that reminded Nkechi of mosquito coil, the one with a big African cock on the packet. Her mother used to burn one in their house every night.

"I wanted to discuss something with you last night, but you didn't answer when I knocked," Nick whispered as the woman began to walk away. "Did you fall asleep early?"

"Yes, I did. Is anything the matter?" Nkechi didn't look at him.

"No, nothing. But I shouldn't have a reason to check on my wife."

Nkechi chewed her lip and shook her head. Pastor Jedidiah called up the next recipient and announced that she would, in addition to the monetary envelope, receive free medical treatment for her leg. She had been in an okada accident and limped as she walked. She had been helped up the stage by one of the church workers. Nkechi said a few words, expressing her sympathy to the woman as the cameras clicked away. Nick bent down with his hands on the affected leg and mumbled a brief prayer. As the woman hobbled away, Nkechi stole another look at her watch.

"Going somewhere?" Nick whispered again, standing close to her, their arms touching.

"This charade is taking longer than I envisaged," she said, still not looking at him.

"Charade?"

"You think I don't understand what's going on here?"

Nick did not respond. The next widow knelt before them in appreciation after receiving the gifts. Nkechi held her by her shoulders to raise her to her feet as the audience cheered.

"We need to talk," Nick said, as the woman made declarations in Pidgin English, inviting the heavens to protect the pastor and his wife for the love they were showing the poor.

"About what?" Nkechi snapped. She wasn't interested in making conversation, in feeding into her husband's narrative.

"The church."

"What about it?"

"I was going to tell you last night that we're getting a jet."

Nkechi looked at her husband for the first time that morning. She saw a total stranger, and she wondered why she had not seen this person the first time he said hello to her many years ago. He repeatedly nodded as if in answer to the question her eyes asked, a smile playing at the corner of her lips.

"Congratulations," she finally said.

"It will arrive just before New Year." He smiled with pride as he spoke. "We shall dedicate it at the crossover service."

"Good." Nkechi turned her attention back to the crowd.

"Our God has been faithful," Nick said.

"Very," she muttered, gritting her teeth.

"A special round of applause for our Mama as she takes

her seat," Pastor Jedidiah announced, signaling the end of the presentation session as the last woman danced away with her gift.

"Just a quick announcement: all the beneficiaries will have a group photo with our Mama and Daddy immediately after the benediction. But before that, let me now invite our daddy, the happening pastor, the caring pastor, the blessed shepherd of God's flock, my father in the Lord, Pastor Nicholas Adejuwon, to bless us with a few words before we close."

AS NKECHI LOWERED HERSELF ONTO her chair, grateful to rest her feet, she thought of the lines she had pre-composed in the message she would send to Ifenna Obumselu, the blogger. She had thought her plans through, sitting up in bed after waking from her dream the night before. It was like those days in secondary school when she wrote James Bond-inspired stories on her bunk after lights out, setting up characters to do her bidding in well-thought-out but overly complex plots. She had stayed up until the lone cock in their estate crowed. Her fears were gone now. Thinking of her plan, as her husband mounted the lectern, filled her with such excitement that she jumped up to scream, "Hallelujah!" in response to her husband's "Praise the Lord!"

TWENTY

Pastor Nick was surprised to find that the meeting had not yet started. He had intentionally set out late. His plan was to slip in quietly and sit at the back. And when it was done and the chit chats started, he would stay long enough to establish that he came and then be the first out of the door. Had he not given Pastor Wale his word that he would be there, he wouldn't have attended. He considered many of the attendees his detractors, and even though the ruckus generated by the blog post had simmered, he didn't want it coming up in any conversation in his presence.

He took off his shades and scanned the room, blinking as his eyes adjusted to the brightness. The room seemed full enough. He recognized many of the attendees, standing in groups, exchanging pleasantries, and chatting. You would think it was a meeting of some social club with deep camaraderie. Nick considered it all fake since he knew the competition among them. Some of the strongest attacks against him had come from the people in this room, these people who were supposed to be his brothers in the Lord.

It was a meeting of the Lagos Chapter of the Pentecostal

Fellowship of Nigeria (PFN). PFN was one of the five blocs within the Christian Association of Nigeria (CAN). The CAN elections were coming soon, and the leadership currently held by the Christian Council of Nigeria bloc was rotating to the PFN for the first time since the creation of the association in 1976. Pastor Wale Ayo-Martins of the Voices of Paradise Church, one of the three contenders, was coming to address them at the meeting to express his agenda and garner their support.

Nick had pitched his tent with Pastor Wale when he'd come to visit him at the cathedral a few weeks back. That Pastor Wale, his senior in the ministry, had deemed it fit to come and see him to solicit his support was all that was needed to convince him. Nick saw it as a great honor and an acknowledgment of his profile within the ranks of young pastors, something he did not often get from the other pastors whom he felt derided him out of envy. The meeting with Pastor Wale had also sown a new idea in his mind. He never gave holding leadership positions a thought, but after coming to appreciate the powers and privileges that came with it, he decided he was going to contest for the leadership of the Lagos State Chapter of CAN when the post became vacant in six months' time. He had entered an agreement with Pastor Wale. A quid pro quo of sorts that guaranteed him Pastor Wale's support when it was time for his own election.

The meeting today was held in the conference room of the PFN secretariat. Nick had ever only been there twice. The first was when Rivers of Joy Church became a member. The leadership at the time said it wasn't enough to pay the registration fees and fill out the forms; they insisted that he must appear in person to be registered and welcomed. The other time he'd come was for the meeting just before the commissioning of his cathedral. He could have sent the invitation card to the Public Relations Officer or sent one of his assistant pastors as was the norm, but he decided to go himself to make a good impression. He'd used the opportunity to gloat about the size of his church and the great works God had been conducting through him. No PFN executive attended the commissioning, and Nick concluded it was because of pure envy.

Now, he spotted Pastor Bidemi of Living Spring Church—Peju's husband—in a corner, discussing with someone he didn't recognize. Nick walked toward them, shaking a few hands, smiling, and nodding in acknowledgment of greetings as he crossed the room. Bidemi was one of the few pastors he was friends with, in whose church he had preached and vice versa. Bidemi introduced Pastor Ezekiel, the person he was chatting with. Pastor Ezekiel said Nick needed no introduction as he took his hands in both of his. Nick flushed with pleasure. Of course, everyone knew him. The trio talked for a bit about the earthquake in Haiti, the introduction of Sharia by the Zamfara State governor, and the threat by the Lagos State governor to ban external speakers in places of worship due to noise pollution. Soon, Pastor Ezekiel moved on to say hello to others, and it was just Nick and Bidemi.

"I read in the papers about the stuff you did for widows," Bidemi said. "I thought you held your charity events in December."

"We decided to do something spontaneous," Nick lied. Then, deciding he could trust Bidemi, he added, "We needed to do something. I'm sure you heard about the blog post."

"Yeah, Peju mentioned it. Something about some lady accusing you of something. I can't recall very much of it. You know me. I'm not so hands-on with all this internet stuff. It is Peju who lives on it."

"Some lady from nowhere sold a story to some blog that we were having an affair." Nick took a deep breath and sucked his teeth.

"No way." Bidemi's eyes widened.

"I'm telling you the truth."

"I bind and cast any jezebel spirit," Bidemi said, snapping his finger and shaking his head from side to side. "Do you know this woman?"

"No, but my people say she used to be in the church." Nick spread out his two palms in from of him to demonstrate his innocence.

"Used to?"

"I'm told she stopped coming a long time ago."

"And this accusation came from nowhere? This is very troubling. What is this world turning into?" Bidemi glanced across the room at some new arrivals who were loud with their greetings.

"You can say that again. When the Bible says we battle not against flesh and blood, this is what it was talking about."

"You need to have her arrested and charged. You shouldn't let this slide." Bidemi had a frank look on his face. "Some people need to be taught lessons."

"I would like to, trust me. But you see, the witch made the accusation from Canada, where I understand she now lives. You see that? That is why I am certain she is being used by some forces against me. Maybe even someone inside this gathering."

Bidemi looked around the room as if scouting for those Nick referred to. He was going to say something but was interrupted by Reverend Clinton Madu, a lanky man who sported jerry curls and looked like a young Kenny G. He approached them with a wry smile on his face, shaking their hands in tow and murmuring his salutation before walking on.

"Has he finally managed to roof his church?" Pastor Nick asked with a nod at the retreating figure of Reverend Madu.

"For where?" Bidemi said dismissively. "That structure has remained like that for five years now."

Nick laughed. "To think he started way before we laid the foundation for Heaven's Gate Cathedral."

"Whatever made him think he would come here and run a ministry? How many Yoruba people go and start churches in Onitsha or Owerri?"

"Will they even give you land?"

"Oho. Ask me o. It's just in this Lagos that we will be doing home for all. Sotey, they now want to come and chase us out of our own land. Do you know in his church only Igbos are among his senior pastors and heads of units?"

"Same thing his master is now doing. Birds of a feather if you ask me."

Reverend Madu used to be the pastor in charge of one of the big branches of Bishop Makinde's church in Ikeja and one of the highfliers in the ministry before he broke away and took along with him much of the congregation to start his own church. He and the bishop had disagreed over his decision to take a new wife, several years after divorcing his first. Bishop Makinde had insisted that as long as his wife was still alive, the second marriage would not be sanctioned by the church, and since Pastor Madu did not agree, he went off to start his own church; then, he flew in a popular pastor from the United States to wed him and his new wife. The issue had caused quite a controversy in the Pentecostal circles, with pastors taking different sides. There had also been a court case instituted by the bishop, claiming Pastor Madu converted church property to his new church. It had dragged on for many years before the leadership of the PFN managed to get them to settle.

"You mean Bishop Em?"

Nick nodded. "I hear now it's not even about being Yoruba. If you are not Ijebu, you can't pastor any juicy parish."

"Well, I guess he can do what he likes in his church."

"I was going to ask you," Nick suddenly remembered, "do you preach first fruit in your church as in Leviticus 23:10?"

"Sure. You don't?"

"Not really. I've never really made it a big deal, but I want to now. Some of my pastors have been harping on it."

"I didn't really put much emphasis on it until this year. I wasn't sure how the congregation would respond. You know how difficult January usually is. I was shocked at the response. So next year, we are going all out. I have already concluded with my people. In January, the only testimonies we will entertain during service will be by people who did first fruit offering this year. If no one comes up, we will arrange for--"

Laughter from a group close to the front of the room

interrupted their discussion. Nick could make out Pastor Wale in the circle, but the loud chuckle had been from the Lagos PFN president. Unlike the rest in suits and collars, he wore a white flowing lace agbada complete with a skull cap, like a Catholic bishop. He was popular for his love for jewelry, and he always had a golden crucifix dangling from a golden chain to his chest, which garnered his nickname of Pastor Blings.

"Why's he laughing like a hyena?" Bidemi raised an eyebrow.

"The guy irritates me," said Nick.

"I hear he is talking of buying another private jet," Bidemi dropped his voice to a whisper. "I keep wondering why he thinks he's so special."

"Aggressive marketing. That's all," Nick said. "I've studied him. He fights dirty. He also knows how to squeeze money out of his congregation. I must admit I admire that part of him. The guy comes up with some crazy stuff. I first learned from him to tell people that if they don't pay their tithes, they're basically stealing from God. Fantastic theology. It works like magic. Recently, I heard he encourages singles in his church to start tithing on behalf of their future spouses that they don't yet know. That's just all shades of smart, but I still can't stand him."

"And he's spreading outlets like they're going out of fashion," Bidemi said, folding his hands across his chest. He was wearing a striped jacket over a white shirt and a priest's collar. A Living Spring brooch was pinned to the left flap of the jacket.

"He has brought the fight to my doorsteps in Apapa. He started a branch, two streets away from my church. You need to see how they are going about it. Every billboard space available is his face. Banners and posters everywhere. Last week they did free medical outreach. As I was coming here this morning, I saw another advertisement saying worshippers will have a chance to win a trip to Dubai for two this Sunday."

"That's the aggressive marketing I was talking about," Nick said, a little absent-mindedly as he retrieved his phone from his jacket and stared at the screen.

Bimbo had messaged him to confirm she'd got him an interview with a journalist from NBC's *The Voice* who was reporting on the spread of Pentecostalism in Africa.

"Come on! Ticket to Dubai? Is that not taking it too far?" Bidemi frowned.

"Forget about whether he's doing bad or good. What you need is a counter-strategy to keep your own members from leaving in droves to him. Can't you see that is what he's trying to do?" Nick returned the phone into his pocket. "The best form of defense is attack. Find something he does and condemn it in your sermon on Sunday. Demonize his actions without mentioning his name. Find passages in the scripture to back your point. You must energize your base. You must keep your flock at all costs."

"Brilliant idea."

"Like that thing he does where he blesses handkerchiefs. He says the fabric can work miracles, so his people pay money to get and keep it in their houses. Is that not idolatry?"

Someone tapped the microphone twice. Pastor Blings stood on the raised platform at the front of the room as he invited everyone to take their seats so that the meeting could start.

"Are you with Pastor Wale?" Nick asked as they headed to their seats at the back of the hall.

"With him, how?" Bidemi asked.

"Supporting him for the election."

"I want to hear all three of them before I make up my mind."

"Me too," said Nick. Because of his own ambition, he had decided to be discreet about his support for Pastor Wale.

"Not particularly excited by all of them, I must say," Bidemi added. "They're all old men. We need to get them off the scene and inject fresh blood. We need people who have fire, who can fight for the body of Christ in Abuja."

Bidemi pulled out one of the white plastic chairs and sat down. Nick took the one to his left.

"You heard about the new directive by the NBC not to broadcast miracles on TV, right?" Bidemi faced Nick, who nodded. "Things like that are what we need to fight. It is a matter that affects us directly, and I am not sure these older pastors get it."

Nick nodded slowly as if just coming to the realization of Bidemi's point.

Pastor Blings's voice over the microphone invited everyone to stand for the opening prayer. Chairs scratched the marble floor as the crowd rose.

"Why aren't you running?" Bidemi asked.

"Me?"

"Yes. We'd support you. We the younger pastors."

"It's too late now."

"Late? Nothing is too late. It's about who has the money to spend. Most of these pastors here will jump on any ship if they get the right inducement."

Nick wanted to respond, but the opening prayer began. As he closed his eyes, he churned the idea of contesting in his mind and thought of just how fitting it sounded that the pastor of the largest church was also the leader of all Christians in Nigeria, the most populous Black nation in the world. The thought made him smile. He decided it was not a bad idea after all.

TWENTY-ONE

"Go jor, smile," Lilian pleaded, staring at herself and Ifenna in the front camera of her phone.

Ifenna made a face and stuck out his tongue just before she clicked. They were on the couch in his living room, and she was sitting on his lap, still in her white nurses' uniform. She had just unboxed her new phone.

"Just look at you!" Lilian laughed at the image. "You look like those mascots at a children's party. Look at your nose."

"Oya, take another one." Ifenna made a serious expression.

When she rolled her eyes, Ifenna relaxed his face and smiled. Lilian clicked many shots of them. Then he placed his lips on her cheeks as though to give her a peck, and she took some more.

"Aww, we're adorable," Lilian said, looking through the images. "Now, I can also take selfies." Lilian clicked as she pouted toward the camera.

"What's that?"

"What is what?"

"You said selfie."

"That's what they call pictures of yourself."

"That's the meaning? I have been seeing it all over. I wasn't sure what it meant," Ifenna admitted.

"That's why I bought this phone. If you aren't using a phone that can take selfies, it's like having no phone at all. I had to just close my eyes and bite the bullet."

"But mehn, the money you can buy a piece of land in this Lagos," Ifenna said, aware that she had used almost her entire salary to buy the phone.

"Land ke?" Lilian laughed. "Maybe in Sangotedo or *inside inside* Ikorodu. That's where you will find land at that rate. That's not the kind of place I am going to buy land o. For what? Has land finished in Lekki? See, my pastor says you must think it to be it. You can't be thinking small. That is why I was like, damn it, I am buying the phone. If you are a child of God, you must be able to speak into existence whatever you desire."

Ifenna, who had been concealing his disgust since she came home with the phone, wanted to argue that none of what she was saying made sense, that buying such an expensive object wasn't wise but decided it wasn't worth it. She was excited, and he didn't want to spoil the mood. So, instead, he reached for her breasts from behind, rested his jaw on her shoulder, and told her to snap another picture. She turned her head toward his, and they kissed. As he squeezed her breasts gently, she lowered the phone to the floor and shifted slightly, throwing both hands behind his neck and responding to his deep kisses.

"You are so amazing," Lilian said when they ran out of breath and pulled apart, her hands still around his neck. "You just get me. I don't know how you do it, but it's like you flick me on like a switch and when you touch me, my whole body just starts misbehaving. I never imagined I could feel this way for any man again. I am so glad I met you."

Ifenna kissed her in reply.

"I just hope you will never change," Lilian said. "I just hope we will always be like this."

"Why wouldn't we be?"

"I don't know." Lilian pulled away. Concern flickered in her eyes. "I guess I am afraid of the unknown, of being without you. Honestly, I cannot handle a break-up. Don't mess this up for us."

Ifenna pulled her closer. "I am ready to swear our love by the goddess of your village.

"I am serious, jor," she said, slapping him lightly on the shoulder.

"I know," Ifenna said in a lower tone. "You are the best thing that has ever happened to me, and I will not trade you for anything. I love you with everything in me, and I know I cannot love any other woman like I love you. Lily, I am fucking crazy about you. Do you know how my heart beats when I set eyes on you? This is not a mistake, my love. It is for real, you and me together. Even the devil cannot try to separate us. I am yours forever."

Lilian stared into his eyes for a while longer as if trying to confirm that he was sincere before leaning into him for a tight hug. It lasted several minutes, and Ifenna felt like she melted into him and sealed her heart inside of his. It was the moment he truly knew he had unlocked the last bar of resistance. She was no longer holding anything back.

"Speaking of which," Lilian said, getting up to go throw

the phone package into the waste bin in the kitchen. "I heard gist. This guy upstairs." She pointed to the ceiling.

"You mean Tunde?"

"I don't really know his name sef," Lilian said as she walked back and sat beside Ifenna on the couch. "But I heard about him and his wife--"

"What about them?"

"About their separation."

"Are you serious?"

"I heard it this morning. My neighbor downstairs told me. We entered the same bus to work. He explained that the woman packed her things and left o, on top of the fact that their child just died."

"You know I told you he came here one night? He looked so troubled. He told me his wife's mother was threatening to take her away. I didn't know it finally happened."

"But what was the matter really?"

"They blamed him for the baby's death."

"How? No be sick the child sick again?"

"Well, no be like that. Disagreements over church entered the whole thing, so it was a bit more complicated."

Lilian tilted her head. "That's what scares me about marriages. All these break-ups. See, eh, I can't even tolerate break-up when I'm dating someone, let alone married. Honestly, I wonder how all these women who have had several marriages handle it."

"Eh … shebi you are Kim's fan. Ask her now," Ifenna teased.

Lilian laughed. "That one? I am hearing that she wants to marry Kanye o."

"Which Kanye?"

"Are there two Kanyes?"

Ifenna was genuinely surprised. "I thought they were just doing the best friends thing."

"No be only best friend. They've been shagging."

Ifenna whistled.

"I am happy for them," Lilian said. "I hope this one lasts for her. People will be shocked when it does."

"And this will make it number what? Four?"

"No, three."

"It is the fourth one, I'm sure."

"You like to argue, don't you?"

"Oya let's bet," Ifenna said.

Lilian sprang to her feet. "Let's just check online."

She started walking to the table. It suddenly dawned on Ifenna that she was going to his laptop. His immediate instinct was to stop her. He began to get up and then decided it was futile. He sat back gently, aware that something unpleasant was about to happen. Later, he would blame himself for not stopping her. He would think then how he could easily have lied that the laptop was dead or that his internet plan was exhausted.

"I've never used your laptop. Is there a password?" Lilian asked, lifting the lid. "There is this vacancy my colleague mentioned that I even want to check out sef"

"No. No password"

Ifenna couldn't see his laptop screen, only Lilian's face. His heart pounded as she ran her finger on the touchpad to take it out of sleep mood. He saw the look of surprise on her face as the screen came alive.

"You've been reading the rubbish blog that published nonsense about my--"

268

Her words trailed off. Ifenna saw her eyes twitch, and he guessed that was the moment she realized he had not been just reading the blog. Shock flashed across her face, quickly replaced by confusion and then disbelief as she scrolled. She turned slowly toward him. You could hear a pin drop. He moved his eyes to the floor so he wouldn't have to meet her gaze and waited for the worst. She said nothing. When it became clear that the outburst he envisioned was not coming, he lifted his head. She stood there speechless, staring at him.

Since he started the blog, he had managed to keep it away from her, doing serious work only when she was out and waking up while she was asleep to moderate comments. Whenever she saw or came home to him at his laptop or stirred to find he had left the bed, he claimed he was writing some news story for *The Nigerian.* She never really came to the laptop to see, perhaps because she hadn't suspected anything. And she had no reason to. Initially, he'd had no real reason for keeping the blog a secret, except that he'd been lying to her about still working for a newspaper. He hadn't wanted to admit he was just a blogger who lived off kabu kabu. Over and over, he'd postponed telling her the truth. It became even more difficult when he found out about her commitment to her church. He did not want to offend her beliefs by telling her he ran a blog whose only aim was to ridicule the pastors and practices she held in high esteem. He also did not want her opinion of his blog to affect his work.

"Can you tell me exactly what is happening here?" She spoke in an even tone.

Ifenna took one unsure step toward her. "I was going

to tell you—"

"Tell me what? That you are…my goodness! That you're the one who…? What am I even saying? I don't even know who you are. Who are you? What else have you been hiding? What else do I not know? Is Ifenna even your name, or are you lying about that too?"

"Come on, don't be ridiculous." Ifenna regretted the words as soon as they left his lips.

"Oh! Now I'm the ridiculous one?" Her voice was raised, and her eyes narrowed to gather her brows above her nose ridge. Ifenna thought she looked different, the way her lower jaw seemed shrunken and her lips tightened. It was the first time he had ever seen her this way.

"I don't mean it like that," Ifenna said. "Of course, my name is my name. Please, calm down, Lily. I was going to let you know, but--"

"But what? A dog stole your tongue, eh? You decided I wasn't worthy of knowing what my boyfriend does, and we say we are in a relationship? Taking me to see your mother, making it seem like I was the one slowing things down when you are hiding things about yourself right under my nose. We live in this same house for fuck's sake, Ifenna."

Ifenna wanted to respond, but he contemplated his words and decided the verbal exchange wouldn't help. He decided instead to walk up to her, to gather her into his arms, and calm her down. As he reached out, she stepped away. Ifenna backed off and tried talking to her, but even as he opened his mouth, it was obvious she wasn't going to listen. She left his apartment that night, slamming the door behind her so strongly that his wall clock fell off the nail, and the glass cover broke into many pieces.

What Ifenna found most frustrating was that she didn't say anything to him as he spat out his explanations, clearing up all the things he had kept from her, including that he had lost his job at *The Nigerian* before they started dating. It seemed like his honesty, instead of winning him some mercy, made things worse for him. The more he revealed, the more the stomping of her feet increased in frequency until she suddenly lurched forward, pushed him aside, picked her handbag from the side stool, and reached for the door. There was a note of finality in the way she banged the door that scared him. The next day, he would come home from his morning kabu kabu round and find all her things in his apartment gone. He'd also discover a note telling him his spare key was under the mat in front of his apartment door.

AFTER HE CLEANED UP THE glass pieces from the broken clock and emptied them into the waste bin, Ifenna sat on the couch and argued with himself whether to call her or not. Though it had been only a few minutes since she left, he already felt lonely, as if a piece of him was excised from his body, leaving the rest of him completely numb. He knew the feeling. He had felt it before.

His first relationship had ended in a severe heartbreak that made him declare he would never have anything to do with a woman again. He had been sixteen in secondary school. The girl, Tomiwa, who was also his classmate, was a year younger. Ifenna had had a strong crush on her; she was the first person he loved. She wasn't one of the girls all the other boys wanted because she was quiet, part of the student's fellowship, and her breasts were barely the size of tangerines. But he liked her so much because when she smiled at him, his body tingled with warmth.

They'd sat next to each other in class. During prep, they talked by passing notes back and forth. He scribbled his best efforts at poetry, and she responded with sketched smiley faces and X and Os, which he would later learn meant hugs and kisses. Ifenna was convinced they were an item and that he would marry her someday and raise a family with her. He would lie in bed at night and imagine them together in each other's arms until he slept off, sometimes soiling his boxers with his excitement by morning. Once, he copied the entire lines of Michael Jackson's "Speechless" and sent it to her in a note, and she responded with the mark of her lips painted in bright red lipstick on a blank sheet of paper. Ifenna had kept that paper like a trophy.

Then, their school hosted an inter-house sports competition. All the boys got to hang out with the girls they fancied because the teachers were too busy supervising the additional students. Ifenna had looked forward to the time he would spend alone with Tomiwa. He imagined getting his first kiss that day. It made him nervous to even think of it, but most of the other boys said she wasn't really his girl if he had not kissed her or caressed her breasts. They said she would even be disappointed if he didn't make a move. On the competition day, she was nowhere to be found. It was as if she fell ill or left school unexpectedly. Finally, someone told him he saw her with a boy around the senior classroom blocks, and Ifenna headed there immediately. The information that she was with a guy had been discomforting, and he had been certain the person was mistaken. When he reached the blocks, sweaty and covered in a film of dust from running, he found them holding hands and whispering to each other. His legs seemed planted to the spot as he watched them from a distance, too shocked to move. The boy, from his uniform, was from the all-boys college in another part of town. Ifenna was even more shocked that his good girl, Tomiwa, could be with such a guy, and it worried him that he stood no chance against him.

When he confronted her later in the evening, he hoped she would react in shock and start offering explanations, but she had replied casually that he was her boyfriend, as if she had been waiting for an opportunity to give out that information. And without waiting for a reaction from him, she shuffled away to join her friends. Ifenna had stood there petrified, and as he watched her walk away, he decided to never love another woman.

Now, Ifenna felt the same way. Lilian's absence made him feel little, like an invisible dot on a page. It was only a misunderstanding, he thought, and she was angry as anyone would be. By the next day, things would change. She would see that he did not mean to hide anything from her, and she would come back to his apartment, still angry but willing to let him explain.

To shut out the crippling feeling of guilt and self-pity that lurked in the back of his mind, he stood up and went to his laptop. He had been in the middle of composing a new post when he heard Lilian's keys turning in the keyhole, and he had just brought down the lid. The story was about an Imam who was caught raping a twelve-year-old girl inside the mosque. Someone had sent a video to Ifenna of the mob dragging the man, long beards and all, naked to his boxers, along a dirty road, while they sang and jeered at him. Ifenna had thought hard about posting it all day. Until then, he had only blogged about Christian men of God, but now he realized that men of God were men of God no matter what their religion.

The story reminded him of similar cases he covered as a metro reporter for *The Nigerian*. They nauseated him, those stories of adults behaving badly, taking advantage of minors. Once, he reported a case of a man who had been raping his own daughter since she was ten. It was quite shocking to the people in the community because the man was a known preacher who led the call for prayers at dawn and hosted well-attended Tafsir sessions during Ramadan. People in his community went to him to settle domestic quarrels instead of going to the police.

The day Ifenna first saw him at the Oshodi Magistrate Court, where the case was being heard, he'd looked meek in his skull cap and trouser that stopped midway between his knee and his ankle. The case had come to the forefront because after several pregnancies and abortions with his first daughter, he wanted to move over to the second one, who had just turned fourteen. His first daughter had suffered in silence all those years and couldn't bear to see her sister suffer the same fate, so she challenged him, and it had turned into a fight. He beat her, as he often did when she resisted, with a koboko whip; only this time, she stood up to him and stabbed him with a screwdriver. The resulting commotion drew the attention of neighbors and the police. A few members of the community thought the case was a family matter and should be taken out of the court and settled quietly, that the girl should be ashamed of bringing such shame to her father. Ifenna was happy that his report of the case had brought the attention of an NGO who took it up and ensured that not only was the man prosecuted but also that the two daughters were safe and taken care of.

Ifenna looked at the video he was about to post. The accused imam had to be over fifty. The person who'd sent the video also sent a short note to tell Ifenna that the imam had four wives and enough children to run a football team. He was also a known preacher at his street mosque, which was supposedly vocal against indecent dressing and promiscuity among young people. He was a proponent of the burqa, and his wives and daughters did not come out in public unaccompanied. Yet, he went on to defile a twelve-year-old sent to him by her parents for training in Koranic recitation. Ifenna couldn't reconcile this as he typed up the brief note that would run along with the video. He had always been fascinated by the heart of man and how it was capable of just about anything.

There was a thrill that came with every successful post. Before now, he had to click the publish button at the exact time he wanted it to go live, but a recent upgrade by the service providers now allowed him to schedule a post to go live at a desired time. Ifenna scheduled the new post for six o'clock the next morning. His biggest traffic was usually in the early hours between six and nine when his readers were stuck in traffic commuting to work and in the evenings when they made the return journey.

After completing the scheduling, Ifenna checked his email, the one linked to the blog. Four new emails. He opened them from the bottom. The first was a spam mail, inviting him to buy an apartment in Dubai at an ongoing subsidized promotional rate. The second was a story about the driver of a church bullion van who escaped with the vehicle after loading it with money from the Sunday service. Ifenna had a laugh. It sounded incredible, like something out of a movie. The sender claimed to be a member of the church, one of those who counted money after every service and packed it in bundles with rubber bands ready for delivery to the bank. Cash collections across the three services the church held on Sundays were so huge that they needed a bullion van to haul it to the bank. The van was usually accompanied by a church security car with one armed policeman in front. On this day, after the bullion van was loaded, the driver who would usually wait for the accountant to complete some documentation before joining him, suddenly zoomed off, knocking down the steel bar barrier at the gate. Then he disappeared. It had been two weeks now, and both the van and the money were still missing, but the church was hushing the story, making sure it did not go public.

Ifenna made a mental note to use the story. A few lines came to his mind as possible headlines. He thought about them briefly, wondering if he should be sensational or matter of fact. The sensational always got the most traffic, but sometimes stories required a frankness that addressed the issue straight up. He was still mulling it in his mind when he clicked on the third email. A brand manager from a beverage company was enquiring about his rate card. Ifenna quickly googled the brand. They were the makers of a new soft drink that he had seen being hawked in traffic.

The last email had an attachment, and the sender did not sign off with a name but rather with a *LMAO* emoji. Ifenna found that curious. The email name, ReplyNot, suggested it had been created for just the purpose of sharing the story.

The few lines of the message referred to the recent story about Pastor Nick and indicated there were more interesting scandals about him in the attachment that the blog should publish. There was a second part, the note indicated, which would be shared only if Ifenna published the first. Ifenna made to click the attachment and then hesitated. He felt the hairs on the back of his neck stand.

"Not again," he said loudly, shaking his head.

His mind went to Lilian. Her reaction about the blog, he was convinced, had been more about the story that embarrassed her pastor than about him keeping the blog a secret. Picking up something else on Pastor Nick would only make her angrier. So, to avoid the temptation of finding out what was in the attachment, he selected the email and archived it.

TWENTY-TWO

"Good morning, Mummy," Bimbo said. She stood just in front of the closed door in an Ankara jumpsuit and blonde hair extensions that gave her a Dolly Parton look.

Pastor Nkechi looked up from her laptop and smiled. "Oh, Sister Bimbo. Come, come, come," she said, beckoning her inside while pushing the cover of her laptop down.

A few minutes earlier, she had asked Funmi to find out if Bimbo was around and to tell her to come to her room. Bimbo walked from the door to the table where Nkechi sat. Bimbo was usually a confident woman who walked like she was on a runway, like she had the sun at the sole of her feet. This morning though, Nkechi noticed she was a little unsettled as she approached, her hands behind her back like a child who had done something wrong.

In the earlier days of their relationship, they had met very often. Bimbo would follow her to her office after fellowships and pop in from time to time just to chat. In those days, Nkechi had fancied herself as a mentor to her, happy to have a younger sister she could take under her wing because her husband, who was trying hard to mold her into a fitting wife of the founding pastor, harped on the importance of demonstrating leadership skills. It was during one of such discussions that Bimbo mentioned she was no longer comfortable at work because her boss wanted to continue an office affair she ended after becoming born again. Nkechi had thought she was doing what a mentor should do, introducing her to her husband and insisting she took on the job of his media assistant. Then the visits began to reduce in frequency until they stopped altogether, and their relationship reduced to smiles and obligatory pleasantries whenever they encountered each other. Nkechi had believed Bimbo was simply busy with her new job and didn't think much of it until Agent X's revelation.

"You wanted to see me, ma," Bimbo said, standing just before the table.

"Yes. Sit down, please."

Bimbo pulled out one of the chairs. Nkechi noticed the glistering stud on Bimbo's engagement ring. She was sure it looked different. She had seen the ring when Kunle first proposed. They had both come to her office to announce the good news, and she had shared in their joy, hugging them both like her children and praying for them.

"I should say, e ku ipalemo. Hope I got that right?" Nkechi said as soon as Bimbo was seated.

"Yes, ma. Thank you."

"How are the wedding plans coming?"

"Great." Bimbo beamed. "It's only two months away now."

"You must be very excited."

"Yes. Just that there is so much to do still. Planning and all."

"I can imagine."

"You know how it is with family. It's like we are just staging a party for our parents. There is always one additional person to invite, an important uncle we must go and invite personally, and someone to who we must send the aso-ebi. It's a lot."

"That's how it is, my dear," Nkechi smiled. "Especially when you come from large families. You must please everyone. It will all be worth it after the wedding. But you must take care not to break down. It is a healthy human being that weds."

"Thank you, Pastor. I will try."

"The material is cockroach brown, right?"

"Yes. Cockroach brown and gold for the bride's family. I already gave Sarah your gele."

"You people and these colors. When Sarah told me, I was like, which one is cockroach brown again?"

Bimbo laughed.

Nkechi could see Bimbo was now a bit relaxed. That was what she'd intended, to make her feel like this was a harmless chat before delivering the message she intended, which had to be served cold.

"You know marriage is such a beautiful thing," Nkechi said after they exhausted discussions on the various new color descriptions for aso-ebi materials.

They had chatted like two old friends who were meeting after some time and catching up on what each might have missed of the other.

"I remember how I felt just before mine. I was very excited because I was completely in love, but there is always this little apprehension, as if you are about to make a costly mistake, and you keep asking yourself if you were sure of what you were about to do. Sometimes you just have to quieten that voice and push it to the back of your mind. But it rears its head again in your quiet moments. From someone who has been in one for these many years, I can still say that marriage is a beautiful thing and one of the best steps one can ever take in life."

"And you have such a lovely one," Bimbo said. "Your marriage is so heavenly-made, Mummy. Honestly, I pray every day for mine to be like yours. I mean, you and Daddy Founder love each other so much. I suppose that having the right partner makes all the difference."

Nkechi shifted in her chair and smiled in a feigned acknowledgment of the compliments, though nausea churned her stomach. "Well, I can't say I had a hand in any of that. It's all to the glory of God."

"Surely, there are some secrets to it. There must be a list of things one must do to keep the relationship fresh and filled with love because, honestly, for me, I feel the anxiety you spoke about earlier, and I sometimes fear that even though I love Kunle, I may get bored."

"Well, it's not only about what to do. It's also about what you must not do. First on the list is keeping the marriage bed sacred. The book of Hebrews says that marriage is to be held in honor among all, and the marriage bed is to be undefiled."

She paused and watched to see if the words had any effect on Bimbo. If there was any, she did not notice it. Bimbo stared back at her like a student taking lessons from a trusted teacher. How she could sit there, calm and looking her in the eye while sleeping with her husband?

"And that brings me to the real reason you are here this

morning."

She saw the confusion creep into Bimbo's face as she stood and walked from her desk to one of the paintings that adorned the walls of her office. With her back to Bimbo, she said, "I want you to send in your resignation today and leave this church."

The office was quiet. Nkechi turned around and started walking back to her chair. She could see that the confusion on Bimbo's face was now full-blown shock.

"Did you hear me? I want you to resign today."

"But...but Pastor. I don't understand!" Bimbo's lips trembled.

"Let me say it again, slowly. I want you to resign from your position as assistant to my husband today and leave this church."

"Why? Where is this coming from? I work hard for Pastor Nick and the church, and I am good at what I do, and he has not had any complaints about my performance."

"Sure, you are damn good at what you do. Maybe too good even, and that is why you have forgotten where your work ends. You've turned yourself into a piece of temptation to an anointed man of God."

Bimbo's mouth dropped open.

Nkechi grabbed a file from her desk and tossed it to Bimbo. It contained the pictures and details of her affair with Nick that Agent X shared with her.

"You think I'm not aware of what has been happening? You this little Jezebel that I welcomed into my home. You are now trying to destroy my marriage and ruin my husband's ministry. I should have known from day one that all your Miss-Goody-Two-Shoes acts were just a smokescreen. I should have sniffed you out when you came to me, feigning a longing for a deeper connection with God. I trusted you, and he also came to trust you. Instead of you protecting that trust, you decided to use it as a weapon against him. Against us. You should be ashamed of yourself."

Bimbo looked from the papers and pictures to Nkechi and back to the documents again, unable to speak.

"Of course, you have nothing to say for yourself. You can't allow a young man to flourish. You must throw yourself at him and open your legs like a dog in heat. You thought I would never know? You thought you were smart? Well, it's all there, and there's more where that came from. So don't sit there asking me questions of why you should resign. Just get up and do it."

Tears ran down Bimbo's face. She tried to say something but choked on a sob. Nkechi pushed a tissue box across the table to her. She pulled some sheets and blew her nose into it, and yanked some more to dab her face.

"You see, I really like you. Or, at least, I did. That's why I haven't made this public. I could easily call Kunle and show him these. Your wedding would be off. You should be sensible and handle this quietly. I don't want you saying a word about the real reason for your resignation to anyone, not even my husband. Just vanish, and I will keep all of this a secret. Do you understand?"

Bimbo nodded.

"Good."

"Pastor, I need to…I don't know how to say this, but--" Bimbo stammered, wadding the used tissues into a ball.

"But what?"

"I did not seduce him. It was him."

"You're lying."

"I'm not. I swear it. I did not seduce him. He came for me."

"You expect me to believe that? Is it not shameful enough that you were sleeping with somebody's husband and a respected man of God? Listen, young lady, everybody knows Pastor Nick is a holy man. No one will buy your story."

Bimbo said nothing, took a deep breath and exhaled with a sigh. At last, she whispered. "This is going to ruin me. This is going to ruin everything."

"The marriage bed must be kept sacred," Nkechi said offhandedly, inspecting her nails to identify the one that she wanted to recoat. "You should know this, Bimbo. Whenever the bed is defiled, it ruins people. It ruins everything."

TWENTY-THREE

Ifenna knocked on the door of Lilian's apartment and waited. He had done so twice now with no response, but he was certain she was inside. She'd left her slippers at the doorsteps, and the lights inside the apartment were on. He was determined to persist until she answered the door.

That morning, he had left early first for his kabu kabu round and to another job interview, this time as a staff writer for a new magazine. He wasn't certain of attending when he got the invitation but lying alone in bed after the altercation with Lilian, he decided it was best he found a proper job and came clean with her. All day, she'd been on his mind. When she didn't pick his calls or respond to the dozen text messages, he convinced himself she was having a busy day at the hospital and that when she got home, they would have the time to talk. He wanted it to be a special night, so he stopped by a "Point and Kill" joint close to their street and bought peppered grilled fish and French fries, which he knew she liked. When he got into his apartment, she wasn't there. Initially, he thought she was not home yet, but it soon occurred to him, as he stepped into his room to change, that her things were missing. Her towel was gone from the bathroom door, the undies she air-dried on a hanger in the bathroom had disappeared, and the top layer of his wardrobe was bare of all her cosmetics and jewelry.

Ifenna knocked once more. He noticed the movement of the curtain over the window that was a few inches away from the door. Encouraged by it, he banged some more.

"Do you want to bring the door down?" she asked in a tone raised to match the loudness of his pummelling.

"I'm sorry. Please open up."

"What do you want?"

"Lily, please, I just want to talk."

"Talk about what?"

"Come on, love. We shouldn't be doing this...screaming our stuff through the wall. You don't want the neighbors to hear."

"And what if they hear? Oh, you are ashamed of people finding out you are a dubious human being?"

"I am not dubious, and you know it. I have not done anything dubious to you or to anyone. Please open the door."

"I can't waste my time arguing with you. Just go away. I am done with liars in my life. But before you go, maybe you can tell me how much they paid you to publish that rubbish story about my pastor."

Ifenna wanted to respond, but the door of the flat opposite creaked open, and he paused, looking in the direction like an antelope caught in a vehicle headlight on a deserted highway. The lady, tying a wrapper across her bare chest, emerged, backside first. Ifenna didn't know her well, but Lilian had often spoken about her neighbor who had a line stroke on either side of her cheeks like the number

286

eleven. Lilian suspected she was an executive call girl because she didn't seem to have a real job, yet she carried around the best designer bags and got dropped off every evening by men in flashy cars. She mumbled what Ifenna assumed was a greeting as she walked past him, the smirk on her face suggesting she had overheard much of his conversation with Lilian.

"Lily, you moved your things out," Ifenna said after the neighbor was out of earshot.

"Is that a question or a statement?" Lilian replied from behind her door.

"Can you please just open this door and let us talk things out like mature adults? Please." Ifenna, feeling very frustrated now, banged on the door some more.

"I have nothing to discuss with you. Just leave me alone. Leave me the hell alone."

There was a note of finality in Lilian's voice, like a judge hitting the gavel after pronouncing a sentence.

Ifenna heard her footsteps walking away from the door. It was futile trying any further, he concluded. He almost bumped into the number-eleven-facial-marks lady as he turned to leave, his shoulders brushing against hers as she approached her door. This time it was he who mumbled apologies. He thought he heard her giggle as he walked off, his shoes beating a rhythm on the compound's interlocking tiled floor. His fingers twitched angrily as he furiously unbuttoned his shirt, cursing loudly to himself as he did so. Lilian was unreasonable. His not telling her the truth about his job was too minor to warrant such a reaction from her. What gave her the right to dictate what he should do or not do, and why did she feel she was in a position to condemn him for blogging what was the truth?

The grilled fish and fries he bought had become cold. He could heat it up, but he did not feel like eating. He wrapped up the grilled fish and tossed it into the waste bin. Back in his living room, he wondered how to calm down. He was seething. Perhaps she was feeling as miserable as he was and had called. He searched for his phone and checked. No message or missed call from her. He slumped to the kitchen and fetched a bottle of drink from the fridge.

IFENNA STIRRED AND LIFTED HIMSELF onto an elbow. He looked around and found he was lying on the floor of the sitting room. The ceiling fan, dancing to the rhythm of the low voltage, spun with a quirky sound as if it needed to be oiled. The empty bottle of alcohol lay close beside him; some of its content had spilled on the floor. He yawned and stretched before rubbing his eyes to squeeze out sleep. The wall clock put the time at half-past three. He wasn't sure what time he'd fallen asleep, but he remembered getting overwhelmed by emotions while he drank. He'd cried like a little girl. Yawning again, he tried to get up, using the sofa as support. He felt light in the head, but much of the alcohol had now been erased by sleep.

As he staggered out of the bathroom after what was a relieving session, Ifenna considered climbing into his bed and continuing his sleep. The bed looked unusually big without Lilian in it. The thought of her made him get a bitter taste in his mouth. He needed to put her out of his mind. Walking back to the living room, he thought of his blog. He had not scheduled a story for that morning. As he opened his laptop, he remembered the email he received the day before, which claimed to have a story about Pastor Nick. That was going to be a perfect way to call Lilian's bluff, he thought. Somehow, he was convinced he needed to get back at her for making him feel so miserable and embarrassing him. Publishing the story was going to deliver the right blow.

He located the email in his archives and read it again. He had missed out a line, which indicated he was supposed to reply to the mail to confirm he would use the story, and the sender would tell him exactly when it should be published. It made him more curious. He didn't wait to see what was in the content. As he clicked to download the attachment, he quickly replied to the email, confirming he was interested in using the story.

TWENTY-FOUR

Tiny floating bubbles with the laughing face of Owo Blow beclouded Pastor Nick's vision as he staggered to the bathroom that Friday morning. He felt exhausted, as though he had been wrestling in his dream. As he urinated, placing his left hand on the tiled wall for support, he repeatedly blinked to clear out the bubbles, wondering why this illusion from his childhood, which he had fought hard to suppress, was reoccurring that morning. But it was not the bubbles that worried him as he walked back into the room and sank onto the bed. It was his exhaustion, which made it hard to even lift his legs off the floor. The exhaustion brought with it a premonition that something bad was about to happen.

He knew that feeling; it was the same way he felt the day his father died. He was in boarding school then, in the second term of his first year. The morning bell had woken him, but instead of jumping up, he had felt a strange numbness and great difficulty lifting himself up from the bunk. It was as if a thousand hands were holding him down. It was such a struggle that, when he finally made it up, he was sweating even though it was the middle of the harmattan season and the mornings were cold. All through the day, he felt as if he was walking in another person's body, as though his real self escaped from his body and took flight. Later that day, after evening prep, the boarding housemaster and his school guardian informed him about his father's passing in a car accident.

So, when he woke up feeling the same way today, he waited in fear for what the news would be this time, answering every call with trepidation. He canceled a scheduled flight to Abuja and sent a message to all his pastors to commence urgent prayers because he could sense the gathering of dark clouds. He was mostly worried that it would have to do with the purchase of the private jet. Since the meeting with his benefactors, he had told so many people about it, and any new development that would change it was going to be damaging. He had spoken about it on the altar during one of his recent sermons at the cathedral. The topic had been on faith, on speaking things into existence, and he had declared to his congregation that he was speaking a private jet into life and added that, if it did not come to pass, then it should be taken that he was not anointed by God. The crowd inside the cathedral had jumped on their feet and broken into a celebratory dance that lasted several minutes. Having raised their excitement to that level, he had gone in for the kill, asking them to come forth with their faith and will whatever they desired into being.

He had been impressed with himself that day because of the spontaneous flash mob-like offering that his words had inspired, but now he felt like he had put the credibility of his ministry on the line. He thought of what could go wrong with the deal. Everything had been signed. He had even done a virtual tour of the jet from his office computer, and after just a bit more paperwork, the jet would be on its way to Lagos in time for the unveiling on New Year's Eve.

He was so consumed by his fears that he had already started planning an alternative story to tell his congregation if he received any bad news that meant the jet would not be there on time. He was going to tell them that he received a special message from God that the jet he wished for was not befitting enough for the kind of mission God called him to. So, when his secretary brought an envelope to him, which he unsealed to find Bimbo's resignation letter, he was so relieved that he turned around several times in his swivel chair like a child visiting a play park for the first time. His secretary, who was still standing there, frowned at his joy, and he quickly dismissed her.

After the initial wave of joy at the realization that the impending sad news had nothing to do with his private jet, Nick read the resignation letter again, and fresh concerns sipped into his veins. Everything about it was strange: the suddenness, the approach, even the words in the letter dripped of an urgency he could not associate with her, especially given that things were perfect between them. It had not been quite a week since they made love on his office table. That day, after they were done, she had requested a break in their affair because of her impending wedding. She said she felt she needed to keep herself for her husband until the wedding night, a request he had found utterly laughable but had accepted without hesitation, partly because he would do anything she wanted, and it was only a break.

He wondered what could have informed this change, so

much that she indicated she was leaving the church and was also changing the location of her wedding service. His first thought was his wife, but he quickly dismissed it. Nkechi was not aware of him and Bimbo. Perhaps, it was Kunle's idea. He had suspected the young man was beginning to get proud since one of his singles became the number one gospel track in the country. Perhaps, he was being poached by another church to lead their choir or was even starting a ministry of his own, pulling Bimbo along compulsorily. The thought angered Nick; he hated treachery. He wondered if he had dropped the ball with Kunle and allowed him to grow wings enough to backstab him.

He tried calling Bimbo, but both her numbers were unreachable. Everyone else on his team had neither heard from her nor seen her that day. He had struggled to keep his tone calm on the calls, aware that if news of her resignation got out, it would cause a stir among his congregation given how close she was to the top. It would allow detractors to spread stories about something going wrong. He knew he had to manage the information well. Being able to control every narrative and make people believe only what he wanted them to believe was how he had come to be so successful in his ministry. He needed to act fast before the news seeped out. Usually, he would have turned to Bimbo for a perfect spin.

A 3D model of the cathedral sat on a side table in his expansive office. He liked staring at it whenever he needed to think deeply about a situation, a crystal ball of sorts. The model of the building brought him inspiration. The idea for the building itself had been the product of unusual inspiration: the design, capacity, pillars, and location had come to him in a dream. He had only narrated it to the architect who translated it into a building design on paper. So, he went to it to think about how to shape the narrative about Bimbo's resignation while trying to dig out the real reason for her departure. He stood over the model and reminded himself he had built that structure, a venture that had seemed impossible when he first conceived it. That self-reminder had a way of making him feel nothing else was impossible, and he could find his way out of whatever the current situation was.

He stood with his arms folded against his chest. His eyes fell on a balcony in the eastern part of the structure, and it held his attention for a minute, bringing back the memories he had fought hard to banish. The balcony held what was perhaps the biggest secret of his life. It was where Pastor Felix had fallen to his death. The events of that afternoon flashed rapidly, making him take a deep breath. It had been an accident. After making sure that his wife Nkechi didn't go to the site that day, he had driven there himself to confront Felix. One of the other pastors had suggested that Felix was helping himself to some of the money he and Nkechi were raising for the building project and using it to plan the establishment of his own church. That explained some of the gaps in the finances, Nick had thought.

So he had gone to the site that day to meet a shocked Felix. The site was empty because the workers had downed tools over a disagreement with the project contractor, and it was just the two of them. He had not got the "I-am-guilty-as-charged" reaction he had hoped for when he first made his accusations. Felix had denied it all. Nick hated being lied to, so an argument had ensued. He must have said too many hurtful things because Pastor Felix began to talk back at him and, in the process, let something slip. In response to Nick's accusations that he was deliberately getting close to his wife in order to manipulate her for money, Felix had retorted sharply that, instead of making a baseless accusation, he should go and ask his wife why she could not keep her hands off him. Felix must've realized the slip. Nick and Felix stared at each other, both knowing things would never be the same between them.

"Are you sleeping with my wife?" Nick had whispered.

Felix had remained silent, his eyes bearing an intense look as if he were staring over Nick's shoulder at a burning house. Nick repeated his question, raising his voice slightly as he began to walk toward Felix with clenched fists. Felix retreated instinctively; oblivious to him, he was approaching the edge of the building. It had happened so fast. He fumbled, lost his balance. Before Nick could switch from wanting to punch the man to saving him from an imminent fall, it happened. He heard the thud when the body hit the ground. He knew there was no surviving such a fall, so he rushed out of the site and drove away before anyone could see what had happened.

Now, a call pulled him out of his reverie. It was the governor's chief of staff. His Excellency wished to attend the New Year crossover service at the cathedral. The news brightened Nick's heart like the first rays of sun after a stormy night. He knew the governor was only aiming to identify with the huge crowd in his church because of the general elections, which was only five months away, but it meant a lot to the reputation of his church, hosting the number-one citizen of the state on such an important night.

For a moment, Nick forgot about his worries, about Bimbo's resignation, and about how to manage the information with the congregation. He thought instead about the new suit he ordered from his favorite designer in Italy for the service. They said it would take more than five hundred hours to design and stitch, using one of the rarest wools in the world. The catalog described it as an extravagant piece of art, and he'd picked it without much thought. Now with the governor coming, he was certain the Holy Spirit had guided him to make that choice.

Another call came through on his direct line. It was Pastor JohnPraise, one of his senior assistant pastors. He was calling to confirm a rumor that Bimbo had left the church. He said a few members had approached him to confirm it, but he really did not know what to tell them. The alarm in Pastor JohnPraise's voice could be heard miles away, and Nick ground his jaw.

"Are you in the cathedral?" he finally asked.

"Yes. I just finished the counseling sessions for intending couples. She and Kunle did not attend, which is very unusual."

"Come up to my office now."

As the call ended, he dropped into his swivel chair. Exhaustion crept back into his bones. The familiar premonition of something bad also returned, this time in the form of chills, like he was suffering from severe fever on a sweaty, humid night.

TWENTY-FIVE

Ifenna's mother called early on Saturday morning. She had traveled a few days earlier for an extended family prayer session. It was the only reason she had gone, the prayers. Since her husband died, she had avoided the village and all his relatives whom she treated as accomplices in his death, but something had happened recently. A string of deaths in the family had prompted some of her husband's siblings to suggest holding a family prayer session. There were talks of ancestral spirits, about the gods their forefathers worshipped haunting them for now abandoning them and not offering sacrifices to them. They all agreed to hold a family prayer, which would help diagnose the source of their challenges and free them all from such evil powers, and every branch of the family had to be represented by at least one person. Ifenna's mother had gone, traveling by a bus that broke down twice on the road. She had called Ifenna when she arrived, and they had talked at length, gossiping about the other family members, many of whom she had not spoken to in years but who had welcomed her, like they were long-lost friends.

Now, on the 6 a.m. phone call, she informed him that something shocking had happened. Someone had been caught burying strange materials inside the compound that night. One of Ifenna's cousins, who also returned home for the prayers, woke up at three o'clock to urinate—the houses built by Ifenna's grandfather were not en suite. Ifenna's cousin walked to the outdoor toilets, he found someone, hidden by the cover of darkness, digging. Not quite sure if the person was a family member, he had walked on to the toilet and back to the room. However, when he mentioned it to his older brother, with whom he shared the room, his brother said they should go see who it was. They found a young man with a hoe who immediately took to his heels on sighting them. They'd caught him just before he scaled the fence.

"The whole thing woke me up," Ifenna's mother said. "When I exited my room, almost everybody was outside already. They had tied the boy to a tree and beaten him."

"Wait, I don't understand," said Ifenna. "What was he doing with a hoe in the compound?"

"The boy was using the hoe to bury those strange items in his nylon bag at different points inside the compound."

"Like charms?"

"Well, they looked like charms, though he said they were fake. but with a person like him, you never know."

"And why was he burying them in our compound?"

"He said he was sent by a man of God. The same one we engaged for the prayer."

Ifenna had never heard anything like that. He had always been amazed when his mother told him stories of how charms buried on people's land were dug up during prayers. Listening to his mother now, he wondered if any of those was real, if it was not the same trick at play.

"You know what worries me more now?"

"What?"

"It was me that suggested the pastor o."

"What do you mean?"

His mother sighed. "They were discussing who to invite. Nobody was agreeing. The Catholic side of the family were talking about inviting Mbaka. Others were calling their own names. Then they asked me. I said, let me ask my pastor in Lagos. It was him that suggested this man and even gave me his phone number. He said they are good friends and that he is very vast in doing family prayers in the east. Truly, when I suggested him, everybody said they knew him, and that was why we went for him. Now, I am wondering if my pastor in Lagos knew his friend was a dubious person."

"So where is the boy now?"

"They handed him over to the village vigilante, but they really beat him o. I am worried for him. His eyes were swollen."

"What are they saying now?"

"Who?"

"Everyone. What is going to happen now?"

"Nothing now. Epele a'yasa go nu. No more family prayer. Everybody is still in shock, but it is clear the prayer will not hold again."

"But what if the man and his team show up this evening. Did you call them?"

Ifenna's mother chuckled. "If they make the mistake of stepping foot here. I am not sure if they will leave alive o. What is paining me is the money we already paid them. He said he was coming with a team of prayer warriors and singers with their music set. Can you imagine all the requests they were making? We must cook their food separately. We must use only goat meat, no beef or chicken. In the morning after the vigil, they will eat pounded plantain and oha soup before they leave. Imagine all that, plus the money they charged us."

"Did you already pay them?"

"Not in full. Just a deposit. They insisted on sixty percent. I am just happy we didn't pay everything."

"How much was that?"

"Biko, the amount is not important now. I am just in shock. How can people be so fraudulent in the name of God?"

Ifenna wanted to tell her that what he did daily was to catalog cases of Men of God being fraudulent and that he wasn't shocked in the least, but he was not ready for that talk yet. So he expressed his own shock and regret that people could be so unafraid of God to do such things and asked for more details of the man of God and the name of his ministry. He wanted to publish the story on his blog. His mother indicated that she had to end the call as her attention was being requested. The vigilante had come back with some police officers from the local station, and they wanted to have a chat with her.

Ifenna decided to type up the story immediately and have it ready to be published as soon as he could get the missing details from his mother. He had published so many stories from others and felt excited to publish one he could tell his readers happened to his family. He wanted to know the name of the pastor and his ministry. He wanted to splash his picture all over the story and shame him publicly. The more he thought about it, the more infuriated he got. He imagined the number of families that had fallen apart because of similar scams of charms dug up and accusing fingers pointed at someone who might just be innocent. He added a line in the story as he typed, suggesting that such men of God should be hunted like witches.

His mother called back about an hour later. The news had now gone around the village, and their compound was besieged by villagers stopping over en route to Nkwo Market, which meant they had to retell the story to curious ears. Members of two other families where the same man of God had previously held prayers confirmed that the charms he dug up were the same materials found with the boy. Usually, he would take it away, claiming that such powerful charms needed to be destroyed and disposed of specially. Though it was much trouble for him to dispose of them, he was happy to help the family do so. A show of how good a man of God he was. Apparently, he was reusing them. Planting and uncovering them repeatedly. Ifenna thought it was funny, the idea of reusing fake charms, and decided that the man couldn't be very smart, that his trade was only possible because his buyers were often too desperate to think things through.

The man of God's name was Apostle Powerful Onyema. In his pictures, which Ifenna found online, he was always dressed in military camouflage, complete with boots, a beret, and a rank hanging on his shoulders. Ifenna wondered about the name. For a long time now, he had contemplated the choice of titles by men of God—why some were called "Pastor" and others "Reverend," what the difference was between

"Evangelist" and "Apostle," and if those called "Prophet" had actually made any prophetic pronouncements. But this Apostle, Ifenna thought, was about to be ambushed. A plan had been hatched by the villagers to capture him. They had made the boy call him to confirm that he had successfully buried the items. Hoping that no one else tipped him off, the villagers waited for him and his team to arrive that evening for the prayers, so they could swoop. This idea had been cooked up after the police claimed they had nothing to charge the Apostle with.

Ifenna left the story in a draft. The ambush, if it happened, would make a great story. Through his mother's phone, he had spoken to one of his cousins and requested that he filmed the entire episode on his phone and share it with him later on. Ifenna had not been this excited in a long time. He felt like a teenager up to some mischief with his mates. Something else made him excited too—the story he finished working on last night before bed. It was a reporter's delight, the kind of story that announced you, that fulfilled your journalistic dreams. He really felt like he was on the cusp of something big.

The email from the mystery lead had said to publish it on Sunday morning by ten o'clock. Whoever was behind the strange email account seemed calculative and precise about their intentions. He guessed it was a lady because they clearly had something against Pastor Nick. Probably another one of his sexual assault victims. He looked forward to the story going live on his blog. It was going to be a different kind of post, a departure from the reposting of stories sent in by readers. He even got to use his journalistic training. There had been data and bits of information, which he had to piece together to produce a good story, an exclusive.

While he worked on it, he remembered the diminutive Professor Thompson with his grey hair afro and black bow tie who taught them "Writing for the Mass Media" in his first year in the university. The professor had started his class with a quote: "In sane parts of the world, the media is the fourth estate of the realm. In Nigeria, there are only two estates: the elite and the rest of us. Your job as a reporter is to write your story so well that through it, a few more of us can become elites while some of the elites join our level."

Those words had infused in Ifenna the belief that he could change society through his work, and it had propelled him every day when he went out to report metro stories for *The Nigerian*. Now, for the first time, he thought he had done something that was close to hitting that mark. His only regret was that, by shaking the table as he was about to, he and Lilian may never be together again.

TWENTY-SIX

Pastor Nkechi felt ecstatic and expectant like she used to feel when she was younger on the nights before road trips from their house in Enugu to their village on the border between Abia and Akwa Ibom States. It was a journey of no more than two hours by road, but the potholes and multiple police checkpoints, which forced motorists to slow down, or sometimes clear off the road to open their trunks and deliberate with police officers who were often just after the "little something for pure water" they could extract from commuters, made it much longer. Her father's old Peugeot 504 conspired to make it an even longer trip with stops to top up water in the radiator like a thirsty adult on a sunny day, or to change an ailing tire overwhelmed by the bad road.

It was always a fun trip for young Nkechi and her siblings. They always enjoyed reading aloud the graffiti on the 911 trucks, the stop they made at the Ninth Mile Corner on the route to Onitsha to buy okpa and yellow bananas, and eavesdropping on their parents discussing the annoying characters in their town's meeting or the incompetence of the state government. On the nights before the trip, Nkechi would be filled with excitement and anticipation, unable to sleep, and when she eventually did, she would dream of being in a moving car tearing through the rain forest, and Mama Nnuku's happy face, smiling and beckoning to them on the horizon.

It was the same excitement she felt now sitting on the pulpit in her usual position beside her husband. Heaven's Gate Cathedral was significantly packed that morning. More people went to church toward the end of the year as they sought divine help for the dangers associated with the "ember" months, while seeking to be in good standing with God so that their New Year would be blessed. But Nkechi also suspected that the news of Bimbo's resignation, which had spread among members with many spinoff stories of what might have happened, had pulled in a few more people who came to satisfy their gossip appetites. An unintended benefit, she thought. A fuller house provided even more audience for what she had planned. All she had wanted by making Bimbo leave was to destabilize her husband. She knew that despite all his influence with the media, her husband was not good at spinning the stories to them. Now that Bimbo was gone, her husband was vulnerable, and this had placed all the aces in her hands.

She looked at her wristwatch. It was nine forty-five. *Fifteen minutes more.* She felt like a movie villain waiting for a time bomb to go off, but she considered that thought briefly and decided she did not like it. She was not the villain. She was the heroine, in the last scene of the action movie, about to deliver a big surprise to the villain that would lead to his defeat. She reached for her water glass, took a gulp, and looked at her wristwatch again.

"Finally, before I leave, open with me to Isaiah chapter fifty-four and let's see what it says in verse seventeen." Her husband's voice boomed from the speakers.

He was standing at the lectern with his back to her. His sermon that morning was longer than normal. He normally wrapped things up in fifteen minutes and got everyone excited for the thanksgiving session, but he had been on it today for close to thirty minutes, touching on a myriad of topics and reading more Bible verses than usual. Nkechi thought there was something subdued about him, perhaps a premonition of what was to come, or perhaps it was Bimbo's absence. On their way to church that morning, he had seemed lost in thought. They did not speak to each other all through the drive, and just when they were about to alight at the cathedral, he had said a little offhandedly, "You've heard about Bimbo, I presume?" And she had nodded as their security detail pulled open the door.

Nkechi picked up her Bible and flipped to the passage her husband just called out.

"Isaiah fifty-four verse seventeen, 'No weapon that is formed against you will prosper, and every tongue that accuses you in judgment you will condemn. This is the heritage of the servants of the Lord, and their vindication is from Me.'"

"Hallelujah!" There was a chorus from the congregation.

"You can say to your child, 'hey, you cannot have any more ice cream,' and that child will feel, oh Daddy or Mummy is just talking, I can go take some more and get away with it. But when you declare it, oh Lord have mercy, when you declare it, because of the frankness, because of the tone, because of the authority in your voice, that child will know that ice cream is a no-go for that day. Do you feel me?"

The pianist played some notes to accompany the chorus from the congregation.

"So, when the Bible says the Lord declares, better believe it. He is not joking about what he is saying. He is damn serious, and that matter is sealed in heaven, full stop. And today, we just read of Him declaring that no matter what is thrown at the servants of the Lord, through them all, He will vindicate them. Can I get a Hallelujah somebody?"

After the ruckus had calmed, Nick continued. "I know some of you may have heard some rumors going around. I am not going to dwell much on it because there are certain things we should not dignify with a response, but just be reminded that whatever is being said, we shall be vindicated, and that is a declaration from the Master himself."

Nkechi re-read the verse again and dwelt on the word "vindication." It seemed ironic to her that her husband would talk about vindication. *Certainly, the guilty have no claim to vindication,* she thought. *Repentance and forgiveness, perhaps, but not vindication.* It seemed laughable to her the way he was now asking the congregation to repeat after him as he shouted "vindication" repeatedly. Despite everything, she could not help but admire her husband's ability to put on a show.

The congregation began to applaud as he walked back to his chair beside Nkechi. She looked again at her watch. It was eight minutes past ten. The story should be up now. What if the blogger failed to publish the story? It was not the first time that thought crossed her mind. But each time it did, she brushed it away, preferring to be positive. He was her best bet to get the story out. No mainstream media would have touched such a story, anonymously sent to them with so many incriminating details about the superstar Pastor Nick. They would have reached out to him first, and that would have tipped him off. Even without Bimbo, she knew he would have mobilized all the influences to kill the story. There were other high-profile persons implicated who would also have stopped it. So really, this blogger was the only option. She had been pleased to find he was the same person who wrote the only critical story about her husband in *The Nigerian*. Agent X had indicated that there was a possibility the blogger had lost his job at the newspaper because of that very story. This could be his redemption, a chance to get back at the man who'd taken away his real job. Her confidence had been boosted by his email responses. He had been upbeat, not asking any questions. His last message to her had been an assurance: The story will be published at ten.

THE DAY AGENT X PRESENTED her the information on her husband, Nkechi felt her jaw drop to the floor. They stood together inside the inner room of the art gallery near the Lagos Business School where they met. Agent X had not struck her as one who would be interested in arts, so she had been surprised when he sent her the location. She was familiar with the gallery; it was one of the places she took visiting ministers to. They had an impressive collection, and it was quiet, rarely occupied by more than three people at a time.

Agent X wanted Nkechi to buy him three pieces of the

artwork as payment for the information. Nkechi suspected he would resell it for twice that rate to buyers abroad. She did not believe his story of being a collector who wanted to have those works grace his home. There was a laptop and a projector in the room where they met. Curiosity propelled Nkechi's legs as she walked in and sat down. Whatever cost so much money had better be worth it, she thought. Agent X was his confident self. Before he projected the information on the screen, he warned her that she was about to access information that was very sensitive, giving her a last chance to pull out, but it had only fueled her curiosity. Plus, what could be worse than knowing her husband was capable of Felix's murder?

"Your husband is at the center of an elaborate money laundering operation," Agent X said. He projected a trove of documents with names, account numbers, and bank transfer documents. "In simple terms, he is helping some powerful people in Nigeria make their illicitly acquired money look legitimate, and in exchange, he gets to keep a handsome fraction of the loot."

None of what he said made sense to Nkechi. She stared at Agent X blankly. He explained that the documents showed inflows of huge amounts of money into a Rivers of Joy Church bank account, different from the one Nkechi knew about. The money came from powerful men. He identified them and stated that they'd all been part of the military era. The new democratic government had set up the Financial Crimes Agency (FCA) to recover stolen government funds, so the men had to find a way to hide the money and keep themselves away from the law.

"The transfers started four years ago." Agent X gestured

to a spreadsheet on the screen. "Your husband got rich fast. He started to put out the money for them in investments both in Nigeria and abroad. Nobody questions the wealth of pastors because they have visible sources of income. The records here show that he has moved mind-boggling amounts for them." He scrolled to another page with more information. "Now, he is helping them to evade tax. They funnel finances through him to mask the amounts they owe the government in taxes. The details are all here."

Pastor Nkechi could no longer feel her legs.

"It might interest you that the cathedral was built with this money. Who builds such a structure in that record time? That edifice is a piece of real estate investment. Every block of that structure hides away illicit funds."

The shock made Nkechi stand up abruptly. "But he had me going all over the US raising funds."

"Well, he had to keep up the semblance of legitimacy. Your husband and his associates are good. They know what they're doing."

Nkechi kept quiet for a long period, during which she tried to wrap her head around what she just heard. It was as though she did not know her life, like she had been living a lie. Some memories began to flutter back, and certain occurrences began to make sense to her, like the first time her husband acquired two brand new Landcruiser SUVs out of the blue and said they were gifts from friends. Another time, the funds for the church building had dried up, and she had been worried, but the contractor had remained on site. When she asked, her husband had said he had worked out something and that "God has been faithful." She thought of how Agent X got the information and wondered why he hadn't handed it over to the FCA instead–they always promised juicy rewards to whistleblowers.

"The government is not my friend," Agent X said when she asked. "I don't work for them. I am a private army. Besides the fact that I break a few laws to get the information, I don't feel obliged to do business with criminals."

Nkechi asked what he would have done with that information if she didn't buy it.

"Many things. You don't know the number of people who will be happy to have the information. Rich people have a lot of enemies, you know. I could also have sold it to him."

"You would have allowed him buy this information about himself? Is that not helping to protect criminals?"

"I am not the morality police, Madam," Agent X said, standing up and pulling out the HDMI cable from the laptop. "I am a businessman, and this is my trade. My information is for sale to a willing buyer. Now that you have the information, what you do with it is up to you. You can either decide to expose him or use it as currency to buy some leverage in the light of his previous misbehavior. Your choice."

As she left the meeting with Agent X that evening, she was certain she was going to expose her husband. The betrayal she felt was deep, like someone had sunk a blunt machete in the groove of her back and then pulled it out excruciatingly slowly. It increased by many folds, especially the pain that nestled in the left of her chest since she saw the junior pastor's wife, who Agent X suspected in his very first investigation for her, had a son for her husband. She had chanced on the woman and her son earlier that day as she walked to her office at the cathedral. As she playfully tapped his cheek after exchanging pleasantries with the mother, she became convinced he was her husband's. The boy looked exactly like the baby she always saw in her dreams, back when her failed IVF efforts planted illusions on her mind. She was not surprised when his mother volunteered that his name was Olufemi, Nick's middle name.

She felt stupid. As the tears began to trickle down, she pulled off the road, stopped the car engine and cried. It was as though the tears brought clarity because after, she felt a readiness to shed it all: the marriage, the church, the status it gave her, everything. As she continued the drive home, her heart heavy with sorrow, she began hatching a plan. She was going to send the details of the money laundering transactions to the blogger to publish. That, she reckoned, would create the perfect storm. Images of how it would play out excited her. He had been the one laughing all these years, she thought. She'd be the one with the last laugh.

NKECHI KNEW WHEN HER HUSBAND became aware of the blog publication. The choir was singing a special number as they did every Sunday when Pastor JohnPraise walked frantically up the pulpit and knelt on one knee by the side of her husband. He had his open tablet in hand. Though she sat right next to him, she could not hear their conversation as they spoke in hushed tones, drowned by the singing of the choir. Nick sprang from his seat, and the two men slipped out the back doors. That was Nkechi's cue. She took out her phone and checked.

Pastor Nick's Empire of Fraud and Criminality

A picture of her husband's head swirling with currency

notes like a halo—the same one used in the recent *Richest Pastors in Africa* publication—accompanied the headline. She did not read through the article. There was no need. She sent out an SMS that she already had in her draft to set the rest of her plans in motion. In a few minutes, those in the congregation who were registered members of the church would receive an SMS with the title and link to the story. Many people now used apps instead of carrying printed Bibles, so they always had their phones on in church. And in case some of them missed it, the story would soon pop up on the digital display screens inside the church. She wanted to cause such a stir that the traditional media channels would have no option but to splash it on the front pages of their Monday edition.

Her husband walked in a few minutes later, alone and looking like he was carrying concrete slabs on his shoulders; the wry smile that was always planted on his face like a mask when he was on the pulpit was gone. She tried to make eye contact as he resumed his seat, but he avoided her gaze.

"Is anything the matter?"

"No, nothing," he said. "Why?"

"Why'd you go off with Pastor JohnPraise?"

"He wanted to show me something."

Just then, Pastor Jedidiah ran up the pulpit. Her husband stood as he approached. There was a brief silence as they both looked at something on his phone. Nkechi grinned as the color seeped from Nick's face. He pushed the phone away and strode to the lectern, cutting short the choir who'd just started their second song.

"Thank you, choir." He spoke calmly, which surprised Nkechi. "We must hurry now so that our people can go. I've been alerted that the weather is going to turn ug—"

Noise in the congregation interrupted him. It started like a little commotion and grew steadily into a loud chatter. The story headline flashed across the church's display screens. Now that everything had gone as planned, it was time to act out the rest of the script. She got up, walked to where her husband stood transfixed at the lectern and whispered, "We need to leave now."

TWENTY-SEVEN

Pastor Nkechi ran her hand through the dresses hanging in her walk-in closet, searching for what to wear. She didn't have any outfit in mind, but she was certain of the kind of statement she wanted to make. There were two racks of clothes in the U-shaped closet. Most of the clothes had not been worn. She had made a rule not to wear the same dress twice, especially to church, after seeing comments she found embarrassing on a society blog where she was once pictured. While the post had been to celebrate her outfit to the Women in Business Conference, where she was invited as a guest because the president was a member of her church, hordes of comments on the post observed—some producing images to back up their claims—that she'd worn the same animal floral print midi dress three months earlier to one of their Sunday services. Jummy, her stylist, a loud twenty-five-year-old she contracted after coming across her fashion blog, had gloated about being vindicated after that episode. She always said Nkechi was too conservative and that she did not seem to understand she was a person of public interest, that what she wore out was now everybody's business.

Just before the opening of the cathedral, they had done a

complete wardrobe makeover. Nkechi and Jummy had done a three-country tour of Europe, visiting the choicest fashion houses in London, Paris, and Madrid. When they returned, they attended the Lagos Fashion show and engaged some of the most creative local designers to make pieces for Nkechi. Jummy did not think there was room for any compromises, especially as *levels don change*. Her boss had to grace the pulpit at the new cathedral with outfits that matched the glory of the cathedral, she'd insisted. They had ended up with a huge collection, and Jummy often joked that she could costume an entire village from that closet.

When Nkechi walked into the closet, she often picked the first dress that caught her attention. This morning, she was conscious of what she wanted, something that made a bold statement and echoed the message she was going to deliver. When she called Jummy the day before, they had discussed something black and bold with dark shades and accessories.

Nkechi pulled out another dress, a black wool-blend sleeveless minidress and placed it against her body. She did not like what she saw in the large mirror. Black made her look like one in mourning. It was not a funeral. It was her victory lap. She decided she needed an attire that screamed celebration. Just then, she remembered it was the last Sunday before Christmas. Being adorned in the colors of the season would do it, she thought. Like one controlled by an external force, she went straight to the section of the clothes rack that looked red. She pulled out a scarlet dress, a replica of Maria Grachvogel's precious dress, encrusted with over five hundred diamonds.

"Perfect," she whispered to herself in the mirror.

So much had happened that week. She thought of it as she walked over to pick a matching shoe from her red-bottom collection. In a way, it felt like she had given more love and attention to her husband in the past seven days than she had in all their marriage. Except maybe the period just after they met, when they could not keep their hands off each other. The thought amused her. He had been her first. Before then, the most she had done with her previous boyfriends was kiss and let the hands stray. But with Nick, she had felt so comfortable that she had willingly given up the virginity she had guarded for years. The last week had felt like those early days. She had planned it to be so. The true show of her fidelity as a good Christian wife was to stand by her husband in his periods of challenge. Not only did it win her validation from all observing eyes, but it also ensured that no one was going to look in her direction as the source of the stormy weather that was sweeping his way. So, from the pulpit a week ago, when he seemed to have frozen seeing the commotion unravel before his eyes, she had been by his side, slipping her hands into his at the right time, whispering reassurances, leaving a smile on her face when she was around him, offering her body like it was their wedding night, and taking the front seat in defending him to every head that offered an ear.

She had led him slowly away that day from the pulpit, her elbow locked in his. They were going to have plenty of time to address things. All they needed to do then was to leave the church. As they left, she signaled a confused-looking Pastor JohnPraise to step up and address the congregation. Her husband did not say a word during the walk to the car. The whole time he gazed ahead like one walking to the gallows.

She had led him into the car and slammed the door herself, after making clear to his security detail to back off. Some of the other pastors had followed them and were gathered around the car like they usually did whenever he was driving off after service. Only, this time, they looked more like lost little lambs than strong, avid followers of God.

"The church of God is under attack as it has always been since the time of the apostles," she said to them. "It is nothing new. We don't yet know where this is coming from, but don't worry, we know our God will go to battle for us and victory will be ours. I want you all to know that we are at war, and this is the time to stand for the kingdom and the church in a special way. Go back in there and calm our people down. It's just best to take Daddy out of here right now so that things don't get messy."

The truth was that she needed to take her husband away to achieve what she wanted. She knew him well enough to know that, if allowed to recover from the surprise that had left him seemingly transfixed, he had the ability to recover fast and calm the situation. He had the uncanny ability to charm anyone with his tongue, but she needed the service to end in confusion. His not being able to address them was sure to lead to speculations and rumors, helping the story go viral, making it the subject of city gossip, which she hoped would set other processes in motion to deliver the kind of blow she contemplated.

She sat close to him on the drive home, rubbing his arm gently. He was quiet for a bit, looking out the window as if he was driving that route for the first time. Then, as they approached Chevron Roundabout, he turned to her as if coming to a sudden realization of everything.

"Where is all this coming from? How did that rubbish get on the screen in church?"

"Nick, I just want you to calm down."

"Fuck!" he cried. He pounded the side of the door with his fists. "Fuck, fuck, fuck!"

"You need to get a hold of yourself, love," she said sternly.

"Who is after me? What have I done to them?"

"We will figure it out."

"And they brought it into my church. They wanted to ridicule me in front of my people."

She did not say anything as she rubbed his arms. She could feel his anger. His arms were shaking.

"Maybe we should go back," he said suddenly. "I should go back there and speak to my people. We should turn around and head back to the cathedral."

"Go back to do what? It was chaotic when we left. We can't go back. Not right now."

He sighed, ran his hand through his hair, and cursed some more.

"Whoever is behind this should be ready for war. I will fight them with everything I've got."

For a moment, Nkechi considered the threat, wondering what he would do if he was to find out who was behind it all. The thought amused her, the stretched possibility of him ever finding out. When they got home, she forced him to the room. He was eager to start working the phones, but she insisted that he do nothing.

"Allow me to handle this," she said, taking off his jacket and making him sit on the bed.

She called Pastor JohnPraise and dished out instructions. The rest of the church communications team had to do something in the absence of Bimbo. They needed to come up with a plan. Counter messages needed to go out. The mainstream news channels should be monitored to see if they carried the story. Nobody was to speak to the press unless they cleared it with her. She wanted hourly updates. After she ended the call, her husband requested that she summoned all the pastors for a meeting. She called Pastor JohnPraise again.

"What's this story even about? Do you know the details of it?" she asked her husband.

"That was what Pastor JP came to show me on the pulpit. You saw when we went out. I didn't read it in full. The much I read was just…I don't know. It's all lies." He sighed. "Something about me being involved in money laundering. Me, Nicholas Adejuwon, money laundering. Can you imagine that rubbish?"

"Money laundering? What sort of crazy accusation is that?"

"Ask me o." He spread out his two palms on his laps. "Ask me."

She slept in his room that night. Things had blown up before they went to bed. The news was everywhere, emphasized by social media. Many other blogs had republished it. It was the number one trending story on Twitter Nigeria. Someone had created a hashtag #ArrestPastorNickNow, and people jumped on it and used it to express their frustrations about men of God in general.

Nkechi, after going to her room to shower and change into her nightie, slipped into bed beside her husband, whom she thought was close to a meltdown. He had gone from anger—screaming, cursing, and kicking things—to shedding tears like a bullied child when he saw the online trends and the things people were saying about him. She held him, and it felt strange. They lay facing each other. She stroked his back and dug for all the words of encouragement she could find. Then, they began to kiss. Awkwardly at first, but then natural, like they'd never stopped.

Early the next morning, they made love again. This time, the sex seemed to have a remorse effect on him. For the first time since she found evidence of his cheating, he apologized for his actions. He spoke like one who could sense death coming and needed to confess all his wrongdoings fast so he could still make heaven. He was sorry. He was carried away. He was tempted. He missed her. He was sorry. She said she understood. She nodded while he spoke.

Afterward, he sat up. "Bimbo. I bet she's the one behind all this. She knew too much. I let her in on runs with my friends. She is the one doing this to me."

When Nkechi asked what he meant, he told her about his benefactors and the money they were pushing through the church. He spoke of them like business partners and admitted the money may have been stolen from the government, that he was getting some percentage of it. Then, he tried to justify it all. "You see, they helped us build Heaven's Gate in record time, and you know that jet I told you about? They're paying for it."

Nkechi feigned surprise and anger. "How could you not tell me? Am I not your wife? Do you not trust me?"

There were more apologies and tears and another round of make-up sex. Then they agreed to maintain that he was innocent in all their utterances. They were going to fight this together. As they got set for the meeting with the pastors later that Monday morning, someone called Nick to inform him that the FCA had taken an interest in the case and advised him to leave town immediately. Elections were coming in a few months, and the president's people were gathering whatever they could to impress the electorate to make up for their boss's empty dossier. It was easy to imagine them taking advantage of the outcry online to score some points and brush up his anti-corruption portfolio by making a scapegoat out of Nick.

Nkechi had hoped for this—that the government would take some sort of interest, but she did not imagine it would happen so quickly or that the online buzz would become so overwhelming. Some groups were mobilizing for a protest at Heaven's Gate Cathedral. Another group said they would submit a petition at the office of the Inspector General of Police for Nick's arrest. There were thousands of negative stories shared about men of God. It was as if the story had caused a release of pent-up anger, and Nkechi felt she had inadvertently lit the match for a wildfire.

NKECHI TOOK HER TIME TO dress up. She was not in a hurry. They were going to wait until she arrived anyways. So she had a bubble bath before settling in front of the mirror to do her makeup. Typically, her team planned her makeup before Sunday service. There was always a stylist waiting at the cathedral for her on Sunday mornings. She would usually be walked into a side room after they arrived for a makeup session before going in to join the praise and worship session, which usually kicked off the service. This morning, she decided she wanted to do it herself. Before they started the church and became rich, she used to do it herself. It was one of the skills she picked up from Ijeoma, her roommate in the university who did makeup for others for a fee. Nkechi had tried it out earlier in the week on Wednesday for the press conference, and it had turned out well. When she saw herself on the cover of the newspapers the next day, standing there beside her husband, like Winnie beside Mandela as he walked out of prison, she had been impressed by how she looked. She finally looked like herself again.

The press conference was held at Heaven's Gate Cathedral's media room. It was packed full of reporters, with TV stations barely finding room to stand their cameras. The decision to address the media was taken at the pastors' meeting that had been held at their residence following the threats of protests at the cathedral. Nkechi had made sure the meeting had ended with one outcome: her husband was innocent, and he'd prove it by willingly turning himself to the FCA. It was going to be a hard sell to her husband, so she had called Pastor JohnPraise beforehand to share her thoughts because he was the most senior of the other pastors. Because he was also older than her husband, he often deferred to him on issues. She had presented the issue to Pastor JohnPraise like a concerned wife trying to do the right thing to fix the challenge her husband was facing. She told him that the easiest way for her husband to show the accusations were false was to do what everyone least expected–turn himself in. This, she said, would save them the damaging embarrassment of arrest if public pressure continued.

The plan worked.

The pastors supported the idea.

Nkechi rejected it, insisting that her husband was innocent and should not surrender to the will of those who fought them. She was impressed by Pastor JohnPraise's performance; the way he pushed back, insisting on his own position, rallying all the other pastors to agree with him. In the end, Nick told her that he would, indeed, turn himself in. But before he did, he was going to address a world press conference to reiterate his innocence. When the meeting ended, and the pastors left, he told her that he agreed to turn himself in to strengthen the pastors' confidence in him and keep them loyal. He needed them to keep the ministry together, and agreeing to their plan was a way of making them feel that their opinion mattered, that he was a listening leader. He believed, however, that he would not stay longer than a day with the FCA because, though he had not been able to reach any of his benefactors on phone since the ordeal started, he was confident they would do what was necessary to make sure the matter died away. Then he told her they were going to have a triumphant entry after his release, and by then, they could plan a grand celebration for the New Year, which would coincide with the arrival of his jet.

The call for his arrest was still the trending topic online by Wednesday when the press conference commenced, and there were fears the FCA would swoop on him before he turned himself in. He read a short, prepared text in which he talked about unknown forces from both within and without ganging up with conspiracies and falsehood to bring him down in an effort to terminate the good work God was doing through him. Those people would fail, he said, and his father would vindicate him. After reiterating his ignorance of all the accusations some faceless publication had leveled against him, he announced that he had decided to turn himself in to the FCA because he had nothing to hide. The address lasted fifteen minutes, and Nkechi stood there by his side, their bodies touching, her eyes hidden behind dark shades. When the news was out, with their pictures splashed on the cover page of most newspapers, she took time to admire herself.

Now, just as she finished dressing, she got a call from Sarah, who was waiting for her in church. It seemed, Sarah reported, that the cathedral was going to be full that morning. There had been fears among some of the church staff that turnout would be low following Nick's arrest and that members would stay away like the apostles after the crucifixion. Nkechi wasn't surprised, though. Everyone wanted to have a first-hand account of the hottest story in the country.

It had been three days since her husband drove to the FCA office in Lagos to turn himself in. The next day, they had moved him to Abuja, and a mugshot of him, naked to the waist, had been leaked in the Friday papers. She knew the crowd Sarah talked about had gathered to see what was going to happen next.

Nkechi took one more look at herself in the mirror and decided she had achieved the look she wanted. All that was left was for her to get on that pulpit and deliver the speech that was going to bring everything to a climax. She had started to memorize her lines from the moment her husband turned himself in, piecing together sentences to clearly state that the church was going to march on under her leadership. Bayo, her assistant, had done a great job coaching her on how to deliver perfect sermons, how to walk the stage, when to turn to which camera to deliver the punch line, which part of the stage to occupy at any given moment, when to vary her pitch, and how to make the most of her feminine appeal.

It was effectively a take-over speech, but she was going to reiterate her belief that her husband was innocent and that she would continue fighting to prove this. And to show that the church was moving on like nothing had happened, the annual Christmas activities were to proceed as normal because that is what her husband would have wanted. Already she had decided that the cathedral be elegantly decorated with Christmas trees and twinkling lights. She was going to leave no one in doubt that it was a new era, and she wondered, as she walked downstairs to the car, if the congregation would notice they had just witnessed a coup d'état.

TWENTY-EIGHT

Owo Blow liked to laugh. He wasn't blessed with good looks by any stretch. Three thick scar lines ran the length on either side of his face, like autographs left by a hunting lioness. A particularly aggressive frontal alopecia, which started quite early in life, had left his head looking like a peninsula of dry land surrounded by greying hair. Probably to shore up his looks, he had resorted to skin lightening creams, though it left irregular pink patches across his face. When he laughed, his head tilted slightly to the sky, his mouth wide open like a wailing child, exposing his blackened teeth.

This image had been stamped permanently, it would seem, on Pastor Nick's memory, like a company seal impressed on conqueror paper, starting two days after his thirteenth birthday when he became homeless. At first, it was a symbol of horror, a mockery of his misery, and a painful reminder of the kind of card life had dealt him. He saw the face, sometimes many of them, like bubbles blown by a harsh wind, when he lay down to sleep at night. They teased him as they danced around and gnawed at his sanity. His mother had come back from Ondo with only enough money to secure them a windowless one-room apartment near Ikorodu waterside, and at night, he and his sisters and their mother rolled out mats on the cement floor to sleep. He did not sleep many of those nights; he couldn't. The bubbles of Owo Blow's laughing face and the accompanying sound of the laughter would not let him.

He had carried those tormenting bubbles with him over the years and made them a daily reminder of the place he never wanted to be at again, a position he was resolved never to return to, powerless and ashamed. He did not realize when it slowly consumed him until it began to rule him, to direct his every action, to make him think of life as nothing more than a race to grab enough power so he was never at the mercy of another person.

When he graduated from the polytechnic by the grace of the loans his mother took from the women's co-operative, his only focus had been to get a job with an oil company. He was going to buy her a house in Victoria Island, get her a chauffeur-driven car, and open a big shop for her in Balogun market. But he was not from an oil-producing state, and his National Diploma in History didn't exactly make him an ideal candidate for the oil majors. His second choice was to work for a big accounting firm. He got into Coopers and Lybrand. For the young Nick, this was his sure way to power. From their induction class, when the staff from the Human Resources Department told them the path toward making partner, he was clear on his ambitions to become one. Partners were powerful; they owned corner offices in the building and walked with a swag that suggested they had not a care in the world. Nick had breezed through his training to become a chartered accountant and made so much mark at work that after only five years with the firm, he got promoted to an audit manager.

The laughing bubbles seemed to have all disappeared with the change in his fortunes. For the first time, he felt like his life was on a straight path, a happy lane. He met Nkechi, fell in love, and got married. Not long after though, his mother died. Then there were talks of a merger between his firm and one of their main competitors. It first started as a rumor but soon became real. The merger brought with it a lot of changes. The work stress doubled and so did the internal competition. He was no longer the superstar, the one on the fast track to partnership. Some of his new bosses didn't think he was good enough. They conveyed their opinions in his appraisals, which took a nosedive. With stress and frustration getting the better of him, the laughing bubbles returned. They blurred the path to partnership. They nibbled at his affections for his wife. They made him feel, once again, like the homeless thirteen-year-old powerless boy.

One day, the thought to start a church came to him. He had been reading books by American preachers and watching a lot of the televangelists. Initially, it was just because he found some solace doing so and because he liked the way they talked, but it soon occurred to him that ultimate power resided in the ability to control the lives of a mass of people and have them obey without question. Nothing could be better, he thought. The decision had been easy. He had taken leave from work, and over a two-week period that he spent mostly lodged in a hotel room while lying to his wife that he was out of town on a work assignment, he had carefully laid out his strategy for breaking into the church industry. The more he thought about it, the fewer the laughing face bubbles clouded his head. Soon, they were all gone, and he thought he had finally gotten rid of them for good.

Now, years later, Nick stared at a large bubble with the laughing face of Owo Blow, floating gently in front of him, looking him in the eyes as if daring him to do something about it. He made repeated efforts to push it away with his hands, to strike it so that it would burst and fizzle away, but it would not. Each time, it seemed as though his hands could not reach. As if in celebration of his misery, the pitch of the laughter that reverberated inside his head increased after each failed attempt. His anger built up fast, and all the things he had wished to do to Owo Blow on that morning of their eviction flooded his brain. He threw a barrage of punches at the face accompanied by curses. His punches soon got weaker, and Owo Blow's laughing face kept floating in his peripherals. When he woke, he was sweating and close to tears.

NICK HEARD APPROACHING STEPS DOWN the corridor outside and stirred, raising his head slightly. He was still sitting, hugging the wooden table, waiting for AB Mustapha to return. The FCA detective who was handling his interrogation had said he would be back in two hours. Though he did not have his watch because they collected it from him along with his phone and wallet, he was certain the man had been gone for much longer. Little light came into the room, making it seem like night all the time, but the day was still young. It was probably close to eleven o'clock. If so, he thought, Sunday service would be in progress now at the cathedral. *His* cathedral. It was still his, no matter what happened next.

He heard keys turn, followed by the creaking sound of the door opening. The momentary gush of light from outside as the door swung open blinded him. It was dark again in a moment. He could make out two figures in the darkness. One walked to the side of the room, running his hand on the wall feeling for the light switch. The other hesitated at the door and began to walk toward the table. Nick sat up and sniffed. The smell of cigarette accompanied the men. The switch flicked and the bulb hanging over his head came on, blinding him briefly again. He squeezed his eyes shut, this time tighter, and when he opened them, the second figure was standing at the other side of the table. It was AB Mustapha looking down at him like he never left, with a wry smile on his face.

"Sorry, I stayed a bit longer than I thought. There was a development that I had to attend to. You know how this job is."

Nick wanted to tell him he had never been a security agent so, no, he did not know how his job was, but he said nothing. Instead, he covered his eyes, which were still adjusting to the brightness. AB Mustapha pulled out the chair on this side of the table and sat down.

"So can I go now?" Nick asked.

"Ah, about that," AB Mustapha said, calmly dropping a tape recorder and a writing pad on the table. "I am afraid not. Like I said, there's been a development."

"And how does that connect with me?"

AB Mustapha opened his mouth to speak and then stopped. He regarded Nick for a while, his head tilted at an angle. Nick could see the bags underneath the detective's bloodshot eyes.

"It connects with you because you are here, in this interrogation room, as a suspect for serious crimes against your country," AB Mustapha said slowly, as if speaking to a child.

"When I turned myself in back in Lagos, I was told I would be taken to Abuja for some questioning and documentation. That's it. I wasn't supposed to be arrested and detained. It's been three days now. You've kept me here, refusing me access to my lawyer and keeping me beyond the constitutional limits. I am a pastor. You know that. I head a church. It's Sunday, and you have kept me away from my job."

"Pastor, we've gone over this earlier," AB Mustapha said, raising his voice slightly. "We have a court ruling to keep you here for up to forty-five days. You're not going home. Frankly, I will not want to talk about this anymore. You know as much as I do that the case before us is a serious one, and you need to begin comporting yourself. And as for your congregation, I am sure they are fine. Maybe they are even better off without you around, don't you think?" He paused. "Things have moved very quickly in the last twenty-four hours, and we will not need to hold you for so long after all. We already have enough evidence to bring charges against you in court, and we will be doing so on Monday."

The room was silent. Nick regarded the detective for a while, trying to see if he was bluffing, if someone was playing a cruel prank on him. AB Mustapha felt his breast pocket and brought out a pack of cigarettes. After lighting one, he tossed the pack across the table toward Nick.

"Do you smoke, man of God?"

Nick shook his head.

"Of course, you don't. What will that make you now? A big sinner, I suppose, but I cannot remember anywhere in the Bible that says smoking is a sin."

"You are not qualified to discuss theology with me."

"Most certainly, Pastor, I am not." AB Mustapha puffed out smoke, sat back, and crossed his legs. "Plus, I'm a Muslim, so what do I know about Christian theology to argue with a renowned pastor like you? My apologies. But I am certain of this one Biblical message, which doesn't need a degree in theology to understand: 'Thou shall not steal.' It is one of the more universal laws that cut across various creeds. It doesn't look like you are very conversant with that particular Biblical pronouncement, Pastor."

"I've never stolen anything in my life. I will not have you call me a thief!" Nick hit his fist on the table. "I have made it clear in my statement that I am not guilty of any of these allegations. I only came to you to clear my name."

"I hear you, Pastor, but the charge sheet that has been put together against you doesn't support your claim. A hundred and fifteen counts bordering around money laundering, enabling tax evasion, and defrauding citizens in the name of God. That is major thievery, Pastor, and it can put you away for a long time. At the very least, we are looking at thirty to forty years here." He paused as if to let his words sink in. "And if you are hoping on your big and powerful friends to come to your rescue, well, you've been with us since Friday. You should know by now that no one is coming. You're on your own."

Nick considered the detective's words. The events of the last three days had left him petrified. It was supposed to be a harmless visit to the FCA office in Lagos, an action to burnish his image and help dispel the accusations. His lawyer had assured him that they would only ask a few questions, probably take his statement, and they would be on their way. They had arranged for some reporters to be outside the FCA building upon his arrival, and he had addressed them, saying he had come as promised during his press conference, as a responsible citizen who had nothing to hide. But the visit had taken a turn. After taking his statement, they had kept him and his lawyer waiting in a locked room for over two hours. When they came back, he was told that an order had come from Abuja that he must be brought to the head office for proper documentation.

He had grumbled all the way because he was made to fly economy class, and he found that insulting. The young FCA agent that accompanied him said that was what the agency could afford, and when he offered to upgrade it for both of them on a different flight, the agent refused. Even his lawyer had to take a different flight. Everyone was cordial until he arrived at the FCA head office in Abuja. There, they stripped him of his belongings and treated him like a criminal, putting cuffs on his wrists and pushing him along as he walked. Before his lawyer arrived in Abuja, they took a picture of him holding a board with his name and charge written on it. Then they'd hauled him into the dark interrogation room with the wooden chair and table. Throughout the two nights he spent there, Nick thought of his benefactors. They had always given him the impression that should anything come up, they would press the right buttons to ensure he was protected from the law. They had connections at the very top of government, and he was confident that they would come through for him. AB Mustapha's words about no one coming for him suggested that they had abandoned him. He quickly pushed the thought out of his mind.

"Since you have all your charges in place like you claim, why are you here, Detective?" Nick asked. "To read me my rights?"

AB Mustapha dropped the half-spent cigarette on the floor and used the sole of his shoe to crush it. He assumed a more serious mien as he leaned forward, his face a few inches away from Nick's.

"You see, we will take you to court, Pastor, and you will get nothing less than thirty years, but that will be unfair because it wasn't just you involved. I mean, you were not laundering *your* money. We have the names of the powerful people you were in bed with, but we need to tie up the case against them before we can make a charge. And that is why I am here."

Nick leaned back, making a face. The smell of the cigarette from AB Mustapha was discomforting. "I don't know what or who you are talking about."

AB Mustapha retrieved a piece of paper from his pocket and slowly unfolded it before placing it in front of Nick. "I am sure these names look familiar to you."

Nick looked at the paper. His benefactors' names stared back at him. He glanced back at AB Mustapha and said nothing.

"All these men...criminal vestiges of the military era... are very corrupt men. They are your friends, your accomplices." AB Mustapha stood and began to pace. "You have been helping them clean their loot. We know that. We have the records. Everything that website published is true, and we have more. We have been investigating them for years now. These men are the real people we are after, not you. Now we have a chance to nail them, to make them pay for all they have done, but we need your help."

He paused as he whispered something to his colleague, who nodded repeatedly and headed toward the door.

"We have enough to charge them, too, but we have a little problem. They're all abroad now. Your friends, Pastor, are on the run. That is why I told you earlier that no one was coming for you. I'm not sure you want to go down for this alone, Pastor. You seem like a very smart man."

Nick studied his cuticles as the detective circled round the chair and walked back to his seat. He suspected that they wanted to cut a deal with him. It could also be, he thought, that the detective was just bluffing about the charge sheet and was trying to trick him into saying something even more incriminating. He was wary of the tape recorder on the table.

AB Mustapha seemed to welcome Nick's silence and continued to talk. He indicated that in order to get the men to come home and answer for the charges, they needed to build a foolproof case against them, which they would present to the governments of the countries they were currently hiding in, to secure their help in extraditing them. They needed a confessional statement about the men from Nick. They also needed information on some of the transactions to fill in the gaps in their own investigation. If Nick helped them, his sentence would be reduced.

"If you plead guilty in court tomorrow and opt for the plea bargain option, we will convince the judge to reduce your sentence by up to five years. It saves everyone the stress of a long trial and saves you the embarrassment of being remanded in one of the federal prisons, coming to court in a Black Maria with chains on your hands and legs. I am sure it is not the kind of image you want your followers to see."

When AB Mustapha's colleague returned, he got up and stretched, indicating he was set to leave. "They will be here to serve you breakfast any moment now. Do you have anything to say before I leave?"

"I'm not saying anything until I speak with my lawyer."

"By all means, Pastor. In fact, a copy of the deal has been sent to him, and he is happy with it, from what I gather. But it is ultimately your decision. Before the court session tomorrow morning, you will have an opportunity to speak with him. You have all the time you need from now until then to think it over and decide."

He leaned toward Nick and spoke in almost a whisper. "Make the right decision. Think of all you will lose if you don't. You've already lost your reputation, and your properties both here and in Dubai. Think of your wife. She's still so young and beautiful. Imagine any of your friends farming on that piece of land in your absence. You know it is not beyond them, right? Because with you out, they will need her sometime down the line, and those men have no honor. You have this one chance to do something right, Pastor Adejuwon. Don't waste it. Make the right decision."

THEY WHEELED BREAKFAST INTO THE room on a trolley table. Usually, it was someone dressed in a white chef's uniform that brought it in and served him, something AB Mustapha said was special treatment because they respected his status as a man of God. This morning, however, the chef stopped at the door. The other agent, who did not leave after AB Mustapha did, received the trolley, dismissed the chef, and wheeled it to the table where Nick sat.

It was the first time Nick could see his face clearly. His bloodshot eyes and black lips provided evidence of his lifestyle. He did not look like he said much or if he was even interested in speaking at all. It was as if he was under strict orders not to talk to the suspect. Nick had asked him what was on the menu, more as a joke because there were no menu options, and he had replied by giving him a long cold stare and continued with what he was doing. It had left Nick feeling a bit uneasy.

The officer methodically poured out the already-made tea from a flask into a mug, and using a dull knife, he spread butter on some slices of bread that he counted out from a loaf. Nick thought he stirred the tea for a little too long, especially because there was nothing inside to be dissolved, before pushing the mug and the flat plate with the bread across to him. Nick looked up at the agent and concluded either the young man did not like his job, or he did not like Nick.

"Can you please give me some space?" Nick snapped. "Or were you instructed to force it down my throat, too?"

The officer seemed to catch himself and immediately straightened, taking two steps away from the table. Nick pulled the small cup of milk close and poured some into the mug. He dropped in a cube of sugar before stirring the mixture. He was a bit hesitant to take a sip. The first few times he was served food there, he had requested that the chef tasted it first. He had been a bit paranoid about being poisoned. Now he felt like asking the agent to taste the tea first, but he waved off the thought. AB Mustapha had just revealed how much of an asset he was to the agency, so no one was possibly going to kill him in their custody. Right? He decided he was just being paranoid again. Raising the steaming mug to his mouth, he took a long gulp.

He would wish, a few minutes later when he felt the first pang of pain, that he had not. The pain emanated like needle pricks inside his gut, traveling to every part of his body in seconds, like his nerves were on fire. When it then began to feel like some great force was squeezing the muscles on the left of his chest and the room was beginning to turn in cycles, he tried to scream, but all he could hear was Owo Blow's laughter ringing through the room.

TWENTY-NINE

I t was a bit unsettling, sitting there, inside Heaven's Gate
Cathedral. For Ifenna, it felt a little like returning to the
scene of his crime, or more appropriately, attending the funeral of a victim he had hacked to death while being perfectly blended into the gathered crowd of mourners and watching the casket being lowered into the earth. He sat back on
a chair and folded his hands across his chest, his eyes on the
podium where a pastor had just stepped up to the lectern.
The noise from the clapping that followed the last testimony slowly died as the man tapped the microphone. The
church was about to be addressed by the woman of God,
he announced, beaming a toothpaste advert smile. Before he
called her up, however, the man indicated that he had some
announcements.

Ifenna looked around the church. It didn't seem like
there was any sitting space left, even in the gallery. When
he'd arrived earlier, he had been quite surprised to find that
the main auditorium was almost full, many worshippers
still streaming in. The sea of heads reminded him of the
day of the opening when he came to cover the event for *The*

Nigerian. How long ago now was it? Covering that story had set everything in motion, a chain of events that led to this very day. If he'd never written about Pastor Nick in the first place, he would not have lost his job, and he would not have started the blog that would publish the damning story that would lead to the pastor's arrest. Perhaps what his mother had told him the morning after his sack, that her pastor promised something good was going to happen to her son, was right after all. The thought amused him, the irony of it all. Who would have thought that the break he always sought in life was going to be foretold by one man of God and that it would be made possible by the downfall of another?

The request to send his account details had come early on the Monday following his publishing of the story. He had woken to another email from the mystery account that sent the material for the story and replied without giving it much thought. His blog was on fire, pole vaulting on the rating chart to be the most visited site in the country. Much of the fun was in the comment section, which was buzzing like the motor park at Oshodi Market during rush hour. As usual, the opinions were divided, and the commenters were going at each other. There were those who condemned Pastor Nick, those who named some other pastors who they believed were worse, and others who argued that it was bad to talk ill of a man of God, especially over phantom allegations. This last group demanded proof for the revelation of the source of the story, for the blogger to be sued for libel. Ifenna was immersed in it all for most of the night, including the banter and insults. He continued from where he left off after replying to the email with his account details.

When the bank deposit SMS notification came, he did

not respond to it immediately. He heard his phone beep but ignored it as he read the last comments that came in after he went to bed. He would later go to use the toilet and afterward go downstairs to meet with Sikiru, his mechanic, who came to deliver a verdict on his unwell jalopy. When he finally read the SMS, an hour had already passed. He saw the amount of money in the alert and counted the number of zeros individually to be sure his sight wasn't failing. After a second count, which confirmed the earlier one, he screamed and dropped his phone to the floor in disbelief.

He had always imagined what it would feel like to have a million naira in his bank account. Once, he and Lilian had fantasized about it while relaxing in his sitting room. They had named the various things they would do with such an amount. They had just watched a man win a million naira in a raffle draw by a mobile phone company. He'd screamed like a girl getting a surprise marriage proposal from her boyfriend on national television. Ifenna said he would do worse if he ever won such, that he would run out of his house down the street shouting for joy.

Now he had five million naira, and even though it was almost a week since the money had dropped into his account, he still feared that he would wake up and it would be gone. So he came up with a plan on how to spend it. First, he would buy himself a car, a good, second-hand, Nigerian car that would not break down in the middle of Third Mainland Bridge like his jalopy. Ifenna planned to use the rest of the money in expanding his blog. He would migrate from a free domain to a paid one, which allowed him a lot more flexibility. He was going to buy a new laptop and a camera so he could start a YouTube channel about men of

God. He'd establish a media empire.

The man at the podium said something about the church's annual Christmas carol holding that evening, and the choir celebrated with cheers and the sounding of various instruments. Ifenna looked around again. Though he came because the email address had sent him a message asking him to be there, he also hoped he would see Lilian, even if just briefly, striding about in her worker's uniform. He missed her. Earlier in the week, on Wednesday when he was at the cathedral to attend the press conference Pastor Nick addressed to declare his innocence and willingness to cooperate with the FCA, Ifenna had hoped that somehow, he would see her. He hadn't.

When the email address told him about the press conference, he had been grateful because having broken the story, his blog had to also be among the first to publish the follow-up stories. He had arrived at the cathedral's media room with memories of his last visit, expecting an elaborate screening before entry or an outright refusal because he was not accredited. There was none of those. The media room had looked smaller than he remembered. He could only find a standing space in the room; he had been uncertain of what to expect, but he hoped there was going to be some interaction with Pastor Nick. When he found out that the accused pastor was only going to read a statement, he had felt a bit disappointed, but he had admired the way his wife clung to him, affirming that she intended to stand by her husband every inch of the way. Ifenna thought it was beautiful, that image of Pastor Nick and his wife holding hands and it made him miss Lilian even more.

As he left the house for the cathedral that Sunday

morning, something else happened that reminded Ifenna of the emptiness he felt without Lilian. Standing on the second-floor landing, he saw Tunde and his wife sharing a quick kiss on the ground-floor landing. He was surprised to find that they were back together. The way their hands were all over each other and their laughter pierced through the morning calm suggested that all was now well between them. Tunde had been extra animated as they greeted, offering Ifenna a hug like an old friend. It was easy to see he was in high spirits. Ifenna thought he was a different man from the one who'd emptied a bottle of cognac in his apartment a few weeks earlier. He also thought Tunde's wife had a nice smile. He had never had a chance to see it. Their previous encounters had been her rude knocks and demand for him to drive out. That morning she had a smile on her face the whole time Ifenna and her husband chatted. It was as if the issue they had created new versions of them. As Ifenna walked past their car, after he and Tunde hugged again and wished each other a good day ahead, he looked in the direction of Lilian's apartment and wondered if their relationship could be saved as well.

THERE WAS A STANDING OVATION to welcome Pastor Nkechi Nicholas Adejuwon to the lectern. Ifenna stood with the congregation, wondering if the lady would not be perplexed by such a reception, especially given what she had been through in the last week since the story about her husband was published on his blog. She didn't seem fazed. In fact, she looked as radiant as ever, her beauty captivating. He remembered the first time he saw her during the opening of the cathedral and how he had wondered then why all the men of God had the most beautiful wives. Now, he felt pity for her in his heart. He thought she was the victim of a reckless fraud of a husband who had left a big mess, which she had to clean up. He wondered how much courage it must have taken her to make that appearance, to face the crowd so soon after her husband's mugshot made the covers of national papers. She must be a strong woman, he thought. The extended applause by the congregation seemed to acknowledge his thoughts.

Pastor Nkechi was surprisingly combative in her opening salvo, which made parts of the congregation who had just settled back to rise again in another ovation.

"They thought they could bring us down," she boomed. "They thought they have wrestled the church to the ground, but we are still standing. Brethren, look around you today. Rivers of Joy Church is still standing, and we are standing stronger than ever because the Lord God, the unchangeable changer, the Elohim Elohai, is with us. Praise the Lord!"

Ifenna did not rise for the second ovation. There was a loud sound from behind him, like someone had blown a vuvuzela. He turned his head in the direction. Then he saw her, Lilian, sitting two rows behind. Their eyes met for a second before she sat back down. It was so brief that he doubted afterward if it was even she who he saw. His heart beat faster. He wanted to turn his neck again to confirm, but it suddenly felt stiff. He willed himself and turned slowly to the right. It was really her. She was staring in his direction as well, and Ifenna imagined she was shocked to see him there. She was the only person who knew he was behind the blog, and he wondered what she thought of him now, after he'd put her beloved pastor in trouble. Many times during the week, as the story caused the stir, he had half-expected her to come banging at his door or send him a nasty SMS to express her anger and disappointment. He thought of how correct she would be if she accused him then, as she had previously done, of collecting money to publish stories about her pastor.

A few other times he had wondered in the opposite direction, imagining instead that she was proud of him for what the story had done, that she had somehow realized that her pastor was a criminal, that she was only too proud to admit she had been wrong earlier, and that was why she had not come to see him. Sitting there now, in the church with two rows of chairs and people between them, he wondered which it was, if he'd fueled her disgust or if maybe, awoken her guilt.

"Me and our daddy built this ministry from the ground up, and God has been so gracious to us. We had a vision from Him, to worship Him in a new way, to tell His people about His grace, which covers all sins, and remind them that he already paid the price for their iniquities, and He blessed us immensely. God is still at work in our lives today, and He is going to show Himself in a special way in the lives of all our people in the mighty name of Jesus."

The loud scream of "Amen" shifted Ifenna's attention back to Pastor Nkechi, who had now left the lectern to prance across the podium. The woman wasn't showing any signs of being weighed down by her husband's plight. He tried following her sermon, but he could not concentrate. He fought the urge to look again in Lilian's direction. He wondered if he could get to speak to her after the service. He thought of what he would say to her if he had the chance; how he loved and missed her; how his world felt hollow without her; and how he could now take her to Obudu Cattle Ranch, which was what she said she would do if she won a million naira.

He thought of telling her how he was certain his mother liked her. When they spoke the day before on the phone, she had asked about Lilian, wondering if she was okay because it had been some time since she heard anything about her. Ifenna had lied, unable to admit to his mother that she had broken up with him, because she would have asked what he did to her, and he knew he would not be able to say. Instead, Ifenna told his mother that Lilian was fine, just busy with work, and his mother had asked them both to come over when she was free. His mother's message would churn an emotion in Lilian. They had got on well the day he took her to visit, and Lilian had mentioned how one of her special requests to God was to give her a mother-in-law that would treat her like a daughter.

"And because poverty and heaven do not rhyme and neither is poverty a prerequisite for heaven, we know that we are destined for prosperity, that every member of Rivers of Joy Church is swimming in abundance of wealth and health and jobs and babies and contracts and visas."

Ifenna suddenly wanted the service to end. Pastor Nkechi's words from the pulpit sounded like an irritated child looking to get his mother's attention. He wished she would just stop talking so he could go to his Lily. Then, it occurred to him that he could lose her in the throng of people as they trooped out after service and miss the opportunity to talk to her. Perhaps he needed to push things forward and make the move before service ended. He could walk to where she was sitting and whisper into her ear to please join him outside. He considered the idea and decided it was a bad one because she could ignore him and it would be embarrassing. He decided he would instead walk out and ask one of the ushers to go tell her someone wanted to see her outside. This plan was his best bet. He was going to do it. He made a fist in both hands to steady his nerves, then shut his eyes and counted down from ten. When he got to the end of his count, he decided to look in her direction one last time before standing up.

She was gone.

Pastor Nkechi's voice rang from the speakers. "And the Bible tells us to sow in season and out of season. So now is the time to jump on your feet and dance forward to this holy altar, bringing Him a befitting offering in thanksgiving, for a new day has finally come!"

ABOUT THE AUTHOR

Sylva Nze Ifedigbo writes fiction, creative non-fiction, and socio-political commentaries. He has published a novel, *My Mind Is No Longer Here* (2018), a collection of stories, *The Funeral Did Not End* (2012), and a novella, *Whispering Aloud* (2007). His short stories have appeared in various publications including Prick of the Spindle, African Writer, Maple Tree Literary Supplement, Saraba, Kalahari Review, True Africa, AFREADA and Thrice Fiction Magazine. Sylva believes the calling of a writer is to study humans explicitly and document this in simple, memorable stories. He lives in Lagos, Nigeria.